City of the Gods - Starybogow

Whispers in the Dark

Edited by Brandon Rospond

ZMOK BOOKS

City of the Gods - Starybogow: Whispers in the Dark
Edited By Brandon Rospond
Cover by Jan Kostka
Illustrations by I. Bilibin, N. Broot, P. Dobrinina, J. Preston
Zmok Books an imprint of
Winged Hussar Publishing, LLC, 1525 Hulse Road, Unit 1, Point Pleasant, NJ 08742

ISBN 978-0-9963657-5-8
LCN 2016912232
Bibliographical references and index
1.Fantasy 2. Epic Fantasy 3. Action & Adventure

For more information on Winged Hussar Publishing, LLC, visit us at:
https://www.WingedHussarPublishing.com
Twitter: WingHusPubLLC
Facebook: Winged Hussar Publishing LLC
Printed in the USA

The Editor's Note

The world, as it has always been and always will be, is everchanging. The 1500's were no exception; the world was ripe with upheaval, especially in Europe. The members of the Knights Templar were branded as traitors by the Church and the order was murdered in its entirety. The Slavic people, comprised of the Polish, Ukrainians, Belarusians, as well as traditions of the Lithuanians and the Balts, were called heretics and rooted out by the Inquisition. Pagan gods of ritual and some of sacrifice were replaced with fear from the holy wrath of the one true God.

But what if there was more to these struggles than what the history books stated? What if these battles were more epic, and that the Slavic people, trying to fight the wave of change, evoked the powers of their Old Gods? They would not be alone in their strange, mystic ways…

For, you see, the Old Gods have combated a foe darker, viler, and more twisted than any mankind has known. To look upon one of these creatures would drive a mortal crazy and cause them to lose all sense of their humanity. Some call them the Dwellers of the Deep, to others they are the Dark Ones, but to those that know the truth, they are simply called the Eldar Gods; and they move through our human world by utilizing their Servitors to cause chaos among the ranks of humanity.

From the Baltic Ocean, the Eldar Gods have rooted their tentacles up through the sea and into the ranks of the humans' 'noble' crusaders, the Teutonic Knights. Using ancient powers of magic and manipulation, their corruption runs rampant through the order, even reaching so far as to convert their leader, Grandmaster Frederick von Sachsen, to undertake their vile bidding – to rekindle the Eldar Gods' powers, long sealed away, back in the realm of mortals.

Trying to combat this darkness, Alexander Jagellonian, utilizing the resourceful Michael Glinski, leads the Slavic people in reawakening the Old Gods. While the Eldar Gods and their Servitors want nothing but to end humanity and replace it in their likeness, the Old Gods, led by Perun, wish to defend the people of the mortal realm and would see them thrive. Many, but not all, share in Perun's vision, as there are those Old Gods that are mischievous and have darker intentions, such as the notorious *vampyrs*, the devilish *skrzaks* or the unholy *drekavacs.*

Ah, but such names must seem foreign to you, in a world where these creatures are nothing but myth. But you needn't worry about that; our authors have brought life to these beings of dream and nightmare alike to the pages ahead, so that you might better understand the world we have created, centered under the nexus for all of the unfolding events. Once an ordinary port-town, an earthquake hit Starybogow, impacting it in a way where it caused the river to physically move away from where it once flowed. This earthquake, wrought from the opening to another dimension, is the first of many events that change history as we know it!

Robert E Waters is one of the several visionaries who have helped to mold and shape this alternative universe. Having published many short stories in the past, his most notable works for Zmok include *The Wayward Eight* as well as "Imperiled in Payson" and "Nation Rising" in the Wild West Exodus Anthology. In Robert's story, "The Cross of Saint Boniface," the motley pairing of a Teutonic Knight by the name of Lux von Junker and a Tartar soldier by the name of Fymurip Azat traverse the ruins of Starybogow looking for a sacred cross, long lost to the Teutonic Order, that is said to have holy properties. However, the duo encounter some terrifying obstacles along the way, including a notorious group that would rather have the duo dead than ever recovering the relic; not to mention the strange chemistry between the men of very different walks of life. Will they find the relic that Lux is after, and even if it does exist, will they survive the journey let alone travelling with one another to bring it back to the Grandmaster?

Veteran author C. L. Werner also joins us in this anthology, bringing his vast knowledge of the time period to the table with his stories, "Blood Bat" and "Hour of the Wolf". C.L. has published many novels, including several under the Warhammer line; as well as the second Jesse James novel for Wild West Exodus, *An Outlaw's Wrath*, and "Brothers in Blood" for the Wild West Exodus Anthology. In "Blood Bat", we follow a grief-stricken man by the name of Dobrogost Radzienski, who enlists the help of a krsnik by the name of Czcibor Niemczk, to track a vampyr who he believes has taken his daughter. The mystic hunter has great power in his strange gloved hand, but is it enough to take down a vampyr? And what of Dobrogost's daughter; could she have survived the wrath of such an unholy creature? "Hour of the Wolf" puts us in the point of view of a Freischoffe from Westphalia by the name of Wulf Greimmer, who is on the hunt for a Teutonic Knight who supposedly seduced and killed a young girl, but in search of him sets Wulf in the midst of a Slavic ritual. Can Wulf hunt down his prey and find justice in his actions?

Michael McCann is a relatively new author who brings his flair for fantasy to this alternative realm of history. Previously with Zmok, Mc-

Cann published "Hell to Pay" in the *Wild West Exodus Anthology,* and much like that tale was about strong familial bonds, "Mad Brothers Three" follows the same connection. We follow the story of 'Wise' Radomir, Nikola 'the weapons-master', and a young warrior named Cyril, as they search for the latter's fiancé, who has gone missing; whether captured or left of her own free will is what the Mad Brothers are on the hunt to find out. After months of exploring the wider world and tracking every rumor, their journey has brought them to Starybogow. Is Cyril's fiancé, 'Sun', to be found in the mysterious ruins, or are there deeper, darker forces that wait for them?

Bill Donahue is a new author for Zmok, "The Swamp Hut" being his first published work. He lives on the plains of Missouri where he makes armor and swords in preparation should the Eldar Gods come to pay him a visit. Jan, Jadwiga, and David are three agents that work for Michael Glinski and have been sent on a mission to re-establish communications in Starybogow and investigate how the Eldar and darker Old Gods were able to open a portal to the human realm. Guising themselves as tinkerers, they join a caravan heading in that direction, but the trail is plagued with obstacles and their riding allies are insufferable. Will the trio make it to Starybogow in one piece or will the Dwellers of the Deep wrap their tentacles around them and submerge them forever?

Jan Kostka is an expert on this time period, especially in Polish history, and he is the brains behind the Starybogow universe; without him, none of this would have been possible. Jan works mostly behind the scenes, but his other published work was "Dogs of Law" in the *Wild West Exodus Anthology.* Having come up with the whole idea of the Old Gods against the Eldar Gods, "A Beginning" sets the scene for what readers can expect in our new timeline. Perun, the ruler of the Old Gods, has come back to the realm of the living, and there is much to be done to stop the Eldar Gods. The other half of the point of view follows a soldier by the name of Damiano Cirrincione, who seems to have a history more rich than even he knows. Meanwhile, "Hallows Eve" follows the exploits of leshiye who guise themselves as priests as they hold the dividing line between the mortal realm and the void. The two stories are intertwined and help to set up the bigger picture of darker things at bay. As it's been stated, not all that are considered of the old faith strive for the same purpose; there are some that would work with the Eldar Gods to see humanity destroyed.

Finally, we come to myself. Being the lead editor of Zmok, I have worked with each of these authors to get their stories as amazing as possible for your reading enjoyment. Besides this anthology, I have edited everything under the Zmok imprint; from the Wild West Exodus series, to "All Quiet on the Martian Front", to the upcoming Gates of Antares Anthology, and even my own fantasy novel, *Rebirth of Courage.* It has been my great pleasure to work with all of these men and women on all that we've published and accomplished over the past few years. That said, I have written three stories for this anthology. Each of them helps to give background on this universe's factions. "Sworn to Secrecy" and "Strength in Faith" go into the workings of the Hanseatic League and the Knights Templar, respectively, while "Torn Asunder" deals with the repercussions of what can go wrong when one Slavic god rushes to cross the opening void.

This anthology is only the start to a wide universe, cast under the watchful gaze of the towering ruins where it all begins – Starybogow. The stories within are only a few of the many tales of courageous men and women that try to scour the land in the aftereffects of the quakes that released the gods of both Eldar and Old. Carry on, dear reader, but take caution; you have been warned of the horrors under the nexus of power. Tread lightly as you join our adventurers through the ruins, and be wary of deep waters; you know not what lurks beneath the shadows of the surface.

Enjoy,
Brandon Rospond

Leshy
by P. Dobrinina, 1906

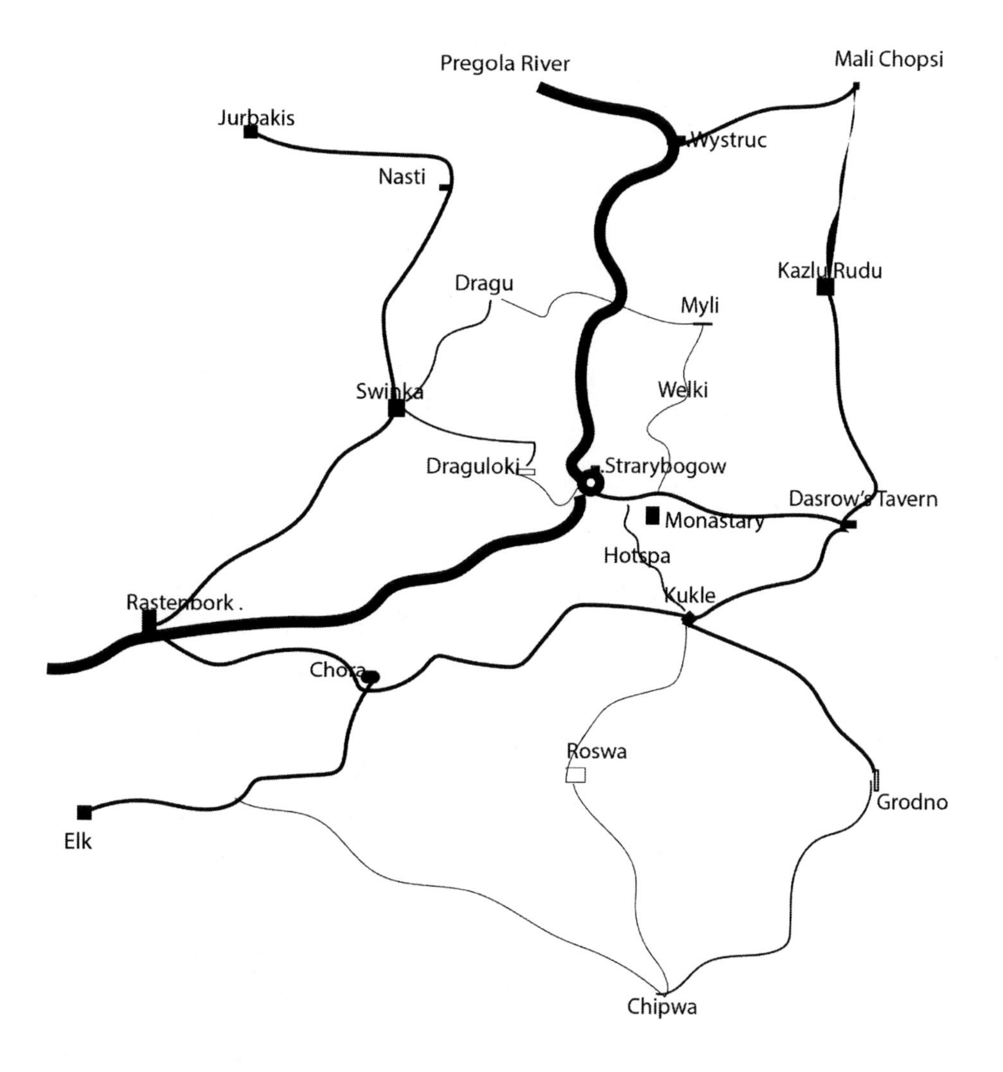
Pregola River
Mali Chopsi
Jurbakis
Wystruc
Nasti
Dragu
Kazlu Rudu
Myli
Swinka
Welki
Draguloki
Strarybogow
Dasrow's Tavern
Monastary
Hotspa
Kukle
Rastenbork .
Chora
Roswa
Grodno
Elk
Chipwa

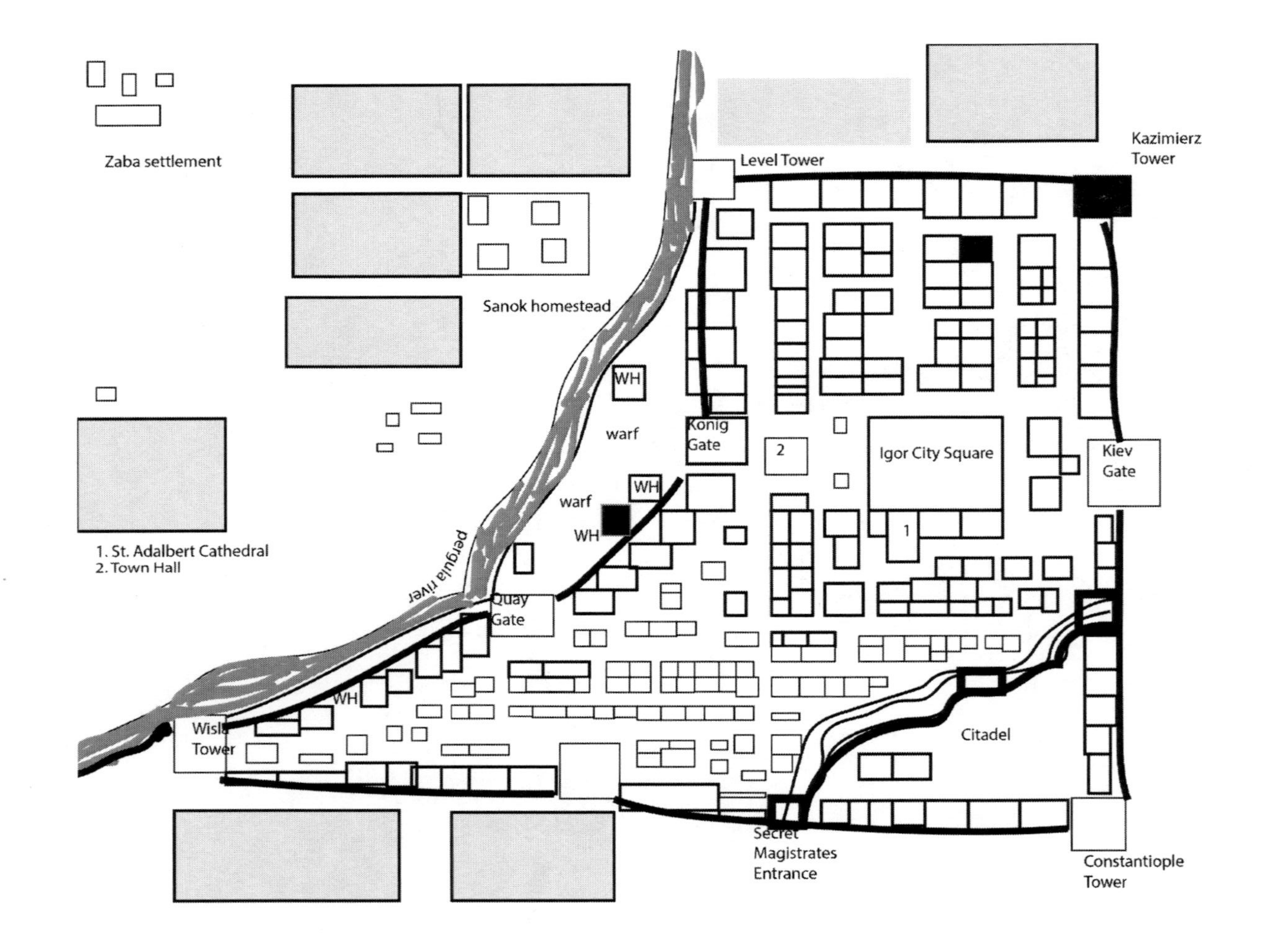
Zaba settlement
Level Tower
Kazimierz Tower
Sanok homestead
WH
warf
Konig Gate
2
Igor City Square
Kiev Gate
WH
warf
WH
1
1. St. Adalbert Cathedral
2. Town Hall
pergula river
Quay Gate
WH
Wisl Tower
Citadel
Secret
Magistrates Entrance
Constantiople Tower

Table of Contents

A Beginning
Jan Kostka

Perun
by Jeff Preston, 2016

Two ghastly blue eyes opened and then shut, even though he knew there would be nothing to see. He awoke and drifted off in fits, not knowing how much time passed between each dozing. This time though, Perun was anxious. He stroked his ever-flowing white beard, staring into the blank nothing all around him. Had it been a year, a day, an hour, a millennium that they were stuck in this infinite nothingness? He worried what was happening to humanity. His stone armor was starting to crack and chip, no longer pristine. He picked at the moss that somehow started to coat the armor; how it flourished in the void was a mystery.

Then again, he eased some of his anxiety remembering that the vilest of the Eldar Gods were of no worry. As long as he and his brethren were sealed away, so were their mortal nemeses. Memories flooded him that felt as if they just occurred yesterday and simultaneously years past, as Perun reflected on his struggles with the dark ones. They waged a millennium-long battle with each other over the fate of the humans; the evil creatures wished to replace the people of the living realm with those of their own design. Perun, along with his many Old God brethren, fought to keep the humans alive; there was a symbiotic relationship between the gods, the humans, and the earth itself. That is why the Eldar race was so dangerous – left to their own devices they did not need humans to sustain themselves. The final battle was fought in a small area in the center of the Slavic nation. It was here that the void was strongest and where Perun had laid the trap. It was a zero sum game, but at least humanity had a chance to survive.

This void, this prison, was by Perun's own hands. He had known that the only way to truly win the battle against the Eldar Gods was to have them sealed away in a void for all of eternity; and that sort of magic resulted in himself and his strongest allies being sealed as well. He was thankful that the lesser deities had avoided the entombment, still working among the humans to muster their strength to combat the lesser of the dark ones that still remained as well.

In the early days of history, the world was a battleground for the gods over humanity. The Elder Gods who arose from the ocean depths would have destroyed humanity and replaced them with beings of their own creation. The gods of the Slavs cared for humanity and the energy they exuded, combined with the life force of the earth, helped to sustain the gods. The Eldar Gods could care less if humans survived. Left to them, they would destroy the earth in a flood and mutate their followers into subhuman slaves. They promised power, but never delivered, and those caught in the net of the Eldar Gods never escaped sane. Rather than see the inevitable destruction of the mortals, the Slavic gods, led by Perun, locked in battle with the Eldar Gods and created a void to trap them both away from humanity. The most powerful of both were locked away to be supplanted by others over time. Some of the lesser deities of both sides remained intertwined with humanity, each trying to amass adherents for the ultimate battle. The Slavic gods left their mark upon some select individuals, and though they might have seemed feeble to the uninitiated, they contained great power; and it was through them that the gods communicated with humans. The Eldar Gods had their adherents as well, bred over centuries and tempted through promises of power.

Yet, something, at that moment, made him stir within the void like never before. He turned to notice Tłun, one of his closest allies, standing beside him; he seemed just as anxious as his leader, sensing the same feelings he did. Once, Tłun had bushy blond hair, beard and mustache, and radiated light. Now, after all these years, there was very little glow. His hair and beard were matted and his once fabulous clothes were tattered. In his glory days he wore a belted shirt and pants of flax and an over-vest of quilted willow bark. But now all he wore was rags tied in place with hair. In this state, his sharp nose stood out like a beak, highlighted in his own light against his diminished presence. He still showed a sense of pride despite his matted hair and beard, tarnished clothes and axe. His weapon was ornately carved flint, hard as iron that glowed in his hands when he went into battle. Now, it just seemed dull and flaky.

"Perun, does the boy have the ability? I feel a power; will they open the portal to us again?" His voice lacked the confidence of prior years, sounding hopeful, as forced as that optimism was. Perun just remained there in silence and stared at Tłun, not sure if he should tell his associate what he was thinking or just ignore him. It had been many years since they felt the energy, since the light had faded and they existed here in the void. But then, Perun spoke.

"The boy that the Grand Duke has found is not the problem. He will get him to the portal as soon as he can. We have waited these many years, we can wait a little more. There are other things at play. Other things that could make our position worse than where we are." Then he fell silent again. 'The void', as it was called, existed in the absence of time as they knew it. Dark, except for the light of blocked portals, it was part misty dream and part nightmare, a black hole in the universe, and they lacked the energy to cross it again to the human world. There were no doubt countless similar voids in existence across space and time, but he shared this one with his brethren – not all of whom he enjoyed. It was a trade-off, themselves for humanity, but there was always hope that humanity could save them without unleashing the others. Until that could occur it would be a stand-off.

"Worse than where we are? We are in a void," Tłun thought aloud. "How much worse could it be?"

*****

Damiano Cirrincione was glad to finally be in the Serene Republic. Even though he had spent most of his life along the coast and in Cefalu, he was not a sailor. His time at sea was never pleasant and this trip was no exception. It was not a long trip from Sicily to Venice, but Neptune always seemed to conspire against him. A storm had delayed their arrival and prolonged his sickness, but once his ship docked at the custom quay, it was like he was given his freedom from a long prison sentence.

The letters he carried from his father, and the small amount of money he had managed to scrounge, would allow him to stay out of debt for a while. The word 'father' resonated oddly in his head; he was to him, in everything but name – at least a recognized name. Damiano was born 'on the wrong side of the sheets', and while his half-siblings enjoyed the status befitting a count, he was held at arm's length. He was given the same education as his father's other children, but the count's wife did not want him there; he was a reminder to her, and thus she seemed to cause trouble for Damiano; not that he needed help – trouble seemed to find him or visa-versa with ease. It did not help that he didn't even look like his half-siblings; they had dark hair and complexions, while he was fair skinned with bright red hair, making him stand out against the rest of the people in the town.

In his most recent bout, however, his father had decided that the boy should seek his fortune, and that fortune was best found off the island. Venice had a vibrant empire, even though it was a 'republic,' and his father had acquaintances who might help the boy. Upon landing, with the day almost half gone, he would try to find the man his father had hoped would set Damiano on the correct path – Ludvigo Zomba.

Zomba commanded a company of Schiavoni in the service of the Doge and the Serene Republic. Zomba was not Italian and his original name was not Zomba – but Zaba. Like many of the Schiavoni, he was originally a member of a Slavic tribe from Dalmatia – a mercenary, but loyal to the Doge. Either through some aid he provided Zomba during the war or perhaps having been an old drinking companion – he was not quite sure which – Zomba owed his father a debt, which was being cashed in via employment. Because of his father's dealings, Damiano had learned a smattering of German and French, as well as a fair amount of Latin and Greek, which did him well in learned society. The Venetian dialect was different from Sicilian, so he had to pay attention when he asked for directions. Eventually, after getting lost three times, he managed to find the barracks and headquarters of Captain Zomba's company. Most were fierce looking men, men who had seen a fight or two, but not all were from Dalmatia. Some had dark hair and features of the Dalmatians, others the look of Germans or north men with blond hair and blue eyes. There were even a few Ethiopians with dark skin. He showed a succession of NCOs and officers his letters, and most of them could not read it until he got to the captain's second in command – Cornet Kerper. Kerper was a German from the northern seas who had made his way to Venice in much the same manner as Damiano. He looked over the count's letters and seal and told the boy to sit and wait.

The captain came hobbling out of his office a few minutes later. The man was not that old – maybe his late thirties, but had obviously been through a few fights and that aged him in some ways that the average person would not have. He had a scar that ran from the top of the left side of his face to the jaw on the right side, giving him a frightening visage. Then he smiled and extended his arms, grasping the boy's hand and elbow in one motion.

"Welcome, my boy. It is a pleasure to meet you and to read the greetings from your father. How is my old comrade-in-arms?"

This took Damiano by surprise; his father had never spoken of his military career. To Damiano, his father had always been a magistrate, yet he had heard whispers around town of other times. Many men boasted of their military careers, but not his father. Men always gave him a knowing nod of respect, but he never considered the possibility.

"My esteemed father is in good health and sends his best wishes, Captain-general." This was a lie of course. His father had just grunted and told him to be wary of robbers and that included the Schiavoni.

"Good, my boy. Your father indicates you are a good swordsman, which will help you, but we will see if you can become a fighter. He has given me a letter of credit to allow me to get you set up, but unless we go on campaign you must watch your ducats." Damiano liked Zomba, but he reminded him of local politicians who were gregarious in public but could be vicious in private. Although the men spoke of his battle prowess, he was starting to gain in girth and he winced when he rose from a chair.

He was passed down the chain of command from one person to another until he was introduced to another nameless NCO.

"Come on, lad," motioned the thirty-something veteran. "We eat at sunset. I'll get you a bunk and some equipment from our arsenal. That will be deducted from your pay until it is paid off, so don't lose it or you will be working for the Republic in more ways than one."

Damiano just nodded as if in a haze, said, "Yes, sir," and continued on his way.

His billet was in a run-down area of the city. While the soldiers worked and dined together, the living quarters were separated into different groups. The non-Dalmatian soldiers were grouped together in one corner. All the soldiers were friendly enough, but he could easily see working clichés in these barracks. The Slavic soldiers stayed to themselves, speaking to each other in their native tongue. They had dark features for the most part so once again Damiano stuck out from the rest of the company. Damiano was given a doublet and breeches, two pairs of hose, shoes, a cap, and of course the straight basket-hilted broadsword of the Schiavoni. He deposited his money and valuables with the company bursar and tried to meet his new comrades. He walked over to the first group speaking in their native language. He tried to speak to them in Italian and they ignored him, then he tried German and finally French. They ignored him, but across the room one of the Ethiopians called to him in Latin.

"Don't bother, man. They won't acknowledge you yet. Come here and have a drink with us."

His messmates were the outsiders – German, French, Italian, and African. There were not many, just ten, out of the seventy-five in the company.

"Relax my friend," said the Ethiopian. "Here, have some Amorone, it's a local wine."

*****

"What of our supporters in the town? Can they help us?"

"The castellan has a blank-fool. He seems right for our purposes if he doesn't blow himself up. He is just a boy. I think Stanczyk has warned the man." As he spoke, Mytiaz started to glow again, giving off an orange glow in the void. Tłun knew that Mytiaz still had enough hope to change color depending on his mood – from optimistic yellow-white to sullen red-purple. It was at least something of interest in the void. Currently, it was yellow and pulsated regularly indicating he expected changes in their status soon.

"You hope for too much, Mytiaz. It has been years since that door was opened. I give you permission to try."

Mytiaz frowned, but he would not relent. "We may not have our minions on this side, but we can still communicate with those faithful to us. We can guide the boy. I fear the others may try to use him as well. If we cannot, there is another potential candidate, however… He is unstable."

Mytiaz showed no sign of nervousness or fear as befitted his status of a deity, but he also knew that darker forms were at work and started to turn orange in frustration. Tłun's brow narrowed in thought. This blank conduit could be a perfect subject to restore them to the human realm. If the Eldar Gods got to him first however…

"Then try. We must stop the others. This is our world. They will only destroy it. They will all try to destroy it."

*****

For the next two years, Damiano learned the way of the warrior as a member of the Schiavoni, in battles against the Turks or other Italian states. At first his unit was used in guard duty for the Doge, but later he was thrust in the line. He scrapped in more than one drunken brawl on the quays and fought two duels with local lads. One of which gave him a swarthy scar on his left cheek – he killed the man for that. Luckily for him they were moving out the next day.

Despite growing up on an island and now in the pay of a 'naval' power, he still didn't like ships and got seasick too easily to the amusement of his compatriots. While many men were heading east in anticipation of war with the Turks, he was sent west to join their new French allies against Milan. For Damiano and his comrades, this was the best option – the lush plains of Lombardy, plunder, and good wine.

The Ethiopian, named Ahmad who most times went by the name of Mateo, was the son of a Spanish mother and a father who arrived and then stayed as an emissary in the Court of Aragon. He was sent by his father to make his fortune in Italy as the Spanish were expelling Moors and the prospects, even though he was Catholic, were not promising. Damiano was glad that the experienced soldier was now with him; he taught the recruit what he needed to know to survive and tricks of fighting in battle where the niceties of dueling didn't matter. An Ethiopian in Venice was not that unusual, but when his company went in-land, Mateo was treated as an object to be seen. It helped that he was tall and muscular. His head and face was shaven except for a small beard on his chin that he kept braided – and he was an expert swordsman, something that Damiano appreciated in more than one scrap with the locals.

Having beaten the Milanese in the war, the Venetian forces moved into territory allotted to them with garrisons to keep the peace. In the summer of 1500, they were posted to a settlement named 'Chiaggo' near Vento when the area was shaken one day by an earthquake. It was not much of a tremor as quakes go – the bells in town rang and some of the shoddier construction suffered, but everyone was safe. The captain of his unit had the men survey the damage and he took Damiano to the local prefect. The captain was a simple man who saw the hand of God in all actions and this was no exception, but the prefect was a man of 'science' who sought to hedge his bet. Damiano had some schooling in such things so the captain wanted him to translate what the prefect said into plain language.

The prefect was always studying such things - the air pressure (he never felt any pressure from the air), the stars in the heavens, and the tremors from volcanoes and quakes. The prefect explained that this was a big quake; very strong and coming from far away.

"It was most surely from deep within the earth, but far away to the north. The closer to it, the stronger it would have been. See, I have these measurements…" and he trailed off to another area of the room. The captain just made a motion to wave the prefect away, turned and left.

"We're just all damned," he muttered and dragged Damiano with him.

As they were leaving he could still hear the prefect just kept on talking as if they were right there beside him. "But my main concern is this reading right here," and pointed to some machine with pencils hooked into it. Noticing he was alone again he slumped down into the chair behind his desk and put aside the paper he had picked up and shouted, "but this discharge of ozone, this is unusual. No one ever believes me when I show them this…" By that time they were beyond earshot.

In the aftermath of the quake, Damiano noticed many unusual things about the people of Chaiggo; the air took on an odd heaviness that made people depressed; the animals started acted unusual – several of them were breech-born, they became aggressive, and birds flew into the walls of the town and the city hall. Adding to this, there were all manner of queer folk passing through the town mostly going north, but some coming south; ultimately they were trailed by a strange assortment of odd and unsavory characters.

In September, a lightweight traveling coach arrived, accompanied by several lackeys and postilions. Later that evening, Damiano was called into the captain's quarters along with several of his brothers-in-arms. In the ante-room of the captain's meeting room several swarthy characters in Hungarian dress stood at the ready. There was the smell of sweat and garlic, and perhaps stale wine in the air. They looked like they would brawl at the drop of a hat, but at the same time also looked like they could not be bothered. Perched on a chair; and he was literally 'perched', was a fool; dressed in a motley coat with bells, he alternatively flopped in the chair and sat on his haunches looking around nervously. The door to the captain's meeting room opened and he walked out with a regal looking woman in a brocade dress and an ostrich plume hat. There were little pearl buttons and spangles on the dress which marked her out as a wealthy woman, but the cloth seemed a little worn.

The guards stood at attention, as did the fool, who took on a mocking copied stance of the Hungarian Guards. She carried herself with a haughty yet familiar manner of someone who was born in the aristocracy and the captain deferred to her as her position required. The Venetians made way as the woman and her guards came through, and Damiano thought she gave him a quick sideways glance as she passed; the fool brought up the rear and also seemed to make eye contact with Damiano and held it for a moment – with a sad, forlorn look on his face. While many court fools were small people or feeble-minded, the countess' fool seemed like an imitation of one. Hers was neither a child and not malformed, but just a small man who seemed like he was always drunk.

The captain called the group in to address Damiano's detachment. Captain Zomba always looked stern when he addressed the men – he could be telling them about the dinner menu and it would still sound like he was scolding naughty children. "The noble lady who just left was Countess Engblad, an aristocrat of the Holy Roman Empire. Countess Engblad needs to get back to her estates near Ducal Prussia, to a town called Starybogow. To get there will require her to cross dangerous areas of the Empire. As she is related to Governor Simka, and a friend of my family, she deserves protection. As she had been living in Venice for some time, she also enjoys the company of our Doge. It is decided that we should help her. Her family's estates have been severely damaged by the earthquake that hit some weeks ago. The route from here to Starybogow is dangerous at best; the route torturous and the food no doubt foreign. With a little luck the wine will be plentiful." He turned to walk away, preoccupied with a series of thoughts going through his mind. When he turned back and saw the men still assembled, he threw up his arms, "Well what are you waiting for? You have your orders, carry them out!"

*****

There was a surge of light like a flash, then the sound of a boom as the barriers in their portal came down. Perun blinked several times, holding his hand up against the blinding light. When he finally saw his hand, he snatched it down, staring at it as if he had never seen it before. "We are free!"

He looked down at Mytiaz, glowing with blue, then back toward the mystic gateway that resonated with the most arcane magic. "Not all of us; we must move quickly before it closes again." The portal that was created opened at several different areas where his fellow entities could escape into the human world, but it would only be open for a short time. He feared not all would have the chance to make it across. Crossing through the portal, Perun turned to Tłun "Get as many through as possible." He took a deep breath in the open air and stretched out his hands. He needed the sun to start to regain his strength. Perun stopped and looked Tłun in the eyes, "Do we still have the boy on our side?"

"For now, the Grand Duke has not gotten him here yet but there are others as well, some we did not see. It was the allies of the Eldar Gods that opened this portal and they have released some of their dark brood. We must gather our forces."

Perun nodded but showed no sign of emotion. He had hoped the dark ones would still be imprisoned, but no; the struggle continued on in the human world once more. They would have to rely on the belief in humans to aid them until they could reclaim their strength.

He already understood what Mytiaz had said. He had prepared for it. He knew if they could be freed, so could the Eldar Gods. At least, in this realm, they could fight back against them. They could use humanity to reclaim their power and protect this world at the same time.

"This world has changed since we were last here," Mytiaz said as he walked around aimlessly, sniffing as if trying to find a familiar homey smell. "I can feel that our power circles are no longer intact. We will need to rebuild."

Perun heard what Mytiaz was saying, but he was not paying him much attention. He was more concerned trying to figure out their location. They were in a catacomb of sorts. As best he could tell they were under a city – their city – what was left from their time was down here. It had been buried by new cities, ever more building; all of that much was for certain. Now there were others that lived above them. Time and war had leveled their land, but humanity built once more. Surely some of their talisman had survived, as he tried to summon his followers. But he was too new back in this world to have any effect. He hoped they had not traded one prison for another.

Perun reached his hand out. He could feel the presence of his people nearby. They would come to him eventually, but he needed to gather his strength, to adapt again to this world, its noises hummed in his head. It would take time though and his kind needed to gather their strength before they were discovered in this weakened state. They were vulnerable now. He opened a passage in the wall and those that had made it through entered before he closed it up again. He could feel the others though, the Eldar ones. This would not do; it would not do at all.

*****

The captain decided to give Mateo command of the troops being sent to convey the countess to her estates. She was intrigued by the man she kept referring to as 'the Moor' and Mateo had proven his bravery and leadership across several battlefields, not to mention commanding the respect of the men. Between the Venetian troops, her lackeys, and other hanger-ons, they moved like a small army for protection because there was no law between the towns. In the backwaters every petty lord thought he was a ruler, and highways were ruled by brigands who made travel between cities perilous unless one had numbers on their side. Some of these brigands were ex-soldiers who could sometimes be bribed, but mostly they were poor people trying to get what they could.

The whole group was mounted, which allowed it to move quicker, but at the same time required more time to get ready and bed down, as the servants took care of the horses. The animals and people needed food, which required more wagons to protect, and thus extended their lines. Although the soldiers were there to protect the great lady, it was their supplies they were most worried about. Each morning her chamberlain, Sir Kinder, with his entourage, would ride ahead to secure lodgings or a campsite and then alert the Venetians where to go and when they might expect trouble. Surprisingly, they had less difficulty on the road than Damiano would have expected. There was the odd highwayman who would appear and quickly exit, but the organized bands they had anticipated were nowhere to be seen. As they made their way through the passes between the Italian, Swiss, and Hapsburg lands, Damiano expected to meet bandits, but the roads were noticeably quiet.

Often the chamberlain would meet them and say there was potentially a problem, but he 'took care of it', then smile with abnormally sharp canine teeth.

The Venetians expected to see the great cities, but the countess's staff kept to the countryside. Bypassing Vienna, they entered Hungary through Presburg, where her family had an estate. The ancestral home dated back centuries. It was sacked by Tartars, rebuilt and attacked repeatedly, but was strong, commanding the trade route in this area. They stayed there for a week to re-supply and gather more lackeys, because the chamberlain kept insisting, "There are many dangers along the way, not all of them man and we need some numbers." These troops amounted to a small private army, but not a particularly strong looking one. Underfed, poorly clothed, but always moving forward; they earned their nickname of 'hardy troops'.

The roads through Hungarian lands followed a series of hills and forests, but the entourage managed to stay at a series of fortified manors along this route – each within a day's ride from the previous, with not much in between. What peasants they met along the way always moved to the side and bowed with hats removed. The danger was always bands of Tartars, Ottomans, and bandits, but it was still eerily calm until they reached the Tatra Mountains. Having found a place to cross the river, the chamberlain stayed close to the group as they moved through the mountains – there was something about these hills that scared him. The countess's lackeys said that they had entered the lands of the Old Gods and would make a strange sign – not a cross but almost a Muslim prayer motion.

The entourage could hear wolves calling in these mountains; the Schiavoni were used to them and treated them like any other threat, but the countess and her crew seemed more afraid of them than Tartars.

Entering into the Crown lands of Poland, they followed the trade routes through Galicia. This area was a crossroads of armies – the Teutonic Knights, the Poles, Lithuanians, Russians, Ruthenians, and Hungarians all fought for control. This expanse was recognized as part of Polish Crown lands, in that part of the Polish-Lithuanian Kingdom ruled simultaneously from Krakow and Wilno by a member of the Lithuanian Dynasty. Each farm was a mini fortress and all the villages and hamlets had a manor house to serve as a refuge. Even though the lands they were moving through were technically part of the Polish Kingdom, there were always raids from Tartar, the free Cossacks of the Sech, Teutonic Knights, and Russian Boyars.

The countess kept to herself for the most part – there was no reason for her to mingle with 'lesser' people. Damiano was given the provisional rank of sergeant and as such, combined with his gentle birth, she would from time to time make small talk with him when he reported to her.

"You seem very polished considering your heritage. Have you read on court life?"

Damiano was shocked the first time she spoke to him. He hesitated, almost not sure if he should speak back to her. He cleared his throat and tried to still remain as militant as possible.

"My father made sure we were all taught in the latest manners. I was schooled with his other children. We learned Latin, Greek, French, and German. He taught me to love learning."

"And yet for all this learning he sent you to be a soldier instead of scholar in the church?"

"I do not have the temperament for the church my lady; and he thought the best way to make my way was in arms. But I still try to read."

"Books are expensive for one on your salary."

"I pick up what I can. When we were in Manuta, I managed to 'liberate' some papers a noble named Castiglione was working on about manners. Not very polished, but interesting."

"That you know manners at all is a relief compared to most of these men." She paused and a devilish smile came on her face. "Do you know chess?"

"But of course, my lady."

"Then you must come play some time. I need a distraction on this trip and the chamberlain is no challenge for me." As if suddenly bored of his presence, her smile disappeared and she waved her hand. "You may go."

Damiano left, feeling put in his place and intrigued that this woman knew chess. He would play when called. The first time he was surprised by her ability, but after that never made the mistake of underestimating her again. He was glad to have a new opponent as well. He tried teaching Mateo how to play, but draughts was more the Ethiopian's game of choice, what with less thinking he needed to do.

*****

Eventually they decided to camp at the crossroads town of Zmigrod. Merchants and traders used this as a resting area before moving in any direction and it was popular in the wine trade. Kazimierz the Great had given its charter, so there were several inns to take advantage of this status and strong walls to protect it. Even with this, the accommodations were not spacious or luxurious, but some of the countess' outriders had gone ahead to secure enough space in a suitable inn.

The roads north consisted of mud or corduroy that cut through dense pine forests. At times, the forest blocked out much of the sun, when it suddenly thinned out to the town before them. There was a constant flow of traffic along the road, and less chance for bandits and raiders, but the Schiavoni kept their arms at the ready. When they finally rolled into the town square, the countess went to her rooms and the soldiers and outriders bedded down in the common room. Damiano was summoned to the countesses' outer chamber where she invited him to some wine.

"A nice tokay. Good enough to wash some of the dust off your tongue, as they say."

Damiano bowed and offered his thanks. She told him to sit and he did so, when he noticed the countesses' fool sitting in the corner having a conversation with himself.

"Ah, Myko." She acknowledged with an arch of the eyes. "You know, in the olden days, kings and rulers employed fools because their minds were not cluttered with thoughts. I suppose it made people come under the impression they were more receptive to the gods. Sort of the way prayer is supposed to work, but most clever people can never really clear their thoughts to be receptive to spiritual beings. The clearer the mind, the deeper they can attain that communion." The countess then took a sip of wine and offered the bottle and an empty glass to Damiano with a hand gesture. "We can afford to be a little familiar at this stage without other eyes on us while we play our parts, eh, Captain?" He could not tell if she was tipsy or playful. It was unusual for a lady of her station, but she was increasingly familiar in private moments.

"I'm only a corporal, my lady."

"Corporal, captain, commodore; what does it matter? You have a broad base of learning. I am impressed."

"I try," he nodded as he poured himself some wine.

"Charming, I'm sure. There are after all many ways to fight, eh, Captain?" She said this with a note of distain and bemusement, then drifted away in thought.

*****

Later that evening Mateo pulled Damiano aside. "There is something wrong with that noble. More wrong than usual. She has a smell of death around her. Beneath a veneer of makeup there are rotten edges. She reminds me of a *diobolose*. My father told me stories of the deathless ones that roamed the plains. Something is not right here."

"She is just an enlightened noble, Matti. All the time with this talk of devils and creatures. Enter the modern age."

"Still my friend, be careful."

Even though he quickly dismissed Matteo's words, he kept coming back to them, and when he did, an odd shiver came upon him as if a chill had blown through. Surely, she was just another of those odd nobles he had encountered throughout his career. Surely.

*****

The survivors awoke to a city transformed. The blank boy they had used to open the portal was no longer there – just his shoes remained. When several of the guards broke through the door to the chambers, they found what was left of the castellan was scattered about the broken room.

Several of the guards broke through the door of the castellan's chambers. The man's head was lodged on a bookcase with an odd grin. Other parts were scattered elsewhere, but for such slaughter, there was a noticeable absence of blood, as if it was drained and then torn apart. There was a great hole in the floor that opened up to what looked like catacombs and tunnels. What could only be described as slime from the river was smeared along the floor and out into the darkness.

When the citizens managed to recover, many came out into the streets. The lucky among them were covered in dust; the others were buried under rubble or found themselves at the bottom of a tunnel beneath the streets. The river had changed course slightly, shifting to the north so that the southern end of the docks was now high and dry. Some of the buildings had toppled over, leaving rubble in the streets. The bells in the church tower were still ringing erratically, and fissures opened in some of the streets to tunnels and caverns below ground. Several people rushed out of their homes into the streets shouting, "It is done, it is done! The Old Gods will be back to us!"

General mayhem broke out and was not contained until night when the militia managed to get things back under control. Along the river front some of the dock workers moved toward town with boat hooks and gaffes; there was a strange light in their eyes. It was the light of death.

*****

"What is the date? I do not wish to be late for my meeting with The Blackbird."

Damiano heard the countess ask her retainer and thought nothing of it. He had gotten used to her odd ways and assumed it was the nickname of someone close to her. However, a few days later they reached a crossroads where Damiano saw an inn called, 'The Blackbird'. He entered the inn with the countess's entourage, as she had now kept him close to her inner group. The innkeeper met the group as they entered. She was an old woman that the Countess called, 'Babcha' or 'Grandmother' in a way that made Damiano think they knew each other. Others in her group seemed to know her as well, but called her 'Baba'.

The furnishings were very old fashioned, but sturdy; the inside was clean compared to many of the other places they had been in.

The evening passed uneventful, but Damiano had strange dreams and the next morning when they awoke and went out to the adjacent stables, Starybogow seemed a lot closer than he remembered the night before. The horses were a little skittish, but Damiano continued to make sure the valets had packed everything securely. They left the inn and got within a mile or two of the town before stopping. Off in the distance to the east, he thought he saw the inn they had just been at, but not where it should have been, as if it got up and moved. He reminded himself that the country was very strange.

The closer the party got to the town, the devastation became more evident. They saw a monastery on their approach but the countess said it was an evil place – one to be avoided. Most of the destruction was from the earthquake and its subsequent tremors. Other places were clearly the scene of a struggle. At some point it looked like Tartars had passed through here on a raid; or at least someone wanted it to look like Tartars. On the plains, many homesteads were like small fortresses. All the way there he saw the remnants of unlucky ones – burnt out shells with bones picked clean by carrion. There were still the remnants of what were obviously sacred groves here and there, which had fairy lights visible in the morning gloom.

*****

The wood sprites watched cautiously from the edge of the glade. They saw the group from a distance, but knew that one of 'them' was among the travelers. Gmiaka, the eldest of the group, sniffed the air and moved quickly to the small spring and back to the edge of the trees.

"There is another with them. We must try to help him; he is one with us."

"Does he know this?"

"Not yet. The closer he gets, the more it is awakened. The more it awakens, the more she can tell. We have to get him out of there and into a safe place."

The smallest of the sprites, named Dzias, came zooming in, almost crashing into the leader. The sprites were small creatures, human in shape but with more slender and lithe frames to match their diminutive height. They moved about in small leaps that looked like they were flying, which allowed them to cover large distances quickly. "There is a problem coming from the east. Horse people coming fast. It looks like the necromancers have raised some for their own purposes. We need to warn the others."

*****

It seemed almost as if the closer they got to the town the slower time passed. Damiano noticed what looked like fairy lights. There were also strawmen or scarecrows about and he swore they moved when he wasn't looking. For a few minutes the party stopped as if in a trance, when slowly, and all at once, they noticed that behind the lights, in the distance, there was a cloud of dust. They began to see that they were riders; and at first they looked like Lithuanian light cavalry, but then someone yelled and they all snapped back to the present, "Tartars!"

There was no chance to outrun the raiders, so the group made for the remnants of a homestead near one of the fields. The building was a short distance from the road, away from the oncoming horsemen. It looked like it had been abandoned years before and would not withstand a prolonged attack, but it would buy them time. Luckily for them, Damiano noted, the raiders seemed like a small party, but that didn't lessen the danger for them. Damiano's guards drew their basket hilted swords from their scabbards and unhooked their bucklers from their saddles. The countess' retainers dismounted and readied bows along with the troops they picked up enroute.

Damiano had not faced these steppe raiders before, but had met their cousins along the Dalmatian Coast. If they got in among the defenders, the raiders would overwhelm them. If anything should happen to the countess, Damiano might as well die defending her because his life would be worthless. The raiders started firing arrows as they closed within fifty yards – using their knees to keep the horse on its path, then turning and circling their position. At that moment only a person unlucky enough to expose themselves would have been hit, but it kept the defenders occupied as they tightened their circle closer on the countess' party. The retainers were neither numerous nor accurate archers, and the Schiavoni were only ready for hand-to-hand combat. They formed a circle inside their compound, ready to deal with an attack from any side, but in the end it didn't matter; the Tartars came at them from all directions. Some of the retainers were shot where they stood, others fell back to inside the circle. The countess and her immediate group huddled in their carriage. Her fool then started running around outside the safety of the vehicle with a short wooden sword as if he was leading a charge.

The countess screamed for him to get back, but he was clearly agitated and would not listen. She sent one of her lackeys to bring him back, but they only succeeded in getting killed by an arrow. Finally, after endangering enough lives, the fellow came calmly walking back amidst the chaos as if on a Sunday stroll, while arrows hit around him. Then upon entering back into the carriage, he mooned the marauders.

The small band of defenders condensed the circle and was able to take down one Tartar who got too close. One lackey was caught around the ankles by a lasso and dragged back away from the protective area and toward the other Tartars. Though he tried to struggle, he couldn't cut the rawhide and he was eventually beaten into unconsciousness. Then it seemed as if the Tartars descended upon him with a hunger of wild animals. One of Damiano's men, a man from Dalmatia named Migos, was caught around the upper body and braced himself to try to cut the lasso. For a few seconds he was able to hold, but the strength of the horse won out and he was pulled across the open ground. At this point, Damiano realized the raiders wanted live bodies and not dead ones if possible.

One of the raiders broke through the defensive perimeter and rode toward the countess. One of Damiano's men stepped up to attack the horseman but was knocked over. The Tartar scooped up his lariat and threw it at the noblewoman. Damiano ran full-tilt toward the ground between the raider and the woman. Then, he noticed a strange thing; it was not the countess, but the fool that the Tartar was going after. He was behind the woman and she had stepped in front of him and caught the lasso in her hand – pulling it tight. The nomad attempted to pull away, but was stopped cold. At that same moment, Damiano jumped into the fray and hacked at the taught horsehide rope with his sword, cutting it in one chop. Both the Tartar and the countess then went flying backward. The countess landed with a thud against the carriage, while the Tartar went flying over his horse. The soldier looked over his triumph and swelled with pride for a second, then quickly ran to the countess to make sure she was alright. He tried to help the lady up and out of the action. The noblewoman quickly shook off the effects of the fall, and scowled at the soldier.

"Fool, I had it all under control." Then as if realizing she said something she shouldn't have, quickly backtracked, "Oh, thank you, sir. But, I was only trying to protect my dear sweet Myko."

Prior to this, he saw Mateo had run through one of the brutes with his sword, but the man kept struggling – more than he had ever seen a man in the death throes move. He kept clawing at Mateo until the brawny Ethiopian grabbed his short sword in his other hand and lopped the man's head off.

Damiano tried to be the cavalier and bowed, with a sweep of his sword, ready to get back in the fray, when he turned and was met with the fist of the Tartar who was thrown off his horse and looked like he had a broken neck. Black, soulless eyes stared out at him before he fell backward. He struggled to get to his feet but felt as if he would black out at any moment. As if in a dream, he thought he heard a trumpet and shouting. Then he felt the hands of the Tartar around his neck. He fought as best he could but was losing control of his muscles. Then he felt a swish of air and the hands slackened. He found himself with the man on top of him – warm from blood. He relaxed back on the ground and turned his head to see the head of the Tartar next to him and a lady's shoes next to it. Then the darkness took him.

*****

When he next awoke, Damiano was in a room, his head bandaged and feeling like a swarm of bees were attacking it. One on the countess' retainers was there and motioned to the soldier to remain lying down. He left and the great lady returned.

"Oh, Captain!"

"Corporal," he grunted as he tried to correct her.

"Well, no doubt you will be promoted to captain when your commander finds out how brave you were." She sat down across from him, smoothing out her dress, and then motioning to the servant to pour some wine.

"What happened… Where are we?"

"About the time you gallantly defended me, soldiers rode out of Starybogow to assist us. They succeeded in chasing the brutes away and saving the day. Unfortunately, not in time to save many of your compatriots."

Damiano could not maintain focus after this, drifting in and out of consciousness, wracked by nightmares and dreams. There was strange music and chanting; sometimes there were shrieks. The soldier would wake up in a cold sweat, but he was too dizzy or nauseated to stand. Every time the retainer would be there, stoic and unsmiling, and summon the countess who would give him something and he would drift off again.

Finally, he had a dream of a wood spirit, what the Venetians would describe as an elf – smaller than a person, with long ears and covered in a bark tunic, chanting to him, beckoning him to follow it. He stumbled along like a drunk man through the corridors following the creature, but never catching him; at the same time unsure why. There was torchlight throwing shadows that showed monstrous figures. He hid in the dark patches, sweating and always feeing like he would pass out, walking with caution as the sprite tried to keep him safe. The creatures, obviously from a nightmare, did not see them, and he was glad as he would almost scream with horror. The creatures scampered around like spiders, clinging to the walls, waiting until they were beckoned by the 'countess'. She was standing in the middle of the ceremony, but not like she was before. The clothes were still expensive material, but she had translucent skin, pulled taunt on her frame and thinned hair. Her mouth was full of blood with long canine fangs projecting from her mouth. She was chanting in an archaic tongue with more and more fever.

Still, it was like a gauze curtain was over his eyes. Finally, he found stone stairs, stumbling, crawling, but moving toward light, he found himself by what must have been an old wharf section along the banks of a river. It looked like the quake that hit Starybogow had shifted the waterway away from the old wharfs, forcing the merchants that remained to build makeshift extensions to the new river edge.

As he reached the open air, Damiano gasped for breath as if the air below ground was foul. He collapsed, trying to rise again, he fell into the muddy clay shore. He had no idea how long he was captive, where his comrades were, but he was free again.

*****

When he woke up, he tried to focus. He wasn't sure where he was; nothing looked familiar as his vision began to focus. It looked like a strange hut, but how he had gotten here, the details were very fuzzy. That is when he noticed he was not alone. An old man with a grizzled look stared at him, concerned. He mumbled something unintelligible, crossed himself three times, and spit over his shoulder.

After trying several different languages, they settled on speaking in German.

"What happened to you, son?" the man asked. Damiano told the man his tale, giving the last of the halting bits of information he could remember.

"You are lucky to be alive my friend. My name is," the man hesitated, his brows wrinkling before relaxing. "... I am the gatekeeper of Starybogow, such as it is now. Even the Tartar attacks never damaged it like this. I was out combing the old river bank for treasure – they say if you look you can find things that have fallen off old ships – when I found you." He sighed and shuffled to a table, then back with a wooden cup, handing it to the soldier.

"Mead," he motioned to the cup with a nod. "It's good for you. Help you clear your head. Better than water if you know what I mean." He reached for a chair and pulled it close to the bed, scrapping along the floor. "There are many things in this area that might seem strange to a worldly man such as yourself but that are quite normal here. The inn you described sounds like Baba Yaga's house. I doubt there is another like it. It has legs that rise and moves it at night to a new location. Baba Yaga is neither bad nor good, but straddles the line between both realms. It is no problem. But, there were horrors in the area, not just the Tartars and bandits. Other *things*. They used to only be outside the town, now they are *in* here as well. There are spirits, both good and bad. You have survived one such adventure with your life. Be happy."

"But what of the countess?" Damiano let the last syllable linger like steam escaping, looking far away, past the old man.

The man shrank back in fear, shaking his head. "If the countess is the reason for your sorry state, then I fear for you more. The countess has been dead for over ten years."

Damiano felt his jaw slacken as he stared at the old man in disbelief.

"The countess and her family first came with the original Teutonic crusade. They annihilated the Prussians and Slavs and brought in German settlers. They destroyed the old Slavic groves, threw the totems in the rivers or burned them. What Prussians still remained lived in the swamps and marsh areas. Occasionally, one would be captured worshipping to their dark gods and delivered to the warrior-brothers." At this he stopped and looked around, almost seeming like he was making sure they were still alone.

"She was present when one old priest was brought before the brethren council. It has been told he promised to cure her of something she had caught from one of the crusaders. Eventually she and others in her family were rumored to be vampyr in league with the Prussians – it was truly an unholy alliance. Around the time of the thirteen years war, Duke Witold took the town and discovered all sorts of foul practices they tried to use to protect themselves. He sacked the town and put them to the sword. About forty years ago, a woman claiming she was the new countess reclaimed the ancestral lands – she supposedly strongly resembled the young lady who held the title before her. That countess died ten years ago, though no one ever saw the body; she supposedly never aged as people normally do. The current countess reclaimed the properties a year after. They all resemble each other so no one ever questioned it.

"If it was the countess you were traveling with, then it is a vile pack of monsters with some foul purpose in those tunnels. If your friends were with you, they are probably no more. If she has you in her sights, you had best run my friend. Seek shelter in some holy place, because there will be no rest for you here.

"Those of us who have grown up here know that this land hides many layers of faith. On top is the Catholic faith, but beneath the surface, lay the old Slavic gods. Below *them* however, are the dark, Eldar Gods, gods of destruction and they still linger. We live here. We always have and we always will. We live with this cycle. You however are from outside and very few outsiders last here. It is best for you to go. Stay till you are well, but go."

Damiano just stared back at him "No. No, I shall seek revenge for my comrades. I can't go back to Venice after this and there is no future under these circumstances. For all purposes I am dead. Tell me about this area; as a favor. Tell me. All I want is revenge."

The old man smiled knowingly, shaking his head in the affirmative. He would use this man against the countess and her kind. For the benefit of all life.

The Cross of Saint Boniface

Robert E Waters

Knight, Death, and the Devil
by Albrecht Durer, 1513

The olive-skinned man in the center of the fighting pit moved like a dervish. He fought Florentine, a Turkish *kilij* sword in one hand, a Kurdish *khanjar* dagger in the other. The man facing him was a brutish oaf, big in the chest with thick, black Armenian hair covering his lacerated skin. He hacked and hammered his way forward, trying to catch the more nimble fighter by surprise, but Lux von Junker could see the exhaustion in the man's eyes, hear the man gasping for air even from his comfortable view from the slavers' loft. The quicker man stepped aside, paused in mid-motion while the bigger fighter lost his balance. Then he struck, sliding his dagger across the nape of the man's pale broad neck with one clean stroke. The blade cut straight to the bone. The brute was dead before he hit the bloody cobbles of the fighting pit.

The crowd roared.

Lux could hardly hear himself think, let alone speak. He pointed at the victorious fighter, shouted, "Him! That's the one I want!"

"Not for sale," Stas Boyko said with a grunt.

"It's not a request, Stas," Lux said, turning to eye the old man. "You agreed to allow me my choice. I've made it. He's the one."

"I've changed my mind. He's far too valuable to free."

Lux pulled a jeweled dagger from beneath his brown robe and placed it on the table between them. "More valuable than this?" Then he reached into a loose sleeve and untied a leather bag dangling from his forearm. "Or this?"

The slaver, his eyes large with surprise, moved cautiously to the items. He ran his dry fingers over the rubies in the dagger's handle and along the blade's gold-inlaid blood groove. Then he hefted the bag, letting the enclosed gold coins click together like Spanish castanets. He smiled, forgetting himself for a moment, then grew serious again.

It was all part of a slaver's game. And Lux knew how to play that game.

"What do you want with a washed-up Tartar soldier?"

"He's a soldier?"

Stas nodded. "Was. . . or so he claims. Though he practically threw himself at me when we found him drunk, destitute, and half dead near the Pregola. He's unstable, erratic. He's got dangerous history I'm sure."

Who doesn't? Lux turned toward the pit again and watched as the fight masters opened the gate and another poor sap lurched forward to meet his executioner.

"Regardless. I want him."

"He's Muslim, too, though I'm not sure how devout."

That paused Lux for a moment, and he considered. What would Duke Frederick say about him using a heretic on such a sensitive mission for God? Nothing, most likely, as the Duke was hundreds of miles away in Saxony, and he would never know of this man if all went according to plan. In fact, no one could know why Lux von Junker was here, in Rostenbork heading for Starybogow.

Stas Boyko huffed as if he were about to say something funny. "Judging by who you are, who you represent, I would think a Muslim in your company would bring unwarranted attention to—"

Lux brought his fist down onto the table, knocking the dagger to the floor and tossing the coins from the bag. Stas jumped, but Lux reached out fast and grabbed the slaver's silk shirt and pulled him close. "The dagger and coins are not just for that man's freedom, Stas. They're for your silence as well. You will not speak of who I am, or what I represent, or speculate among your slaver friends as to why you think I've returned. For if I find out that people are aware that I'm here, I will blame you. And then I will use that man's dagger to gut you from balls to brains." He let go of Stas's shirt. "Now. . . I will ask you once more: do we have a deal?"

The slaver fixed himself, cleared his throat, adjusted his neck, and tried to keep his anger and fear in check. "Very well. Take him."

Lux smiled and nodded politely. "May God show you mercy." Lux turned again to the pit and watched as the fast man easily finished off his next opponent with a swift undercut of legs and a sharp jab of steel through the liver.

Lux nodded. The duke – and even God – might disapprove of his choice of partner on this mission. But the cursed city of Starybogow looming so large down the long road that he yet had to travel, required the best, most savage fighters to survive. Lux allowed himself the small vanity that he was one of those fighters. The man in the pit, holding his bloody weapons aloft to the enraptured glee of the crowd, had already proven that he was one of them as well.

"One more thing," Lux said. "What's his name?"

*****

Fymurip Azat sat shackled in the back of his new master's wagon. It was an uncomfortable ride. It was bumpy, and the dry, cracked planks creaked back and forth as the weak, aged team stammered through the uneven ruts of the path. They were heading east; that much he could tell. And along the narrow bank of the Pregola River as well; he could smell its deep muddy flow. Where were they going? To Swinka, perhaps? Or maybe Kukle, where he had fought in another pit to the satisfaction of a blood-thirsty crowd just a few months ago. What did it matter, really? When he got there, he'd be required to kill again, and again and again, until his master's coffers swelled with coin. And perhaps this master would be generous enough to throw him a few as appreciation for a job well done. Fymurip huffed at that notion. White masters were never so generous.

He took a deep breath and laid his head back against the side of the wagon. Amidst the faint light leaking through the tears in the canvas cover, he studied the crates and the few barrels packed around him. There were even a few bags of barley; for the horses no doubt, and sizable too, which meant that the man had travelled far. But there was no distinct smells in the air beyond the barley, no indication that there was anything in the crates or barrels of any merit or substance. He pushed a barrel with his sandaled foot; it moved easily. There was nothing in them. Travelling with empty containers, and east as well, where mercantile activities were scant at best. Fymurip screwed up his brow. Things weren't making sense. *Who is this man, and why is he travelling with empty boxes?*

The wagon stopped, and the driver stepped off. Fymurip waited quietly as his master walked toward the back. The man opened the flaps, motioned with his left hand, and said in broken Turkish, "Come. Come on out."

He hesitated at first, his eyes adjusting to the sharp light of the setting sun. Then he crawled to the end of the wagon, letting the chains of his manacles drag along the slats.

"Please, step out."

He did as instructed, though the flay marks on his back from his last beating were growing stiff with scar tissue. He stretched his taut skin as he emerged, then straightened himself as best he could to stare into his new master's eyes. A sign of defiance; some might say, disobedience. But he was tired of looking away.

They were big, brown eyes, inset in a long, gaunt face, covered with a thin beard of graying hair. He was older than Fymurip, that was clear, perhaps twenty years or more, but the thick, loose dark robe that covered his tall frame seemed small, draped gently across his broad shoulders. He was wider than he had seemed at first; not fat, really, but big-boned, his hands larger than Fymurip's but with fingers longer, narrower, pointy like brush needles. His nose was long and thin, and he stared at Fymurip with a wry smile on pale lips.

He pointed to a rock at their feet. "Lay your chains over rock."

Fymurip hesitated again, then knelt and pulled his chains tight until the links were taut and straight.

Before he could look up into his master's face, the big man drew a sword and cut the chain in half.

Fymurip fell backward, his arms splayed out fully to his sides. He lay there like an image of Christ Jesus on the cross, spreading his fingers out, then making a fist, then back again. The only time in the past three years that he had ever felt this free was in the pits, killing. And now here he was, lying in the muck and mud, before a giant of a man whom he thought owned him.

"I apologize that I remove your shackles cannot," the man said. "That horrid man of an excuse Boyko refused to give me key. But we'll find a way to cut them up."

Fymurip stood slowly, uncertain that he had heard the man's words correctly, his Turkish imprecise. Fymurip replied in more correct German. "You are letting me go?"

"Ah, you speak my language." The man smiled and chuckled. "And far better than I speak Turkish. Very well, then, German it is." The man reached into the back of the wagon and pulled out Fymurip's sword and dagger, cleaned and wrapped in leather. He unwrapped them and held them in the light a moment, admiring the bright glint off their newly sharpened edges, then held them out as if offering them as gifts. "Take them. They're yours. And yes, I'm letting you go. From this day forward, you are a free man, unless through careless judgment you should find your way back into Boyko's grubby hands. You may go by God's grace. But I would like to offer you an alternative path, if I may."

He offered his hand. Fymurip neither moved nor took it. The man cleared his throat, then put his hand down. "My name is Lux von

Junker. I've come a long way on an important mission, and I would like you to help me complete it. Your skills as a fighter are most impressive, and I daresay that a man who can survive Stas Boyko's pits for more than three years can survive anything."

Almost anything. "Where are we going?"

Lux pointed through a tree line on the east side of the path. "Through those woods, to Starybogow."

The very word made Fymurip shudder. "It's a cursed place."

Lux nodded. "Yes, and more dangerous than any other place in the world. Or so they say, though again, I'm sure a man of your talents can survive it."

"What is your purpose there?"

"Treasure. Or, rather, one particular kind of treasure. A goblet, in fact. One that used to belong to my grandfather. He acquired it through distant relatives whose ancestors shared in Marco Polo's journey to Cathay. I never lived in the Town of the Old Gods myself, you understand, but my father would speak of it often, so much so that I can describe every jewel, every line of gold along its foot, stem, bowl, and rim. It's a priceless family heirloom. . . and I want it back."

"And you believe it has remained in Starybogow?"

Lux nodded. "When the city was ravaged by earthquakes, my father and his sister and little brother escaped. My grandfather, an old stubborn goat, refused to abandon his home. My father spoke of a tableau where he waved goodbye through gathering grey smoke as his father clutched the goblet to his breast while being consumed by the crumbling spires of St. Adalbert's Cathedral. If so, then my grandfather is buried there, his white boney hands still clutching the goblet in prayer. I want it back."

"This is all for greed."

For a moment, Fymurip thought he had erred, that taking such a confrontational tone against a man who had just cut his chains was not his best move. He had no doubt that, in a fight, he could best this tall stranger. But despite his lanky appearance, Lux von Junker was strong, and fast. He had cut those chains straight through with one swift stroke. It was not a move that Fymurip had seen often in his days as a pit fighter.

But the pale-skinned German merely paused, nodded, then continued. "One would think so, indeed. But I assure you that my reasons are pure. If anything, I wish to recover said goblet to ensure that it does not fall into the hands of a cutthroat who would exploit its value to make other lives unbearable. I do not seek to find then sell the item. I merely wish to find it and take it back home so that my family can enjoy its history."

"You have a family?"

Lux nodded. "Indeed I do. A wife and a young son."

"I'm surprised that you are here, then. Risking your life for such a silly thing as a cup."

"Silly to you, perhaps. But as I say, it's a part of the history of my family, and I intend on finding it. So I ask you again. Will you help me find it?"

Fymurip fixed his sword and dagger to his belt, adjusted them so that they were equidistant from one another, the dagger on his right side, the sword on his left. He fiddled with the angle of the belt so that the sword sat a little lower on his hip. He preferred it that way; it made for a quicker draw.

He stepped forward and stared up into Lux's big eyes. "What is in it for me? You get your goblet. What do I get?"

Lux opened his palms as if in prayer. "I have already given you the greatest gift a man can give: freedom. But, if it makes you happy, you may keep all other riches that we may find among those ruins. As I said, I'm not here for glory, fame, or fortune."

It was a tempting offer, indeed. Rolling images of gold coins and jewels swirled through Fymurip's mind, and it all had a favorable glow. But the man was correct. The greatest gift he had now was freedom. He had the freedom to choose, which was something he had not had for a very long time. And he was not about to let that lay fallow with indentured servitude to a man he didn't know. For that is certainly what would happen if he agreed to Lux's terms. Accepting his offer would merely replace one form of slavery with another.

Fymurip shook his head. "Thank you, sir, for my freedom. But I must decline. You may handle your own affairs as you wish, and I shall handle mine."

Lux paused, then stepped aside. He motioned to the woods. "Very well, then you may go. May God keep you safe."

Fymurip stepped carefully, afraid that it was some trick, that the man would suddenly produce another set of chains and clap them on his wrists with the same swiftness that he had cut the first set. But he reached the wood line, and nothing happened. He took a step into the wood, nothing happened. Then another and another, and suddenly he was alone. He kept walking, picking up the pace, a newfound energy in his stride. He stepped over fallen trunks, pushed through brambles, ignoring the scratches from thick needles. He brushed aside a rotten limb. He took more steps, and then the old fears returned, through the dark haze of his memory. A pair of eyes stared out at him through that haze; large, uncompromising, savage, and blood, blood red.

Vucari eyes.

He paused, right on the lip of a ridge line, right before falling down an eroded escarpment thick with exposed roots and jagged rock. He wavered on the grassy lip, regaining his balance. He stared into the river valley below, and miles away, the ruined spires of Starybogow reached up into the clouds like broken fingers scraping a deep blue sky.

The City of the Old Gods.

He didn't even notice that Lux had come up behind him.

"She's a wondrous sight, isn't she?" Lux asked, moving to stand beside Fymurip. He pushed out a long breath, then continued. "See how the evening fog off the Pregola is drawn over the walls like a man drawing smoke from a Hookah pipe, and even from this distance, you can hear the thousand sounds of those who still walk its streets. The screams, howls of the destitute, the crack of whips, the snarl of savage teeth, the clamor of steel on wood, rock against bone. Light from the setting sun casts its shadows long and deep through the detritus and filth, giving it an almost solemn, thoughtful veneer, but at its center beats a heart that God has forsaken. Scandinavians, Cossacks, Moscovites, Imperial thrill-seekers, Poles, Lithuanians, Romani and, dare I say, Tartars, all come to bask in its danger, its promise of riches and unearthly delights. Worshippers of Perun and Dazbog, Veles and Jarilo walk its cluttered streets, sounding clarion calls for the return of the Old Gods, while Prus pagan tribesmen chitter out their foul incantations in hopes of keeping those Old Gods in dominion over the Eldar Gods. Indeed, it is not a place where humble, spiritual men like us should venture, and yet, there is no other place that I want to be. . . where I *must* be."

Fymurip turned and stared into Lux's face. "For a man that has never lived there, you sure know a lot about it."

Lux ignored the statement, turned and said, "I know I don't have a right to ask you to help me, given your life these past few years, but I ask once more. Come with me to Starybogow and help me do God's work."

God's work? I do not worship your Christian God, German. But Fymurip did worship Allah, though he had not been given the honor these past three years of praying each day, bent on his knees to face Mecca. It would be nice to do that again. But there would be little time for that in Starybogow. Every step down its cobbled streets, its darkened alleys, would be a danger. It was madness to go down there, and yet, it was madness to be out here alone.

The red eyes of the vucari invaded his memories once more.

He turned to Lux, but instead of accepting, he pulled his *kilij* and thrust it above the German's head and into the swollen belly of a dog-sized black-and-gold spider that dangled above, readying its stinger. Lux ducked reflexively and shifted to the right, and lucky he did so, for the spider, pierced straight through, tried spraying its poison. Fymurip pulled his blade free, let the green toxic fluid squirt to the ground, then with one swift stroke, cut the spider's silk strand and let it fall to the ground. Its wounded belly popped open like a tick, and for good measure, Fymurip hacked the vile creature into three even pieces.

"God's grace!" Lux said, recovering. "What a horrid beast!"

Fymurip wiped his sword clean on nearby weeds, sheathed it, and said, "A *Pajaki* Death-Spitter. If that poison had hit your face, you would have died instantly."

"I owe you my life."

"No, sir. On that score, we are even. And yes, I will go with you to Starybogow against my better judgment. Because if I do not," Fymurip said, staring down at the gurgling pieces of the giant spider, "you will be dead in a day."

II

Lux paid a farmer six copper coins. The old man agreed to keep the wagon hidden and the team fed and well-rested. "We'll be back in a couple days," Lux said as they readied meager provisions and fastened their blades to their belts. With a few crude chisels and a hack saw that lay in the farmer's barn, Lux removed Fymurip's shackles.

They then made for the ferry that would take them across the Pregola and up to the Konig Gate, but they would not cross until nightfall, Lux explained to Fymurip. It was a risk to cross the river by day.

"What does it matter if we wait till dark?" the Tartar asked, as they entered the tree line. "You are taking us through the front door."

"By night, there's little chance of being targeted by snipers or distrustful Romani from the outer wall."

"I thought you said you had never visited."

Lux shook his head. "I haven't. I've been told of the threats."

Another lie. If a cat-o-nine-tails were convenient, Lux would beat his back for the constant lying, but what choice did he have? He could no more tell this Tartar soldier the real reason for their mission any more than he could accomplish it on his own. *I lie for God*, he kept telling himself, and it helped. *I must keep it secret until the mission is complete.*

An hour later, with the sun fully setting in the west, they stood at a guard post on the bank of the Pregola.

"No, no, no," a foul-smelling Belarus guard said with his bulky frame blocking their passage. "No one gets into Starybogow. . . especially on the ferry. It only goes north to Wystruc. It never lands on the opposite bank."

There were many Lithuanian and Belarus guardsmen strewn about the perimeter of the city with orders to keep out any thrill-seekers, vagabonds, beggars, what have you.

"But it is such a pleasant night for a river ride," Lux said, rolling a thick gold coin between the fingers of his right hand. "Be a shame to lose the chance of catching that cool breeze blowing upstream."

The guard stared down at the coin, his eyes widening. He remembered himself and cleared his throat. "There are two of you."

Lux sighed and fished into his pocket for another. He handed them over with a firm handshake. He squeezed the guard's hand a little longer, and a little stronger, than normal, making it clear that negotiations were over, and that if they persisted, the next offer would be in blood. The guard understood. He pulled away, massaged the pain out of his hand, and flipped one of the coins to a henchman.

"That could have gone badly," Fymurip whispered as they stepped onto the ferry. "You paid them too much. They will never see the likes of that coinage again. That kind of money loosens lips. They are going to talk."

Lux said nothing, but perhaps Fymurip was right. Six coppers to keep an old dirt farmer quiet was reasonable. Gold coins for a ferry ride was obscene. But he couldn't risk not getting to the other bank, couldn't waste time bargaining with foul, inconsequential guards. Now that he had gotten this far, there could be no interruptions, no further delays. He'd risk the publicity. But Fymurip did have a point.

He pulled a bag from beneath his robes and handed it over. "You are in charge of negotiations from now on."

Fymurip took the bag, stared at it through the ferryman's torchlight. It was probably more money than the Tartar had ever held in his life. He opened the bag and fished around in it, letting the gold, silver, and copper pieces tumble over each other. "This. . . this is Royal coinage. Where did you get it?"

The ferryman pushed off from the bank, and Lux shrugged. "A German nobleman travelling to Posen refused to pay my toll. I asked for it politely, but he didn't agree to terms until I stopped twisting his neck."

Fymurip huffed. "You expect me to believe that?"

Lux pulled his robe tight against the chill off the water. He leaned forward and glared into Fymurip's eyes. "You doubt me?"

The Tartar stared for a long while, then blinked, shrugged, and turned away.

Lux relaxed and straightened, turned his head to the far bank and watched as the tiny sconces along Starybogow's high walls flicked in the wind. He closed his eyes and prayed that God would forgive him for yet another lie.

*****

No one lifts this much Royal coin from a traveler, Fymurip thought as they left the ferry behind and made it quickly up the worn escarpment toward the Konig Gate. It was an absurd statement, and perhaps a mistake by his large companion, who up to this point, had carried himself fairly well. Now, the German seemed nervous, agitated beyond comprehension. But perhaps it was not unusual. If what he said were true, getting this close to Starybogow was a milestone, and cause for concern. So close, yet so much to do to find this goblet Lux spoke of. Was there a goblet? Fymurip did not know, and in their current situation, now was not the time to press him on it.

They found the gate easy enough. The Konig entrance was a big, double wide iron banded door that, these days, sat askance against the crumbling stone wall. One of the earthquakes that had ravaged the area had nearly torn it off its hinges. Now, it hung there on rusty joints, daring anyone to come and touch it, and risk it falling on them and smearing them into the mud and grime. They did not dare, for again, another set of guards needed tending to. These, however, were more amenable to bribery, and cost a third what Lux had paid the others. They took their money and stepped aside.

Fymurip had to admit that it was wise to enter the Konig Gate, for it was closest to the Town Hall and Igor Square. That area of the city had been ravaged by earthquakes and years of looters. Even in the poor light of their torches, he could see the detritus and filth that had been strewn along the cobbled streets, the cluttered back alleys, and enclosed neighborhoods that lined their passage. But this part of the city was the most open, and far harder for any wandering brigands or cutthroats to try an ambush. Fymurip pulled both blades and kept them out and visible for anyone, or anything, that dared try a move. Lux did likewise.

The German pointed down a narrow passage through piles of broken work stones. "This way. The cathedral is near."

In its day, Saint Adalbert's Cathedral was a marvel to behold. Fymurip had never seen it without massive cracks along its base and blood-stained prayer chambers, full of rat dung and the bones of unfortunate thieves, but he had heard of its majesty upon his first arrival. The stories that the old citizenry would tell marveled any tales of Christendom and its glory days here in East Prussia. And then the earthquakes came, and then the Teutonic Knights, who slaughtered most of the citizenry in an attempt to rid the dying city of its sin and its slide back into paganism. Such an attempt had failed, of course, and now the city and its cathedral, whose ruined spires lay before Fymurip as a testament to man's infinite skullduggery, died a little death every day.

Fymurip could feel eyes upon them. Every glance left, right, behind, always seemed to flush out a streak of some shadow, some blurry mass that moved from debris pile to debris pile. Off in the distance, he could hear the howls of the ravenous, the screams of victims. There was a flush of balmy wind off the Pregola as fog drifted over the walls and settled around everything like virgin snow, and yet he felt no comfort in it. Not that he should, but behind the grey billows of condensed water, with weapons in his hands, and beside a large man wielding a massive sword of his own, Fymurip felt that he should feel more comfort, more security. He did not. It was true that every man had a destiny out there somewhere, and in this place of Old Gods, that destiny was usually a sword or a steel bolt through the heart. The difference being, most did not know when the end would come. Fymurip, however, did know his fate. *My destiny is out here somewhere*, he thought as they reached the cathedral entrance, *and it's waiting for me with teeth and claw.*

He made a move to the left toward a pathway along a line of old apartments and ruined single homes. "No," Lux said, pointing to the right and toward a dark gap between fallen columns. "Through there."

"But that will take us below the cathedral," Fymurip whispered, trying not to arouse the interest of anything watching from a distance. "Surely your grandfather's home is in this—"

"It was buried in the earthquake. It will be this way!"

It did not make any sense to Fymurip, but he let it go. He did recall Lux's comment about his grandfather being buried by falling debris, but it was very unlikely that his home would be underground. More likely the home's remains would be under piles of rock, in the direction Fymurip had suggested. *Something is not right here.*

They slipped through the gap. The way was pitch black and smelled of moldy dead things. Lux held his torch high to reveal a passage downward. Fymurip followed, keeping tight control of his blades, letting his feet fall in the exact same places as Lux's. The boards along the ground were spaced as if they were walking down stairs, but Lux's massive feet took them in stride, two at a time, as if he had been here before and knew the way instinctively. Fymurip kept close behind, letting the tall man clear the path of spider webs and loose debris that Lux kicked out of the way. He looked back over his shoulder constantly, making sure that no one followed.

He coughed. "Are you sure you know where you are going?"

"Yes," Lux said, his voice echoing through the dank tunnel. "Not much further."

The passage leveled and became wider, until it opened into a circular chamber, with three exit colonnades before them, just as dark and brooding as the passage they had entered. Lux raised his torch.

What the light revealed trapped Fymurip's breath in his throat.

Stacked against the far wall were bodies, mangled and contorted into one giant mass. Limbs of half flesh, bone, and rotten wool stuck out everywhere like weeds in a field. The corpses' heads revealed damp, moldy hair of fair blonde, red, and black. The eyes inside shrunken sockets peered out in long, deadly stares, as if searching for their lost souls.

Fymurip dared take steps toward the pile, and the closer he drew to it, the more disgusted he became.

"Children! Every one of them!"

"God have mercy," Lux said, nearly dropping the torch. "They must have all died together. In the quake. A nursery, perhaps."

Fymurip found the courage to step closer and use his sword blade to push aside strands of dark hair from the sallow face of one of the victims. He leaned in and studied the exposed neck bone.

"These children did not die in the quake," he said. "Look at the deep cut on this girl's neck bone. And this one. . . and this one. No, Lux, they were murdered. Their throats cut. Probably in sacrifice to the Old Gods to *keep* the quakes from happening."

"Monstrous!"

Fymurip nodded. "We should bury them."

Lux shook his head. "I agree, but we don't have the time or the tools to do so. Perhaps later, when—"

His next word stuck in his throat as his eyes grew large and fearful in the shadow cast by his torch. The German was staring like a statue past Fymurip and into the pile of dead children. Fymurip dared to turn and see what Lux was staring at.

A body rose out of the pile, one of the children most certainly, and yet, this one had eyes that could see, hair prim and well-kept, with a clean white dress. It was like a spirit of one of the girls, and yet, its skin was dark and patchy. Then she changed, her dress fouled, her skin paled. From her mouth grew thin roots, from her ears fungus. She smiled a dark set of rotten teeth, opened her mouth wide, and screamed, "Baptize me!"

The shock of her voice knocked them back. The torch scattered. Fymurip held to his weapons, but tumbled backward, hitting his shoulder hard against the floor. "What is this?" He howled, trying to right himself against the waves of piercing sound flowing out of the dead girl's mouth.

"A drekavac!" Lux said, regaining control of his torch and fighting to stand.

"BAPTIZE US!!"

The ceiling was beginning to crumble. Dust and small rocks fell like rain from the cracks.

"Run!" Lux said. "Run—"

But Fymurip was already up and running, down one of the colonnades, deeper into the catacombs below the cathedral. Lux caught up quickly and they ran, together, not caring where they were headed. Fymurip knew that the only thing that mattered now was escape.

Escape from the drekavac who continued to scream as it pursued them down the tunnel, followed by an army of dead children.

III

Lux gasped for air as the dead children rumbled behind him, screaming their request for baptism and reaching out with boney hands to grasp at his robes. He could not stop running, for the impetus of the unholy shamble behind would plow him asunder, and how would he escape a pile of rotten children intent on tearing him to shreds? The key to this affair was their leader, the drekavac. Lux could not see the evil spirit amidst the undulating pile of bones, but if it could be brought down, then maybe. . .

"We cannot run forever," Fymurip said, a mere pace ahead of Lux. "I am tiring."

Lux was exhausted as well. The heavy clothing, the armor, the lack of sleep and food, combined with the stale, thick air of the catacombs made his lungs and flesh weaker than he realized. The Tartar was right. They had to stop, turn, and make their stand.

Lux was first, sliding to a stop across moldy damp cobbles, swinging around with his torch, and letting the flame serve as a sword. And just as he predicted, the bone pile hit them square, knocking them back against the wall of the tunnel. Lux let his torch drop. Its flame set alight several of the children, who did not seem to notice or mind that the dry stitching in their muddled clothing turned scorch black like burning leaves. They poked and scraped and gnawed at Lux's arms and legs, and the only thing that saved the big man from being eaten alive was his thick robes and armor.

He tossed them off handfuls at a time, kicking and pushing them away with but a flicker of his wrists. They were paper thin and frail, their dried bones unable to handle any significant pressure. His sword, incapable of being swung in such close quarters, served more as a hammer, and he turned it around to use its hilt as a stabbing tool, knocking child after child away with crushing blows to their ribcages.

Fymurip was fairing the same, but his superior speed and sword skill allowed him to cleave heads clear off their brittle necks. His dagger was small enough to wave through the thick air and send skull after skull tumbling away.

Three bone children leaped onto the Tartar's back and began clawing at his shoulder blades. Blood was drawn, but the swift man plucked them off one by one and ended their assault by dashing them against the rock wall.

They were destroying scores upon scores of them, yet the pile never seemed to dissipate. Then Lux saw why.

Near the back of the onslaught, the drekavac waved its corporeal hands over a pile of bones. The pile would shiver and then reanimate into another deadly skeleton. The newly formed shamble would then take its place in the ranks. An endless stream of unbaptized bones to bite and claw through his mortal flesh. Seeing this, Lux realized that there was only one thing to do to put an end to this madness.

He stood, and punching a hole through the ravenous skeletons, he produced an amulet that hung from a gold chain at his neck. It had been buried beneath his robe and hauberk of chain, but now that it was free, it glowed like the Northern Star.

He held the amulet aloft as he walked toward the drekavac, and said, "Unholy spirit. . . I cast you down with this amulet of Saint George. Go now. . . and threaten the world of the living no more!"

The drekavac reared up, letting the tendrils of is undulating form swirl into a funnel. It tried to scream its dissatisfaction, baring a mouth of teeth and flicking its ghastly tongue at Lux as if it were spitting poison. "Baptize us—"

"I will do no such thing," Lux replied, holding up the amulet and letting its light bathe the entire corridor. "There are no souls left to cleanse. You have consumed them all and condemned these children to the fires of Hell. And so I say again. Leave this place!"

The drekavac tried again to resist the powerful light emanating from the amulet. It reached out to try to strike it away from Lux's hand, but the charm was too powerful, too dipped in the word of God to destroy. It shrieked, then flew through a gap in the ceiling. It was gone, and the remaining child skeletons dropped dead to the floor.

Lux paused to ensure that the drekavac had really disappeared, sighed, then tucked the amulet away. He turned and there stood Fymurip, blades held forward, ready to strike.

"You are a Teutonic Cleric."

He saw no reason to lie about it now. "Yes, I am."

"I should have known. Your Grunwald sword, your robes, your speed and strength. I should have known that you were a warrior from the start. You lied to me."

Lux shook his head and sheathed his sword. "I freed you from your bondage. I gave you your freedom, and you made a choice."

"I would not have agreed had I known your affiliation. Teutonic Knights killed my father, a loyal servant of the Sultan. They bled him out before my eyes. They raped my mother and left her for dead. You killed my father, raped my mother."

"*I* did these things? Or did dishonorable men, agents of the devil, do so? I cannot speak for every member of the Ordo Teutonicus. I can only speak for myself and for my lord commander, Duke Frederick. We are honorable men with an honorable purpose. I can promise you that before God."

Fymurip took a step forward. "Tell me why we are really here, cleric! And don't lie and say it is to find a golden cup. A man who walks on unholy ground with so much gold in his purse does so under more meaningful reasons. Speak the truth, or you will lose your throat."

The Tartar placed his dagger against Lux's neck. The cleric swallowed. "I doubt you have the stamina to make the slice. Step back a pace, and I will tell you."

Fymurip held his blade against Lux's neck a few seconds more, then stepped back. "Speak!"

Lux cleared his throat. "Many, many years ago, long before you and I were born, Simon von Drahe, the Grand Commander of my order, had a premonition on the night before battle. That premonition told him that he would fall against a Lithuanian and Polish force arrayed against him near the town of Dragu. So powerful was the premonition that he decided to entrust in his cleric, Gunter Sankt, with the honor of protecting the Cross of Saint Boniface."

"The Cross of Saint Boniface is a myth."

Lux shook his head. “No, my good man, it exists. Held by Christ himself before the Last Supper, he kissed it, blessed it, and imbued it with all his heavenly goodness. A pure, yet wondrous silver cross that can destroy any evil it encounters, heal even the most egregious wounds. But only in the hands of the righteous. Such a man was Saint Boniface, until he succumbed to his own mortality, where it passed from generation to generation through peace- loving hands, until it reached Commander von Drahe. But he was worried that if he fell in battle, then pagan hands would corrupt and corrode its goodness. So he gave it to Gunter the Good, who vowed upon death to keep it safe.

“The Grand Commander’s premonition proved true. He fell in battle, hard, his body quartered and catapulted over the Teutonic battlements. My brothers fought bravely to avenge the death of their commander, but it was not meant to be. In the fighting withdrawal that followed, Gunter the Good fell as well, but neither his body nor the cross was ever recovered. Therein lays the legend, as you say, of Saint Boniface’s cross.

“But most recently, through intelligence obtained by travelers of good character, a man has been seen walking these unholy ruins. The stories claim that he is a cleric of my order, and that he wears a cross of pure silver about his neck. And thus, I have been sent here by Duke Frederick, the lord and Grand Commander of my order, to ascertain if these travelers speak the truth. If so, I am to take this cleric back to Saxony and thus return the cross to its rightful keepers.”

Fymurip huffed, but he put away his blades. “A foolish, *foolish* mission. Your cleric is most certainly dead after all these years. And the cross could be anything.”

Lux nodded. “Indeed, but that is why I’m here. It’s not my place to prejudge the authenticity of the stories. It is my duty to see if the stories are true.”

“And if they are not?” Fymurip asked, eyeing Lux carefully, searching his face for any sign of waver or doubt. “What then? Will you kill this man whom *they* claim is a cleric. . . whoever *they* are. Will you rob him of whatever lies about his neck?” Fymurip opened his hands and swiveled in place, motioning to the naked child bones at his feet. “Look around you, Lux. This is a mere taste of what awaits you in these ruins. You go floundering around here without care or clear purpose, you will wind up dead. And that is not what I signed on to do.

To find a Christian relic for an order that has brought so much pain to my people, to my family."

Fymurip seemed near tears, but Lux could see that the rage the Tartar felt kept his sorrow in check. "I am well aware of the risks in this place. That is why I asked you to help me. But we have had this conversation already, my friend. The question before you is the same as it was the moment I broke your chains. Now that you know the truth, will you still help me?"

Lux could see the uncertainty behind the Tartar's eyes. He could tell that the man wanted to say no, and yet something stayed his hand. But in the end, Fymurip shook his head.

"No. I say again, this is not what I signed up to do. I will not be party to this mad endeavor. Your mission is your own. I want no part of it."

Lux watched as Fymurip walked back down the corridor from where they had entered, picking his way gingerly through the piles of bones and tattered clothing. He wanted to call out, to try once more to convince Fymurip of the value of the mission, the righteousness of it. But he held his tongue and simply watched the man walk away.

*****

Fymurip picked a baby tooth from a bite in his forearm and let it drop to the ground. He cursed, rubbed away the pain and blood from the wound, then knelt momentarily behind a pile of stone slabs and discarded wood planks. Ahead a few hundred feet stood a group of men, talking in a circle, one pointing toward the east. Who were they? Where had they come from? What nationality? He could not discern these details through mere moonlight, for that was all he had. He had left the torch behind in the catacombs. He told himself that he had done so out of respect for Lux, despite the man's deceit. But in truth, he had just forgotten about it, so angry he was at the cleric's lie. *Foolish old goat*, Fymurip thought as he waited behind the stones for the men to move on. *Floundering around in catacombs looking for a phantom.* And they had indeed found one, but not the one Lux was looking for. He'll never find what he seeks. Of that, Fymurip was certain. So what was the point of helping?

The men moved on and Fymurip rose carefully and continued toward the Kiev Gate. He would, once and for all, leave this evil place and never return. He would go home, perhaps, or pledge his allegiance to the Sultan, become once again a warrior in the Turkish ranks. Those had been good times, indeed. Why he had ever left the Sultan's service he did not know. Ancient history. But what mattered now was getting to the gate and leaving Starybogow. Then he would figure out his next move.

He moved from shadow to shadow, keeping low and tight against walls and dilapidated statues that had been pushed out of Igor Square by broken crests of ground. The earthquakes had devastated this area of the city, leaving mighty crags everywhere. It was perfect for hiding, for moving stealthily, but one false step, and a person could be lost forever down one of those crags. He tucked away his sword but kept his dagger in hand. He needed at least one free hand to use for balance as he made his way through the debris piles. A left turn, then a right, another left, and there it lay: the Kiev Gate, its door still intact, but guarded heavily outside. It would be easy to knock on that door and request departure, but difficult to pass through it. The guards were far less accommodating when it came to letting folks out. But if need be, he'd give every coin he had to be free of this place.

The coins!

Suddenly, he remembered that he had walked away with the bag still tied to his belt. For a moment, he considered turning around and going back. But no, that would be foolish. He would not go back into those catacombs . . . *never again*!

Fymurip breathed deeply, stood straight, and took a step toward the Kiev Gate.

A massive clawed hand came out of the shadow and knocked him aside. Fymurip hit stone hard, cried out in pain, and nearly dropped his dagger. He hit the ground and rolled, trying to adjust his eyes to the darkness now formed by a massive creature blocking the moon's light. He rolled again as a large, clawed foot slammed down an inch from his face. Fymurip gained his feet, slashed out with his dagger, and caught a bit of the beast's hide. But it did little damage, for an arm, roped with muscle and patches of black fur, grabbed Fymurip's shirt and hoisted him up into the air. He slashed and slashed with his dagger, but he found no hide, no meat. The beast roared and slammed him into a stone block, then pulled in close to stare into his face with red, furious eyes. The beast's rancid breath stung his lips.

"Vasile Lupu!" Fymurip managed to mumble as the vucari's

malformed face snapped with bloody teeth and spit.

"You remember me," the beast said, slurring his words in broken Turkish. "I certainly remember you, Fymurip Azat. I have been waiting for you a long, long time. You are the last. You are the one who wielded the blade. You will die."

"It was not me, I swear." Fymurip tried to speak, but the vucari's hand was pressing hard on his throat. "I was ordered to do it. I. . . did not know. I. . . did not understand."

The vucari ignored his pleas and flung him aside. Fymurip soared through the air and broke his fall by stretching out his left arm and plunging into a tuft of weeds, soft mud, and ornate pebbles that lay at the base of a marble statue. The vucari pursued, tried grabbing Fymurip's leg, but was stopped cold by a bolt that struck him square in the shoulder.

The beast roared, stumbled forward, and Fymurip took this opportunity to lash out with his dagger. He swiped left to right and drove a deep cut across the beast's chest. The vucari roared again, reached up to his shoulder and broke off the bolt. Another struck him near the first, but only a glancing blow. Fymurip tried to cut the beast again, but the vucari fell back, moving to attack the person who had struck it with crossbow bolts.

That person was Lux, and though he stood on high ground overlooking the square, he could not reload his crossbow fast enough. The vucari was on him. Lux threw the crossbow aside and drew his sword, but was only fast enough to block the beast as it lashed out with both hands, trying to maul the cleric's throat.

Fymurip did not hesitate. Though weak and dizzy with pain, he drew his sword and rushed the beast, jumping a small gap in the ground and striking the vucari across the back. It was an ill-timed lunge, however, and the beast easily shrugged him off. Yet the strike distracted the vucari enough for Lux to swing his sword and lop off the left hand.

The vucari's agonized screams echoed through the ruins, and Fymurip was sure that everyone within a mile could hear it. He feared the unknown dangers the screams would bring their way. But, one crisis at a time. Lux's strike ended the fight.

Clutching the bleeding stump on his arm, the vucari jumped a large gap in the ground, turned and roared his rage. "I will find you again, Fymurip Azat. I will find you again!"

Then it was gone, and Fymurip fell exhausted to the ground. Lux stood beside him. "That should take care of it."

Fymurip shook his head. "No conventional blade or bolt can kill it. When it is in its wolfen form, only the power of a strong talisman, or silver, can break it. I doubt that even the trinket you wear about your neck can drive away the evil in that man's body. No. Some day he will find me again, and next time, I might not be so lucky."

"Hmm!" Lux grunted, taking a seat beside him. "Seems you have been keeping secrets as well. Care to explain what that was all about?"

Fymurip hesitated, reluctant to divulge the truth. He wiped sweat from his face, stretched his back to massage away the pain running through it, and said, "I came into this area five years ago. A young, immature – dare I say, stupid – kid, fresh out of the Sultan's service. I left his army because I was tired of killing for scraps, for nothing really, other than the glory of Allah. That in itself was a good reason to fight, but at the end of the day, I was weak and wanted more. Fame, glory, and gold. And Starybogow promised all of that.

"But I quickly fell in with a band of Muscovites cutthroats. I was quite surprised that they cared not that I was a Tartar of Turkish descent, and that I worshipped Allah, peace be upon Him. Like you, they cared only for my skills as a fighter, and fight I did. But soon I realized that these despicable men were not here for treasure or for glory. They were here for revenge. They just wanted to kill and rape and plunder, until every last person – Lithuanian, Polish, Cossack, you name it – who had wronged them in some way, suffered and died. I justified staying with them because we would, on occasion, enter the city and make war on those evil, horrid denizens that lurk in the shadows. . . like those dead children. That was Allah's work, I argued to myself, and so I stayed on, participating in all manner of vengeance.

"One day we were working through the ruins near The Citadel and we caught rumor of a vucari hunting in that area, stealing little gypsy children and eating them whole. We went in and found her. But it was clear that the rumors were false. This wolf creature was just living in the area, you see, trying to survive like the rest of us. When the truth of it came to light, I tried getting them to stand down, to retreat. A vucari is nothing to trifle with, as you have seen. But they had their blood up, and nothing I could say would stay their sport. We tracked her until she was cornered. She managed to slit the throat of one of the Muscovites, but in the end, she lost her strength.

"By that time, my blood was up as well. Someone thrust a silver dagger into my hand, and I plunged it into her belly, three times. It was over, and she lay there dead. It was only afterward that we realized that she was pregnant, with two pups. We left her there on the cold marble floor and never entered the city again. But shortly thereafter, the vucari's mate, his name being Vasile Lupu, tracked us down, one by one, and took out his vengeance. I was the sole survivor, and that is when that bastard Boyko found me. I was more than happy to be in his service, even if that meant being a slave. I wanted nothing more than to be rid of that vile creature.

"So you see, Lux. I cannot travel with you, for my curse will affix itself upon you. Wherever I go, that beast will surely follow. He waited years for me to reemerge. He will not stop this time until I am dead."

Lux listened to it all, nodding appropriately at various places. Afterward, he was silent. Then he stood, cleared his threat, and said, "I understand. But we all have our secrets, and there is no shortage of dangers lurking in these ruins. My request still stands. But if you are intent on carrying this burden on your own – a respectful decision – then I will see you to the Kiev Gate and have you on your way."

Just like that? Fymurip stared at the Teutonic Knight, not certain what to do. The man hadn't even asked for his coins back. *Is he playing me?* Fymurip wondered. When they reached the gate, what then? Would this cleric fall upon his knees and beg him to stay?

Fymurip looked deeply into Lux's eyes, trying to divine the truth. There was no malice, no deceit, no deception there. He would see Fymurip to the gate, and then happily bid him farewell.

"This cross of Saint Boniface. . . how important is it to you?"

"I have sworn an oath to the Grand Master that I will return with it or not return at all."

"And you honestly believe that it resides somewhere within these ruins?"

Lux nodded.

Allah, forgive me for what I am about to do.

"Very well," Fymurip said, standing and turning toward Igor Square. "Follow me."

"Where to?"

"Lux von Junker," Fymurip said, not bothering to turn, "you

may have Royal coin, but I am not without resources of my own. Come. We will do this *my* way."

IV

Just outside the little town of Draguloki, they watched the withered old man fish for carp. He had neither bait, nor pole, nor net, but he thrashed around happily in the knee-high water of the small stream that flowed a few feet from the entrance of his hovel. He would grunt and jab his hands under the water, flail around aggressively, but would always come up empty-handed. The failure didn't seem to shake his resolve. "I'm gonna get you, fishy. I'm gonna get you."

Lux shook his head. "This man is going to help us?"

"Looks are deceiving," Fymurip whispered, hoping that he was correct. It had been a long time since he had seen the hermit. He was crazy back then. Hopefully, he wasn't absolutely senile now.

Fymurip picked up a small rock and tossed it into the water near the man's legs. The splash startled the carp, and the old man fell to his knees, cursing. "Damn the gods! I nearly had it!"

"You haven't caught one since I've known you!" Fymurip said from brush cover. "Nor will you ever."

The hermit scrambled backward toward his hut. "Who is it? I warn you. . . I have strong magic."

Fymurip emerged from hiding. He smiled and put up his hand in peace. "Would you harm an old friend, Kurkiss Frieze?"

The hermit pushed strands of greasy grey hair out of his face. He squinted. "Who are you? And who is that with you?"

Lux emerged then, his hand on the pommel of his sword. Fymurip motioned toward Lux with caution. "Careful, he's not kidding about the magic."

Fymurip took a step into the water. "It is I, Fymurip Azat. Your old Muslim friend."

Kurkiss didn't seem to believe at first. He squinted again, moved forward cautiously, looked Fymurip up and down. "Impossible. He was torn to shreds by a wolf."

"Not yet," Fymurip said, lowering his hand and taking another step forward. "And I won't be until you can catch a fish with your bare hands."

Kurkiss giggled. "It's good to see you again, old friend. I had written you off." He motioned to Lux. "Who's the giant?"

Lux seemed insulted by the comment, moved his hand again to his sword. "An impatient fellow, for certain," Fymurip sighed, "and not one who can take a joke, apparently."

"No time for jokes, my *friend*," Lux said. "Daylight is wasting, and people are dying."

"Welcome to Starybogow!" Kurkiss cackled and did a little dance. "Where death is cheap and life. . . well, that's more complicated."

"Agh! We'll get nothing from this bloviating fool. Let's be off!"

Lux turned to leave, but Fymurip grabbed his arm. "Patience, cleric. Kurkiss will give us what we need."

"And what is that?" Kurkiss asked, straightening his back, though it seemed as if the weight of the world pushed down on his shoulders. The past few years had been hard on the old man, Fymurip could tell. He seemed more broken, more unsettled. Fymurip could see a tremor in the man's hand as he spoke, and he appeared to always be on the verge of collapsing. "I don't treat with Teutonic Knights."

"How did you—"

Fymurip was just as surprised as Lux at Kurkiss's statement. Nothing in the German's outward appearance gave away the truth, though the sword might have been a clue, or his height, or his arrogant impatience.

"He is a knight indeed," Fymurip said, deciding there was no reason to lie about it, "and he is on a very important mission. We need to find a man, a Teutonic cleric in fact, who has been seen in Starybogow."

Kurkiss waved off the request. "I don't travel in those ruins anymore. Bad for my arthritis."

"No, but you still know everything and everyone. Surely that hasn't changed."

Kurkiss paused, stared at them cautiously and rubbed his chin as if he were deciding their fate. Perhaps he was. "Very well. We can talk. But he won't fit in my house."

They followed Kurkiss across the stream and into a small clearing on the left side of his hut. There, a pot of water boiled over a small fire, and dried ash stumps had been set up to use as chairs. Atop the stumps were what looked like black, shrunken heads, but on further scrutiny, were simple macramé balls affixed with button eyes and dried corn husks for hair. "Meet the family," Kurkiss said, motioning to each as he lifted them gently and set them on the ground. "*Batushka and Matushka*. . . oh, and of course, my wife, Helena. They like the cool breeze of a morning and the warm flames of the fire as they await breakfast. But sit, sit. . . they are happy to give you their chairs."

Fymurip and Kurkiss sat quickly, but Lux could not find a comfortable stump. He settled on the damp ground next to *Matushka.*

"The gods have cursed you with so much girth," Kurkiss said, giggling at Lux's misfortune.

"There is only one God, old man, and my girth, as you call it, has served me well."

"Perhaps. But what do you do, I wonder, when hiding from mice, or from roaches, or from—"

"Kurkiss!" Fymurip snapped. "Focus, please."

The hermit shook his head as if to clear away the fog, then nodded. "Of course, of course. So, tell me whom you seek in the old city."

Fymurip laid out the mission as best he could. Lux chimed in on occasion to fill in any missing pieces. When they were finished, Kirkiss reached down and scooped up a handful of dirt, dried leaves, and sticks, and tossed them into the boiling pot.

"An old Bosnian woman taught me this little trick. Then I found out that she was Baba Yaga and had to kill her." He chirped like a bird. "I do miss her cooking."

He swirled the dirt mixture with a wooden spoon, then let the inertia of the stir die down. Fymurip stood and gazed into the pot, watching as the boiling water sizzled and popped around the dirty pebbles. To him, the mixture had no distinctive shape, nor did it suggest anything resembling a location or a direction in which they might go. It looked like nothing more than wet dirt and leaves.

But Kurkiss gasped, stepped back from the pot, made the sign of divinity over his chest, and fell back onto an ash stump.

"What is it? What do you see?" Lux asked, rising from the ground.

"Your deaths," Kurkiss said. "Both of you. Abandon this mission. Now."

"Did you see the cleric?" Fymurip asked.

The hermit nodded. "Yes."

"Where is he?"

"I don't know. He was in motion, near The Citadel, I think. The vision was not clear. Romani surrounded him. He is being protected by them. They will kill you if you try to find him. So I say again, abandon this mission. It is not safe."

"Why do they protect him?" Lux asked. "We will do him no harm."

Kurkiss shook his head. "It isn't you that they fear. They are afraid of who else wants the cross."

"Who?" Fymurip reached out and put his hand on the hermit's frail shoulder. "Who wants it?"

Kurkiss shivered as if cold, but he stood, opened his mouth, and tried to answer. "The Han—"

Before he could finish, a shaft came out of the thicket behind his hut and struck the hermit in the neck.

Kurkiss Frieze fell dead at Fymurip's feet.

*****

Before the hermit's body hit the ground, Lux was up and setting a bolt in his crossbow. Fymurip had already reached the woods' edge in pursuit of the assassin. Lux followed closely behind, finding it difficult to negotiate the thick underbrush, the branches and nettles ripping at his clothing and skin. The Tartar moved with ease, but the assassin was fast, agile, and it was clear from Lux's position that a confrontation had not occurred. Lux burst his way through the wood, crashing and plowing the brambles like a mad boar.

Finally, the bolt was ready. He raised the crossbow to his shoulder, aimed as carefully as he could as he stepped out into a small clearing. He pulled the trigger. The bolt found flesh in the assassin's hip. Lux smiled at his accuracy, until he realized that he had shot a dead man.

"He's already dead," Fymurip said. "He cut his own wrists with a poison blade."

Lux clipped the crossbow to his belt and knelt down beside the assassin's body. The poison had worked fast. Already the corpse's eyes bulged purple. His throat was puffy and red. His veins ran dark green, giving his face a striped marble appearance. His lips were bloodless.

"Nasty poison," Lux said, picking around the body, looking for clues, anything, to indicate who he was, who he worked for.

"He must have been tracking us from the city," Fymurip said. "Maybe that is why it was so easy to leave."

Lux nodded. "I would say so. And clearly, he didn't want the old man to tell us why we shouldn't find Gunter Sankt."

"But why?"

Lux rolled up the corpse's sleeve, and pointed at a blood-smeared tattoo. "That's why."

Fymurip leaned in and gasped when he saw it. It was a tattoo of two black birds, back to back. Both had red beaks and talons, and in the center of their bodies, lay a plain red-and- white shield. In the corner of the white part of the shield lay the capital letter **H**.

"The Hanseatic League."

Fymurip whispered the term as if doing so aloud was a curse it-self. Lux had to admit some apprehension at uttering the name as well, for the Hanseatic League was nothing if not diabolical. Headquartered in the city of Lübeck, in the German state of Schleswig-Holstein, the League served primarily as a collection of merchant guilds. Though its mission seemed sincere – on the surface, at least – it dominated European trade by any means necessary. But its influence had fallen on tough times in the east, primarily in Poland and Russia. Why had they employed an assassin to work in a ruined city? And why did they care at all for an old cleric with a silver cross? Surely they had no clue as to its power, and even if they did, how would it benefit them?

Fymurip put words to Lux's thoughts. "Why is the Hanseatic League here?"

Lux shook his head. He laid the corpse's arm across the man's chest, said a silent prayer for the lost soul despite his anger, and stood. He looked into the woods. Are there others? He wondered. *Are they watching us now?*

"I don't know," he said. "But I suspect the reason they didn't want Kurkiss to discourage us from finding Sankt is because they too are looking for him. They haven't been able to find him, and they must think I can do a better job than they for I am Teutonic."

"Can you?"

"No, it doesn't work that way, Fymurip. I do not share any kind of spiritual connection with a member of my order simply because we worship and serve the same God. Does it work that way with you and other Muslims? I thought not. No. We have to do the leg work. We have to find Gunter Sankt by searching Starybogow. Brick by brick, building by building, if we must. And at least the old man gave us some clue as to where to start looking."

"If we go back in, Lux, we may lead the Hanseatic League right to the very thing they want most."

"Yes, and I suspect that's exactly what they intend. And we should give them what they want. We need to let this play out as it may, if we are to learn who all the principles are in this game. I owe that much to myself, to my order, and most importantly, to Duke Frederick. We need to find Gunter Sankt before the Hanseatic League finds him, or things may escalate beyond our control."

V

Realizing that they hadn't eaten in a full day, they chose to stay at Kurkiss's hut for a few moments longer to find succor and prepare for another foray into the ruins. Lux found the notion a little unsettling: ransacking a dead man's hovel for food, and over his corpse no less. But it was either that or go back into Starybogow weak of body and spirit. They had already seen what lay waiting for them in those ruins when they were at their best. Lux shuddered to imagine what it might be like if they were fatigued.

Fymurip dug a small grave for his friend and laid him to rest. Lux had no practical idea how Muslims buried the dead, nor did he particularly care. When the Tartar wasn't looking, Lux said a small prayer of his own for the old man, and then got back to the matter at hand: finding food and clean water.

Fymurip took this time to pray to Allah.

Lux imagined that it was the man's first chance to do so since his enslavement, and it looked cathartic. Fymurip did not have the traditional Turkish seccade prayer rug, and for a moment, Lux wondered if the Tartar remembered in what direction Mecca lay. Then all fell into place as Fymurip found a dry-rot potato sack and spread it out in compensation, then went to his knees in the center. Lux crawled into the dilapidated hut and gave Fymurip all the time he needed.

He found a loaf of half-moldy bread, tore off the bad portion and ate half of the good part in one massive bite. After prayers, Fymurip did the same. They also found a wineskin of bitter dark grape, but otherwise, it was drinkable. They also found a store of cured squirrel meat, which they finished off quickly. Then Lux cleaned himself in the creek while Fymurip ran his dagger across his face to eliminate the stubble which had grown there over the past few days.

Then they let out. The sun was well past its zenith, and they dared not wait any longer. Kurkiss's hut lay close to Starybogow so their trip back was quick and ueventful. They also had little problem getting back in, the guards at the Konig Gate remembering them and put out their hands for coin the minute they were spotted. Still in charge of their finances, Fymurip dipped into the bag and produced a few silver coins. The guards quickly stepped aside.

The Citadel lay in the southeast corner of the city. In its day, it had served as a natural defensive position for the citizenry, a stone-fortified keep, with its tall, Constantinople tower looking out for invaders winward. It sat atop an escarpment, and atop that lay a sturdy curtain wall which had faired relatively well in the earthquakes. The main passage up the escarpment, unfortunately, had been devastated by the quakes, and was nothing more than a long, snake-like pile of stone barely navigable by anyone without grapple hook and maddened determination. If one were bold and foolish enough to try climbing those stones, there were entry points through the wall that lay guardless, but Fymurip had a different idea.

"There's a staricase that winds up through the eastern battlement, which lies between the tower and the Kiev Gate. Few know of this entrance. The city watch would use it to move quickly from the square to the battlements if the town had ever been breeched."

"Seems like a weak point in the defense," Lux said, but then changed his mind when he actually saw its construction.

A third of the way up the staircase, Lux noticed that some of the steps were false: strong enough to support a man-sized body, but easily cracked open. Once open, it offered a clear view to the winding stairs below, and thus burning oil or other flamable substances could be tossed in the approach of any invading force. And with the stairs so narrow, once burning bodies began stacking up, it would be near impossible for armed hostiles to get up the staircase in any orderly fashion.

They reached the top, and it took Lux several minutes of driving his thick shoulder into the splintered wood of the steel-enforced door to knock it open. Too much noise, he had to admit, but Fymurip, with his slender dagger and sword, could not break the locks free. There was no other choice.

It finally gave, and they paused a moment to let the echo of the cracking door die away. Then, they moved to a small pile of marble near the base of the barracks that lined the eastern wall.

"The old man didn't give us a clue as to where in this mess to start looking," Lux said.

"He probably didn't know."

Lux nodded. "Well, we'll have to search stone by stone. Find a door, perhaps, or a passage leading down into the hill where the old structures lay."

The Citadel had been built atop centuries of older stone work. Some claimed that the structures below the keep offered miles upon miles of corridors and hidden rooms bereft of life, and yet swarmed with all manner of ghosts and other devilment. That was one of the reasons why it had been left alone by most thrill-seekers, but that was the only logical place for Gunter Sankt to be living, if he was here at all. Lux had no desire to venture into such a dark, musty netherworld. But he saw no other option.

"We could split up," Fymurip suggested, pointing across the yard to the other side of the complex. "Sweep the ruins from the ends, inward. That'll allow us to cover more ground."

Lux shook his head. "No, that isn't a good idea. It'll be dark soon, and truth be told, I'm not inclined to search these ruins without support."

"I'm indespensible now, eh?"

Lux could see a tiny smirk spreading across the Tartar's face. He huffed. "I wasn't the one who stalked off in a fury just a day ago. If you wish to work independently, be my guest. But with this sore shoulder now, I might not be so readily available to provide assistance should your wolf come howling."

"Very well," Fymurip hissed. "Let's start over there."

They searched the ruins, starting with the barracks and working their way into the center of the complex.

They moved from building to building, many of which lay in overgrown disarray. Lots of crows, ravens, larks, and other fowl had built nests throughout the cracked stonework. Lux shooed away a hawk and snatched her eggs. He tapped one open and ate the yolk right there. Fymurip did the same with a few small sparrow eggs, then snatched a snake from its perch in a stone cruck, not to eat it, but to gather its poison and spread it along the edge of his dagger. He then tossed the snake aside and resumed his search.

An hour later, as the sun began to set, Lux's foot broke through a rotten slat.

Fymurip managed to catch him before he tumbled down the hole that the slat had covered. Lux adjusted himself, knelt down, and pulled away the remaining planks.

They stared down an old dry well. Someone had placed a ladder in it that disappeared into the darkness. Lux grabbed a torch from his hip, lit it, and set it over the hole.

"That's a good thirty feet," Fymurip said, whispering so as to not allow his words to echo down the well.

Lux nodded. "I'll go first."

Fymurip held the torch until Lux was settled onto the ladder. Then he handed it down. Lux moved carefully, slowly, so as to test the ladder. But it was relatively new and well- constructed, more than capable of holding the German's weight. He moved a little faster, which allowed Fymurip to clear the top of the well and pull the slats back over to cover their descent.

Nausea struck Lux's stomach like a thunder clap. "I don't feel well," he said, pausing to let his stomach adjust.

"Neither do I," Fymurip said.

Lux tried to keep moving, but every step became harder, until his eyes could no longer adjust to the poor light. The stone shaft of the well began to quake and surge, and Lux felt the yolk of the hawk egg lurch into his throat.

He dropped the torch and barely managed to hang on. "What's happening to us?"

But Fymurip clung to the ladder as if he were about to be sick. "I—I don't—I don't—"

The last thing Lux saw before falling to the bottom of the well was the blue-green etheareal face of a blud spirit.

*****

Fymurip awoke to a white face. The face smiled as if the man possessing it were a friend, but he didn't know who it was. Certainly not Lux, for the face was very old, the man's cheeks a pasty grey with a full white beard down to his chest. Around his neck sat a rusty gorget, and from what Fymurip could discern through the dried crust in his eyes, pieces of chain mail adorned the man's shoulders and hung loose to his waist. Somehwere below that set of thick steel links lay a white leather shirt that bore a gold cross set in a red field.

Fymurip reached for his dagger, was surprised to find it still affixed to his belt, but strong hands held him firm on the stone slab.

The old man raised his hands in peace. "Calm yourself, my Turkish friend. There is no need for violence here. . . not yet anyway."

"Who. . . where am I?" Fymurip glanced around the dim room. Torches burned from sconces in the walls. At least ten men—*were some women?*—stood in the shadows of the torchlight, holding curved blades, long swords, and bows. Lux lay on a wooden table nearby, unconscience.

"Kebrawlnik does his job well," the man said.

"Who?" Fymurip asked.

"The blud spirit that aggravated your descent down the ladder. His job is to disorient, confuse, and if the moon is right, nauseate. I cannot afford to have the wrong sort enter my home."

"Who are you?"

"The man you've been seeking." He opened his arms and bowed low. "I am Gunter Sankt, knight and cleric of the Ordo Teutonicus. Welcome."

On cue, Lux began to stir as if from a deep sleep. The Romani that had held Fymurip down now took their place beside Lux, and when he finally came to, his reaction was the same. He reached for a weapon and struggled under the tight control of the Romani. It was not quite as easy to hold Lux down, his strong arms tossing one of the Romani to the floor. Gunter Sankt moved quickly, despite his age, to calm the younger cleric.

"Peace, my brother," he said. "There is no need for that here. I assure you, you are among friends. You have found the man you have sought these past few days."

Lux stopped struggling, and his eyes grew large. For a moment, it looked as if he were going to kneel before Gunter Sankt and pay homage, but he paused, collected himself, and said, "The cross. Where is it?"

"In good hands, under my personal protection."

"I must see it. Now!"

Gunter sighed, shook his head in disgust, then nodded to one of his Romani who quickly left the room. "The impatience of youth. I thank God every day that I am beyond it."

"Patience is indeed a virtue, my brother," Lux said, "but I am on a mission for our Grand Master Duke Frederick, and its mandate takes precedence. Time is not a luxury I have."

Gunter did not reply. He waited until the gypsy returned with a small cedar box. He took it and opened it slowly. There, in the center of a small piece of purple felt, lay a silver cross.

It was smaller than Fymurip had imagined it. He could tell by Lux's reaction that he too shared that surprise. It was simpler, more workmanlike than he had imagined as well. Not simplistic, not at all, but it could easily be mistaken for any other silver cross worn by clergy or royalty. It could fit in the palm of a hand. It looked as if, over the years, it had been tarnished and cleaned, tarnished and cleaned. In many places, Fymurip could see the markings of polish, and at one point, it had been worn as jewelry around the neck; he could see the small clasp at the top where a chain used to lay. Apparently it had not been worn like that in a long, long time for no chain existed now. And it did not possess fine jewels and gold filigree as the stories told. The only adornment it had was a small, oval-shaped ruby in the center of the crossbar, representing the blood of Christ.

"That's it?" Lux asked, letting his voice rise.

"What were you expecting?" Gunter asked. "One big enough to carry on your back?"

"Do not blaspheme, Gunter Sankt. You are in no position to make light of this. You are in violation of your oath. Why are you here? Why have you not delivered this cross back to its rightful owner, back to the Order?"

"Its rightful owner died on his own cross centuries ago. Saint Boniface, God bless his soul, was only its caretaker, until he died in Frisia. You do not know the whole story, my brother."

"Then enlighten me," Lux said, turning to face Fymurip. "Enlighten us."

Gunter closed the box and handed it back to the Romani. Then he began. "At the Last Supper, Jesus did indeed bless this cross with his kiss. But what you do not know is that at his scourging, the whip itself hit the cross and made an indentation that imbued its finery with doubt, with anger, greed, fear, all of the terrible aspects of such a brutal act. Jesus in his final moments tried to reinvigorate the cross with another kiss, but he was too weak, had lost too much blood. And thus, the cross passed from him into the wider world, where it moved from hand to hand, unclean, cursed if you will, until it reached the Ordo Teutonicus, and to Simon von Drahe, my Lord Commander.

"By sheer will and good conscience, von Drahe almost brought it back from darkness. But his premonition of his own death before the Battle of Dragu stopped the cross's revival, where it fell into my hands. . . my, unclean, unworthy hands. For years, I tried, as von Drahe had, to bring the cross back to its glory, but I could not do it. What I could do, however, was protect it, and with the help from these fine men and women around me, I have done so. I have kept it out of the hands of sinners and of evil men who would see it used for dark purposes."

Fymurip could see that Lux's head was about to explode. He'd never seen a man's eyes bulge so red.

"What are you talking about?" Lux asked, his chest rising angrily with forced breath. "How can you possibly protect it in this godforsaken place? There is evil *here*."

Gunter nodded. "Yes, there is. But I would rather it fall into the hands of those who worship the Old Gods, than to see it back in the hands of the Order, in the hands of your duke."

"Duke Frederick is a saintly man, a pious soul! You do not know him."

Gunter wagged a finger. "Oh, but I know whom he serves, and I know what they want."

"Who?"

"The Eldar Gods."

The old man tensed as if the words themselves struck pain in his heart. Lux wanted to reach out and slap Gunter's coarse face as if doing so would somehow force the lie back into his throat.

"That's a lie! Why would Duke Frederick be in league with the Eldar Gods? That would be an irredeemable sin. I do not believe a word of it."

Gunter scoffed. "I can assure you, Lux von Junker, that I haven't risked life and limb all these years simply to keep a silver bauble out of the hands of a saintly man."

"How do you know my name?"

Gunter chuckled. "Ferrymen have loose lips, my brother. You should not have used Royal coin."

Fymurip couldn't help but smirk as Lux gave him the evil eye. But the big man recovered quickly. "Perhaps I did that on purpose. Perhaps I knew that word would get back to you that a Teutonic Knight was in town."

"Perhaps," Gunter admitted. "But now that you have found me, you refuse to believe what I say."

"Because it's ridiculous. As I've said, Duke Frederick wants the cross simply to bring it back to Saxony, so that it may lay in state as a reminder of our charge and duty to fulfill God's promise. That is all."

Gunter shook his head, moved forward. Fymurip reflexively placed his hand on his dagger, then thought better of it. The old man wasn't moving in anger, or to place hands on Lux. He was simply moving closer to whisper his next words.

"My young brother, one of the hardest of the deadly sins to avoid is greed. Greed for money, for fame, for women, for power. It could very well have been the duke's original intention to heap praise and security upon the cross, as you say. But trust me when I tell you, such humility is no longer in his heart. Duke Frederick is in contact with the Eldar Gods, and they seek the cross so that they might use it as a doorway through which to cross from their ethereal realm to ours. Imagine it: What mortal army could withstand a Teutonic Knight battalion with Eldar Gods in its ranks? Why, your Duke Frederick could cut a swath of death and desolation from here to Nippon. Trust me when I tell you that this is our future... if we allow this cross to fall into Duke Frederick's hands."

"And what of the Hanseatic League?" Lux asked. "Why do they seek the cross?"

Gunter shook his head, sighed. "That motive is harder to divine. It's unlikely that they want it simply for its silver, for its jewel. I daresay that there isn't enough raw mineral in it to pay for a night's carnal pleasure. They may or may not know its power. I suspect that they have a buyer for it, someone who knows of its nature and wishes to do the very same thing that Duke Frederick wants. There are necromantic wizards who I'm sure would love to get their boney hands on it. It's someone who's willing to pay a God's bounty, I can tell you that. And from the League's perspective, it's simply a business endeavor, one that they're willing to kill for. It cannot fall into their hands either."

Lux jumped off the table and motioned for Fymurip to follow him. They huddled in a corner, out of earshot of the Romani. "What do you think?"

Fymurip rubbed the growing stubble on his chin, breathed deeply. "I think he's an old, senile goat. But, he may be right."

Lux shook his head. "I can't believe that Duke Frederick is working with the Eldar Gods, a man I have loved and respected for so long. It's. . . it's not possible."

Lux turned to Gunter and said, "If what you say is true, then why did you risk exposure by letting us come here? Why not kill us beforehand and keep your location a mystery?"

"God teaches us that in the midst of life, we are in death. I am in death, Lux von Junker. I am old, tired, enfeebled. My time is over. I have done all that I can do. It is your time now."

"Mine? What do you mean?"

Gunter reached for the cross again, held it up so that the torch-light caught its simple beauty. "I pass the Cross of Saint Boniface to you, to hold and to cherish, to protect, until the end of your days."

Lux shook his head, and Fymurip grabbed the man's arm in order to keep him from moving too swiftly toward Gunter, lest his actions be misinterpreted by the armed guards nearby. "Easy, my friend."

"I'm not worthy of such a charge, Gunter Sankt. I cannot—"

"Any knight, who would take the council of a Muslim Tartar as easily as you, is the right man. You are a brother of God, but you have a practicality of mind and of spirit that is obvious by your demeanor, your carriage. No. You're the one."

Lux dropped slowly to the floor and sat there quietly, perhaps in prayer, for a long time. He never clasped his hands together, and Fymurip could not see his mouth move as if reciting words from scripture. It surprised Fymurip that Gunter Sankt said nothing nor did he move, for the entire time Lux contemplated his situation on that hard, dusty floor. Perhaps they were connected mentally in some way, worshipping together, seeking truths in the ethereal plane, where all truth resided. Fymurip remembered himself having such cathartic moments in the worship of Allah before a battle, setting his mind straight for what he was required to do.

Fymurip backed away and let his friend have the time he required.

Then Lux stood, quickly, his eyes fixed on Gunter Sankt. "They're coming, aren't they?"

The old cleric nodded. "All of them, scores, perhaps hundreds. They are gathering now in the city. They will have breached The Citadel wall by morning."

"Unless we stop them," Fymurip said, surprised at his own determination. In truth, this was hardly his fight. This was a Christian battle, between Christian forces. Why not just walk away? But was it really just that? A Christian squabble? If released onto the world, the Eldar Gods would make no distinction between Christians, Muslims, or Pagans. They would kill anything that stood in their way. Fymurip wondered if the Hanseatic League, in their desire to sell the cross for profit (if that was indeed their motive), understood that. Probably not. Men whose minds were clouded with greed were always blind to the truth.

"Very well," Lux said. "We'll face them, and we'll do what we can to turn them back. But if there's one thing I've learned in my time as a knight, it's that sometimes, the best weapon in war is chaos."

"What do you have in mind?" Fymurip asked, his interest piqued.

"They are expecting us, the Romani, the cross." Lux placed his hand on Fymurip's shoulder, and winked. "Let's give them something that they're not expecting."

VI

Lux dragged a blade over Fymurip's exposed arm. Blood spilled from the wound. The Tartar did not wince or howl in pain, but Lux could tell he was unhappy.

"This is a foolish plan," he said. "It is madness."

Lux shook his head. "Mad times demand mad tactics. It will work. It has to work. Blood of Christ," he said, patting Saint Boniface's Cross that now hung from his neck on a cord. "Blood of Fymurip Azat."

Lux let droplets of Fymurip's blood fall on a rag, then he tied the rag around a bolt, notched it in his crossbow, and let it fly over the wall and into the morning darkness of the streets below. He tied similar rags around three other bolts, and let them fly as well, all down the wall, much to the chagrin of Fymurip who walked along with him, wounded arms crossed, eyes filled with rage and fear. Lux ignored the silent protest, though he had to admit at least to himself, that the Tartar was right. It was a risky move, and one that might backfire. But they had no other choice. None that Lux could see, anyway.

"Gunter refuses your council of safety?"

Fymurip nodded. "He wishes to go out in a blaze of glory."

"Then he shall, praise God. Is he in place? And what about his guard?"

"They are ready, and waiting for whatever will come."

Lux turned and placed his hands on Fymurip's shoulders. "Then let it come."

An hour later, it came.

An entire Hanseatic army, or so it seemed to Lux. Scores of men, dressed in dark red-and-black cloaks, pouring out of the fog of Igor Square, moving in mob form – though in unison – toward the escarpment of The Citadel. From his perch on the battlements, it was difficult to know what weapons they carried, but he figured the usual swords and bows were present. Perhaps some even had crossbows, but that was unlikely. Lux looked again down the line. Every twenty feet stood a Romani with a bow, an arrow notched, waiting. Fymurip anchored the end of the line, near the door where the spiral staircase lay.

Lux raised his arm, letting the small red rag in his hand wave in the wind. He waited, waited, until the first line of men reached the wall. Down his arm came, and the Romani pulled their bowstrings back, and let their first volley loose.

Several Hanseatics fell at the base of the wall. The moving mass paused, took shelter in the rubble, returned fire, but their shafts missed the wall or ricocheted harmlessly away. Another volley followed, continuing to pin the Romani but causing no damage. Lux knew that wouldn't last for long. Seeing the ocean of men hanging behind their bowmen skirmish line, it wouldn't be long before men were climbing the escarpment, and there was no value in wasting so many shots at such long distance.

But Lux gave them the sign to fire again, and again, and again, until their supply of arrows ran low. Many men were falling dead to the ground below them, but not enough.

"Halt!" he said finally, "And draw swords!"

They would come now, for Gunter and his Romani did not have enough power or resources to stage a fortified defense.

Within the hour, the Hanseatic League set grapples, and sticks of ten, twelve men worked their way up the escarpment and The Citadel wall. They were supported by bow fire, which was just frequent enough to keep the Romani hiding. On occasion, Lux would order counter fire, but it did little to stem the rising tide. A Romani even cut one of the grapples, and they watched as the line of men fell screaming into the rocks below. But they couldn't cut them all, and soon the battlements of The Citadel were swarming with Hanseatic goons.

Lux tossed aside his crossbow and drew his sword. He swung it against the hasty defense of a man who had just scaled the wall, and sliced through his face with one mighty stroke. He pushed the man over the wall, hitting other men trying to reach the top, sending them falling as well. Then three came at him, swinging maces and what looked like a paddle with iron spikes. Lux let a mace graze his arm in order to find security against a block of stone. He hesitated a second, then thrust his Grunwald into the chest of another man. The blade cut clean through the ribs, getting caught as it exited the back. Lux pulled desperately on the blade as he fended off man two with his arm. The man hammered at Lux with his nail paddle. Lux ducked, placed his boot on the stuck man's chest, and finally kicked him off. He swung up with his free blade and cleaved the paddle man's throat in two. The final threat was taken down by Romani blades.

At least a dozen Hanseatics were racing toward a small clump of men in the center of the complex. Gunter Sankt stood in the middle of that clump, short sword raised in defense. Lux jumped down the battlement and raced to the old cleric's aide.

They met in the center with a crash of steel, bone, and flesh. This group of invaders was tough, skilled fighting men, clearly mercenary types employed by the League for nefarious purposes. Lux knew immediately that Gunter had not been kidding. The Hanseatic League was in it to win, to bring them all to heel and steal the cross for themselves. Clearly these men knew that Gunter was their target, but of course he no longer held the cross.

Gunter was strong, though. He tore into his assailants as if it were his last battle. And of course it might very well be. The man seemed content with that knowledge, letting his now frail body move once more like it most assuredly had when he was young and full of hope and purpose. Lux took down another with a clean hack to the shoulder, pushed the corpse aside before it hit the ground, and then stood back to back with Gunter as the attack continued.

"Do you miss it?" Lux asked.

"Miss what?"

"Being in the field. Marching under the banners of God."

Lux could not see the old man shake his head, but he imagined it. "Never. I was never good with a blade."

"Don't take me for a fool," Lux said, ducking one sword swipe and fending off another in parry. "I know skill when I see it."

The old man grunted but said nothing. He swung his sword, and Lux responded in kind by protecting their left flank. On and on it went, until Lux could see that the fight was all but gone from Gunter. The Romani who had protected their charge were dropping one by one. Gaps in the defense became pronounced, and Lux tried plugging the holes as best he could, turning and twisting and carving up assailants as if they were warm bread.

Fymurip screamed. Lux reflexively took a step toward the shout, then paused.

"What are you waiting for?" Gunter asked.

"I—I can't leave you here. Not alone."

"I am not alone."

It was true. From behind them, through the shadows of the ruined keep, the blud spirit, Kebrawlnik, reached out like azure fog and enclosed the attacking Hanseatics. The spirit twisted around them like a funnel cloud, working its way through their clothing. All but one hesitated, lowered their weapons, seemingly confused. One even bent over and vomited into the weeds. Gunter Sankt reached down and grabbed up a spear in his free hand. He moved through the confused, lethargic attackers, painting mad throats with crimson stroke after stroke. "Go," he shouted. "Go and help your friend."

Lux nodded and pushed his way through the remaining attackers.

Halfway to where Fymurip stood, Lux could see the reason for the Tartar's scream.

*****

Fymurip held the gaze of the vucari. It had bounded up the winding stone staircase, killing Hanseatics as it came, tearing them to shreds in fact, and painting the walls with red gore.

"I could smell your blood for miles," Vasile Lupu hissed, licking his wet fangs with sharp tongue.

Lux's trap had worked. Fymurip really had no doubt that it would, assuming that the vucari was somewhere in Starybogow waiting. But now it was here, and in the light of early day, the beast seemed larger, taller, and more muscular as its violent breathing puffed its rippled chest.

"I give you one opportunity, Vasile Lupu, to abandon your lust for my death," Fymurip said, gripping his dripping dagger and sword. "This is not a fair fight. Go, and be gone forever."

The Hanseatics turned their attention to the vucari. Since it had killed everything up the staircase, they naturally assumed the beast was working for Gunter Sankt. What fools they were, caught up in the bloodlust themselves, not realizing why the wolf man was here. Fymurip did not divest them of that belief. He stood back and let them tear into one another, but the vucari gave as good as it got. Better even, for its oversized paws hammered and scraped and clawed through the mounds of Hanseatic flesh that stepped in its way. And though it received multiple cuts, and now bled from those cuts, Fymurip knew that no amount of damage to its corrupted, evil flesh could put it down.

He screamed, like Lux had instructed, then dove into the fight.

Fymurip slashed and hacked and ducked and dove through the vucari's huge arms. Now, he was on its back, stabbing down with the *khanjar*, hoping to slow the beast enough to keep it occupied. It could not die of wounds from normal blades, Fymurip knew, but it could weaken, tire. *Just enough for. . .*

He erred and failed to duck. The vucari's paw struck him in the chest and drove him against the wall. Fymurip dropped his sword, but held firm the dagger which now he used to deflect another paw strike. He could barely breathe, the pain in his back strong as he tried to recover. But the beast was on him again, punching and kicking. Some blows found skin and bone; others were deflected, but over and over the vucari attacked, keeping his focus on Fymurip while fending off Hanseatic men who kept trying to bring their feeble weapons to bear. The chaos of the moment was overwhelming, and Fymurip drifted back and forth between understanding what was happening around him, and feeling the mist of confusion. Out of the corner of his eye, he could see the blue tint of the blud spirit whisk its way through ranks of attackers, but where was Lux? Was he dead? The blood trickling down his face obscured his vision. *Is that him? No, there he is. . .*

Fymurip felt the vucari's claws wrap around his throat. "I'll give you one last chance," he managed to squeal through the pain. "Leave, now, or face certain death."

Vasile Lupu snarled a laugh through his fangs. "I don't think so, Azat. I have waited a long, long time for this, and now I will have my vengeance."

Though he was nothing more than a blur, Lux charged forward through the press of Hanseatic men, and shouted, "By the grace of God!"

Fymurip raised his hand and caught the silver cross that Lux had thrown to him. It felt slick and cold in his hand, but firm and solid. He wrapped his weakening fingers around the crossbar, raised it above his head, then brought it down forcefully into the vucari's eye.

Only a tiny spurt of blood followed the thrust, as Vasile Lupu dropped Fymurip and fell back, clutching his wounded face, trying desperately to pull the cross from his eye; it would not budge. Then light glowed from inside the silver, a clean, white blinding light as the vucari fell and howled in agony. Fymurip shuffled backward, but kept his eyes on the tortured wolf man.

The glow now was blinding, and Fymurip raised his hands to cover his eyes. Then he heard a wet pop. He forced his eyes open and saw that the vucari was no longer fighting, that his face had grown twice its size, and then burst open at the sheer power of the silver glow. It was the most terrifying thing Fymurip had ever seen, and for a brief moment, he felt sorry for the beast.

The vucari's thick claws and hide faded away, absorbed by the wan light of the cross. His snout – what was left of it – changed too, reforming into a man's shattered face. A moment later, its entire body had reshaped itself to a naked man.

The light of the cross slowly dissipated, and then disappeared.

Everything was silent. The Hanseatic invaders were gone. The battle was over.

"Cutting it close, weren't you?" Fymurip said as Lux offered his hand. He took it and stood on weak legs, wincing at the pain shooting through his back.

"Sorry. I was otherwise detained," Lux said, putting his hand on Fymurip's shoulder. "But you look no worse for wear."

Fymurip tried to smile, but his face hurt too much. "Say that to my ribs."

They walked over to Vasile Lupu and stared down at his taut, emaciated human form. The wolf curse had ravaged the man, and now he was nothing more than a bleak corpse. "Devilish," Fymurip said, as he stepped aside to let Lux bend at the knee to retrieve the cross that now lay harmlessly at the corpse's side. "I wonder who he really was."

Lux wiped the blood off the cross and put it back around his neck. "Probably just some farmer, who took the wrong turn one day going home, who never imagined living such a cursed life, and allowing that curse to consume him, body and soul." The knight reached up and closed the man's remaining good eye, then mouthed a silent prayer.

They walked to where Gunter Sankt lay among a pile of bodies. The dead cleric was covered with stab wounds and arrow shafts.

"The cross is yours, Lux," Fymurip said. "There is no way to refuse it now."

Lux nodded. "Indeed, it is. But we won't remain here with it. Now that the Hanseatic League knows where it lays, they will never stop until they have it. We must leave at once."

"Where are we going?"

"To Saxony."

"So you intend on giving the cross to the Duke?"

Lux shook his head and walked to the battlement. "No. Though I cannot in my heart believe that Duke Frederick is in favor of the Eldar Gods, it would be too risky to hand it over to him at this time. No, we go there for my family, that I may secure their safe passage to France. And then, we shall go to Constantinople."

"Why? What is there?"

"I know a man, a mystic, who resides in that ancient place. If there is anyone in all the world that can tell us what Saint Boniface's cross is, and what it is capable of, it is he."

Lux turned to Fymurip and offered his hand. "Are you with me?"

For a moment, it seemed as if the Tartar would decline. Now that the vucari was dead, there was nothing to hold them together. And what purpose would it serve a Muslim anyway to venture further into Germany on a quest to ascertain the nature of an ancient Christian heirloom? But as he had done from their first meeting, Fymurip surprised him.

They locked hands. "Why not? Besides, someday, we will return to this cursed city, and you're going to need my protection."

Lux smiled. "Very well. Then let's be off, before Starybogow grows dark and comes at us once more."

Together, Lux von Junker and Fymurip Azat made their way out of The Citadel and toward the Konig Gate.

Torn Asunder

Brandon Rospond

A Statue of Triglav, circa 1500

This infernal prison had held him for so long that the melody of battle and the rush of blood felt like some sweet summer dream. Damn Perun for sealing them in a void. There was no gauge of time passing; the moments seemed to stretch endlessly, and for all he knew he could have been trapped here a day or a millennium. It all felt the same. He longed for the thrill of battle, the rush of adrenaline, and yet here in this accursed void, there was nothing. He clung to the memory of when he was first sealed away, for it was one of the only things of note to happen here. He thrashed like never before in his life, swinging and clawing at the blackness that surrounded with uncontrollable rage, every bulging muscle threatening to burst.

After the voices of all three of his heads burned raw and his limbs felt like jelly, he finally listened to his brethren that told him his fits were for naught. For once in his existence as the god known as Triglav, he felt powerless. He fought tirelessly with Perun, scolding him for his stupidity; they could have fought the Eldar Gods and eventually prevailed in the human world. But here? There was nothing for any of them – Old God or Eldar alike. This was not life.

Triglav learned to channel that burning madness into his bulging muscles as he floated in the emptiness, his eyes shut as he focused his efforts on the immortal enemy. His breathing would speed when his thoughts got the best of him, but after days, months, years, however long he spent in this torturous existence, he learned how to calm himself and focus.

All six of his eyes shot open. Even though he could not see anything but blackness, his instincts were as keen as ever. He could *feel* it – there was a stirring in the void. At first, it was just a pulse of energy; such a light throbbing that he almost missed it. But then, the sensation grew past a heartbeat and into a surge of power – the first of which he felt all the while having been trapped! It was a rush of emotions; joy and excitement at being set free, but then anger and rage as he planned his revenge!

A bright light blasted his vision, threatening to set his eyes on fire with how bright the flash was. He thrust his arms out to his side, welcoming the release from his prison, and then when he thought he would be finally setting foot on solid ground once more, all went black.

*****

The light was blindingly bright. He raised a hand to block out the giant white orb in the sky as he groaned. He turned his head and blades of grass rose up to kiss his cheeks with dew. Strange strands of red fell down across his vision and he brought his hand to pull at them. He winced when he found out they were connected. Was it... his hair? He had red hair?

He thrust his body up, pushing stray hairs out of his face. Where was he? There was nothing but open stretch of field around him in every direction; strange structures stood on the edge of the grassland, but they did not move. They must have been dwellings of some sort.

He looked down at his hands. The bare skin was lightly tanned on the long fingers. He held up his arms; bare as well. He was not sure what he expected to be there, but when he looked down at his legs, some sort of material, the word 'cloth' resonated somewhere in his mind, covered his lower half, and yet his feet were bare.

He put both his hands to his face, touching his features; his strong jawline, his stout nose, high cheekbones. His hands dropped off his cheeks, feeling the broad blades of his shoulders, as if expecting something to be above each that was not there. Then the most prevalent question hit him.

Who was he?

He backed up and his back touched something cold and hard. He spun around, his fists coming up, even though he could not say why. He stood back, staring at the statue that he had not realized was behind him. The metal creature had three heads that each stared down at him, judging him, with all six of its eyes. The middle head was that of a lion's, while its left was a ram's, and the right a dragon's. He could not say how he knew the names of these creatures; he just *knew* the right words.

He turned back to those – the word came to him – huts on the far end and noticed there were shapes moving toward him quickly in quite a commotion. He was not sure what to do, but he backed himself up against the three-headed statue, holding his hands up in what he somehow knew was a defensive way. The strange people, clad in even stranger garb, encircled him, staring with wide eyes.

"It is him! The mighty Triglav has come back to us!"

The red-haired man looked around, as if searching for this man they called 'Triglav', almost thinking they were talking to the statue, but when their eyes remained glued on him, he shook his head.

"Tree-... What?"

"O, great Triglav! Only you could have come from the very sky itself to bless your followers with your great might!"

"The… sky?" The man, who they apparently thought was Triglav, looked up and then back at them. He could not remember much, but he could not believe that such a feat was even possible.

"Yes, my lord," this time, the man's exuberance wavered as he fidgeted nervously with his fingers. "The sky opened and as if by some power greater than any human mind could imagine, a swirling vortex of winds brought forth a bolt of lightning, and with it we saw you come to us!"

The man put his hand to his head, shaking it back and forth. He felt the man coming forward, his hand held out to reach for him. The red-haired man grit his teeth and shoved him back. He was surprised by his own strength as the man tumbled back head over heels twice before a small rock broke his impact. The man lay motionless as his aggressor stood tall, leering over him.

He stood straight as a board, his fists balled, as he looked around at the other men that encircled him. Their weapons were raised and whatever jubilance they might have once showed at the man who apparently came from the sky, was now replaced with snarling looks of defiance. The tan-skinned man could not say why, but the thought of a fight made the corners of his lips curl and he felt his brow draw down.

"Heretic! He is not our lord Triglav!" He turned to the agitator in the front of the crowd, his dagger held high, shaking, his voice a frenzied pitch. "Triglav would never turn upon we that have been so faithful! Kill the impostor and string his limbs up for each of Triglav's three heads to feast upon!"

"Sacrifice!"

The calls of 'sacrifice' rang out all around him and the man swung his arm through the air.

"Come upon me with your blades and the only ones sacrificed to your god will be my enemies!"

The words worked themselves out of his throat before he could even think. He stood before at least thirty armed men, and he had not even a covering over his body. He could not even begin to explain who his mind thought he once was.

It was not the man who had shouted that led the charge, but another feisty youngling. The amnesic man ducked under the blade as it whizzed by his head, sticking into the statue behind him. Leaning into the attacker, he drove his fist into his stomach, sending him back with just as much surprising strength as the push. He whirled back around, grabbing the dagger from where it was stuck. He turned toward the next attack and saw the raise of the blade; the dagger would do nothing against it. He feinted back as best as he could, but the blade found bite in his arm. He hardly noticed as he drove the dagger into the man's eye, pulling it back out only to plunge it into the other.

He tossed the dagger back and forth between his hands before he reached back and threw it into the throat of another oncoming warrior. Ducking under the next few attacks, he felt some scratches on his back and arms, but he delivered savage blow after blow with his knuckles that were covered in blood.

He snatched a spear from one of his attackers, smashing his foe's skull in with the butt. Whirling the shaft around, he punctured the blade through the chest, and as his opponent struggled to fight the attack, he pulled him further down the blade. The blood splattered across his face and he licked his lips, the taste of tangy metal pungent. Continuing forward, he impaled a second and then a third, and then even a fourth, before the spear could hold no more. The shaft buckled under the weight of the bodies, snapping in half as the bodies lay in a pool of congealing liquid.

He turned back toward the remaining warriors, if they could even be called that, and let out such a massive scream, he almost blacked out from the force. The men dropped their weapons where they stood, some even shouting out the name of that damned deity they worshiped, as they ran with their tail between their legs. The man grunted, his bloodlust unfulfilled, but it was hard to tell that from looking at him. His arms and knuckles dripped in red and he could still taste it on his tongue. He was not sure what was his and what was his opponents'.

He tried giving chase to those that fled, but found that it was useless. They were pitiful cowards; there was nothing to be gained in their deaths. As he slowed down, continuing to saunter aimlessly onward, he started to think about the fight. What *was* to be gained from their deaths? Why had he been so ready to slaughter each and every one of them? Something about looking at that idol had worked him into a frenzy.

Could he really be the Triglav that all these strange cultists believed him to be? He had no idea who their deity was or what he stood for, but the facts he had before him were that he excelled in fighting far superb over his opponents, he had a wealth of strength in his bulging muscles that he did not know how to properly harness, and he had no idea where he was or where he came from before he had awoken. They could have been right; he very well could have come from the sky for all he knew.

His steps became slower, his feet feeling like they were dragging on the ground with every push forward. Twinkling lights dotted across his vision and his head spun with great strain. He fell to one knee, using his left arm to stabilize his balance, but it did not help. His head started circling of its own accord. The last thing he remembered seeing before the blackness took over was that he was staring down at a red liquid that was pooling directly under him.

He was sure that time that the blood was his own.

*****

The man, who still had no idea what his own name was, felt himself keep waking in blurs. The darkness receded slightly, revealing the outline of a strange enclosed structure, but the details never were clear enough. Vision would only come to him for a few seconds every time, and then it would fade out again. On a rare occasion, he thought he could see a figure on the fringe of his vision, but it was covered in shadow and impossible to make out.

The shadow seemed to draw nearer every time his vision returned, until he felt the shade hovering over him, as if he could hear the breath being drawn into the being's lungs. Something in his brain clicked. He snapped up and grabbed the entity hovering over him, holding them in the air. His vision returned instantly and he saw the man dangling in the air, his face reddening from lack of oxygen.

He heard footsteps approaching and turned when he heard a feminine voice.

"Father...?"

A girl stood in the doorframe, long chestnut hair tied into a braid, and a confused expression on her pale face. Something clicked in his mind again as he came back to the present, dropping the man he held before him, unsure why he had the sudden fit of aggression.

"Sorry," the word was barely heard out of his own mouth as he grunted it, looking down at the floorboards.

"That's... uh... okay there... friend." The man he had choked stood next to his daughter, laughing nervously with each word. "We're just glad you finally woke up."

"Finally?" He looked up at the man. He had short gray hair and a full beard. From the look of his clothes, he was some sort of farmer. Looking around the quaint wooden room, it all started to fit together. "Just how long have I been unconscious for?"

"Well, hmm." The man looked at his daughter and then started counting on his dirtied, calloused fingers for several moments. "I'd say about... a month or so. Give or take."

The man sat back, staring up at the farmer incredulously. "What? I... There is no way."

"Oh yes, at least a month. With the wounds you had when we found you, I would have thought you'd have passed some time ago. But you've got to figure, a month for wounds that deep and that severe to heal completely... That's pretty good, sir."

He looked at his hands. There had been blood before he passed out; a copious amount of it. He had not been sure whose blood he had been covered in at first, but before he fell unconscious, he *knew* it was his own. Somehow he knew it, and yet his wounds seemed fully healed. He shook his head, coming uneasily to his feet.

"I'm sorry for any trouble I may have caused you."

"It's no problem, sir. We figured you weren't from around here – what with your skin and hair color, pardon me for saying." The farmer hesitated before stepping forward, extending his arm. "I'm Konrad Eberstark."

The man looked at the offered hand and narrowed his eyes. Something told him that he should grab the man's hand, but another thought in his head told him it was a custom he did not partake in. The stocky, bearded man must have felt the apprehension because he dropped the hand, but then quickly brought it back up, indicating to the girl beside him.

"Th-This is my daughter. Victoria is the one who found you."

The young woman stood beside her father, a nervous smile on her face as she bowed lightly. She had working clothes on too, yet something in his mind made him think she should be clad in elegant dresses or strong armor. Even though her attire seemed out of place, his gaze lingered on her face for several moments.

"Thank you. For finding me. And for tending to my wounds." He stretched his arms, making his muscles bulge several times to test their strength. He felt sore, but there were absolutely no signs of wounds or scars.

"I am just glad you're feeling better, mister…?"

He froze, keeping his gaze pinned on the floor. He still had not figured out his name. He looked back and forth between Konrad and Victoria a few times before speaking.

"I… cannot remember my name. Those that attacked me called me Triglav."

Konrad chuckled, rubbing his hands together nervously. "Like the Slavic three-headed god of war? You're joking, right?"

He almost told him that he was not and wanted to recant the battle in great detail, but the look on the farmer's face made him think otherwise. He simply shook his head. "I do not know my name and that is what they insisted on calling me. Until my memories come back to me, it is the only name I know. I doubt there is a connection between myself and this deity. You say that this god has three heads? I have but only one."

"Ah, of course… of course."

They remained in silence for a few moments, with Triglav – since he might as well get used to having a name – sitting on the bed and the farmer and his daughter standing by the door. He was not sure what they expected him to say and so he said nothing. Konrad was finally the first to break the silence, making a strange sound as if he had something stuck in his throat.

"So… Triglav. Heh, still strange to say… What are your plans now that you're awake? Where were you going before you were attacked?"

"I… don't know." Triglav shrugged his shoulders. "I have no path that I am set on. I awoke in the middle of a field with no direction or memories. My future is a blank slate."

"Ah, I see." The man looked to his daughter and then exhaled with a smile as he shrugged. "Well, if you have no other plans, you're welcome to stay here for the time being, until you figure everything out."

Triglav stood slowly, realizing he towered over the other two. "If you are to extend your hospitality in such a grand gesture, then allow me to repay you. As long as I stay here, I will help you with any tasks that my might may aid you in."

The farmer stood there, surprised, but eventually nodded with raised eyebrows. "Why, yes, of course. There are always things that we can use help with. Yes. Yes, thank you."

*****

It took Triglav some time to get used to the work outfit Konrad provided him. The pants were itchy and the shirt was too tight. So to avoid the aggravation, he usually went shirtless when working in the fields, the sun bronzing his already tanned skin. The shirt was mostly worn out of respect when they went into towns; especially since he would usually go with just Victoria.

He had been fascinated with the girl for reasons beyond his understanding. He worked with Konrad out in the fields and was explained the basics of what they were doing, but Victoria would enlighten him on things she thought anyone should know, amnesia or not. The first time they had gone to market had been the most surprising.

"Where are we going again? *Yur-bak-eez?*"

"No, no. Close, but you're saying it wrong!" Victoria's giggle was infectious. Sometimes he tried to make her laugh just to hear it. "Jurbakis. We're going to market."

"I do not understand the point of this… market. You bring items of your harvest just to trade with others who possess different harvests? Why do you not just obtain the items yourself?" There had been a darker idea niggling in the back of his mind to suggest sacking other towns for what they needed, but after getting to know the farm girl, he realized she would probably not find that acceptable.

"If it were only that easy. There are only so many hours in the day to do so much work. We devote our work to farming instead of logging or weaving. It's with these people we trade for firewood, or new tools, or clothing." She pushed a lock of her hair back behind her ear, turning to glance at him. "You remember such strange things. I would have thought the purpose of a market would have surfaced through your memories. It's like you're from a different age altogether."

Triglav did not respond. He sat back, glancing at her out of the corner of his eye, but then turned to stare at the forest pines as they passed them. There were concepts and words that he could remember, some basic ones that he shared with Victoria, but then there were the more… difficult ones. Concepts like 'death' and 'bloodshed' rang very vividly and violently in his memories even though other thoughts decried those notions as 'evil' or 'wrong'.

The men he had been attacked by, they seemed to embody all of those more savage thoughts; but Victoria seemed to represent a completely different set of ideas altogether. Her face did not perpetually scowl like his; her demeanor was always pleasant despite her demure frame. The slightest mishap in their farming did not set her to fits like it did he. Everything about her radiated with positivity, and just looking at her seemed to soothe him to great tranquility. He felt himself drawn to that opposition of his thoughts and greatly enjoyed being around her.

He could hear the roar of a crowd even before he could see the town. The thrill of a battle rushed through his veins as the adrenaline pumped heavy. It startled him into action, grabbing for the dagger that Konrad had given to him. It felt so puny in his hands; like he could fend off an aggressor easier with his bare fists. He swiveled his head toward Victoria, and what he believed at first to be fright, he realized was laughter. He let the dagger sink back into its sheath as she placed an arm over his chest to settle him.

"Triglav, calm yourself. I still don't understand how you have no memory of a market. That's just the excitement from all of the people, there's no cause for alarm."

He looked toward the source of the commotion and scowled. He pulled at the fabric covering his body and itched at his leg; these garments were insufferable.

Inside the market was even worse. He tensed as they passed the guards and reached for his dagger, although he could not say why. As Victoria guided them through the dirt roads, the tension and anxiety sweltered as people moved around them at every angle, raised their arms as they called out to others, and those with wares to buy were the most obnoxious in their bellowing. Every time Victoria found something to trade for, he had to rush to get out and retrieve the goods before she started loading them herself, the confusion threatening to paralyze him otherwise.

Subsequent times were better. Once the novelty of the market wore off on him, he got more accustomed to the raucous, but he never quite became comfortable with it. Even though he never dealt directly with any of the other merchants, his looming presence as he stood behind Victoria was enough to always get them the best deal.

The months passed and the man known as Triglav continued his work on the farm. He thought less about what past he awoke from and concentrated more on how he could help this family in any way possible. The dark thoughts had their moments where they threatened to consume him, but they were mostly quiet. He found it somewhat comical that the cultists first called him Triglav and often considered changing his name to something more fitting.

*****

Triglav voraciously tore into the haunch of meat. He knew he should have been eating a bit more properly like Konrad and Victoria, but he had worked up quite the appetite. He was determined to help the farmer push the most out of his crops this season and he had been working out on the field since sun-up.

"Well, Triglav. Eat your fill. You've more than earned it today, my friend."

"Thank you. I do not know what use I had of these muscles in the past, but I am determined to put this strength to good use."

"Indeed." Triglav watched as Konrad leaned back, wiping his mouth with his sleeve. In the other hand, he coddled his ale, rocking the mug back and forth. "So, my friend… It's been some time. Have any memories come back at all?"

Triglav paused, placing the hunk of food down. He wiped his arm across his mouth before he leaned back. "No. Strange dreams now and again – sometimes violent infernos, sometimes I walk endlessly through a dark mist, others I argue ceaselessly with an old man – but no concrete memories. Nothing to tell me who I once was or anything about my life."

Konrad nodded, drinking deep. "I cannot begin to imagine how that must feel – living a life with no memories. If I could not remember my farm, my daughter, anything that brought me to this point, I honestly don't know what I would do. Heh, farming is the only thing I've ever been good at."

Triglav stared down at his food while Konrad spoke. What had he been good at? His muscles bulged with strength and he knew how to keep his own in combat. Maybe he was a guard or a soldier, but no memories surfaced of protecting or serving for any nation or person. The only thing that kept nagging in his mind was the thought of blood and spilling it against any that stood in his way.

But then again, why had those thoughts never come to light about the people he was staying with? Beside that first initial reaction when Konrad had stood over him, he had never even considered lifting a hand against his benefactors. Konrad had been exceedingly kind to him and Victoria helped him on relearning everything he should have supposedly known… but any other person that they met, the thought of killing them where they stood was always present.

"But that said," Konrad cleared his throat, as if sensing Triglav's mind had been elsewhere. "You know you're welcome to stay with us as long as you need to. God know you've been a great deal of help to us. You've helped us to accomplish more than anything we could have on our own. Just worried you're missing out on some big, beautiful life you forgot about."

Triglav nodded and slowly began to turn back to his meal, his mind spinning.

*****

He could not get Konrad's words out of his mind. Despite how many times he and Victoria went into town, despite how hard he worked in the Eberstarks' field, he could not escape the thought that there was a life he could not remember. As subsequent days passed, he had fallen sullen, not engaging as much with Victoria when she spoke – at first it was not on purpose, but once he realized what he was doing, it was hard to stop. There had been days when she would try to hold full conversations with him, that normally he would have been enthralled to listen to, but all he did was grunt in response.

At first, she spoke at lengths more than ever, as if noticing his depression and trying to pull him out of it. But when he refused to speak with her, she let him stew in his thoughts. He resented the cold that took over his persona, but again, did nothing about it. It was not until after a full week of his moodiness that she tried to speak to him again.

"So, who do you think you once were?"

He turned toward her and cocked an eyebrow. "What?"

"Well, clearly you're stuck thinking on the past, so why don't you share your thoughts with me? Who do you think you were before the amnesia?"

"I don't know," he grumbled, shrugging his shoulders. When he realized she expected him to elaborate, he sighed. "I really do not. A warrior. Of some sort. I don't know. Someone who was good at fighting."

"Well, your size would definitely work in your favor if that was the case." She slapped him on the arm, beaming wide with a smile that pulled him slightly out of his thoughts. "Could you imagine if you were a baker? Being stuffed in a tiny room, suffocated with the heat of the oven? I can see you wearing an apron, meticulously kneading each roll of dough!"

Her laugh did him well, and for the first time in a while, he smiled. "I would do no such thing. I can little stand to wear these itchy shirts, and you think I would wear an apron? Not likely, my lady."

"Okay, fine. How about a spinner? You seem to have quite the picky sense for clothing. Sitting at a wheel all day spinning thread must have been how you built up all those muscles!"

"Oh, sure. And I wager that I sang songs waiting for a princess to save me from my labor."

She bent forward as she laughed, almost losing the reins. The smile spread across his face a little wider. He was not sure why he had been so preoccupied with his past. What was past, was past. He could not do anything to change it, and he supposed eventually the dreams would cease. What was actual was the present and all of the work he was doing with the Eberstarks.

He heard an unfamiliar noise and looked down at the horses. They whined strangely and it looked like Victoria had to struggle to keep them on the path.

"Whoa, whoa boys." After some struggling, she was finally able to get them under control. "That was… unusual. They never act up like this."

Triglav's brows bent as a scent assaulted his nostrils. He knew what it was, having smelt it whenever a fire was lit, but the strength of the odor threatened to choke him.

"Is that… smoke?" Victoria's voice wavered as she looked

around nervously, her eyes finally locking on a plume that rose above the tops of the trees. Triglav had been so preoccupied with his mood, he must not have noticed it.

They passed the last group of trees that blocked the way to the farm and Victoria's jaw dropped, only the slightest quivering sound emanating, the reins dropping completely from her hands. The farm, the plots – everything – was aflame. It looked like something from his dreams, the way the flames covered everything, engulfing the once prosperous town in death. Triglav grabbed the reins and pulled the horses off to the side of the road. Once they stopped, whinnying loudly as they turned away from the heat, he leapt out of the wagon, taking a sword out he had procured at the market some time ago. He turned once to Victoria, cutting the air with his free hand.

"Stay here! Do *not* get out of the wagon!"

"But..."

"I said *stay*!"

He took off running before she had a chance to respond. He realized he had been more forceful with her than he wanted to be, but he could not risk anything happening to her. As he drew near, he saw people standing in front of the source of the blazing inferno. He recognized them instantly from the attire.

Cultists.

"Ah, Triglav. So we were right to believe this is where you have been hiding out, my lord."

The man leading the group he had not seen before, but among those surrounding him he remembered as some of the survivors of the first group. They had that same wild look in their eyes as they clutched weapons that Triglav noticed with anger were coated with dripping red liquid.

"Your people have called me that name before, but I am not the deity you believe me to be! But for the destruction you have wrought upon this family, who I will be when I send your souls to the underworld will make no difference!"

Triglav raised his sword in the air, but the leader raised his hand and shook his head. The man stopped, for what reason he could not say, but something about the way the cultist leader held himself made Triglav believe he was more important and knowledgeable than any others he had met.

"Ah, great lord. Your coming back into this dimension must

have torn your memories asunder. Were there a way that we could have better heralded your coming, we would have embraced it. However, those of the Eldar used their fool before we were able to finish with our own summoning rituals. I am just glad that the dark ones were not alone in returning."

Fool? Eldar? Summoning…? They all touched spots in the empty bank of his memories, making him believe there was great weight to them. His head hurt more than ever before.

"I don't…"

"Of course you don't remember, my lord. As I have said, we had no way to prepare for you coming back to our world. But now, you are here with us once more! Come with us, my lord, and we will help all that we can to restore you back to your former strength and reunite the three heads!"

Then it hit him again; the words, especially speaking of the three heads, caused his brain to work in overtime, trying to recall lost memories as they threatened to burst forth from the depths of his mind. He almost relented, thinking going with these people to be the best course of action, but then he saw the pyre and came back to the moment.

"The only fools I know are those before me," he said through grit teeth as he readied the sword once more. "If I am truly the god you believe me to be, do you know what you have done in desecrating this farm?! The people that lived here are good people." Then he paused, realizing that he had not seen Victoria's father anywhere. "Where is Konrad?"

The cultist leader closed his eyes, bowing his head. "We had heard that you had become attached to these mortals, clearly the result of the amnesia. In order to restore you to your former glory, we knew what had to be done."

The man stepped aside and behind him, the rows of their followers parted to reveal a statue, smaller than the one of 'Triglav' that he had seen when he had first awoken. It took him a moment, but his heart dropped in his stomach when he realized that body parts were strewn about the three heads. In the mouths of the lion, ram, and dragon were two arms, two legs, multiple organs, and at the base was a human head, the eyes rolled back and the mouth open to reveal the cut out tongue.

"We have offered him, the man you called Konrad, as a sacrifice in your name."

Nothing could stop the rage he felt, flowing through his body, through every muscle and bulging vein. He rushed at the leader with his blade held high, but another stepped in his way to take the killing blow that swept across his entire body. As the first drop of blood hit the ground, Triglav was an unrelenting force of destruction. He leapt forward in great bounds through seas of people to try and get to the leader, but he wove back behind lines of supporters, deeper and deeper until Triglav found himself surrounded by men in every direction.

His blade became one with his arm, swinging and slicing in every direction possible. His foes barely could mount a defense as he came at them. With his spare hand he would occasionally strip the weapon from his foe's hands and use that as a temporary offense. When the weapon would dull or break, he grabbed at his foes and threw them into one another, and occasionally would slam his head into the face of another and crack their nose.

His fury could not be quelled. He stopped caring about finding the man who had incited all of this and decided he would save him for last. He would kill each and every one of these bastards who had defiled the Eberstarks' home; the place he had been taken in and worked so hard to keep prospering.

One by one they fell, slaughtered beyond recognition as the silver of the sturdier blade of his could not be seen beneath the thick coat of blood. It was then he realized that the cultist leader was the last man standing. He stood at the base of the statue, a sadistic gleam on his face as he held both hands up.

"Yes! Yes! The sacrifice worked! Before this statue, every life you have taken has been to make you stronger! You are the demon of the battlefield that you once were! None can stand before your might!"

It was the first time Triglav had stopped to think about the overwhelming count of bodies. He looked about him and realized there had to have been seventy to eighty-five dead people all around him; men and women of various ages, and even, he realized with great disgust, some very young cultists who all fought to believe he was the great three-headed god of war. He was disgusted with himself for all of the carnage, but then, when he really reflected on the fight, he realized with some sickening feeling, that he felt alive. Traces of memories of battles fought millennia ago starting becoming clear in his mind.

They started returning, at first like a slight spark of light, but then like the flames that burned so bright all around him, he started remembering who he was. Years worth of struggle against the Eldar Gods, the argument with Perun over their seal, the damning void, and who he was. He was Triglav, the three-headed god of war. And this man had reawoken him.

"Thank you." Triglav held his sword low as he walked forward, his expression inscrutable. "Allow me to repay you for your efforts."

The priest was practically drooling at the deity as he stepped forward. Triglav's expression turned sinister as he stood before him, scowling down at the man who waited for his prize. Triglav wrapped his free left hand around the throat of the cultist, lifting him up off the ground. He could have crushed the windpipe if he really wanted to; he could feel the muscles buckling under his grip, but it was just enough to cause the agony he desired. He raised the kicking body two feet in the air and looked ahead of him.

Thrusting his arm forward he impaled the body on the horns of the ram, grinning sadistically as the man howled in pain. He stepped back as the blood spurted on him, drenching him in the thick liquid. It was the first time that he had fully embraced the dark thoughts and he felt an overwhelming rush of emotions; but on the forefront of his mind was an unbridled glee.

He waited until the body stopped squirming before sheathing his sword and retrieving the parts of Konrad off of his idol. He looked toward where the cultists had their wagons and found a large tarp to swaddle the parts in. He covered them all; the limbs, the entrails, and with a great sorrow he took the head and wrapped it up. He placed the wrapped pieces on the ground beside him and then looked toward the statue. He could not lie to himself. He was Triglav, and this idol, damnit all, had given him a gain in battle prowess. In the past, he would have welcomed with open arms such a sacrifice, but Konrad was not one of those people that should have been killed in his name.

He picked the statue up with both hands, the priest still dangling, and raised it above his head. To a mortal man this feat would have been impossible, but with his herculean strength, the object felt weightless. With a thrust of his arms, the idol flew into the burning wreck, caving the remains inward as it joined the inferno.

Triglav exhaled deeply. The bodies of his followers at least deserved to be burned and he still had to bury Konrad's body, but he felt himsel freeze, colder than ever his returning memories could fathom.

Victoria stood about twenty feet away, her hands held over her mouth, tears flowing freely down her face. Triglav looked down at the ground, at the pieces that lay wrapped up, that Victoria believed to be a full body. His heart hurt. He had never felt this way about a human before, but these people had been beyond kind. They had shown him generosity like none ever when he needed it the most.

"Victoria…"

"Did… Did my father suffer?" The words were choked by emotion, barely understandable.

Triglav considered telling her the truth, telling her he made them all pay for what they had done to her father and their farm, but ultimately, he did not want her to feel the same kind of pain that the cultist leader had felt before he perished.

"He fought against the men that attacked and they killed him quickly. Your father died bravely, with no pain."

She turned away from him, sobbing deeply. The smile that had brought him so much joy and taken his mind off all of the self-anguish was nowhere to be seen. She wept out of a loss greater than any he had ever experienced. He stepped forward to her and turned her around, trying to think of what to say to ease her pain. He had taken so many lives and so many had been sacrificed in his name, but he did not know how to deal with grief.

She wrapped her arms around his torso, burying her head into his chest. He had not realized his shirt had been torn off in the fighting until he felt the warm liquid that poured down her face, dripping down his chest. His arms dangled limp at his side as he struggled to look down at the mess of auburn hair. Eventually he brought one hand up to hold against her head and the other held her back, doing what he thought the mortals called a 'hug'.

*****

While the fire stilled burned, Triglav threw the bodies into the blaze. Two to three at a time he would heave his once-followers, saying silent prayers for each of them. Despite the nauseating stench that human flesh gave off as it burned, Victoria refused to return to the wagon. She insisted on digging the grave for her father. He would not let her touch the body though. Once they had both finished their tasks, he let her say her final goodbyes before placing the body in the grave.

She covered his resting place and let a few more tears seep through.

Triglav turned away, looking to the distance past the tops of the trees.

"Victoria… I am deeply sorry. All of this happened because-…"

"I know." He turned back at her. She was looking down at her father's grave, but her gaze was a bit more resolute, her expression hardening. "I… I don't understand how, but somehow… you are the god Triglav. I do not know why or how, but you are he. I should have known from the start, but I thought it was impossible for a deity to walk among mortals. It truly makes no sense, but with all of the strange happenings around these lands lately, I suppose I should not be surprised. I had heard tales of your followers, of supernatural beings that came with the quakes, myths that once upon a time your kind lived among us… But I could not believe there was any truth to it."

"Believe it. All of it is true. My kind has fought to save humanity against an evil known as the Eldar Gods for millennia longer than I can remember. Our followers have always existed, and this quake that you have spoken of, I am sure that is the result of our release from the prison that housed us, known as the void."

"I see… That is very confusing, but I will try to understand." She nodded but still did not meet his gaze. "What will you do now?"

He looked back toward the distance where he had been focused on originally. "Now that I know the truth, I need to go to the place where my brethren once called home. Starybogow."

She turned to him, her gaze quivering as she stared. "Whatever home you once held there is no more. You have heard the word about the darkness linger-…"

"They are minions of the darker gods of old." Triglav tried to keep the cold out of his voice, but as his memories returned, so did much of his personality. He was filled with hatred for the people that were responsible for bringing him back. Was he better off sitting in the void, stuck forever without coming back into contact with humanity? "I need to return to Perun. There is much I need to discuss. While my memories have started returning, there are still many holes. I believe my three heads have been separated and reuniting with them is the only way that I can ever be whole once more."

"Then I am coming with you."

Triglav looked at her, pressing back the sneer he felt coming to his lips. "No. I thank you for all your help, but you cannot-…"

"I am going with you."

He was stunned. No other human dared speak to him that way, but no other human had seen a side of him he thought nonexistent. She had seen, arguably, his most mortal side and helped him recover from the brink of death. She was indeed different. The sneer completely faded and a smile began to form.

"Alright, Victoria. If you wish to come with me, I warn you that this quest will be dangerous. As you have said, Starybogow is not a place of peace anymore. The city is fraught with dangers beyond my control, but I will protect you if you are determined to go."

"I have to." She stood tall, pushing the hair behind her ears. "Everything I have is gone. I am in the same position you were when I found you. To repay me, and my father, for everything, I request to go with you. I can fight if given a weapon; I am not some damsel in distress. I am a hardworking girl, and do not forget it, *deity.*"

He raised his eyebrow as she punctured the last word with no fear. He nodded, the smile still there.

"Then come, we must be off at once."

They got back to the wagon and he took the driver's seat for the first time since he ventured out with her. She looked at him, confused, but he nodded as he grabbed the reins and she settled next to him.

"While what you knew was one side of me, there are also some parts that you do not. In my day, before I was sealed away, I was quite the horseman. Watch, my lady, and pray these horses still have fight left in them."

With that, he whipped the reins hard, forcing the horses into action once more. Victoria had to grab hold of his arm tightly. As the wind whipped through his long hair, the speed of the horses propelling them forward, he smiled broadly. He was Triglav, and despite being separated from the three mystic heads, he felt alive for the first time in a very long time. This human guise would do just fine until he was reunited.

Blood Bat

C. L. Werner

Elizabeth Bathory, the ‘Blood Countess”,
Artist unkown, 1600

The moon hung gibbous and full in the night sky, its sinister rays conjuring ghastly shadows from the rubble and debris that had once been a great city. Empty windows stared malignantly from the splintered facades of ruined houses, the broken doors of abandoned workshops gaped like hungry mouths. The autumn wind groaned through crumbling rooftops and cracked chimneys, whistling with the eerie cry of mourning.

Zoja recognized the frightful aspect of her surroundings, but they made no impact upon her. There was only so much terror a human vessel could contain, and she was already filled to the brim with fear. Her heart pounded relentlessly beneath her breast, throbbing with the fury of a furnace. Her breath was hot, stinging her lungs as she drew it down into her chest. Her legs felt like lumps of dead iron as she forced them across the broken cobblestones, each impact of her feet sending a lance of pain speeding through her nerves.

Behind her, in the darkness, Zoja knew it was following. She didn't need to see or hear it to know it was there. She could feel its presence in her soul, a ravenous chill that pawed at her with spectral claws, an icy whisper that filled her mind with hopelessness. *Lie down*, it said, *lie down and let there be an end to it.*

Somewhere, deep within her, Zoja found some unguessed reserve of strength. She raced through the shattered streets, raw terror feeding her flight. She thought of her family, safe back in the village. Perhaps her father was waiting at the door, wondering why she was so late returning from tending her sick great-aunt. It was too much to think that he was alarmed, to hope he was out there looking for her. More likely he'd decided she was staying over with his aunt and gone to bed. Even if he was looking for her, even if he did find her, what could a simple farmer do against the nightmare that now hunted her?

Ahead of her, Zoja could see a wall of darkness. It took her a moment to understand it was no trick of her fear, but indeed an actual wall that rose before her. She'd reached the edge of the broken city, the perimeter wall that had once defended it against raiders and Teutonic Knights. Sight of the barrier caused her step to falter, the hopelessness inside her to swell. Then she spotted a scratch of light amid the darkness. A crack in the wall, a gash left behind by the earthquake that had devastated the city. Desperately, Zoja hurried for the cleft and the promise of escape that lay beyond it.

Mustering herself for one last great effort, the girl hurled herself at the gap. Even her lean body found the gap too narrow. Only a few inches and she became stuck. A panic greater than anything she'd yet experienced swelled inside her. With her face turned to the fields beyond the ruins, she had no way of seeing what was happening in the city behind her. She had no way of knowing what might even now be stalking toward her from those broken streets, ready to seize her in its claws and drag her back into the shadows.

Squirming and squeezing, Zoja forced her body through the breach. She bit down on her lip as pain flared through her body. She was scraping her skin raw, slashing herself on the jagged stones. Blood dripped from her cuts, seeping through the ragged tatters of her dress. Despite the pain, the girl forced herself on, sliding and shifting until at last she was free!

Zoja collapsed in the field just beyond the crumbling city wall. The grass felt cool against her cheek, the hearty smell of the soil was rich in her nose. A cool breeze flowed across her bruised body. Around her the land was bathed in moonlight, dispelling the ghoulish shadows that had closed in upon her within the ruins. A sound, half-sob and half-laugh, rose from her mouth. Jubilation that she had escaped. She had survived!

Then, in the moonlit fields, Zoja's eyes fastened upon a dark splotch of shadow. The sound of relief caught in her throat as she stared in horror at the black thing. She hadn't escaped, not at all. The thing hadn't abandoned its hunt. It had gone ahead of her, been waiting here for her when she left the ruins.

In the moonlight, Zoja could see every detail of the monstrous thing. It sat upon its haunches in a circle of dead grass, emaciated arms folded around its withered knees. Grey skin, so thin it appeared almost translucent, stretched tight across its bony frame. A coarse black shroud was wrapped about its body, whipping around it in the breeze, the folds expanding into the semblance of batlike wings. The thing's head was shriveled, little more than a leering skull. The nose was rotted away entirely, leaving only a pit at the center of its face. The mouth was impossibly wide, a gash that stretched from ear to ear. The eyes that smoldered deep within the shadows of its visage were a ghostly white, chips of marble from which all warmth and humanity had long ago fled.

The vampir sat there, staring at its prey. It raised a blackened claw to its mouth, opening that gash-like maw to reveal its wolflike fangs. A long, lupine tongue lolled out, licking the claw with feline attentiveness. The monster was in no hurry to seize its prey. It kept its cold eyes focused on Zoja while it licked each of its claws clean. She knew it was savoring her mounting terror, that it was simply toying with her like a cat with a mouse. She also knew that the time would come when it would tire of its ghastly play.

Zoja tried to move but found that her strength had abandoned her. She lacked even the ability to cover her eyes with her arm, to shield herself from the monstrous image of the vampir. Her mind was her own, awake and aware, but her body was frozen in a hideous paralysis.

At last the vampir rose from its crouch, unfolding its limbs with a grisly motion that suggested a spider creeping from its web. Standing upright, the monster evoked some echo of human shape and form, though the semblance only heightened its ghastly appearance. The black shroud draped down its shriveled body, tears in the cloth exposing the rotten form beneath. As the vampir stole toward Zoja, she could see the grass withering under its step. A fell, charnel reek struck her senses as the fiend prowled closer and a spectral chill slithered across her skin.

The vampir's slow, mocking advance persisted for a few awful moments. Then a hungry light shone in its dead eyes. In a burst of motion, the monster pounced upon Zoja. Spidery limbs wrapped themselves around her body, a skeletal foot stamped on her neck and pushed her face in the dirt. Zoja screamed into the dust as she felt the vampir's loathsome tongue licking at her cuts, lapping up her blood.

The vampir shifted its hold, irritated by Zoja's muffled scream. Its ghastly strength was far in excess of its starveling frame. The peasant girl was like a rag doll in its grip. Easily it wrenched her up from the ground and pulled her close to its chest. One clawed hand seized a fistful of her hair and forced her head to one side.

For a moment, Zoja saw the vampir's fangs glistening in the moonlight. Then, like a striking serpent, it lunged at her, stabbing its fangs into her throat.

After that, for Zoja Radzienski there was only darkness.

*****

Dobrogost Radzienski glowered at the men around him. A delegation from the village of Swinka, his companions represented friends and neighbors, people he'd known all his life. Or had he? It was only in moments of great tragedy that the true quality of a man revealed itself. Listening to them now, he appreciated more fully what kind of petty, miserly people these were. There was Maciej Bogacki, whose sheep had been victimized all winter by a bold she-wolf until Dobrogost helped him track the animal back to her den and stick her with a spear. There was Waclaw Tokarz, whose harvest had been commandeered by a gang of roving mercenaries and who'd relied upon the charity of the Radzienskis to carry his family until the next harvest. There was Rafal Kucinski, whose brother Lucjan had been held for ransom by bandits, a ransom gathered together by all the men of Swinka.

Now it was Dobrogost who was in need and he found that these same men he'd helped and stood by through their own trials were dissembling. True, they'd made the long trip to Wormditt with him, representing no small investment of time and risk, but now that they were on the cusp of accomplishing their purpose, they'd finally decided that the expense was too great.

"They say that this man's services do not come cheaply, Dobrogost," Rafal whispered as the four Poles walked through the narrow streets of the German town. "Even with our tithe to the church forgiven by Father Henryk there is no guarantee we can pay this man."

"You did not sound so thrifty when Black Wladimir had your brother," Dobrogost snarled back.

"That was different," Maciej said. "As a village we agreed to pay the bandit because doing so could save Lucjan." The sharpness left his tone when he met Dobrogost's gaze. When next he spoke, his words were laced with shame, but that sense of guilt didn't keep him from saying them. "Your daughter is dead. Paying this man won't bring Zoja back."

Waclaw dodged away from the gutter as a bowl of night dirt was dumped from the window of the house he was walking past. He scowled at the residue that spattered across his boots and wool leggings. "Be practical, Dobrogost," he said as he wiped the filth off with his hat. "We are all of us saddened by Zoja's death. You know I had hopes my son and your daughter would make us family." He paused, frowning at the now soiled brim of his hat.

Dobrogost rounded on his friend. "What if it had been your son who was taken? What would you say then, Waclaw? Would you cry and whine about money or would you do everything you could to get justice?"

Waclaw retreated before Dobrogost's anger, turning an imploring look to the other peasants. Rafal rose to his defense. "If it is justice, then we should have entrusted the matter to Baron Ksawery and left him to deal with it."

A bitter laugh hissed over Dobrogost's mustached lip. "His lordship has no time for superstitions," he scoffed. "Hasn't he told us so many times? Have his men even once stirred themselves to look for this monster? How many have been lost from the other villages? How many travelers and strangers have been found lifeless just outside the city walls?"

"It isn't justice you want, Dobrogost," Maciej said. "You want revenge."

The last word seemed to hang in the air. Dobrogost felt it jabbing against his chest like an accusing finger. Still, it wasn't enough to deaden the anguish and anger that raged through his heart. "If it is revenge, then it is revenge that is to the good of us all. Our lives are hard enough without the worry that our families will fall prey to a vampir."

When he spoke the dreaded name, Dobrogost at once regretted it. Not only his companions, but many of the townsfolk in the street around them, turned pale at the word 'vampir'; many of the Poles made the sign against the evil eye before hastening away from the four peasants, some of the Germans crossed themselves and did likewise. A few wealthy burghers made a point of laughing at the sudden fright provoked by Dobrogost, but instead of a condescending snort it was a nervous titter that rolled from their tongues.

One man, a wizened old campaigner by his military swagger and the gray scars that marred his face, didn't share the timidity of the others. Instead of hurrying away, he approached the men from Swinka. Doffing the fur cap that covered his balding pate, he addressed Dobrogost. "Forgive my intrusion, good sir, but as you can see, I could not help overhearing your speech." He gestured at the retreating townsfolk at either end of the street. "It will be some time yet before the folk of Wormditt forget their own dealings with... the undead." The grizzled veteran pressed his palm against the little copper cross fixed to the breast of his tunic.

Rafal shook his head. "We heard that the trouble here was over, that the shadow was gone from Wormditt. That is why we came."

"Just so, just so," the veteran said. "But even when dawn breaks, it is hard to forget the night." He turned a scowl toward the fortress that loomed over Wormditt. "Of course the Knights still refuse to admit what it was that took eighteen souls these past ten months." He tapped his brow. "They know, though. That is why they have been digging up the victims and checking for decay. Any body that looks too fresh..." He made a slashing motion across his neck. Beheading, among other rituals, was essential to ensuring a vampir was truly destroyed.

"We came here hoping to find help," Waclaw said.

"Then it is the krsnik you've come to see," the veteran nodded. "I thought as much."

Dobrogost grabbed the man's shoulder, fingers digging into his bony flesh. "He is still here? You know where we can find him?"

The old soldier pulled away from Dobrogost's clutch. "I should say that I can. Was it not Mateusz Niziolek who assisted the krsnik in finding the secret grave of Anton Gornik? Was it not I who helped burn the foul corpse when Gornik was brought to ruin? Yes, of course I know where he can be found." Mateusz looked over the four peasants, studying them with a practiced eye. From the state of their clothes as well as the accent of their speech, he knew they had come from far away. "Your need must be great to seek out the krsnik. I am sure you will not scruple about a few coins if I am taking you where he is." He held up a warning finger. "Mind, I do not promise that he will help. I think he has lingered so long in Wormditt in case one of Gornik's victims does rise and he can collect another fee from the Knights. If that is his intention, I doubt he can be induced to leave town."

Dobrogost looked over at his friends. Before any of them could speak he gave Mateusz some coins. "We've come this far," he declared. "We won't leave until we've at least spoken to the man."

*****

For most of an hour, Mateusz led the four peasants through the cramped lanes of Wormditt. Word had spread about Dobrogost's injudicious utterance, for at every turn Poles and Germans and even

Jews shunned them. No one in the town was anxious to associate with anyone who would remind them of the horrors their community had so recently endured. The sole exception was Mateusz. The old veteran regarded the recent horrors not with fear but pride. Helping to rid the town of its vampir had lifted him from his beggarly existence for one brief moment. With each step, he regaled the men from Swinka about the monster's destruction, exaggerating his own role until the peasants wondered if their guide would claim sole credit for slaying Gornik before they reached the krsnik.

It was with a touch of reluctance that Mateusz brought a halt to their journey. He waved one of his grimy hands at a sign hanging from the second floor of a half-timbered building ahead of them. Painted onto the sign was the image of an upraised sword with a cat transfixed upon its point. "That is the *Katzbalger,*" he announced. "Czcibor Niemczk has made this tavern his headquarters since he arrived in Wormditt." He smiled and gave Dobrogost a reassuring clap on the back. "The krsnik is a man of the people," he said. "The Knights offered him lodging in the fortress but he turned them down. Maybe if the good God looks kindly on your purpose, Czcibor will prefer peasant copper to knightly gold." Bowing to the peasants, Mateusz walked off down the dirt lane, his fist clenched tight around the coins Dobrogost had given him.

Dobrogost led his companions into the tavern. The common room within was a long hall, its floor strewn with sawdust, several long tables with plank benches dominating the space. A small fire smoldered away in the depths of a large stone hearth, its glow and that of a few rushlights providing what little light could be had. A forlorn-looking man leaned against the timber bar that stretched across one wall, a flash of hope passing across his heavy features when he saw the peasants enter. It seemed that word of their purpose had reached even this place, for the taverneer's expression darkened and he returned to a dispassionate study of the scratches on the counter he was resting against.

"Don't be unsettled by Otto," a voice called out from the shadows. "His custom has suffered of late. When you opened that door, I imagine he thought his troubles were over. Instead you simply bring him more of the same."

As their eyes adjusted to the gloom of the tavern, the peasants could pick out the speaker from the darkness around him. He seemed to be the only customer the Katzbalger was entertaining at the moment. Rafal called out to the man. "You are Czcibor Niemczk... the krsnik?"

"And you are the men who have come so very far looking for me," Czcibor replied. He waved his arm, motioning for the peasants to join him. "Otto, bring my guests beer. And cheer up, these fellows are trying to extract me from your premises." The last comment did seem to cheer the taverneer and he hurriedly filled two braces of steins from one of the barrels behind the bar.

Now that they were in the presence of the man they'd come so far to find, the peasants felt a tingle of fear crawl down their spines. Tales of the weird powers of a krsnik filled them with a sense of dread. A krsnik was said to be a sorcerer, able to call upon dark magic and occult energies. Some claimed they entered into pacts with the Devil to learn their arcane secrets, forfeiting their eternal souls to command eldritch forces.

Dobrogost was the first to overcome his unease and walk to the table where Czcibor sat. He was shocked to find that the krsnik wasn't some hoary old wizard but a young man no older than Rafal's son. Czcibor was clean-shaven, his skin possessed of an almost feminine softness. His features were handsome, with a strong chin and wide brow. His hair was a pale blonde, almost snowy in its fairness. His raiment was fine, but not opulent, a crimson doublet with slashed sleeves and an azure lining beneath, little clasps and buttons of silver adorning the breast and cuffs. Only a single ring graced his hands, a simple band of gold on which was set the coat of arms of some noble house. Dobrogost might have found the man unremarkable had he not seen Czcibor's eyes. The steel-gray eyes were as sharp as any sword, possessed of a wariness that belied the ease and welcome of his inviting visage.

"It seems that you are to be spokesman," Czcibor said, motioning for Dobrogost to seat himself. "Explain your situation. Leave out no detail." He tapped his finger against the table. "Whether I assist you or not depends on what you tell me now more than the size of the purse you would offer. So choose your words with care."

Dobrogost looked back at his friends, but the other peasants were still holding their distance, willing to concede the task to him. When Otto brought the beer, he took the stein and drained a third of its volume in a single gulp. Then he set about describing the menace that hung over their village and the death of Zoja.

As he recited his tale, Dobrogost studied Czcibor, noticing things he'd failed to see before. The man did everything with his left hand, from cutting the meat on the trencher sitting before him to drinking from the stein lying beside his meal. His right hand was clothed in a bearskin glove, the symbol of a cross branded into the fur. A little pillow was under the hand, keeping it from resting directly against the table. Words were embroidered into the pillow, but Dobrogost could only guess at their meaning or the strange custom that made Czcibor pamper his hand in so curious a fashion. Had he been injured in his fight with Gornik?

Czcibor noticed the direction of Dobrogost's gaze. He smiled, but waited until the man had finished his story before offering an explanation. "First let me reassure you, friend Dobrogost, that I suffer neither wound nor infirmity." He raised his gloved hand from the pillow, making a point of clenching his fingers into a fist. "Just as a knight doesn't tire his warhorse with the drudgery of daily toil, so a krsnik must preserve his sword arm for the moment when it is needed in battle." He set his hand back upon its pillow. "You have heard, no doubt, that a krsnik has special magic all his own? Such power makes its own demands of those who would command it." He tilted his stein, displaying the milk that filled it. "Neither beer nor wine may pass my lips, only the milk of goats." He thrust his knife into the meat lying before him. "I may eat only that which Surma kills for me."

"Surma?" Dobrogost asked.

"My wolf," Czcibor answered. "Right now he is chained in Otto's yard, but you will meet him if I make the journey to Swinka."

"If it is money..." Dobrogost began.

Czcibor shook his head. "The Teutonic Knights have given me enough to keep me for some time. It isn't money that makes me hesitate. It is doubt."

"You are afraid?" Waclaw gasped. "If even a krsnik is afraid, then what hope have we?"

"You mistake me," Czcibor said. "It isn't fear that makes me hesitate. It is uncertainty. You must understand that just as there are many breeds of pestilence, so too there are many breeds of vampir. There is the *vjesci* and the *strigoi,* the *nachzehrer* and the *wupji*. My powers are honed to combat two specific breeds of vampir, the *kudlak* and the *varcolaci*."He stared into Dobrogost's eyes. "You have told me much, but not enough. I don't know if the fiend that took your daughter is a *kudlak* or not. I don't know if I will be any help to you."

Dobrogost shook his head in despair. "If you won't help us, I don't know where we can turn. Perhaps what they say is true, that the ruins of Starybogow are cursed and all who dwell too near it share in that curse."

The vampir hunter leaned back, tapping his fingers against the side of his stein. "Starybogow," he muttered several times, then fixed Dobrogost with a hard look. "You didn't mention that your village was near the city."

"Is that important?" Rafal asked.

"In my experience every detail is vital, especially the battlefield I am expected to fight upon. Kudlaks prefer places forsaken and abandoned," Czcibor said, then laughed. "So too do many other breeds of vampir. Still, the lure of the ruins may have drawn all sorts of evil into them that they might prefer to prey upon the blood of men."

"You will help us?" Dobrogost gasped, clutching desperately at the hope within Czcibor's words.

Czcibor took a last swallow of milk and rose to his feet. "I will go with you back to Swinka. That is all I can promise. It may be that it is some normal adversity that preys upon your community, or it may be that the evil which hangs about your homes is one I cannot overcome. If such is the case, then my services will be to no avail." He looked at the darkened hall around him. "Of one thing, at least, I am certain. I have been in Wormditt too long. As fear of their vampir fades, the townsfolk come to fear my powers. It may not be too long before the Knights decide they can recover their fee if they declare me a witch and hang me in the town square. Yes, I think if nothing else, a journey to Swinka will give me a needed change of scenery."

*****

Though there were better homes in Swinka that could have played host to the krsnik, Czcibor chose to stay with the Radzienskis. The loss of his daughter, Czcibor said, would make Dobrogost a more capable host than any burgher or baron. Sincerity, not splendor, was the real measure of gratitude.

Questioning the people of Swinka about the rash of killings and grisly bodies found in the area took up the first days of Czcibor's stay. With the grudging indulgence of the priest, some of the bodies were exhumed for the krsnik's inspection. The priest didn't scoff at the powers Czcibor was said to possess, rather he felt they were unholy magics derived from Satan. The fear that gripped his flock, however, made the priest hesitant to oppose their superstitions with anything more forceful than the occasional disparaging remark.

The next week was spent traveling to nearby villages and towns. Czcibor called upon Dobrogost to handle these inquiries, using his knowledge of the area and familiarity with his neighbors to pose his questions with more discretion than the krsnik would have managed. Czcibor was careful to impress upon the farmer that he must always return to Swinka before nightfall and that, until they knew more, he mustn't stay over in one of the other villages.

After two weeks, Czcibor called Dobrogost to join him at the table in his hut's common room. Spread across the table was a crude map of the area that the krsnik had drawn. The peasant shuddered when he noted all the little crosses drawn upon the map, each marking where the bodies of the monster's victim had been found.

"You were right to believe this fiend is a vampir," Czcibor stated. "The bodies from Swinka's own churchyard bore the unmistakable marks of such depredation. Yet none of them bore signs of becoming undead themselves. That is an important thing. Many breeds of vampir pass their corruption on to those they kill. We can safely dismiss these monsters from our consideration. That leaves far fewer possibilities. Among them is the kudlak. The peasants you spoke with, the ones who claimed to have at times seen a great black wolf and a giant bat haunting the environs of Starybogow, they make me think even more strongly of kudlaks, for among the traits of these monsters is that of changing their shape to assume the guise of birds and beasts – but always of a black and sinister aspect."

"Then you will be able to destroy this monster?" Dobrogost asked.

"Perhaps," Czcibor mused, tapping his fingers against the map. "I think the vampir has hidden itself somewhere in the city. Finding its lair will be no easy prospect. It will be better to draw it out, to lure it with bait and kill it on ground of my own choosing."

"How will you do that?" Dobrogost wondered. "This isn't some simple wolf you can catch with a haunch of meat and chain in your yard." The peasant thought of Surma, the massive gray wolf Czcibor had brought with him and which must kill any animal before its master could dine upon it. Feeding the krsnik and his beast was an expense the peasants of Swinka hadn't taken into their calculations when agreeing to hire Czcibor.

Czcibor pointed at the map. “The answer is right in front of you.”

Dobrogost leaned over to stare at the markings, but could make no sense of them. “I don't know my letters,” he apologized.

“Then let me explain,” Czcibor said. He tapped at one of the marks. “This is Swinka,” he stated, then indicated the marks that denoted the other villages and the great symbol that indicated Starybogow itself. “You can see that these attacks have claimed travelers and natives alike. All of the bodies have been discovered close to Starybogow, concentrated here on the western side of the city.” He swept his hand across the crosses which indicated where the victims had been found. “There is little to be gained learning where the vampir's prey was left once the monster drained them. But,” the krsnik raised a finger to emphasize an important point, “there may be much to be gleaned from where the victims came from... or more precisely, where they *didn't* come from.”

The peasant peered closely at the map, trying to discover the secret that Czcibor seemed to have found. “I don't understand,” he confessed at last. “The strangers were from everywhere and nowhere. The locals who've been killed were taken from each village.”

Czcibor shook his head. ”There, my friend, you are wrong. Each traveler, be they pilgrim or peddler, was going somewhere. And there is one village which has lost none of its inhabitants.” Like a knife, the krsnik stabbed his finger down at one of the marks on the map. The illiterate Dobrogost understood the significance only when Czcibor gave a name to the place. “Krynka.”

“No,” Dobrogost protested. “You are wrong there. People have been taken from Krynka. My poor Zoja was on her way to visit her aunt when she was...” The peasant broke off, choking back his emotion.

Czcibor gripped the farmer's shoulder, motioning for him again to look at the map. “Many of those who have died were going to or from Krynka. Travelers heading north or south, their path taking them through the village. Locals gathering wood or making charcoal in the vicinity of Krynka. Wherever their bodies were found, it was near Krynka that they were last seen.”

Dobrogost's face became a vision of rage and hate. "Then the vampir is in Krynka!" he snarled.

"The truth is far worse, I fear," Czcibor explained, drawing Dobrogost down into one of the chairs. "Those who have died were close to the village, but except for a few of the earliest victims, none of them were from Krynka."

The peasant stared at Czcibor, shaken by the ghastly implication. "What are you saying?"

"Nothing, for the moment," Czcibor said. "I will need to visit Krynka again, but this time I will announce my purpose in coming to this region. If my suspicions are unfounded, then nothing will come of it."

"And if your suspicions are right?" Dobrogost asked, his words redolent with an undercurrent of fury.

"If I am not back by nightfall," Czcibor told the peasant, "then you are to unchain Surma. He will be able to find me, whatever my circumstances." The krsnik looked down at his gloved right hand. "If I am not back by nightfall, I will need Surma's help."

*****

The village of Krynka was close upon the crumbling walls of Starybogow. It was much like Swinka in general appearance, a simple collection of half-timbered huts with a barren strip of muddy road winding between them. The only large building in the settlement was a two-story structure that acted as both tavern and meeting hall for the community, Krynka's headman making his residence on the upper floor.

It was to this comparatively opulent building that Czcibor rode. As he passed the collection of huts, he could feel the eyes of the inhabitants watching him from behind cracked doors and shutters. The krsnik could sense the fear emanating from the villagers, detecting the emotion with an arcane talent that had served him well over the years. For Czcibor, knowing when a community was angered or afraid was the first warning that the very people he was trying to help might turn against him. It remained to be seen, however, if the people of Krynka wanted any help.

Czcibor dismounted outside the tavern. It took a few commanding waves of his hand to summon the grimy boy out from the shadow of the building and a few equally imperious words to get the lad to lead his horse to the stables. The krsnik could sense the fear wafting off the peasant, but in the boy's expression there was a sullenness, a resentment that lent that fear a sinister aspect. It was an attitude he'd found often among the abused servants of a cruel lord.

Dismissing the boy from his thoughts, Czcibor stalked into the tavern. The hall was filled with villagers, men and women of every age sitting on the benches nursing leathern jacks of beer. They turned to regard him as he entered and he saw the same glower of resentment on their faces. The taverneer behind the counter made no move to greet him, but kept wiping at a clay stein, trying to remove some imaginary speck from its surface.

Czcibor walked over to the man, careful to keep his gloved hand resting upon the hilt of his sword. "I find Krynka less hospitable than it was on my last visit," he told the man. One of the peasants sitting on the benches turned and spat into the hearth.

"You were with Dobrogost and Rafal when you came here last, stranger," the taverneer said.

"Ah, and your hospitality doesn't extend to strangers, I take it?" Czcibor wondered.

One of the old peasants rose to his feet, pointing a gnarled finger at Czcibor. "Not ones who pretend to be something they aren't," he growled.

Czcibor turned toward the crowd, drumming his fingers upon the hilt of his sword, reminding them of its threat. "If you know who I am and why I've come, then you must know I'm only here to help."

"We don't need your kind of help," a plump farmer's wife declared. "We don't want it."

"And what about the people in Swinka? Or those in the other villages?" Czcibor challenged. "They seem to need my help very much." He could feel the fear boiling off the peasants, but more he could feel their anger. They'd found a way to protect themselves and they weren't about to let anyone put them at risk by disturbing things.

Czcibor spun around with a speed that would have shamed a viper. The taverneer was caught by complete surprise as he caught the man's descending arm and the heavy clay stein gripped in his hand. The krsnik smashed both stein and hand against the counter, shattering the vessel and driving clay shards into the fingers that gripped it. The bleeding taverneer staggered back, howling in pain, the bones of his wrist cracked by their brutal meeting with the timber counter. Czcibor was already whipping back around, the sword leaping from its sheath. Staring at the vicious length of steel in his gloved hand, the peasants of Krynka abandoned the sudden surge that had threatened to overwhelm him. Glowering at Czcibor, they returned to their seats.

"So, you won't be frightened off." The statement issued from the shadowed stairway leading up to the headman's residence. Czcibor shifted position so that he could both see his accoster and keep an eye on the villagers. The man on the stairway was older than Dobrogost, with only a few flecks of black left in the grey mane that covered his head, but there was an almost familial similarity about his features. His raiment was slightly more elegant than that of his neighbors, but the only trace of ostentation about him was the bronze chain he wore about his neck as a badge of office.

Czcibor gestured at the peasants. "There are a lot of frightened people here," he said. "I am not one of them."

The man on the stairs nodded his head. "Of course you aren't. I am Lukasz Walczak, headman of Krynka. I must apologize for my people, but we have learned to be wary of strangers. Especially ones who claim they can help us." Lukasz studied Czcibor a moment. "Perhaps you are different. Come, we will talk and I will decide if it is truly so." He waved his arms at the villagers gathered in the common room. "Back to your homes. There is nothing for you to do here. What needs doing, I will do. Go." Turning back to Czcibor, he motioned the krsnik to follow him upstairs.

Lukasz led Czcibor down a narrow hall and into a small room that had the appearance of both study and storeroom. The headman seated himself behind the table that flanked the room's only window. He waved his guest to assume the only other chair. Czcibor ignored the invitation, instead walking about the chamber and exploring the contents of the boxes and sacks piled about the floor. Dust had accumulated on many of the containers and he noted that mice had been gnawing away at some of the grain and furs bundled into the sacks.

"Your people must have missed the last few market days," Czcibor observed. "Their labors are going to waste."

Lukasz frowned at the remark. "It has been some time," he admitted.

"Since Krynka's troubles began?" Czcibor asked, turning over a silver plate he'd withdrawn from one of the chests.

"I've been told that Dobrogost went all the way to Wormditt to find you," Lukasz stated. "The rumor is that you're a vampir hunter."

Czcibor set the plate down and faced the headman. "It is more than rumor. That is my profession."

Lukasz licked his lips anxiously, a desperate light shining in his eyes. "Have you killed many of them?"

"One doesn't kill a vampir," Czcibor corrected him. "They are already dead. They can be destroyed, but they cannot be killed. To answer your question, I have destroyed fifteen of the creatures to date, the last of these in Wormditt a few months past."

The headman stroked his graying mustache, weighing Czcibor's claim. "We hired a man who said he could help us when these troubles began, you know. He was a Hungarian, a sellsword knight who said he knew all about vampyr. He took our money and rode away laughing. I can still hear him laughing at us."

"I have already been paid by the people of Swinka," Czcibor said. "There's no reason to fear that I'll steal from you."

"No, there isn't," Lukasz agreed. "But you might do us even greater hurt." Before Czcibor could react, the headman drew a pistol out from under the papers piled on the table. "Lay your sword over with the other treasure the vampir has left us. Don't think I can't hit you with this. Since its last owner left it with us, I have become an excellent shot."

Czcibor slowly unbuckled his swordbelt and set it down atop the pile of chests and sacks closest to him. "Your fiendish master has paid you well. It is a shame you're too miserly to profit from your spoils."

"This isn't about plunder," Lukasz declared. "It is about survival. After the knight betrayed us, we saw no choice but to reach an accord with Wera. We promised to bring her victims if she would spare our village. At first she was content with sheep and pigs, but soon she came to demand human offerings." Tears glistened in the headman's eyes. "Don't you understand, if we didn't give her someone, then she would come for us?"

"I can stop her," Czcibor said. "All I need is to know more about her. Know where her lair is."

Lukasz laughed, a sound bitter and forsaken. "She's found some hole in Starybogow. If you searched the ruins a hundred years you'd never find her. And that's allowing she doesn't move to a new grave each night. No, the only way is to appease her until God, in His mercy, sees fit to lift this plague from us."

"Perhaps God sent me to do just that," Czcibor said. "I don't boast when I tell you that I've faced these monsters before. I don't lie when I tell you I've destroyed vampyr in the past."

"But can you promise that you will prevail?" Lukasz demanded, shaking the pistol at his prisoner. "Is there any guarantee that you will triumph? If you die, we would be left to Wera's vengeance. She would know we sent you to destroy her. She would prey upon us with even greater abandon than before and this time there would be no appeasing her." He shook his head. "No, I cannot risk such a doom falling upon my people. We must hold to the pact we've made with Wera."

"A pact with the Devil isn't an easy thing to break," Czcibor warned. "But if you would save your soul, it must be done."

"It isn't souls I'm trying to save, it's lives," Lukasz said. There was a knock at the door and four stout peasants entered the cramped room. The headman pointed at Czcibor. "Bind him with ropes and take him into Execution Square in the city. Prick his arm with a knife and then leave him." He looked apologetically at Czcibor. "The smell of blood will bring Wera to you once the sun is down. I'm sorry, but this is for the good of my people."

Czcibor fixed the headman with a steely look. "Necessity has birthed darker evils than greed ever did. Remember that there will be a reckoning one day."

"But it won't be today," Lukasz declared as he motioned his men to bind the krsnik.

*****

The cold of the stones he was lying on was leeching the warmth from Czcibor's body. It was some hours since the peasants had left him in Execution Square and the sun was fast fading from the sky. The gathering darkness managed the impossible, rendering a still more sinister aspect to the shattered buildings that fronted the square. The scaffold, charred by fire and cracked by earthquake, leaned across the plaza at an impossible angle, the arm of the gibbet thrusting itself at the sky as though to threaten the moon and stars. The broken remnants of the thirteen steps that had borne so many to their doom lay strewn about the platform in a nimbus of scorched wood.

It had been difficult for the krsnik to wait for the onset of darkness. While the sun was still in the sky there had been the risk that Lukasz might repent the villainy he'd plotted. He'd felt the regret and guilt pounding through the headman's heart when he'd been ushered into the treasure room. The people of Krynka weren't trying to profit from the vampir's depredations – they were simply trying to escape them. With that in mind, there was a chance the villagers might come back to release him. Czcibor wanted to give them that chance for penance. Otherwise they would find no forgiveness from their neighbors and their liege lord once the nature of their perfidy came to light.

Now, of course, that chance was gone. No villager would risk being in the ruins after dark, regardless of their arrangement with the vampir. Even if this creature Wera did display enough restraint to spare them, Starybogow was reputed to be the haunt of all manner of ancient horrors, things drawn back from the frontiers of civilization by the desolation of the city.

Czcibor watched as the last light slipped away. It was time now to draw upon the mystic talents he'd sacrificed so much to learn, the arcane arts that had imperiled his very soul to acquire. Abilities far less passive and subtle than his heightened senses and power to read a man's innermost intentions and emotions. The old craft that was being burned away by the fires of the Inquisition in France and elsewhere - the power men called magic.

The krsnik closed his eyes and worked the fingers of his right hand in a series of scratching gestures. From his lips there hissed a babble of eldritch notes, sounds midway between speech and snarl. He cleared his mind, focusing his thoughts upon one image, pouring his very being into it until the image expanded to consume him utterly.

On the cold stones of Execution Square, in the shadow of the gibbet, Czcibor's bound form began to change. The man's arms became pallid, a growth of white fur exploding across them with blinding speed. His hair fell away from his scalp as more white fur pushed itself up from his skin. His face began to lengthen, mouth and nose stretching outward to merge into a weasel-like muzzle. The krsnik's body began to diminish, shrinking into the folds of his clothing, leaving the still-tied ropes behind as hands and feet became too small to restrain. Soon, the transforming hunter was lost completely within the mass of clothing.

Yet something moved within that heap of seemingly empty clothing. Squirming out from the neck of the shirt, the long lean shape of a ferret emerged. The animal was pure white in color, as though coated in new fallen snow. The ferret rose up onto his hind legs and sniffed at the air with his whiskered face, two gray eyes peering into the growing darkness. Transformed by the ancient magics he'd learned, Czcibor had found it easy to slip free of his bonds. What remained to be seen were if his powers would be a match for the vampir Wera.

A foul scent, a sickening admixture of old blood and carrion, sent the white ferret scurrying underneath the scaffold. The vampir was coming.

A grisly cold beat down upon the square as the carrion-reek intensified. A monstrous shadow fell across the stones. The next moment saw the thing herself descend, dropping down upon the ground like some foul scavenger bird. Czcibor could see the shape the vampir wore, the form of a great bat, black and furless, her limbs withered and drawn close to the bones beneath. The abomination sniffed at the air with her shriveled nose, a pink tongue flickering across the knife-like fangs that protruded from her mouth. Then, using the clawed fingers of her wings to pull her along, the grotesque bat scrabbled toward the pile of empty clothing lying where she'd expected to find a victim.

The vampir cocked her head to one side in confusion when she found the empty clothes. She reached out with the finger-claws and drew Czcibor's shirt toward her face, sniffing at the raiment. The unfamiliar smell only increased her perplexity, for the scent of a krsnik is not like that of normal men. In her befuddlement, Wera let the bat-like shape slip away. The vampir's limbs cracked and creaked as bones twisted and reformed, as wings diminished into skeletal arms and the minuscule feet of a bat lengthened into the longer legs of a woman. Even in a more human shape, the vampir was ghastly, a desiccated husk in which the only specks of life were the smoldering eyes and the glistening fangs.

Stooping over the clothing, Wera began to inspect each article, trying to learn what sort of man had worn them and how he had been able to slip free. Czcibor, watching from the shadows of the scaffold, had seen enough. He knew which breed of vampir he was faced with, recognized Wera as one of the infernal kudlaks. He could see her crimson eyes grow wide as she smelled the bloodstains on his sleeves. The vampir's long, lupine tongue snaked out from between her fangs and licked at the red blot. Then she swung around, a low growl rattling through her gangrel body, her nose twitching as she pulled the smell of Czcibor's blood from the air. Her eyes narrowed to vicious slits as she glared at the scaffold.

Czcibor stepped out from the shadows, no longer wearing the shape of an animal. "Yes, kudlak, I am here," he snarled at the monster. "Here to put an end to your infamies."

Wera stared at the krsnik for a moment, confused by the man's impertinence, uneasy by the lack of fear she sensed in her intended prey. Then a savage hiss rasped from the vampir's throat, bestial rage boiling up from the depths of her undead heart. With the speed of a striking snake, she lunged at Czcibor.

Despite the inhuman swiftness of the vampir, Czcibor was swifter still. As Wera rushed at him with bared fangs and outstretched claws, the krsnik swung around. From behind his back, clenched in his right hand, a jagged strip of wood torn from the planks of the scaffold was thrust at the attacking kudlak. The sliver raked across Wera's forearm, gouging it from wrist to elbow. The decayed skin was split open and a mist of foul black ichor steamed out from the vampir's wound. Wera leapt back, howling in shock and pain, glaring at the injury that had been visited against her. Hungry eyes looked up from the steaming wound to glare at Czcibor. Her tongue licked across the gash in her arm, her venom sealing the cut and stifling the flow of smoking ichor to a trickle.

Czcibor retreated back toward the scaffold, ducking under the platform and creeping under the gallows. The special enchantments that had been conveyed from his hand into the sliver of wood had been enough to harm the vampir, but he knew it would take much more to destroy such a fiend. The means to destroy Wera wouldn't be found in the ruins of Starybogow, but rather outside the city's walls. To be victorious, he had to lure her to a battlefield of his choosing. To do that, he had to arouse Wera's rage to a degree where it overwhelmed her caution.

"Yes, blood-worm, you bleed," Czcibor mocked the vampir. "How does it feel when your prey can fight back?"

Wera's eyes narrowed, transfixing those of the krsnik. The vampir took a few steps toward the scaffold, always keeping Czcibor's gaze. He could feel her predatory will scratching at the doors of his mind, trying to overwhelm his resistance like a serpent transfixing a bird. Even for him, it was no easy thing to fend away the vampir's hypnosis. When he did, Wera's reaction was immediate and vicious. Charging for the krsnik, Wera's claws raked across his flesh, opening deep gashes across his shoulder and abdomen. Blood splattered across the kudlak.

Again, Wera drew back in shock and pain. Ugly blisters erupted from her decayed flesh, livid sores that marked where Czcibor's blood had splashed onto her. The strict diet and ascetic lifestyle of the krsnik had endowed his blood with properties toxic to the kudlak. As she staggered back, the hunger drained out of the vampir's eyes. She knew now that she couldn't make a meal of Czcibor. She knew now what he was, and that even if she couldn't drink his blood she couldn't allow him to live.

Czcibor clutched at the gash across his belly and hobbled back out toward the square. He'd aroused the kudlak's fury, but would he live long enough to make use of it? Already Wera was prowling toward him again, stalking him like some great cat. The vampir's next attack would be more wary than her earlier ones, making her all the more dangerous. Czcibor had to draw the monster away from her hunting grounds.

"You've left your smell on me," Czcibor told Wera, sliding one of his fingers across the wounds along his belly. "I've got your scent now. I'll be back, when the sun is high and you are helpless in your grave." Mustering his strength, the krsnik spun around and threw himself out from the shadow of the scaffold. The moment he was again in the open air of the square, his body underwent a swift transformation. Feathers sprouted across his naked body, his feet became slender talons, his arms stretched out into broad wings. An enormous white owl rose into the sky, climbing away from the desolation of the square.

From below, the transformed Czcibor could hear an inhuman screech of rage. A huge black shape flitted upward. Once more wearing the shape of a giant bat, Wera was pursuing her adversary, determined that he shouldn't escape and make good his threat to find her hidden grave.

Czcibor lead the blood bat far across the ruins of Starybogow, the cracked streets and crumbling buildings flowing away beneath them as hunter and hunted sped toward the lands beyond the walls. Though the owl was smaller and swifter than the grotesque form Wera had assumed, Czcibor was weakened by the wounds he'd suffered. Many times weariness threatened him, causing his wings to stiffen and leave him to merely glide above the ruinous city. At such times, the bat would sweep forward, diving down at him with the ferocity of a hawk on the hunt. Only the greater agility of the krsnik's aerial shape saved him from being caught in the bat's claws or knocked from the sky by the vampir's leathery wings.

Forcing himself to greater effort, Czcibor at last found himself soaring past the abandoned walls of Starybogow and over the fallow fields and overgrown pastures beyond. The kudlak was close after him, her rage and anxiety moving Wera to stray far beyond her familiar haunts. Once more she was forced to range over the lands she'd stalked before making her compact with the peasants of Krynka.

The lights of the duplicitous village shone like a beacon in the night. Czcibor flew toward Krynka with such strength as he could coax from his owlish form. In his mind he estimated the distance between the settlement and Swinka. Yes, he decided at last, there had been enough time since the sun's setting. If Dobrogost had followed his orders!

The white owl fell toward the muddy lane that wound its way between the huts. As the bird descended, feathers fell away and wings thickened into muscular arms. It was the feet of a man rather than the talons of an owl that struck the road. The impact of his speedy descent sent Czcibor tumbling through the mud, but as his body lost momentum he turned his fall into a sprawling roll that brought him diving under the overhang of a woodshed.

Diving in pursuit of the krsnik as he tumbled down the street, Wera's claws were grasping for him even as he slid under the roof of the shed. Instead of human flesh the bat's claws sank into the wooden roof. Shrieking in frustration, Wera tore the roof to splinters, her monstrous wings beating furiously as she rose once more into the air.

Czcibor scrambled out from the other side of the shed, his right hand gripping a splinter from the torn roof. Unerringly he hurled the sliver of wood at the hovering bat. It lanced through the vampir's leathery wing, producing another burst of mephitic smoke as the kudlak's ichor reacted to the krsnik's enchantment. Howling in pain, Wera dropped from the sky and smashed through the thatch roof of the hut below her.

Screams of terror rose from the hut, but there was nothing Czcibor could do to help the occupants as the enraged vampir turned upon them. The weapons he needed to destroy Wera were locked away in Lukasz's treasure room. Without those, it would be all he could do just to protect himself. Looking away from the doomed hut, he quickly oriented himself and loped off in the direction of the tavern. The wounds across his belly were bleeding again, each halting step he took draining a bit more of his strength. He could see his goal standing off in the distance, but it seemed as far away as Wormditt's castle.

A snarl of bestial wrath caused Czcibor to look back. Wera had resumed her ghastly, corpse-like form, standing amid the wreckage of the hut's door. Blood was splattered across her mouth and chin, the lifeless body of a peasant dangling from one of her emaciated hands. The kudlak's injuries had faded away, no longer was mist seeping from her cuts or her deathly flesh marred by blisters. The excess of blood upon which she'd feasted within the hut had restored her hideous vitality. Aware now that she could undo whatever hurt Czcibor could inflict on her, the vampir was doubly eager to fall upon him.

Wera sprang from the threshold of the hut, but as the vampir leaped toward the street her body again shifted its form, stretching out into a long lupine shape. Abominably wasted and thin, it was the semblance of a huge black wolf that rushed down the lane to overtake Czcibor.

Before the vampir could fall upon him, Czcibor threw himself forward in a sprawling lunge. Like the kudlak, the krsnik's body transformed as he leaped, taking the shape of a white dog. Lithe and supple, the dog ran ahead of his black pursuer, distancing the withered wolf as he fled down the muddy lane. Each bound sent a tremor of pain coursing through Czcibor's canine frame and the gashes that had closed with his transformation were soon ripped open once more, crimson blood seeping across his white fur.

Smell of the krsnik's blood drove Wera into a frenzy. The vampir surged onward in a burst of maddened speed, her jaws snapping at Czcibor's tail. He could feel her undead chill stealing over him, curdling the blood in his veins and making his flesh crawl. The lights of the tavern were only a few dozen yards ahead, but Czcibor knew he wouldn't make it.

Then, from the shadows of an alleyway, a great gray apparition pounced upon the black wolf. A snarling tangle of claws and fangs rolled through the mud, ripping and slashing with savage abandon. A cry of agony rose from the black wolf, steaming mist whistling from her jaw. With a panicked burst of might, she threw aside her attacker and sent it tumbling down the street. The vampir resumed her cadaverous form, clutching at her injured face with a skeletal talon.

Wera's late attacker growled at her as it lifted itself from the mud. A great gray wolf, larger even than the lupine shape the kudlak had assumed, stood glaring at her from the middle of the street. Surma, loosed by Dobrogost, had followed Czcibor's scent. Now the wolf stood between the vampir and her prey.

The kudlak sneered at the wolf's threat. The hypnotic powers Wera possessed were even more effectual against beasts than they were against men. She'd turn the animal against the krsnik and kill him with the teeth of his own defender. Yet as she tried to bring her powers to bear against Surma, she found a hateful glow shining around the wolf, a shimmering aura that burned in her brain and refused to permit the focus needed for her enchantment. She saw the cause at once, the injury against her mouth had been inflicted when her fangs sought the wolf's throat. Now she saw that the animal was guarded by a collar of beaten silver into which was woven several slivers of hawthorn.

Further down the road, Czcibor limped toward the tavern. As the krsnik's blood continued to seep down his side, his mind lost the focus that allowed him to hold his canine shape. By degrees his human form was restored so that it was his own battered and bloodied body that sagged beside the building's door and rapped against the portal with knotted fist.

The vampir suspected there must be some purpose to Czcibor's retreat, some protection he hoped to find within the building. A wrathful glint shone in Wera's eyes as she followed his creeping progress. Whatever the krsnik's plan, it would die unfulfilled when she rent him limb from limb. Returning her glare to Surma, the kudlak began to transform once more, her arms stretching out into great leathery pinions.

"You will not escape!" The enraged voice howled from the darkness. Wera felt something stab into her side, interrupting her transformation. She turned to confront her attacker, the man who'd slashed at her undead flesh with a scythe. The force of vengeance and hate eclipsed whatever horror pulsed within the peasant. Even as the kudlak brought her talon smashing down into the heft of the scythe and split it in half, there was only the flush of rage in Dobrogost's eyes.

"Whore of Satan!" Dobrogost railed, flinging himself upon the vampir. With the iron blade of the scythe still embedded in the creature's side, he instead drove what was left of the shaft into her ghastly visage. Again and again he battered away at her, raining upon her blows that had split the skulls of cow and swine.

The vampir, however, was possessed of a supernatural vitality and against her even the fiercest of mortal implements were as nothing. Deftly she plucked the shaft from Dobrogost's hand, tossing it down the lane. Then, with the back of one claw, she dealt the peasant a blow that sent him crashing against the nearest hovel. He landed in a moaning heap, blood bubbling from his split lip and battered chest. The scent of Dobrogost's wounds brought a hideous smile to the vampir, the gesture rendered all the more abominable for the mist seeping from her own injury.

Before she could pounce, Wera found herself once again confronted by Surma. The giant wolf sprang at her, its jaws snapping at her throat. The kudlak spun around, lashing at the animal with her arm to ward it away. She shrieked as her unclean flesh brushed across the blessed metal and wood of the wolf's collar. A thin spray of mist dribbled from her cut skin as she retreated from Surma's assault.

The kudlak turned her focus upon Dobrogost. Unlike Surma and Czcibor, the peasant had no protection from Wera's hypnotic gaze. Almost from the instant the vampir's gaze fell upon him, he was enslaved. Ruthlessly she compelled his battered body back onto its feet. While she fended away Surma's snapping jaws, Wera directed her slave to recover the broken heft of the scythe.

Dobrogost took up the improvised club and stole toward the wolf from behind. Even as he raised the weapon to strike, however, a fierce grip took hold of him and pushed him aside. At once he felt the vampir's influence lift from him. He blinked in bewilderment as he saw Czcibor standing beside him. The krsnik was bereft of raiment and the grisly wounds in his side were yet bleeding, but in his hand the vampir hunter held a weapon that seemed aglow with a brilliance that eclipsed both moon and star.

Wera cringed before sight of Czcibor's steel, hissing in repulsion at the fiery blade. Every detail smashed against the vampir's senses as the krsnik raised his sword. The metal was an alchemical fusion of steel and silver that hearkened back to the mythical science of long-drowned Atlantis and upon this impossible alloy had been etched symbols of arcane potency. The crossguard and pommel were fashioned of gold and studded with gemstones of equally magical significance. Locked within the rounded pommel itself was a tiny reliquary within which the tiniest splinter of cedar was ensconced.

"Doom is upon you, tomb-leech," Czcibor pronounced as he advanced upon Wera. The kudlak spun around, tried to flee from the krsnik. At that moment, Surma leapt upon her, smashing the undead fiend to the ground. She clawed at the beast, heedless now of the injuries wrought upon her by its collar.

Dobrogost snapped from his confusion when he saw vampir and wolf struggling. The thirst for vengeance came flooding back and he hastened toward the melee. "For Zoja!" he shouted as he brought the broken heft of the scythe stabbing down into the kudlak's breast. The vampir threw aside Surma and reached for the peasant with her clawed fingers.

"Deeper," Czcibor warned the peasant. "It is not enough to pierce a kudlak's heart! The fiend must be pinned to the earth!"

Obeying the krsnik, Dobrogost forced the stake deeper into the vampir's breast, punching through moldy bones and rotten organs to at last sink into the mud of the street. Impaled upon the spike, Wera was rendered immobile, her fiendish strength ebbing away into the ground beneath her.

Czcibor warned Surma away with a snapped command, then motioned Dobrogost to do likewise. He stared down at the paralyzed vampir. Wera glared back at him, hissing and spitting with the craven viciousness of a cornered rat. "A kudlak can be rendered powerless by a stake which pins it to the ground, but to do destroy them needs stronger measures." He stepped around the vampir until he stood above her snarling head. Raising his sword, he brought the glowing weapon slashing down. The stroke cleaved through the monster's neck, severing the head from the body. For an instant, Wera's eyes still blazed with an infernal energy, but soon their malignant glare cooled into the long-defied chill of death.

The moment of Wera's destruction saw the eldritch glow of Czcibor's sword wink out, the blade becoming only a few feet of sharpened steel with a silvery sheen. The krsnik sheathed the weapon, then knelt in the road with the sword before him and bowed his head in a prayer of gratitude for his triumph. When his devotions were complete, Czcibor slumped into the street. Instantly, Surma loped over to his side, a concerned whine rasping from its jaws. The wolf sat down beside him, laying its muzzle across his foot.

Dobrogost walked over to the vampir's severed head, spitting on it and hurling curses upon the vanquished fiend. Now that his vengeance was sated, he found it small recompense for the loss of his daughter. Tears streamed down the peasant's face.

"Nothing can replace what you've lost," Czcibor said, "but I think if you asked Lukasz, you would find the people of Krynka only too eager to pay wergild to their neighbors for their losses. It is a small penance for their part in all of this but it is a start." The krsnik looked around at the huts lining the road. During the fray not so much as a light had betrayed the presence of their occupants. Now there was a babble of excited murmurs and the occasional face peeping out from behind a shutter.

"Get the villagers to help you," Czcibor told Dobrogost. "The kudlak's head and body must be burned separately and the ashes scattered in a river." He raised his right hand, the hand that was devoted solely to his gruesome business. "First you must cut out the vampir's heart. It is to be boiled down into a broth." A weary smile crossed his bruised face. "Something to keep up my strength. The best hunters always have something of their prey inside them."

Dobrogost shuddered at the grisly suggestion. Supping on meat killed by a wolf was outré enough but this flirted with the profane. Then again, from what Czcibor had said, there was much about Krynka that bordered on the profane. Had these people truly been a party to the vampir's depredations? And if they had, why should they help to dispose of the monster or make recompense to its victims? He voiced his concerns to the krsnik.

Czcibor laughed. "You don't give yourself enough credit, friend Dobrogost! You are braver than you imagine. It wasn't enough for you to set Surma free when I failed to return. No, you had to follow him, dogging the tracks of a wolf through a benighted forest."

"I was safe enough," Dobrogost said. "Surma is your wolf."

The krsnik reached down and scratched at the wolf's ears. "There you are wrong. Surma isn't some tame and broken beast. He is my companion, but not my pet. Without my influence to restrain him, he is as wild as any of his kind." Czcibor shook his head. "It is well that Surma had more important things to occupy him while you chased him alone through the woods. You are fortunate indeed that Surma doesn't like to go into a fight with a full stomach."

The Tale of the Mad Brothers Three

Michael McCann

Leshy
by N.N. Broot, 1906

"Cyr, catch!" A deep voice cried out as a dagger was tossed through the air and into the hands of another, younger, man. Cyril's tanned leather overcoat swayed through the air as he spun on his heel. Catching the weapon without any strain, and bringing it down with force intended to do damage, the young swordsman jabbed the blade between the eyes of the creature that hissed and convulsed as it went limp. Its claws loosened from Cyril's overcoat and dropped to his feet.

Some feet away an identical creature with hair that resembled more leaves than that which belonged to a human was quickly ran through by a stout man wielding a spear in both hands; its blood splashed to the ground upon the loosely armored man's jerk backward, the head of his polearm slick with the viscous liquid. Nikola the weapons-master breathed heavily and quickly looked toward his 'brother' Radomir, who was busy with his own target.

The cloaked scholar strafed his own creature, whose needle like teeth dripped with purplish venom. Radomir was the largest of the three of them and despite his ability to overpower most men, including his companions, he was perhaps the most calculating and weighed every decision, every step, and monitored his opponents with an unrivaled intensity. It was because of this that when the creature sprung, its claws extending outward, that the man briefly turned into a blur of blue cloth and upon the monster's rebound, it found a small yet deadly sharp axe buried in-between its pitch-like eyes.

Cyril checked his chest for blood, but luckily the mail beneath his coat absorbed most of the creature's slash. Nikola smirked, planted his spear into the ground, and rotated his arms in some post-battle stretch. The patchwork set of armor he adorned shifted and clanged as he began to unbuckle the round shield attached to his wrist. Wise Rad, as the other two called him, wretched his double bearded axe from the creature's skull and let out a smooth and even breath between pursed lips.

"Ha, those creatures were fierce. Fun fight though." Nikola said as he turned over his kill with a steel plated boot.

"You think anything that is trying to kill you is a fun fight, Nik." The shaggy auburn haired Cyril said handing back the dagger. Searching the clearing in which the Mad Brothers were jumped, Cyril became elated when he located his favored sword. *At least I won't have to clean it,* the youngest of the three thought as he sheathed the curved blade.

"Mmm." Wise Rad murmured aloud. With his left elbow planted in his hand and his fingers stroking the thick, red beard that ran from his jaw and cheeks, he was studying the dead creature whose wood-like skin seemed to turn brown and decay, as if it were an ancient tree.

The other two went to his side, Nik chugging from his waterskin and Cyril biting his lip. "What is it, Rad?" the latter asked.

"You fallin' in love? These things are dead. No meat on him. Maybe we could burn them for kindling, though." Nikola exclaimed with a stifled laugh.

"Don't be so crass, Nik. These are leshiye," the scholar noted, bending down and lightly touching the hardened hide of the creature.

"*Leshiye*? I think I had a hound named that once. Damn thing nearly bit my father's hand off."

"Leshiye are forest spirits, guardians of the wood." Cyril answered. "It might mean we're getting close." In the Mad Brothers' research, Rad's idea, Cyril discovered that Starybogow was not a place to be taken lightly and it was rumored that spirits, and even some ancient deities that the Slavic worshipped, seemed attracted to the place.

"Which also means we should be wary of our movement. Keep our noise to a minimum, our bonfires low. Our clumsiness may have given us away to these leshiye," Rad stated. Years of reading, rereading, and studying any book or tome he could get his hands on proved invaluable on their journey. More times than they could count, Rad understood and explained some of the things they had come across; many vile and malevolent, while there were some rare peaceful ones.

"Clumsiness!?" the weapons-master belted incredulously.

"Here we go..." Cyril whispered.

"Yes, we were speaking too loudly and your... incident at the creek probably put every spirit or animal on alert." Rad scolded.

Nikola's finger was pointed accusingly and his mouth open to defend himself. At the mentioning of the creek however, his eyes went wide and his mouth promptly shut.

"Sirs, may I suggest we move along? I don't want to be in this clearing-…" Cyril took one more look around at the large, sun bathed opening in the forest's canopy and was reminded of a similar spot his Sun and he would spend afternoons talking and drinking what felt like a whole cask of wine. *We're coming, love, I promise you that.*

"Clearing...?" Nikola said, bringing the younger Brother back into reality.

"I don't want to be in this clearing if any more leshiye are to show up. Besides, it'll be dusk soon and gods know what crawls out from the caves at night."

"Point made, Brother. I'd be more worried 'bout what crawls out of the grave than what beast hunts at sundown though. We only got the one dagger made of silver. And sometimes that don't even work. Have I ever told you the story of when I-"

"Was nearly killed by a drekavac? Yes, you have. At least a dozen times, Nikola." Cyril answered.

A hearty laugh from Rad, followed by a nod in the direction they had been headed, was all it took for them to be on their way. Cyril adjusting his riding gloves - though their horses long abandoned, Nikola cursing a split in the shaft of his spear, and a playful low hum from the Wise was an image that perfectly embodied the Mad Brothers.

The young, emotional Cyril quietly and casually made sure his gear was in place, his overcoat sitting perfectly so it didn't chafe the back of his neck, constantly pushing back the auburn hair that came beneath his ears. His weapon was a curved blade that would cut flesh quickly and deeply; his father once gave it a name but the son viewed that as pretentious and meant for seasoned warriors like those of the Teutonic Knights or the weapons once wielded by the legendary Templar. Coupled together with a bow primarily used for hunting, Cyril was not the epitome of a warrior; but those who knew him understood just how quick the young man could move and slash his way to a victory.

Nikola the weapons-master was a brash yet agile man. Quick to action with a tongue that would always make haste in conversation, the warrior was a former sellsword whose 'career' brought him all over the land. Though their friendship caused him to keep putting one foot in front of the other, the chance to see Starybogow was perhaps one of his largest driving forces of their quest. Anxious to slay creatures that many only saw in their nightmares, the two short swords, a shield, a half dozen daggers and knives strategically placed on the armor he wore would be the only tools he needed to make himself famous.

Wise Radomir was an intense individual and some would even be off-put by his demeanor, confusing intelligence for arrogance.

Though he was not armored like Cyril, nor armed like Nikola, Radomir needed nothing more than his mind and the ever growing journal he kept in his robe's inside satchel. While Nikola convinced him to take up an axe in case it was needed, Rad was quick to believe in peace before violence.

Cyril narrowed his eyes as he tried to stare through the tops of the trees. If what Rad had said was correct, it would not be long before they saw the peaks of Starybogow's battlements; and behind those walls were fabled to be some of the vilest monstrosities ever conceived by the Old Gods, rivaled only by even darker forces living in the murky waterways.

But one creature in particular was on the prowl tonight, stalking the unaware young warrior and his allies. While its yellowed eyes glowed in the moonlight, tracking their movements, it lapped at the blood and viscera that soaked its claws.

*****

The three walked the dirt pathway through the forest, mildly jumpy at any strange sound or chirp that echoed through the dense woodlands. It felt like forever since they had set out on the path in search of Cyril's fiancé, the woman he affectionately named Sun.

The woman vanished and nary a clue was to be found. Some say a spirit or demon claimed her for their own otherworldly bride, others spoke of a creature roaming down from the mountains and snatching her for its meal. But Cyril was not to be so easily defeated and accepting of such a fate. Grabbing a sword, bundles of arrows, and a bow, the young man set out to find his lover.

He had been readily joined by the two men that walked now beside him; Nikola the self-proclaimed weapons-master, and the studious Radomir the Wise. Together the three walked all ends of the earth, searching for some trace of Cyril's fiancé. Many weeks went by and they found nothing but implausible stories and fabrications. That was, until one night, having a drink in a local tavern, they heard a shadowed figure speak of a woman matching her description heading to a northern city. They finally had hope. Hope that was quickly dashed once they heard the name of the northern town; a name that caused the Wise Radomir's face to go pale underneath his red beard.

Starybogow.

They were looked upon as mad for even attempting the trip, yet it can be said that their bond with one another kept them going even into the maws of such an enigmatic place. Villages began to speak of the Mad Brothers as they passed through, three travelers on an unending quest that would bring them to the steps of the Old Gods so as long as they remained companions. It was upon the trail for the lost woman, nicknamed Sun by Cyril, for her flowing, blonde locks, that this tale begun.

For countless moons now they had traveled through many kinds of terrain, but they all agreed that this particular forest was the most difficult. If it weren't for Nikola's seasoned traveling experience, they assured one another they would have been lost some time ago.

As the sun began to set and the sky turned to a kaleidoscope of oranges and faint purples, the three decided to make a fire and set up their bedrolls. A quick kill at the hands of Cyril's bow made venison their dinner that evening. The skin was beginning to crisp and the meat grew tender as they expelled the last of their salt and spices that Radomir brought as a bit of a reprieve from their harsh journey. The seasonings brought a curl to Cyril's smile. They had learned early on that their priorities in civilized locations were each very different.

Cyril would take to the tavern for a drink and to converse with the locals about rumors and often come back with news of the Inquisition or the Teutonic Knights attempting to eradicate another area of the Slavic tribesmen; sometimes even hopeful word of the Knights Templar striking back to defend the Slavs. Luckily the young man's skills with people and his natural charisma would often net them with something useful to their journey, and more than once they were able to dodge the Inquisition or worse, the Teutonic Knights.

Nikola would often be quick to the blacksmith to assure his weapons were in top shape, and he was often chastised for his ability to spend far more coin than they had to spare; whether it be for a new scabbard, a piece of armor, or even just get them kicked out of town for criticizing the smithy's work. But, if it weren't for his constant need to perfect his craft of killing, the other two might have ended up dead some time ago.

Wise Rad was a curious case, for he was always hard to locate when the three decided to make a brief nest for themselves at a town. Whether he was busy adding more script to his journal, or sketching a particular type of leaf, the man was always out and about; usually getting himself lost among the local foliage. Or in one particular case, arguing with an elderly man about the history of the Knights Templar and dismissing the man's wild accusations against the Romani.

But this particular evening however, sparse on supplies, and weathered from their battle with the leshiye, the three sat in their usual formation with their dim fire in the center. A whetstone in each of their hands, the fire danced and made shapes upon their faces.

"You know what I don't understand about you, Cyril." Nikola said in a brusque but not accusative fashion. "The skill you have with your sword is some of the best I've seen in a long time. You can dodge, roll, even pirouette yourself out of an enemies swing or swipe. Yet you adhere yourself to the use of a curved blade, a weapon that is extremely foolish to use against someone wearing plate. Why never invest in something you could stab with? Even a short sword."

Cyril smiled and stared into the fire, longing for their dinner to be ready. "I was taught that there are many creatures, monsters if you will, in the world which are feral and attack with the utmost rage in their black hearts. Spirits whose sole mission is to cause harm or to drive a man mad. My teachings with a sword are explicitly meant to be the opposite. Flowing, like water - some might even say dancing - I can weave in and out of an opponent's reach and strike back before they even realize where I am. I can move in a way that my enemies cannot and that gives me an advantage. Besides, I do well to not pick fights with men in plate, Nikola."

"Smart words, they are." Rad chimed in. "I've seen you fight and it is quite a sight. I've read from time to time that there is a group of individuals out there who disguise themselves as mere peasants, merchants, and sometimes even royalty. They stick to the shadows; they operate in pure darkness and can poke you full of holes before you even realize they are there. To be so attuned to the elements around you? That, my brothers, that is true skill." Wise Rad said, with a wry look at Nikola who sat with his short sword across his lap, the newly oiled surface shimmering in the fire's light.

"That's not to say that your capability to run up toward a fiend and overwhelm them with ferocity is not effective." Cyril smirked, Nikola nodded his head in approval.

"Well," the eldest sat up from his prone position and gently closed his journal. "Let's get this deer in our bellies before the smell attracts some more unsavory monsters from the woods."

"Hear, hear!" Nikola cheered, gently sheathing the blade.

*****

The three men ate their meals quickly and quietly, as was usually the case. Before they had even begun to douse the fire in dirt and call it a night, Cyril's eyes grew heavy. Within thirty minutes all three of the companions were asleep. The night carried on and just at the peak of the starlight, a faint crunching of twigs sounded some feet away. Cyril woke out of instinct, unaware of the sound that had disturbed him.

He rubbed his eyes, ran his hand through his hair, and sat up. His throat was dry and as he felt for his waterskin, the movement sounded once again. Alerted and at the ready for a leshy, wolf, or something far worse than both, Cyril slowly slid his hand to the falchion at his side. In the pure darkness he would not be able to defend himself well and so he sat as still as possible to allow his eyes to adjust.

I may end up dinner for something but at least I'll know what it is. He thought to himself, leaning toward Nikola's legs to shake him awake. But, before he could, his eyes met something in the woods, the very thing that had caused him to tense up in the first place.

There they were, two milky blue orbs staring at him from behind the thicket of a nearby bush. Unmoving and shadowed in the darkness of the night, the eyes seemed to stare directly at him. Judging by the height of them, Cyril observed, the thing was as tall as a grown man. In mere seconds he recollected the tales he had heard about in his youth, or that Radomir had taught him.

Baba Yaga? No, we haven't seen a house for days... Likho, maybe? Can't be that we have encountered anyone we have wronged or made a deal with... vampir? By the gods I hope-

But as the swordsman and the entity stared holes in one another, a shriek like nothing Cyril had ever heard sounded from deeper in the forests. The sound seemed to almost boil the young man's blood and filled him with instant dread.

It alarmed him even more when the two other Mad Brothers woke up suddenly, Nikola with a small knife in his hand pulled from his boot, Wise Rad lay with his eyes open and a single hand out to calm the others. Cyril turned his head quickly as the commotion at the bonfire caught his attention, but when he went to look back to the eyes, they were gone, only the faint sound of something bounding through the woods could be heard.

"Are we being attacked? Do I need the silver?" Nikola asked impatiently. Without a clear answer he was already searching wildly through his gear to locate the other dagger, discarding the pig-sticker he had in his hand.

"Calm yourself, you fool! Stay perfectly still," Cyril demanded. Rad himself had sat up and monitored the surrounding area.

"Both of you shut your gobs," the Wise rasped.

The three sat, half in their bedrolls, for nearly ten minutes before the only sounds to be heard were the chirping of birds, the rustle of grass, and the noise from insects.

"I think we are safe." Cyril said finally. He rose to his feet and continued to look around. "I swore I saw something in the wood, there." He pointed a finger in the direction of the eyes that stared at him.

Rad sat up and started flipping through his journal. Dragging a finger across the well-inked pages, he sat murmuring to himself, attempting to find an answer in his notes.

Nikola was already up and fastening his swords to his back, always anxious that he'd be caught unawares. "What exactly did you see?" he asked innocently.

"Eyes." the single word caused Wise Rad to look up and bite his own lip.

"What kind of eyes? Yellow, red, one or two?"

"Blue. Two of them. Stood just as tall as a man, I'd say." Cyril said, rolling up his bedroll. Dawn was a little ways off, but clearly the Mad Brothers were no longer safe, strange creatures looked upon them as they slept, and even stranger ones shrieked some distance away. Nothing would allow them a well rested night any longer.

"Great. We have ourselves an admirer. Maybe it's a woodsman with a pet dog or wolf or something. Every man worthy of calling himself a woodsman can make a fine stew. Love me some of that." Nikola said, tightening the small belts that sheathed his knives.

"I don't think woodsmen would stray this near to Starybogow, Nik. We have better chances-"

Rad held up one hand, his bedroll still sprawled out, his head shot up and slowly looked back at them. "You say wolf... and it comes."

"What are you going on-" a sudden snap of twigs and the shuffling of underbrush caused Nikola to put one hand on the hilt of his sword and the other wrapping around the silver dagger at his waist. Cyril too drew his falchion and stood, two-handing the weapon.

Wise Rad slowly got up and stood next to his 'brothers', axe in his hand. "Oh, mother of..." he whispered.

Out from the line of trees, it came. Its paws covered in thick, reddish fur ending in long black claws. It walked upon all fours, unaffected by the uneven landscape it traversed. Stalking them with its snout open, revealing yellowed fangs dripping with saliva, its body hunched, indicating its capacity to walk on two legs, ears perked up like a hound smelling a pheasant. Its eyes glowed that milky blue Cyril had seen... that was until it walked into the moonlight-exposed clearing that the Mad Brothers had made their camp where their true yellow shade came to be seen. Faint scars glistened in the pseudo-darkness along its back, bristling fur covering every inch of its muscled body. A low, and terrible, snarl came from its massive lungs.

"Vucari..." Nikola gulped, even the seasoned warrior was too tense to make a move knowing that the wolf-man before him could easily pierce the plate on his chest and turn his bare skin into ribbons. "...and here I am forgetting my shield on the ground..."

"Do not move. If the creature leaps we can easily overwhelm it... Nikola, have that silver dagger at the ready," Cyril said. "Rad... any knowledge in that thick skull of yours that can help us out here?"

"Yes, pray to Porewit and hope Flins does not take us so soon." the Wise said.

"I don't think your Old Gods are going to help us now..." Nikola growled.

With an ear-shattering bark and snapping of its jaws, the vucari startled all three of them so suddenly that instinct seemed to take them over, for Nikola moved in, sword in hand. He charged toward the beast belting a war cry at the top of his lungs.

"NIKOLA!" Cyril shouted, but before they could grab their brother from what would be certain death, the wolf-man turned its attention to its would-be attacker and simply back-handed him to his feet, and snarled.

"What the-" Wise Rad noticed the vucari hadn't had its eyes on them after all. He snapped his head around and even he couldn't help but let out a scream of sorts.

There was a second creature that had tracked them down and now stood flanking what escape they would have had. But unlike the vucari who was beast-like, a ferocious predator whose appetite was its driving force, this second one was not quite of the natural world.

"T-topielic..." Radomir shuttered.

Cyril had quickly gotten Nikola to his feet, but both froze when they saw the newest threat to reveal itself. When the creature let out a deafening shriek, they were forced to cover their ears.

It stood as tall as a man, with the posture and shape of one as well. Its grey, mottled skin was covered in hideous boils and carbuncles that hung to its joints like some ghostly armor. It was sickly thin with a ribcage that threatened to pierce its skin, and its collarbone seemed to protrude from underneath like a corpse that had been wasting away. Thin, soaked hair that was as black as pitch covered its head, framing the vilest feature of its already hideous appearance.

Just one look at the putrid, gaunt face made Cyril feel bile rising in his throat. If it weren't for the small reflection of the moonlight coming from the black orbs that sat in them, its eye sockets would have seemed to be empty with the gray skin stretched monstrously tight against it. The cheek bones and jaw seemed to too angular to be human, ears that were non-existent, and its mouth puckered with a lipless grin; the skin seemed to split against its sharp teeth and leaked out some foul ooze. The nose was flat and almost fish-like, the tiny slits heaved as it watched the scene like a stone sentinel; webbed fingers curled around a tree branch that had been fashioned into a spear.

The vucari made its presence known once more by growling deeply and rose to its hind legs, revealing its true height. Cyril and Nikola's eyes went wide and their mouths opened in a gasp.

Wordlessly, the topielic tapped its make-shift spear against the earth five times. Before they could react, the Mad Brothers began to hear a low, gurgling moan come from seemingly all around them.

"You have gods that answer the prayers of the royally fu-…" Nikola's curse was cut short by the vucari suddenly pouncing from its spot, blowing past Rad like a whirlwind and sending itself crashing into the topielic. As the wolf creature caught itself on all fours and spun around for a second pass, the water spirit was already on its feet, carrying itself like the bones beneath its skin were too heavy for it.

Nikola went to join the sudden fray, but a gray-skinned arm rose from below him unnoticed. Pulling itself from the earth, a second topielic emerged, covered in dirt and slick as though newly bathed. Its clawed hand grabbed Nikola's arm and pulled as it wriggled free from dirt and mud.

Thinking quickly, Cyril swung his falchion and sliced a huge gash across the creature's face, sending it reeling, its grasp on Nikola broken. But this however, did not stop it.

"Get up you idiot!" Wise Rad shouted, but just as he finished his warning, a sharp pain erupted from his right arm, and he turned to see a third water spirit readying another thrust from its spear. Luckily, Wise Radomir was left handed and when the second thrust came to pierce his hand, he parried the blow with his axe, though the creature's weapon of choice made it far too clear that he would not be able to amount an offensive from that range. He opted to back away, trying to remain just the right distance from the sharply tipped branch.

"I've never seen creatures mount such an attack!" Cyril said, finally pulling Nikola up off of the ground. It was then that he noticed two more of them shuffling through the forest, spears in hand. "There's more!? This is crazy!"

"No, Cyril!" Wise Rad shouted; awaiting the next thrust from the topielic that he faced, he managed to catch the branch in his right hand and forced strength into a downward slash from his axe, splitting the creature's weapon in half. With all of his weight down on his right foot, he leapt slightly, shoving his shoulder into the creature, knocking it off of its clumsy feet. "This... this... this is what awaits us at Starybogow."

Nikola, fuming from his humiliation, was finally on the offensive. Unfazed by the hideous enemies in front of him, he charged toward the two that Cyril had noticed before. Moving at a steady pace, he parried a thrust from the one he had put on his left, its spear bouncing away harmlessly. With a quick, full spin, he brought his short swords with him, using the momentum to thrust both forward into the spine of the topielic. Without so much as a cry of pain, it fell to its knees. The one on his right craned its neck and clumsily tried a thrust at his torso, the tip snapping against the breast plate. Without missing a beat, he took the sword out of the first dead one's spine, and then in the same motion went for a killing blow on the second.

In one quick, lion-like swipe, Nikola the weapons-master brought the silver dagger from his belt and planted it in the topielic's neck. With a shriek that caused Nik to wince, the creature's mouth fell open unnaturally wide, as it seemed to convulse and shrivel. Taking the small blade out, it seemed to return to the ground from whence it came. Noticing the first topielic crawling its way toward his ankles, Nikola planted the silver into the creature's skull as he half-turned and fell to one knee, using the momentum to utterly decimate it.

Meanwhile, Cyril had been busy with Nikola's original attacker. With almost serpentine like movement, the young swordsman allowed the creature only slight movements before he unleashed devastating slashes upon it. Skin, carbuncle, and bone splattered his overcoat. Gashes were open all over the creature as it mounted a mindless attack against him. Finally, with a quick flurry of one-two, one-two slashes, Cyril put all of his momentum into a quick spin that beheaded the creature.

At the same moment, as Wise Rad's target rose from where he had knocked it down with a shoulder thrust, he returned to his usual strategy of combat. Watch, and learn. As the small, grape-sized orbs bore holes into him, Rad walked closer, ever-weary of the still sharp spear he had split asunder. Just as he edged in closer, looking to cleave away, a reddish blur bounced on top of it, nearly sending him on his back. For the vucari had struck again, this time, covered in black ooze that he only guessed was that of the original topielic.

The bearded Radomir nearly leapt a foot when Nikola's hand came down on his shoulder and pulled him back toward the original campfire. The three of them stood, silent and weary, as all sorts of viscera flew through the air as the vucari slashed and bit its victim into a second grave.

"By the gods that is disgustin'..." Nikola said pointing to the heap of unidentifiable parts that had been the topielic that emerged first. "Quick, I'll get it with the silver while its busy eating." Nikola added, and put a single foot forward before he was stopped by Cyril, his blade flat across his chest.

"No, wait... if that thing had wanted us dead…"

"Vucari do not kill for sport, or so the rumors say." Rad said, grimacing at the blood that soaked through the right arm of his robes.

"*And so the rumors say...*" Nikola said in a mocking tone.

As they all wordlessly thought of a plan to avoid a second encounter with the much dangerous foe, besides run for their lives, the vucari stopped its assault on its long-dead victim and slowly turned its head toward the Mad Brothers. The clicking and clacking of their various weapons slowly rising into attack position was all that was heard.

That was until the vucari sighed, and wiped its snout with one, massive forepaw. With little fanfare, the monster stared at them for what felt like hours and just as suddenly began to stride into the forest with a trot that wouldn't have been uncharacteristic of a domesticated hound. The three of them all watched, confused and unsure of what to make of the random encounter, until it barked in their direction.

"You've got to be kidding me..." Cyril said under his breath.

"What?" Nikola questioned.

"It... wants us to follow it...?" Rad asked no one in particular.

"Chyeah, there's not much I fear in this world. But the two things I do are vucari and you being unsure of yourself, Wise."

Without permission or even acknowledging them both, Cyril had already taken the leap and began to follow the vucari who stood, on all fours again, watching them as if impatiently waiting.

"Cyril, you git! Would you follow a damn Servitor just as quick!? Come on, now!" Nikola shouted, looking back at the corpses of the topielics to make sure his sudden increase in volume hadn't revived them a third time.

Again, without words, Wise Radomir began to follow Cyril and the wolf-man as well.

"Oh, this is bloody brilliant! Let's follow the thing that just eviscerated those creatures! Why we must follow in the steps of something that only silver can kill is beyond me!" Nikola stood still, arms crossed. Taking one last, long, shiver accompanied look at the fallen water-spirits, and their blood soaked bedrolls, the second oldest Mad Brother began to follow. "We'd have better luck with the damn Servitors, I swear it…"

Servitors, Cyril thought as he carefully followed the wolf-like beast, *the cursed followers of the Eldar Gods.* Stories had made their way across the known world about the nightmarish beings that pledged their lives to the Dwellers of the Deep seemingly forever. Campfire tales of men rising from the waters of the sea, clad in armor like that seen on crabs and tentacles jutting out from their chins. They'd creep onto the shore and steal children from their beds as sacrifices to their gods. Horror stories of men in cloaks decorated with dried up starfish, cracked and sharpened sea shells sown into their sleeves, and their hair transformed into slick sea weed; speaking in tongues as if they were underwater.

After he shook the imagery from his head Cyril decided he would much rather take his chance with the vucari any day.

*****

For the rest of the night, the three of them followed the now calm vucari through the forest. Rad tore a piece of his robe off to wrap his wound, Nikola's hand never strayed from the handle of his silver dagger, and Cyril seemingly mindlessly followed the wolf-being.

Rad winced as he wrapped the make-shift bandage as tight as he could without cutting off circulation. Nikola briskly walked next to him.

"You really think this is a good idea, Rad? I didn't keep myself alive for years fighting things like that," he said pointing an accusing finger at the vucari, "by trusting them and letting them take the lead. Are we mad?"

A slight chuckle erupted from beneath the beard. "Well, that is what they call us right? The Mad Brothers Three? Fancy we live up to it by some regard, eh? Besides, you and I met years ago, Nikola. You in turn knew Cyril's swords-master and we were recruited to find that young man's would-be bride. I do not have it in me to suddenly turn away from him. Lest we be in a situation in which we are forced to choose, I love him as a brother far too much to abandon him. And I know you can say the same." As Rad lectured, Nikola sighed and scratched at his neck.

"Yeah, you be right. But still. Leshiye I get. We were in a forest. The topielic..."

"Must I bring up your involuntary swim in that creek again?" Rad asked, a single eyebrow raised. "You might have disturbed some of the restless spirits that resided in the water."

"It certainly explains why that one seemed to like you the most, Nik!" Cyril shouted from the front of the line. Rad and Nikola looked at each other. They were unsure how much of the conversation Cyril had heard, until he spoke the next words. "But, thank you both. I know this journey hasn't been easy and how we truly are the Mad Brothers now, but I cannot put into words just how much comfort it brings knowing that I have you two. My blood brother joined the Teutonic Knights some years ago, and afterward I hadn't known what to do. Follow in his footsteps, strike out on my own. It was a confusing time where I questioned everything I had believed in or had wanted in this world. That was until I met," he fought back tears just thinking of her.

"Until I met my Sun."

"Aye, we'll be with you every step of the way... no matter what you make us follow." Nikola said, smirking. "Though I stop the line at anything with tentacles."

The three of them shared a hearty laugh as the tension of combat finally eased away and they began to see the sun rising from just below the treeline.

*****

As dusk was nearly upon them, they all marveled at the sight that revealed itself. They stood atop a large, moss covered hill, overlooking only three more miles of woodlands that broke away into rolling hills and meadows. The picture perfect sunrise would have warmed their hearts and eased their spirits, if it weren't blemished by the gloom seemingly emanating from just beyond that. For there was Starybogow.

"I'll be a right fool." Wise Rad said. The three of them had stopped and took in the sight. Cyril crouched down, his hand on his mouth, positive that his lost love was growing every closer. Rad bore his teeth in pain as he held his journal in his bad arm to quickly check to see if the description he had written down some months ago matched what he was seeing. And finally Nikola stood, his hands on the back of his head, whistling his wonderment.

But, as the three travel-weary men took a breather, their sightseeing was quickly broken up by a bark from the vucari who they hadn't realized was already half way down what looked like steps leading into the last remnants of the forest.

"Ruins?" Cyril asked pointing to the cracked and crumbling stone.

"Cyril, if this thing is leading us into its den to feed its family, I'll have you know that I'm changing my deal, and I certainly want coin for this."

The three of them swiftly followed, their achy legs and knees not aiding the shaky descent that the vucari made look so easy. As they entered into the forest, the fragrance of fresh water and pine trees consumed their senses; a welcome scent after their exposure to topielic. They were also amazed that the stonework hadn't stopped at the stairs, as they found themselves walking a hobbled walkway, though it had been long since its construction and countless stones were broken away.

"Look there, lads!" Cyril exclaimed, the vucari had taken a bit of a lead on them and now awaited beneath the ruins of what was once a stone archway. Its massive frame obscured what awaited past it, but the three men were too entranced at the sight. It had been far too long since they saw anything resembling civilization.

The Mad Brothers nervously followed, Nikola's hand once more firmly planted on the dagger and his other had twitchy fingers that were quick to reach to the sheathe upon his back. Cyril's eyes remained squinted and his face contorted in a confused fashion.

And so when the vucari had kept along the path, and the Mad Brothers found themselves at an ancient waystation, where traders taking the road to Starybogow could stop to rest or trade goods. Thick, yet long crumbling stone walls closed off all sides of them, save for the two exits leading to and away from the long-fabled city; two quaint battlements arose where guards must have taken post assuring nothing had happened when traders passed through. A second set of steps led upward to a second floor not even a man's height taller than the original. It was a welcoming respite for them to behold.

As they drew closer, the first thing to stand out was a bonfire upon the second level. It held a small, makeshift spit to cook meals, a bedroll accompanied by two books at its head, and a small bench that was piled with a large traveler's pack and a pile of assorted clothes. Someone had been living here.

Before any could speak on the oddity, they noticed the vucari had not stopped. It walked toward the steps leading toward the camp, and their mouths opened wide at what they saw next.

The wolf-man began to ascend the stairs but went on its hind legs to walk up them. The creature seemed to shift, shrinking as its posture corrected into a more human-like stance; the fur seemed to recede back into skin, the claws giving way to regular, human fingers, and its paw like hands and feet shrinking back to human proportions. The hair atop its head gave way to strands of long, ashen blonde hair and its snout vanished.

In front of them stood no longer a creature feared for its killing ability, but a naked woman. Her bare skin glistened in the fresh sunlight, her naked arms reaching upward as she extended herself on the tips of her toes. A faint, yet very human yawn came from her lips... as she turned and looked at them from over her shoulder. Her chin delicately rested on one of the numerous scars she bore on her back, the same Cyril had noticed on the vucari the woman had transformed from.

"That was some night wasn't it, my Moon?"

He could not believe the face that turned to greet him, but when he heard the sweet, melodious voice of his long-lost fiancé, he could not stop the tears that seeped down his face.

"Elena..."

Without any hesitation he unbuckled his overcoat and raced toward her, taking the steps she stood at the top of in a single bound. He stood in front of her, looking into her blue eyes and admiring the beauty of her face for the first time in over a year. Wrapping her up in his overcoat and embracing her so hard, he found *himself* wincing, taking note of just how much muscle seemed to be hidden underneath her petite frame.

And in typical Cyril fashion, all he could think to say was, "I'm so sorry that this coat is covered in blood."

The two kissed passionately and refused to let each other go. Wise Rad had nudged Nikola and signaled to give the two privacy as they walked back toward the road that they had taken.

*****

It was roughly two hours since they had arrived, and after some angry looks from Cyril, Nikola had finally unfastened his swords and unbuckled his armor. The four of them sat around a fire, two rabbits spinning on the spit. Elena freshly garbed, and Rad's wound cleaned and bandaged, the brothers welcomed true relaxation now they were at journey's end.

"So... you ran away due to the vucari that runs through your blood?" Rad asked, removing his traveler's cloak revealing the inexpensive yet respectable tunic beneath.

"You could have told me, Sun." Cyril said, his head in her lap.

"Yes, that would have gone swell! Lover, of course I'll join your family in holy matrimony but as a warning, I have the ability to turn into a wolf creature at twilight!" she jested with her thick, northern accent.

"Sure would have made running through the glen with your kids a bit more interesting." Nikola joined in.

"Funny man, this one." Elena said through her own giggle.

Rad laughed himself, drooling over the fresh ink and quill Elena had given him. "I take this is why you sought Starybogow?" he asked.

"Aye, I wanted to tell you, Moon, but... I feared that if I stayed in the village any longer, I'd have ended up being burned at the stake or tortured." she answered.

"I'd have protected you. You know that." Cyril said, squeezing her arm in reassurance.

"I'm sorry, Brother, but I don't think this particular damsel would be in distress. We all saw what she could do to topielic." Nikola piped in.

"Nasty things, they are. Taste even fouler."

"You can stop there, my love." Cyril's face scrunched in disgust as he stuck his tongue out. "I'm quite looking forward to this rabbit."

"This is what confuses me. You find out I'm a vucari but you're not running for the hills or coming at me with that silver dagger of his." She noted, pointing to Nikola.

"We've seen quite a bit on the road, lass." Wise Rad said.

"Besides, if there truly is a cure in Starybogow like you said. We can at least accompany you and help." Cyril sat up and wrapped his arms around Elena, turning his gaze back to his brothers. "That is... if you two wish to remain Mad Brothers and further aid me in this quest."

The three of them exchanged looks and finally Nikola smiled.

"As I said earlier, Cyril, you've become my brother. I'm with you until the end." Rad answered, the three turning their attention to Nikola.

"I'm with you, too." Nik playfully smacked Cyril's arm but raised one finger. "But, first. We have to come up with a name."

"A name? Of what?" Elena asked incredulously.

"Of us! You're a she! A toothy, clawed she at that! How about the Mad Brothers and the Wolf Sister?"

"Oh, Nik..." Cyril shook his head and rolled his eyes.

"The Mad Brothers and the She-Wolf?" Wise suggested.

"Are they always like this, love?" Elena asked as the other two continued to shout out names for their new company.

"Always..." Cyril sighed.

Hallows Eve

Jan Kostka

Domovoi
by Ivan Bilibin, 1934

Brother Adalbert could tell when Brother Anselmo had the visions coming on. He would start to play with his rosaries before bleeding from his nose. They were usually in prayer together, when the visions hit, and Anselmo always did as the Holy Father had taught him to keep himself under control and from what he told Adalbert, to keep the demons out. Whenever they spoke, Anselmo always said that he fought back with his faith, concentrating, focusing on one point, then as if glass breaking, his world shattered into darkness. This moment was one of such times.

Adalbert perched next to his fellow and he could see that the world must have been coming back to him slowly as Anselmo's eyes reopened. He, alongside Brother Witold, helped Anselmo sit up. There was confusion in his eyes, and it took a few moments before Brother Anselmo recognized the other two. Brother Adalbert tried to stop the blood as best he could, but the trail, now dried, still came from his nose, down the front of his cassock, and all along the palms of his hands. His long black hair, now streaked with grey, hung limp and straggling across his face. Brother Witold leaned in toward Anselmo and smiled when he got his attention.

"Be still, Brother. You have successfully fought the demon. The Holy Father is right to have faith in you. Give yourself a second."

Adalbert knew that Witold did not really care about Anselmo. He was not even sure that Witold believed in Anselmo's powers, but Witold knew if other people believed in Anselmo's gifts, he would by association be looked on with favor, by being close to him. Adalbert reached his hand to the prostrate monk. He touched the monk, but then backed away as if he was struck by lightning. Anselmo was still pulsating for a moment or two after one of his 'visions' and Adalbert knew that if he made direct contact, skin to skin, he could feel the residual effects. Brother Nachtel had been thrown against a wall with smoke coming from his hair, when he had touched Anselmo once. Through the blessing of the lord, he used this force, this 'electricity' to keep the demons in check.

"Come, Brother. Let us clean you and give you some nourishment so you may rest and prepare."Adalbert had a small but muscular frame that made it easier than Witold to help up Anselmo. He didn't have the facial hair the other brother had yet, but he started to show light blond fuzz. He was one of the tallest brothers in the monastery after the masters, but never used that to intimidate the others.

"Yes," Witold repeated with a look of concern that was forced, "so you may rest and prepare."

The prone monk leaned over on an elbow, then with the help of Adalbert, got onto his knee, then stood up. Adalbert was quickly elbowed out of the way by the sycophant Witold. "I will take him back to his cell, Brother. No need for you to worry. Just clean up the floor."

Adalbert stood for a second, knowing that two people were supposed to be with Anselmo at all times. As he watched Brother Witold walk away with Brother Anselmo, he knew he would have to say penance for contemplating kicking his fellow brother. He would worry about that at confession; for now, he needed to attend to the floor. Brother Misko was there to help, but Adalbert decided he would work in silence by himself. Sometimes, the young novices did not do a thorough job and the stones were stained over the years by the brothers that bled from the transformation. Now, more than ever, the brothers needed to be vigilant to protect Anselmo and whoever might replace him.

In the old age, Perun and the others had sacrificed themselves to bind the old ones inside a portal. Over the years, cracks had appeared as some of the old ones escaped. Brother Anselmo was used to reinforce the wards; the monastery resided on the doorway between worlds, connected to one of the waylines of power and energy. Nearby lay the town of Starybogow, the center of planes between worlds. By holding the wards in place they assured that outside forces could not release the Eldar Gods, but someone had effected a major breach. In some cases the lesser gods had been co-opted by the Christians, some like the brothers in this monastery had just remained hidden in place, replacing the guise of pagan priests for Christian ones. The town of Starybogow was the nexus of the portals. There was a shrine to the gods where they sacrificed themselves against the old ones and over time Prussians, Slavs, and Balts gave way to Teutonic Knights, Lithuanians, and Tartars. Towns rose and fell, but the brothers stayed immemorial as watchers and protectors. Now though, a breach had been effected as they had not seen for many generations. There were forces at play here as there always were that could break this wide open.

When Adalbert first came to the monastery he was a simple peasant boy. His family was killed in one of the raids in the area and the brothers took him in. He learned the ways of the monasteries, the faith, and because he was called a 'clever' boy, he was taught to read and write. He eventually accompanied Brother Wojtek to transact business in the town for the monastery. Only certain brothers were allowed to enter the town walls. At first Adalbert thought it was to keep them pure, but eventually he discovered that some of them 'couldn't' go into town. When they did they became ill – some violently so, but he was safe enough to go. There was something in the town – in the town itself – that they were susceptible to.

Once in a while he would sneak out to the sacred grove that still stood near the monastery. The brothers knew that sometimes the people would be there to pay their respects to the Old Gods. The statues of the Old Gods had been thrown in the pond when the Teutonic Knights had controlled the area, but the local people did not forget Perun, as they saw the wonder that the four sided statues of his still stood upright below the surface. Sometimes, to appease the spirits, the people would come with straw effigies to appease the spirits that still lingered. Adalbert would go as well to spend time and contemplate; he did not bother them, they did not bother him. He was there on the night of Kupala, the summer solstice, when some of the young and old gathered for dancing, drinking, and loving. They lit fires and threw a bread lady in the pond. The water sprites gratefully took the sacrifice. The men and women wore crowns of flowers in their hair as they danced in circles before pairing off. He left the folk to their merriment and returned to the monastery. This spot however, was still stained. There was a blood sacrifice here and in the city center. When the Teutonic Knights first came in, they slaughtered many of the inhabitants – some were of the old Prussian faith, some were Slavs, but to the knights they were all pagans and deserved to die. The memories of those events still hung heavy in the air and the soil.

The brothers practiced martial skills for an hour twice a day, to be prepared in case the pagans or heathens attacked the monastery. It was during practice one day that the first tremor hit. After that, the talk of tremors in the area was all the brothers could speak of. The only thing that replaced such talk was when Anselmo had a vision that indicated a nexus of the Old Gods. Adalbert lit a candle in the corner with the icon of the Virgin and prepared himself for morning prayers.

*****

Adalbert was going into town with Brother Wojtek to bring manuscripts to the castellan and goods to trade with the merchants. For the most part it was business as usual; they were at the town gates with their cart when it opened and passed through after a cursory inspection. After visiting the castellan, accompanied by his fool, the monks visited the tanners with sheepskins, then set up their cart in the market and started to buy some supplies.

After their duties had been done for the day, they had some time to relax. Adalbert breathed in deeply as he looked up toward the sky, a hand held up to shield his eyes. From the position of the sun in the sky, and the traders packing up in the market, it seemed to be about noon. He smiled as he turned to Brother Wojtek.

"Peaceful, is it not, brother? Even with all that has gone on lately."

When Wotjek did not answer, Adalbert cocked an eyebrow in his direction. He stood, still as stone, but his face was pained. Adalbert leapt to his feet as he approached the brother, and it was just in time to catch him. The man staggered as if he has been hit in the chest and toppled over into Adalbert's arms.

"Wotjek?! Wotjek, speak to me!" Adalbert shook the man, but felt his stomach knot as he noticed the color had drained from the man's face and his eyes had rolled back to only show the whites. He looked to the sky again, this time for a sign from God; he was terrified with what he saw. Black clouds filled the area overhead until black smothered the light.

Lightning came in bright flashes and the ground shook. At first, he could barely feel it, but with Brother Wotjek in his arms, he was thrown violently to the side; the tremors were so severe that cracks appeared in the ground where buildings toppled.

Wojtek reached out and was going to fall, but Adalbert caught him as the ground shook again. Cracks appeared in the ground in some places and several buildings toppled. He could see what appeared to be a giant wave along the river front and he could hear water splash and wash. Then there was silence; for a second or two, then the world exploded with sound. The bells of the church were ringing and people were shouting. He could hear rumbling and it seemed other parts of the town collapsed.

Adalbert felt hands on him and came back to the present as Brother Wojtek was pulling at him and talking with a strained voice.

"Get back, back to the monastery. Quickly." Then he slumped as dead weight and slowly fell to the ground despite Adalbert's efforts to hold him up.

Brother Wojtek was a big bear of a man, muscular and hairy, so it took all of Adalbert's strength to throw Brother Wojtek into their cart and then try to make their way out of the town. There were people in the narrow streets that made it difficult to go, until finally, he tried to carry the brother over his shoulder. That worked for a very short distance, but his muscles began to scream in agony, and he realized he could not carry the brother any longer. Several people were pointing toward the northern end of town – a purplish-green smoke was forming a cloud over the area. Other people ran by saying the earth had opened up a fissure to Hell. Adalbert was not going to be able to go much further, so he put Brother Wojtek down near a stable, avoiding the horse manure on the street and finding some clean straw. He propped Wojtek up against a support pole, but he was out of the way. Adalbert picked up a pole to keep people away, waited there, and guarded the brother in the hope he would regain consciousness.

As the day wore on and evening started to creep in, there were less people on the street in this area, but Adalbert could still see the glow of fires and that eerie smoke plume. During that time Wojtek came in and out of consciousness.

"You need to go boy." Then drifted away only to drift back a short time later, continuing in mid-thought, "if the Gods are released some of us are susceptible to them, people in town as well as the brothers.You need to go; now." Then he drifted out again. All Adalbert could do was keep an eye on him.

He was watching this when Wojtek let out a gasp and bolted upright, his eyes milky white and a raspy voice released from his throat.

"I thought I told you to go boy."

"Brother Wojtek…? What has happened to you?"Adalbert crept forward but held his guard. "Are you alright, I…?"

Before Adalbert had time to react, the man was upon him. He had drool from the side of his mouth, his milky white eyes stared blankly at the boy and his nails seemed to have transformed into small talons. Wojtek got tangled up in his cassock and fell forward. Adalbert hesitated for a moment as he tried to move away from his companion; the wild look on his face sent a chill through him as he lunged forward again on hands and knees. Adalbert just turned and ran, not sure what had happened, but sure he needed to run.

He ran toward the gates as fast as he could, dodging rubble and fallen bodies strewn along the way. He dodged and darted, losing his outer robe for his hose and jerkin beneath. He felt hands were grabbing at him along the way, but he pushed them aside, not looking back until he reached the gate. It was closed, which meant that he was locked in till morning – no one left or entered the city after dark. There were no guards visible. He pounded on the door of the tower, but no one answered. He looked around when he saw a figure emerge from the far street – it was Wojtek, but he was not moving well – starting and stopping with spastic movements, but always toward the youth. Without knowing where he was going, his legs carried him onward, back into the city. He didn't know anyone in the town other than those they traded with and he knew them only from the market. Perhaps the river would be the way to go.

Those people who were on the street had a hollow look on their faces as could be seen from the firelight. They were huddled in small groups and made a menacing gesture if Adalbert got too close. Occasionally a scream for help or a shriek could be heard, but he never could tell from where. He kept checking if he was followed by Wojtek, but he could not see him, though the little light available made monstrous shadows appear. The closer he got to the river, the more dilapidated the buildings were, to the point where there were some caved in. Only the older buildings that dated from the early history of the town, where they were still visible, seemed to have weathered the upheaval alright.

Once he got close to the riverfront, he stopped in shock, then ran quickly again. The river was no longer at the docks, but had shifted its banks at least thirty feet away from its original location. Where the river had stood along the docks, was now mud glistening in whatever moonlight had hit on it. He saw men down there hauling small boxes up to the wharf. Tunnels were now exposed along the bank – several feet down and seemingly beneath the town. He thought he might try to make his way out along the muddy banks when a roar rose up to his right. A mob erupted from that direction and suddenly there was a battle along the riverfront as men and women armed with all sorts of knives and blunt instruments started to fight each other. He tried to flatten himself in a doorway and was sure he had seen Wojtek amongst the battlers. At one point he thought he saw the man try to bite his opponent. His face took on a macabre visage in the dancing light, dripping and pressing forward. At that moment another cry came from the opposite end of the block as the town militia started to press in. He leaned back against the door and it gave way. He fell in, but instead of floor, there was a hole that dropped down ten feet or more and he hung there in the air on the door handle with his feet flailing as if he could fly with his legs. He pushed the door back with his feet to a ledge to get his footing, then swung the door back closed. With no other option, he tried to climb down the ruins and rocks, into the tunnel.

Now, there was only moonlight to guide the way. There was an opening to the left toward the water, but that only led to chaos. There seemed to be another tunnel to the right which was dark as pitch. Behind him was more space, but he couldn't tell if there was a pit a few steps ahead or more tunnels. A light suddenly appeared in that space twenty or so yards away in what appeared to be a gentle slope downward. The person coming toward him was holding a lamp – not bright, but projecting enough light to see ahead in a concentrated beam. The shadow made it seem to be a big person, tall as it was broad, but as it got closer, the being seemed like a young boy; but once the figure came in sight it was clearly a short man by the lines on his face and thick beard.

Almost as if the man expected him to be there, he strode purposefully toward Adalbert and came to a stop in front of him. He held a pry bar in one hand, about equal to his three foot height. In the other hand was a lantern like a miner would carry with a series of succeeding doors to expand or focus the light. He wore a black round felt cap with side flaps that were tied across the flat top. His tunic was also black, tied in the front, brown hose and ankle height boots completed his outfit. His hair and beard was carefully combed and braided with silver rings holding them in place. A battle was raging above him, but all Adalbert could hear in this tunnel were the soles of the boots on the limestone ground. The small man motioned to Adalbert to come, and without hesitation he followed him. A *karzełek* – a dwarf abiding in the underground – that is what he looked like. As they went back about the twenty yards he had come, there was an opening on the right. As they started into it, Adalbert turned back to see people starting to fall down the opening into the area they had just come from, and new people or creatures were coming down the opposite tunnel.

Adalbert followed the *karzełek*, still as if it was the most natural thing in the world, and when they turned the corner, the small man pushed a boulder along and covered the opening so that there was no seam to indicate it was there at all.

The man set the lamp in a nook in the wall and it was then that Adalbert noticed there did not seem to be a candle or wick in the lantern.

"Come," the man motioned again, and the passageway seemed to light-up as they passed down it, then darkened. "As long as you are with me there will be light. Stay close and don't dawdle." His tone was annoyed as if speaking to a small child. They traveled for what seemed like an hour, but probably took less time. It seemed like there were a couple of side galleries, but they kept moving forward. They finally got to a dead end, when the dwarf opened the wall and pushed Adalbert through – leaving him in the common room of the monastery.

*****

The primate looked up from his papers in annoyance at the knock on his apartment's doors. His secretary poked his head in hesitantly. The primate hated interruptions when he was trying to collect his thoughts like this. He motioned for the man to come in.

"Holiness, I have received these responses in the post from various magnates." He dropped the papers on the primate's desk and backed away.

During the interregnum when the nobles were to meet to elect the King of Poland, he was the head of state. He quickly scanned the responses and moved the papers to the side. During this interregnum he needed to make sure he reunited the crown of Poland with the Grand Duchy of Lithuania again and keep the Teutonic Knights in check. He was also following the portents from his 'friends' in the Abbey that there were stirrings in the void. He waved the man away again, and the secretary started shuffling toward the door, stopped, and raised his hand as if lost in thought.

"A thousand pardons, Holiness," he turned, bowed, and pulled another note from his coat pocket, then backed away. "This came earlier from Rotmizter Robach."

The primate's head jerked up from his papers and grabbed at the note snarling at the cleric. "I thought I told you to let me know right away when he sent anything…" he ripped open the seal and read the report. His eyes scanned the paper quickly, then focused on certain sections. "Damned! Damned, damned, damned!" He grabbed some paper and wrote out orders; stopped, crossed out a section, and wrote some more. He folded the note and sealed it with his ring, then handed to the scared man. "Bring this to Rotmizter Robach, now. Do not stop, do not forget, and make sure you give it to him directly." He paused to compose himself, "And if you ever wait to give me news I will make sure you will accompany the next mission to Moscowy."

The frightened man quickly left the room. The primate got up from his desk and went to the corner of the room with the icon of the Madonna. He crossed himself and opened the small box below that – the one for the domovoi, the 'household spirits' and threw a crust of wafer in there as an offering. If an opening had occurred, they would all be in trouble. No telling what the German Knights would do, or the Muscovites. There was always a bad time for a breech, but at this point in the royal election too many people would be distracted. The nature of royal politics, be it the King of Poland, Holy Roman Emperor, or Tsar meant that there were always forces at work that would try to swing the election in their favor. By getting Alexander elected King, both nations would be united under one ruler and they would be better suited to combat the Teutonic Knights, and perhaps put an end to them once and for all. Not many people knew the true history of the knights in the Baltic and the dangers they posed.

Alexander was a Grand Duke who understood the forces they were facing. While Jan Olbrach was a strong King, he also was a carouser. Alexander was more cerebral, and knew the folklore of the areas under his rule. From what the primate understood, he also had his own secret agents at play to counter moves the dark ones might take. Jan Olbrach was supposedly injured during a drunken brawl on his way around the city. In reality, the Knights had a hand in his death. The barber-surgeon who initially attended him noted small punctures on his neck, discolored from the poison that was injected in him. By the time the medical doctors had arrived it was too late. "A shame to have to kill the barber, but can't have loose tongues gossiping."

"I am a good and loyal servant of the church," the primate declared to no one in particular, "But even the church tries my patience with the people it protects." With that he slumped in his chair, took a deep breath and started in on his correspondence again.

*****

Grandmaster von Sachsen paced back and forth in his study. At one point in their past the knights might have been ascetics, but now he liked his comfort. He moved closer to the fire to try to get warmer. He tightened the belt on his robe and tucked the tentacles back under his beard. The Grandmaster of the Teutonic Knights, Frederick Wettin von Sachsen, began to review his reports from the countryside. He nodded to himself with a smile of satisfaction. Their assassination of Jan Olbrach had bought them more time and forestalled another war. His reflection was interrupted by a knock on the door.

"My lord, this bird has just brought some correspondence from our man." The knight-brother placed the small pieces of paper on a silver dish, then backed away.

The Grandmaster waved him away and picked up the paper to review. Reports from the castellan in Starybogow indicated that the opening would be moved forward and the old masters released. He smiled to himself and relaxed, reaching into the small box and pulled the small bird out, then quickly gobbled it down. There were some in the order who still believed they represented the Christian God, but those of the inner circle knew. They knew the old masters could be brought back. They could disrupt the guardians. With a little luck, their agents could bring them back.

"*Ph'nglui mglw'nafh fatgn.*" The longer they kept the election in limbo, the most they could consolidate their forces. He would order a troop of men toward the Lithuanian border; surely the boy-Duke would try to move people across to block any moves the Knights and their agents might make. He would move some agents toward the town as well. Better yet, use some of the unsuspecting ones under the guise of a quest.

*****

Adalbert felt himself slowly coming around. It was not like waking up from a sleep, but how he imagined it would be after drinking too much wine – if he drank wine. Slowly he was able to focus and he came rushing back to reality like jumping from a height; then he was able to concentrate. He was in the common room, but with little recollection of how he got there. His cassock was torn and muddy, and he was starting to shiver, but at the same time he was sweating profusely. He tried to stand and lost his balance. He grabbed the side of the bed and steadied himself. He stood there clutching his arms together, then fell into a heap. The next thing he knew, several of the brothers were surrounding him as well as the assistant Monsignor Urza.

They brought him to one of the benches and sat him down. As usual, Witold was in the front feigning concern. Brother Urza moved them all aside and gave Adalbert some water with a little brandy in it.

"Brother," Urza placed a hand on Adalbert's shoulder. He bent down to Adalbert and spoke in a low clam voice. "What happened to you? Where is Brother Wotjek?" Urza's eyes were piecing blue and once focused on Adalbert, felt like it would reach into his soul.

At the sound of his companion's name, Brother Adalbert sprung back to the present. He could not remember much, but something about his brother jarred his memory. "I… I don't know. Brother Wotjek convulsed, then there were quakes, and then, I… I…" and his voice trailed off.

The brothers mumbled to each other and Adalbert felt his head swimming. The rest of the brothers started talking amongst themselves. Some spoke to Adalbert, but to him it all sounded like a dull hum flowing through his brain.

"Silence!" A voice boomed across the room, but there was no mistaking it; it was Brother Ulric the brother-militant, the disciplinarian of the monastery. "Bring him to my chambers," his voice dropped lower, but it was just as stern. The brothers knew to just do as they were told and helped Adalbert toward the brother-militant's cell. Brother Ulric had white blond hair that was unruly and always with stubble, but never quite a beard and never clean shaven. His long moustache drooped around his mouth. His flaxen robe was tied with two ox-tails made into a belt and he always carried a staff of myrtle-wood.

There were some hurried whispers along the way. Several of the brothers had suffered fits when the quake hit. He passed Brother Anselmo's cell with people running in and out. There was blood in several places along the walk as if a brutal, fight had occurred. He was brought to the brother-militant's cell and placed in a chair opposite Ulric, who waved the rest of the brothers away except for Urza. "What do you remember?"

Adalbert attempted to put the pieces back together. There was the earth moving, shaking; houses falling and people in the street. He was helping Wojtek, then it all went hazy. He only remembered fire and blood and the little man. The karzełek. Or maybe it wasn't real. He was not sure. He just shook his head and repeated he wasn't sure.

Ulric looked up at Urza, who was standing to the side of Adalbert and raised his eyebrows. The brother then leaned in to Adalbert and spoke to him in a low voice. "Brother, we are at war with many evil things today. Our monastery has been grievously hurt, but it is time for you to take a more active role. You are not aware yet, but you possess important powers for the upcoming battles. I know that you spend time with the faithful of the old Slavic ways. Be prepared to use your faith of the old ways with those of the new faith. We shall guide you in what must be done."

*****

Ulric and Urza entered the chambers of the Monsignor Stanisław. The head of the monastery was hunched over his table as if asleep. Ulric gently shook the old man. He gave a quick start but then recovered.

"Too tired; too much going on to hold back the darkness with our meager forces. Is Anselmo better?"

Urza sat down opposite him, while Ulric stood behind him. "Brother, they have affected a breech. Anselmo has closed it for now, but we don't know what has made it through – some of ours, some of theirs. We need to take action. It may be time to return to our ways."

Stanisław sat up and it seemed as if twenty years disappeared from his face. There was a commotion in the corner and all three turned to look. It was the Lekka and Vekka, the *domovoi* and *kikimora,* or household spirits of the monastery. They had been listening and fell off their hiding place when they heard Urza's statement. They were small hairy creatures, these house spirits. Although they were nominally male and female, it was difficult to tell which was which.

The one called Lekka stood up and helped Vekka up, or maybe Vekka helped Lekka. He could never be sure. "I think that is a good idea, Belobog."

Stanisław held up his hand to stop the creature, "Stan-is-swav," he said slowly. Pointing his finger as if to accent each syllable.

Lekka lowered his head, but kept eyes on the monsignor. "Oh

yes, sorry Bel-…Stanisław. I have heard things; things from the bannik and vodyanoy that the rusalka are coming back in numbers, while the leshy and vila have seen things beyond the Bies. They say the ladies have returned."

Urza rubbed his beard through all this, trying to take this in. The rusalka were the mermaid like creatures that skulked along the river. They were always there for as long as he could remember. They were both good and mischievous, but the ladies were another matter. *Polunocnica*, 'Lady Midnight', and *Pscipolnitsa*, 'Lady Midday', were demons who hunted down children at night and attacked workers in the field. They were not seen for years, and under normal circumstances they would be bad enough, but what had happened in the town required desperate action to protect the people of this area.

"We have to act quickly to restore the balance. The vampyr and undead have taken over parts of the city and some of the rusalka have started attacking ships."

Ulric jumped in. "We can send some of the brothers to help the militia. They will be overwhelmed if they haven't been already. See if our friends among the karzełek can help us through the caverns. If we don't keep the dark ones in check the city could be lost."

*****

Grun checked the street for any sign of the creatures. He knew that once there was a lull in the fighting they would have an opportunity to search for treasure. The battles had gone back and forth in the streets for what seemed an hour. The town militia had pushed some of the monstrosities back until those shadows of humanity attacked. Some of the locals then joined in to clear out this section of the city. It was quiet for now, but it was an uneasy quiet. There were opportunities here. Everyone had heard the stories of the Scythian treasures buried beneath the city, but no one had ever found anything. But now; now there were tunnels, and where there were tunnels, there was the possibility of treasure, granted they survive long enough in the unknown below.

There were still some fire smoldering where houses had been aflame; what had saved them from spreading was that many had collapsed into holes, which in itself was a miracle. He spit three times and crossed himself. He gave a short whistle and what was left of his associates appeared. The only one that did not come out was Zek. He was dead, he had turned and Grun had to kill him. He had seen it all living on the fringe. He grew up hearing stories of those people that mysteriously turned back in the days when the knights ruled the city, and he knew what to do when that happened. The first time he'd seen it he was a little slow and almost got himself killed, so when Zek's eyes turned black he knew what to do – take off the head; everything else was temporary.

"Alright, boys. Let's see what we can find before the authorities stop this little party." Technically they were not all men, but Wanda and Rose fought as well as any of them. Living by the docks did that to a person.

Grun gave Jan One a nudge to lead the way down one of the sinkholes. Jan Two followed him along with Wanda, Rose, Bolek, and finally Grun.They had the blackout lamps they used for smuggling along the river. The lanterns they carried spread little light in the tunnels – this was done purposely so they didn't alert people of their presence. Grun was always concerned that somehow his red hair would still give him away in the dark. While some of the areas looked as if they were hued out of limestone, others appeared as if they were part of buildings that were covered up over time. There were some niches in hallways that looked like doorways, but were solid; then there were rooms off other halls, one with a pool formed. The structure that was above must have been empty. There was no silver or even brass at the bottom of the sinkhole. Only the remnants of burnt wood were left in most places. It seemed like anything salvageable had been destroyed or taken by other people.

In addition to the hallways, there were stairs leading up and down – carved or chiseled out of living rock, but in some cases it was clear they were built by masons. There were a couple of times when they thought they heard someone or something approaching and closed the shutter on their lanterns, hiding in one of the niches. When they thought it was safe, they emerged only to find themselves face to face with what looked like Zek only to have him blink out. They let out an audible breath, Jan One stammered a "Maybe we should be going", which was seconded by Jan Two. They all started moving in the opposite direction, while Grun kept looking down the other; nodding in agreement to no one there.

Grun followed his crew without knowing where they were

going. They came up to a large room off to the right. There were stone columns interspersed throughout, surrounding a pool. Torches lit some of the central area, but there were shadows around much of the room. It smelled bad like turned meat, with a metallic tang in the air. On either side was a stone platform with the remnants of bodies visible, which brought the group to a crunching halt – the last people in the group bumping into the forward folks.

There were several rooms that were barely visible off the main room, but the glint of gold got their attention. At once, the group abandoned the torches and moved as one body toward the riches; greed painted plain as day upon each of their faces. It wasn't treasure lying in a heap like some abandoned karzełek horde, but a series of oddly shaped golden statues. The crew fell on them like ants trying to hack off bits to carry off or move them from their pedestals even if they were not going to be easily moved. The figures carved as statues seemed to be parodies of humans – misshaped with feral characteristics. They were placed in niches in locations that seemed like they were ready to jump out of the shadows. Grun was in the middle of carving apart one of the statues when something caught his eye further in the room, and then made his stomach drop, feeling ill at the sight before him.

The Teutonic Knights had been mostly thrown out of Starybogow after the Ten Years War of the early 1400's, when it was called Querstadt. It was said the knights that garrisoned the town participated in unholy practices. They did not leave willingly when they did go. Grun then realized these were mock visages of knights – tattered surcoats, lesions on their faces, exposed flesh, and a dead look in their eyes. Their swords were coated with a dark patina. The lead one pointed his gloved hand at the small group and started to mumble in an incoherent tongue. The smell of heated metal soon filled the room and it seemed the pool began to glow. The parody knight stepped forward and grabbed at Wanda, who had wandered close to him. Prior to that she was almost sleepwalking, but at that moment she and the others awoke to the realization of what was happening. Her screams died quickly as the swords stabbed her on one of the stone blocks. Those that were left were under-armed and their only means of escape blocked.

Grun quickly realized if more of the monsters followed, they would all be dead soon enough. If they could keep the one at bay and take them on one at a time, maybe time would give him an answer; he pushed Rose and Bolek forward. Although they had short knives against the sword, the knight had very little room to maneuver and they didn't have a reach, so it quickly settled into a standoff of parries and thrusts with each side waiting for the other to overcommit or make a mistake. Years of street fighting were perfect for this, but it could not last. When the three knights behind the lead were done killing Wanda they tried stabbing at the gang behind their commander, pressing forward. At one point Bolek found an opening and stabbed the knight in the chest, but he was stabbed by one of the knight behind whom then pushed into the room.

Bolek fell to the ground and was pulled out by one of the creatures. The stabbed knight then pulled the knife out of chest and took a step toward the survivors when a bright light flashed.

*****

The brothers were quickly organized by Ulric and they advanced through the passageway and quietly down the stone hall. Turning a corner, they came up against two of the demon knights. The knights assumed a defensive stance, as if by muscle memory with shields up and swords pointed. The brothers were armed with swords and halberds provided by Ulric. Finally, the special training that Ulric had put them through finally came to benefit. The sword felt light in Adalbert's hand. As they got closer to the sound of fighting and the dead knights appeared, the sword started to glow in his hands. This was not happening with the other brothers, but Adalbert felt power growing in his sword and his arm. The dead knights had slower reflexes, which were taken advantage by the brothers who quickly overwhelmed them. Adalbert rushed to the front, parrying several thrusts and decapitating the creatures after a short fight. Ulric followed behind, armed only with a staff when they entered the summoning room.

The pool was already filling with blood and water and more demonic knights had some humans surrounded - ready to finish them off, while a human held a scroll calling out an incantation. A portal was opening in the pool as a red scaly talon was just breaking the surface of a swirling vortex. Ulric stood for a second in concentration. He had not been able to summon lightning for many years, but he felt the power surge in his body and casting his hands toward the pool, he let loose a light bolt to neutralize the incantations, filling the room with light and a loud crack. The human with the scroll was thrown back against a column. This was quickly followed by a howl as the entities trying to come through the portal were returned to where they came from. All that effort took energy from Ulric and he slumped for a second, leaning against his staff. He felt dizzy for a moment, but quickly recovered.

"This never gets easy," he muttered, moving forward.

The decadent knights were stopped in their attack on the humans and turned to face the brothers. The monks moved with enhanced speed with Adalbert leading the way, isolating and killing the creatures before coming upon the humans.

"Who are you?!" Ulric's voice was already amplified by the acoustics in the chamber, but he had enhanced it using his inner voice. The humans tried to form a circle to protect themselves, confused by the arrival of the monks but really they couldn't do much against the brothers in the open. "Put down your arms." He paused; when they hesitated Ulric boomed, "Now!" The humans hesitated for a moment, then milled around in a circle, they seemed half in a trance and half drunk, but not sure what to do. Then they complied. He point to the one who seemed to be in charge with the red hair, and motioned him along with the rest. The ruffian pulled himself up into stiff, formal pose, and smoothed out his hair; he seemed far more awake than the others.

"Who are you?! What are you going to do to us?" He jabbed with his knife, keeping them away. Adalbert shook his head at the shaking blade.

Ulric approached with palms down, "Calm down fellow. We mean you no harm, but you need to put those weapons away."

"I've seen you," he stammered, "I know you. You're from the monastery. But you're no priest. You want this gold don't you? It's ours. We found it." And with that he moved back toward the statues.

"No one should take that. It is cursed, made with blood and madness," Ulric then motioned for them to leave. "Go, go now while you can. I'll send one of my men to show you the way out."

With hesitation, Grun heard the words from Ulric and seemed to nod, but didn't move at first, as if he heard but didn't necessarily understand. Then, as if it suddenly sunk in he nodded and started to shuffle away. The others blithely walked as if they were dazed. As he went past Ulric, the priest paused him.

"One more thing," then blew dust he had in his hands into the face of the human and he dropped like a stone. He then motioned to Jan One and Two to take their companion and follow one of the brothers. "He will have a knot on the side of his head where he hit the floor, but he won't remember why. Give him a couple of coppers for stalling those creatures, then block up this entrance so the servants of the old ones can't use it. Burn the bodies of their companions so they can't come back to life," then he turned on his heel and led his companions in search of any more portals. The brothers eventually returned to the monastery to regroup.

At that point Adalbert realized he had been touched by the Slavic Gods. By concentrating and summoning that power he could unleash the wrath of the gods, but it took its toll on him. While it surged through him he felt great power, but after he started to shake with cold as the power drained from him.

He braced himself on a wall for a moment, shaking the spots from his eyes as the dizziness from his mind, before he prepared for the return trip.

*****

Grun woke up in an alley near the *Spitting Pig* tavern with the other three, not the least bothered that the others of the gang were nowhere to be seen. He had some coppers in his pocket and a bottle. He must have gotten into a row after drinking – his head hurt, he was fuzzy, and didn't feel well. One and Two were sprawled out along with Rose. "I guess it was a good night."

*****

The town began to attempt to rebuild, but it would take time. Several of the wealthy merchants in town disappeared when their homes collapsed into the sinkhole. The new castellan, Piorik, thought he would use the wealth of the missing families to rebuild, but their treasures seemed to have disappeared with them. Piork was in a bad mood in his rooms above the city in the keep of the castle. His fool, Lambert, sat in the corner playing with his knife. Lambert, wasn't actually a 'fool' like most blanks, but just a short boy that Piork had conscripted into the position because he knew a person of his status needed one.

The captain of the militia, Sturtze, walked over to the table and poured a cup of mead in a familiar manner. The castellan was a veteran of King John Albert's excursion into Moldavia and the homage of the Grandmaster Frederick von Sachsen. In the end, he was mustered out and came east with a letter from the king to take command of the town militia and the small lance of Cossack used in keeping an eye on the area. While the castellan was a minor szlatcha and the captain a commoner, he did know people and he had the muscle to back up his position.

"It's been two weeks since the terror. It's God's punishment for the evil ways of this town."

The captain slowly placed the cup back down on the table and tilted his head to avoid the direct light in the window. "If that was the reason for God's vengeance, I think more than this town would be in trouble right now."

"How do we know what is going on beyond our walls? Father Kolma…"

"Father Kolma is a very old and foolish man who drinks too much and reads less. Couriers have come back from Vilnius to say they are fine. I am still waiting on news from the west."

"Why wasn't I informed about these couriers? I am in charge!"

"I just told you, Castellan. Besides you were indisposed at the time, but more important matters. We have been able to restore some sort of control. The wharfs are still not operable because the river has changed. There have been several mysterious deaths in the north sector, I have the barber checking for plague." He turned to walk away and stopped at the door turning back to the castellan. "By the way, we have had several of the wandering caravans from the south come to town. I have put some of them to work on clearing and rebuilding. I will keep an eye on them." Then he left to make his rounds.

Castellan Piorik slumped back in his chair. He poured himself something to drink and gathered some papers. "No tolls for the river, no market taxes, means no tithes for me," he said to himself while counting on his fingers. He threw his hands up. "Bah, we need to do something or I'm ruined."

*****

Captain Sturtze took a couple of men to the docks before heading up to the northern sector of the city to patrol. The former quay was twisted and buckled from the moving ground, and part had actually sunk about fifteen feet. The river had shifted in such a way that boats could not effectively unload cargo and would be forced to bypass the city. That was, unless the castellan and the city fathers could get their thumbs out and rebuild the waterfront.

He was staring out at the mess for a second when he felt a presence below the wharf in the riverbank. Sturtze quickly looked over the edge to the sandy bank, but saw nothing and no one. It was dusk and there were no regular lamplighters out anymore since the quake, and what would normally be a raucous waterfront was eerily quiet.

He saw a figure staggering toward him and he grabbed for his sword, but let it go when he saw it was only Grun, still coming down to the docks even though there was nothing new to rob here. The gang stopped when they saw the patrol and stiffened warily on the defensive, then realized it was the captain. He grunted at the militia and made a move to walk the other way.

"Hold on there, Grun." Grun turned back toward the captain. He seemed like he was sleepwalking or drunk, but didn't smell of alcohol as usual.

"Captain, what are you doing out and about? These streets are not safe anymore."

"Is that a threat you boozer?" It was half stern, half joking, but Grun's face turned blank as if he was thinking and scared.

"No, Captain. This place is getting bad, the north side especially. I may take my chances with the Tartars than stay here!"

"What are you babbling about? And where is the rest of your motley crew?"

"I don't know where they are; I can't remember, but I need to get out, get away." Then he moved his arms as if pushing and stumbled. That is when Sturtze caught a whiff of metallic smell and grabbed his arm.

"Grun, are you okay? What's wrong?" Then he noticed a a large lump on his head.

"Nothing, nothing. Leave me alone." Then Grun stumbled back toward the town square.

"Have that neck checked out! You dumb..." then he just trailed off.

*****

Zoltan eyed the house from the shadows. The count and countess had not occupied the house for many years. Some people thought they were dead, but here they were. The count had arrived two weeks before and the countess arrived yesterday after her entourage was attacked by Tartars outside the city. Zolton and his brethren had other issues, his master would want a report soon. He took a pinch of zmatek and his senses exploded again. He had been watching this place for two days now, if not for this drug the boss had given him he would have fallen asleep a while ago. But he was wide awake, alive, and perceived all things around him. His third arm began to twitch again. He was getting used to it, a gift from the masters. He kept it hidden under his tunic when he was out. For a noble house there never seemed like there was much going on. Occasionally some minion would come and go, but very few visitors, and when they did, they stayed for hours.

Eventually Horta came to take over at the post, and sent Zoltan to go back to their quarters. Several of the brothers and sisters were there chanting, trying to bring the old ones back. There were promises after all, promises of power.

The house of merchant Schmidt looked like many other townhouses and like other German merchants in the town, it was as orderly as it could be under the circumstances; the inside was a fortress of sorts. Members of the Order used it to keep an eye on events in Starybogow and now the time was right. The portents were right and they had brought in their own mediums. They had almost succeeded in releasing the old masters. One more push and they might accomplish what they had all wanted. The forces of the Countess and those monks, though not aligned, had stopped them for now. But not much longer. First to the *Black Goat of the Woods Inn* to meet and plan.

Hour of the Wolf

C. L. Werner

Teutonic Knight of the early 16th Century

The white stone walls of the church almost seemed to glow as the dusky rays of the setting sun fell upon them. Except for a gnarled old oak, the building stood alone on the little hill just outside the Silesian village of Karlsdorf. A low stone wall circled the hill, encompassing the rough gravestones and simple wooden crosses that rose from the churchyard. Just beyond the burying ground, on the other side of the wall, a few crude markers denoted the resting places of the few suicides and witches Karlsdorf had produced in the two hundred years of its existence. Such grievous sinners were too corrupt to place in consecrated ground alongside the faithful and God-fearing.

As he spurred his horse toward the church, Wulf Greimmer wondered which side of the wall the man he hunted would be buried on. If there was any justice, Klaus von Auerbach would rot in some unhallowed place, fodder for worms and crows. Wulf was determined that justice would find the Teutonic Knight. He would be the instrument of justice.

Wulf tethered the reins of his horse to one of the stone crosses that sprouted from the churchyard and walked toward the white building. His hand closed about the leather-wrapped grip of his sword, easing it from its sheath. Disgust welled up within him. The vile nature of the crime committed by his quarry made him despise von Auerbach as he'd never hated any man before, but for the villain to flee to a church and try to avail himself of Sanctuary brooked an unspeakable cowardice. The knight should at least be able to die with honor.

Approaching the church, Wulf drew back when he saw the oak door swing open. The sword was ripped from its scabbard before he realized the man who stepped out across the threshold was too slight and aged to be the renegade knight even if von Auerbach had set aside his white livery to disguise himself in priestly vestments. The clergyman bowed his tonsured head in greeting, his gaze focusing upon the naked steel in Wulf's hand.

"You come bearing your sword into the house of God?" the priest said, his words weighted with sadness rather than condemnation. "Heavy must be the sin that weighs upon your soul, my son."

Wulf glowered at the elderly priest. "The sin that burdens my mind isn't my own. It is the crime of the one I hunt."

"It is written to judge not lest ye be judged," the priest cautioned.

"He has been judged," Wulf answered. "Not by prince or king, but by the people themselves. The Vehmic Court has found him guilty and condemned him for his crimes." He nodded toward the church. "His trail has led me here. Don't try to stop me from taking him."

The priest shook his head. "You would shed blood in the sanctuary? You would work violence before the very altar of Christ?"

"My cause is just, commissioned by the Holy Order of Vehm," Wulf said. "The man I hunt is unworthy of God's protection."

"Who among us is worthy of His grace? Yet God has bestowed His forgiveness upon us all the same." The priest stepped into Wulf's path as the hunter tried to move past him and enter the church. "Sheathe your sword. The man you hunt isn't here."

Wulf stared into the priest's weary face, gauging the depth of the clergyman's sincerity. "He was here, though. The knight Klaus von Auerbach came here."

"I took his confession," the priest admitted. "Then he left, to perform penance for his deeds."

Fury boiled up within Wulf's heart. Penance! Atonement! Exoneration for his crimes! "Father, you took von Auerbach's confession. You know what he did! He seduced a young girl, a burgher's daughter, and when she was with child he killed her. There can be no forgiveness for such atrocity. He thought to hide behind the protection of the Teutonic Knights, but the Vehmic Court condemned him just the same. Now he thinks to hide in the grace of the church."

The priest reached out and laid his hand upon Wulf's shoulder. "Leave justice and vengeance to God, my son. Men cannot know all that has been or must be. Turn back from the path you're set upon. Return to your home, tell the judges that your quarry slipped beyond your reach."

"That would be a lie," Wulf sneered. "I am reckoned the best Freischoffe in Westphalia, the enforcer of the Holy Order of Vehm. I have been the court's avenger for ten years now and never have I failed to bring justice to those found guilty by the Vehmic Court."

"Pride is the sin by which Satan fell from Heaven," the priest warned.

"A man must be steward of his own honor, otherwise he ceases to be a man," Wulf said. "If I fail, then I will fail because it was God's will."

The priest turned, pointing his wizened hand toward the southeast. "Perhaps when you hear the penance I have set von Auerbach you will relent. He has gone to the ruins of Starybogow, to ply his sword and his courage against the unclean things that now infest it. It is there my nephew will find redemption."

The color drained from Wulf's face when he heard the priest mention Starybogow. The once mighty city had become infamous as a place of darkness and evil. Ghosts and vampyr were said to haunt the ruins, demons and witches to make sport among the desolation. All the evils of the world had come crawling back from the shadows to claim Starybogow for their own.

Fear faded from his heart when Wulf heard the priest speak of redemption for von Auerbach. There could be no atonement for the crimes the knight had perpetrated. The very thought offended Wulf's sense of justice. Too often had he seen the noble and powerful escape punishment for their misdeeds. The Vehmic Courts had risen up as a response to such infamies, a way for the people to wrest an accounting from those who inflicted harm upon them. It didn't matter if the knight had fled to the very gates of Hell, the avenger would follow his trail and carry out the verdict brought against him.

"You have my sympathies, Father," Wulf said as he turned from the priest. "I didn't know he was of your blood. It explains why he rode all the way to Prussia to make his confession here."

The priest followed Wulf to where he'd tethered his horse. "Would it make any difference to you if I said my nephew's crimes aren't what you think them to be?"

Wulf climbed up into the saddle and looked down at the old clergyman. "Judgment has already been brought against him." He shook his head as he turned his horse from the churchyard. "No good can come from you violating the sanctity of his confession." He cast one last look back at the priest. "Pray for me, Father, that I am spared the evils of Starybogow."

As he spurred his horse away, Wulf heard the priest's voice one last time. "I will pray for you. I will pray for you both."

*****

Guided by plumes of smoke, Wulf came upon the ravaged caravan. Arrows and spears projected from the sides of wagons, fires flickered from burning tents and overturned carts. Slaughtered oxen and mules lay strewn about the despoiled encampment. German merchants struggled to salvage their wares from the wreckage while Slavic laborers dragged bodies away from the debris. Several men arrayed in heavy leather hauberks and steel helms kept a wary watch, their eyes roving across the edge of a nearby wood for any sign of threat. At Wulf's approach, two of the armed men advanced toward him with bared swords. As they came near, he could see they were Poles, likely mercenaries hired by the merchants as guides and guards. Their wariness lessened when they saw that Wulf was alone.

"What happened here?" Wulf asked, gesturing at the destruction.

One of the Poles, a tall man with a scarred nose, scratched at his black beard for a moment. "Wends," he said. He waved his sword at some of the bodies the Slavs were dragging away from the wagons. Even in death they had a savage, dusky aspect, their feral features matching the rough hides and skins in which they were arrayed.

"Wends?" Wulf repeated.

The other Polish guard, slighter than his comrade and with a few fingers missing off his right hand, scowled and spat on the ground. "Wends," he said. "Brigand raiders stealing anything they can carry away and killing anything they can't steal."

"It was my understanding that the Wendish Crusade saw an end to them long ago," Wulf said. "Their kingdom was broken and their people brought to Christ."

"Not all of them," the taller Pole declared. "Some of them fled, retreated into the wilds. Parts of Lusatia are still thick with them. Oh, most of them make an effort at being civilized, most of them play at being Christian, but who knows how many still revere the Old Gods?"

"These Wends don't bother to pretend," the other mercenary said. "They follow their pagan gods just as they did of old. They subject themselves to their *volkhv*, a sorcerer called Horjan."

The tall guard crossed himself as his companion spoke the volkhv's name, fear shining in his eyes. "It is ill to speak of their shaman," he reproached his comrade, looking up at the circling crows. "Who can say what bird or beast might be one of his spies?"

Wulf pointed at the dead the Slavs were laying out in the grass. Only a few of the bodies looked to belong to the caravan but there were at least a dozen that had the barbarous cast of raiders about them. "For all this sorcerer's power, his followers have seem to have come out worse for crossing your trail."

The smaller Pole nodded excitedly. "We were rescued by the grace of God. The Wends set upon us from ambush and would have surely overwhelmed us. Just as it seemed we would all be killed or worse, a rider came charging down upon them! Arrayed in white with the holy cross in black across his breast! You should have seen him as he strove against the brigands. His sword was like lightning as he brought it slashing down into his foes. However many of them came at him, he beat them back, smiting them with righteousness."

"It was steel the knight used," the other guard commented, more restrained in his outlook than his comrade. "He must have felled four or five Wends in the first charge, then accounted for three more when they tried to rally against him. When the brigands started to flee, he rode two more of them down and harried the others all the way back into the woods."

"What became of this rescuer?" Wulf asked, trying to keep his tone diffident. The Teutonic Knight who'd saved the caravan might be von Auerbach. If so, he didn't think the Poles would be happy to learn the Freischoffe was hunting him.

"After seeing that our wounded were being attended he rode away to the east," the tall guard said.

"I heard him ask one of the merchants if Starybogow was near," the other Pole interjected. He shook his head, worry creeping into his voice. "He might be looking for the volkhv, for there are many rumors that the Wends have raised a temple to the Old Gods in the ruins."

Wulf looked away from the mercenaries, casting his eyes across the green fields that spilled away toward the horizon. "East you say?" Before either of the Poles could answer, he set his horse galloping across the fields.

The knight had been von Auerbach. Wulf was certain of it. The attack upon the caravan couldn't have been more than an hour old. That meant his quarry was close, closer than he'd been since Wulf had set out after him.

Justice would soon be visited upon the murdering knight.

*****

A brooding malignance clung about the ruinous expanse of Starybogow. Wulf could feel it closing tight around him like the walls of a grave, pressing down upon like the lid of a coffin. Every shadow seemed to harbor some lurking menace. Strange shapes flitted at the edge of his vision, flashes of motion that evaporated as soon as he turned his head to focus upon them. Eerie sounds whispered across the fringes of his hearing, weird aromas teased his nose, uncanny chills plucked at his flesh. The hunter's every sense was tautened by the capricious gloom of the ruins. Despite his mind's best efforts to control his emotions, he couldn't quell the almost primal agitation that gripped him.

His horse had fled soon after he entered Starybogow. The animal had bucked in response to some threat unseen by Wulf. Surprised, he'd been thrown onto the cracked cobbles of the street while his steed went racing off toward the guarded city gates. The hurt of his fall didn't discomfit Wulf nearly so much as the loss of his horse. Docile or unruly, obedient or rebellious, at least the animal had provided a sense of companionship. A feeling that he wasn't alone. Alone among the roguish inhabitants and inhuman horrors that now ruled the city.

When Wulf found signs of von Auerbach's trail, the relief he felt was more than simply that of a hunter pursuing his quarry. To know that the Teutonic Knight was here, somewhere in the ruins served to provide a counterpoint to the unreal, phantasmal atmosphere of Starybogow. Pursuit of the knight provided Wulf with focus, something familiar to oppose the enigma of the fallen city.

Through the broken husks of warehouses and across the rubble of workshops, the hunter made his way. Here and there, in a patch of dust or on the splintered panes of a fallen window, Wulf would find the imprint of an armored boot. Patches of moss clinging to the crumbling walls rubbed away by something brushing past them. Weeds broken or crushed underfoot. Once, caught upon the jagged edge of a wooden doorway, he found a few threads of white cloth – perhaps torn from the white surcoat of a Teutonic Knight.

The uncanny, inexplicable wariness of his hunter's instincts brought Wulf to seek cover behind a dilapidated ox cart lying sprawled across the street. For several long minutes, he crouched against the side of the cart, his every sense keyed and sharpened to a razored edge. When the sound of a crow croaking in agitation and taking wing reached his ears, Wulf knew that something was drawing near. Soon the rattle of armor came into his hearing, the approach of someone in mail. His heart quickened as Wulf felt the certainty that his quarry was close at hand.

Across the street, cautiously making his way through the rubble of a devastated city, a tall man draped in white stepped into view. Sunlight glistened from the steel helm that enclosed the man's face, though the blued metal of the sword clenched in his mailed fist betrayed no such brilliance. The heavy white folds of the surcoat and cloak that fell about the man's body were marked with a great black cross, one upon his left breast and another that stretched across the back of his cloak. Only the Teutonic Knights displayed such insignia, and there was only one of that order Wulf expected to find prowling the streets of Starybogow alone. Klaus von Auerbach, the perpetrator of infamies in Westphalia, was before him.

The avenger kept silent as he watched the knight moving among the rubble. It was obvious to Wulf that von Auerbach was vigilant as he prowled the ruins. For a moment he worried that the knight had somehow discovered that the Freischoffe was on his trail. He quickly disabused himself of the idea. Perhaps in Westphalia he might have worried about the Vehmic Court hunting him, but here on the frontiers of Poland the knight would think himself beyond their reach.

The smell of blood gave Wulf a more reasonable explanation for the knight's caution. There was evidence of gore spattered about the white surcoat and dark stains on the sword in his hand. Much too fresh to be residue from the caravan raiders. Von Auerbach had found some enemy here in Starybogow. From the methodical way the knight inspected his surroundings it seemed he was trying to find his late foes rather than hide from them. Perhaps he'd found the rest of the Wends and their sorcerer-chieftain.

Wulf brushed aside such thoughts. The Wends and their volkhv were of no concern to him. He had only one enemy in Starybogow, and he was looking at him. Exhibiting a stealth that would have shamed the great jungle cats, Wulf slipped away from behind the ox cart and crept down a passageway between the crumbling shops and warehouses. His route put him parallel to his quarry and the faint rattle of the knight's armor allowed him to shadow von Auerbach as he marched deeper into the ruins.

Though resolute in his determination to carry out the judges' command, Wulf was realistic about the task set before him. The Teutonic Knights were dedicated warriors, trained to a hardness as cold and uncompromising as the armor they wore. Von Auerbach was a veteran of many battles, a warrior accustomed to the swift brutality of combat. It would be a grave mistake to let his loathing of the man's crimes discredit the formidable nature of his foe. To be certain of success, to ensure that justice was visited against the knight, Wulf would have to strike fast and without warning. If he gave von Auerbach any chance at all to defend himself, then the results might go against the judgment of Vehm.

Gauging the position of his quarry by the sound of his advance, Wulf hurried ahead and darted down an alleyway. Hastening to the opening at the far end, he held his breath and waited for the knight to appear. After what seemed to him an eternity, the rattle of armor drew closer. Tightening his grip upon his sword, Wulf lunged out from the alleyway and fell upon his enemy.

There was shock in the eyes that stared at Wulf from behind the knight's steel mask. Von Auerbach was stunned that an enemy had ambushed him despite his vigilance. Such was his incredulity that he made no move to raise his sword while the avenger drove upon him.

Then it was Wulf's turn to be surprised. Even as he brought his sword stabbing at the knight's body, a sudden gust of wind set the heavy surcoat and cloak whipping forward. The hunter's blade became snagged in the heavy cloth, fouling the impetus of his thrust. The keen edge raked harmlessly across the steel mail.

Wulf didn't waste time trying to free his weapon but instead caught at von Auerbach's arm as the knight started to bring his own blade into play. Straining against one another, the two men fought for control of the Teutonic sword, their struggle bringing them staggering against the wall of the building beside them. The knight's armored weight was taxing Wulf's resistance, forcing him to combat both the brawn and bulk of his foe. As plaster flaked away from the wall when the two men struck it, a desperate idea came to the avenger. Mustering such might as remained to him, he spun his foe around, slamming him full into the wall.

The rotten timbers and cracked plaster gave way beneath von Auerbach's mass. The knight went hurtling inside, dust and debris pelting his armored frame. Yet even as he went tumbling through the hole, he refused to relinquish hold of his sword. Wulf was dragged after the knight, crashing down upon him as both men struck the floor.

Wulf blinked dust from his eyes and glared down at his enemy. With one hand still locked about the knight's sword, he pawed among the debris around them, his hand curling around a piece of rubble. Viciously he brought the crude weapon slamming against von Auerbach's head. The chunk of plaster disintegrated as it cracked against the steel helm.

Heavy padding within the helm dulled the impact of Wulf's blow. Unfazed, von Auerbach brought his leg kicking up under the avenger's body. The strike broke Wulf's hold on the sword and sent him careening overhead, thrown across the room. Boards splintered under the impact and the hunter found himself plummeting into the cellar below.

All the breath was knocked out of Wulf as he slammed into cold, unyielding stone. Sparks flashed across his vision as his head bounced against the floor. Before his awareness was smothered by darkness, he could see the knight standing at the edge of the hole staring down at him.

Then the Freischoffe collapsed into unconsciousness.

*****

Wulf was not certain how long it was before he came to his senses. The cold of the cellar had roused him, setting his flesh shivering and his teeth chattering. Tugging his cloak tighter, he tried his best to fend off the cold. The temptation to lie back down was, he knew, a dangerous one. Many men had perished in the chill of winter because they lacked the resolve to resist.

When Wulf struggled up from the floor, pain crackled through his body, stabbing into places he didn't know could hurt. He choked back the agony, refusing to give it voice. He wasn't going to betray his presence until he took stock of his surroundings.

Night must have descended upon Starybogow, for the building above the cellar was just an indistinct shadow. Wulf could discern the jagged edges of the hole he'd plunged down, but nothing more. He chided himself for the passing thought that von Auerbach was up there, as though the Teutonic Knight would linger around all day waiting for him to awaken and offer him honorable combat. The grim reality was that his quarry was long gone. He'd have to pick up his trail again. Once he found a way out of the cellar.

The avenger set to examining the cellar into which he'd fallen. Some perversity of nature had brought luminescent moss to flourish underground, rendering it brighter than the murky building above. The walls the moss grew from were constructed of heavy stone blocks, pitted with age. Certainly they were out of sorts with the building above, which had been nothing more profound than a granary in its day. It was obvious to Wulf that the vault represented some remnant of far older construction and as he looked about in vain for stairs leading up into the building, his suspicion was confirmed. Before his violent descent there had been no communication between the cellar and the granary.

Wulf looked again to the hole overhead. It was a little more than twenty feet, but well away from the walls. Without rope and grapple he wouldn't be leaving the way he'd come. He moved toward one of the walls, inspecting the construction. He scowled when he realized the stone was too tough to easily chip handholds into it with his knife. The effort would be daunting enough, but then he'd have to smash his way through the floor overhead.

Following the curve of the wall, Wulf discovered that the vault he was in wasn't isolated. There was a dark recess ahead, an opening into some further chamber or passageway. Appreciating the dismal prospects his current surroundings offered, he marched to the opening and made his way down the tunnel beyond.

Wulf's trek through the weirdly lit subterranean world was the strangest of his experience. Aside from rats, bats, and crawling vermin, he was alone in the vaults. At least so his senses told him. His hunter's instinct kept nagging at him, stirring him to a heightened wariness. Sometimes he would hear a distant sound that was uncomfortably like that of footsteps or catch a momentary impression of something too articulate to dismiss as the chirps of bats.

Then, amid the dank gloom of the tunnels, Wulf found tracks in a patch of slime on the floor. They were the marks of feet, at least four men judging by the print of their shoes. Scratches in a nearby wall made Wulf question whether they were the work of rat claws or a sign left to guide visitors to this underworld. He'd paid small notice to such marks before, but now, coupled with the evidence of human activity, the hunter kept a closer watch for them. When he noticed another of the peculiar scratches, he made a careful inspection of the surroundings. His effort was rewarded when he found the imprint of a heel captured by a splash of mud. It was enough for him. The marks were guiding someone through the tunnels. That meant one way or the other, they must lead to a way out.

Not knowing how far back the marks might have started, Wulf decided to press ahead, following the same path taken by those who'd preceded him. The knife he'd drawn from his boot felt small and puny in his hand when he considered who, or what, might be ahead of him.

The sound of voices carried back to him now, though in a language strange to him. Wulf hesitated a moment, then became aware of a hideous realization. He could hear sounds behind him as well, footfalls tramping through the mud and slime of the vaults. He was caught between two unknowns, trapped by those ahead of him and those following behind. Fingering his knife, Wulf decided that his best chance was to confront the nearer of the underworld travelers.

Wulf sprawled himself across the scummy floor, hiding his knife hand underneath him. He was depending on the curiosity of the owners of those footfalls, that they'd be more puzzled than alarmed at finding a strange body lying in their tunnels. A moment's incaution, and Wulf would have the advantage of them.

The footsteps drew closer. From where he lay upon the floor, Wulf could see the rough hide boots and fur leggings of three men. When they started talking among themselves in the same strange tongue, he decided there were at least five in the group. One against five were odds to sicken anyone's heart and Wulf had few illusions that the men approaching him would prove friendly. He'd seen rough clothes like theirs recently – on the corpses of Wendish raiders.

After some discussion among themselves, one of the Wends approached Wulf. He prodded the avenger's body with his boot, seeking to turn him over onto his back. The moment the pagan put pressure into his action, the 'dead' body erupted into violence. Wulf lunged up, catching the shocked Wend and slamming him against the floor. Before any of the other raiders could react, Wulf had his knife at the first pagan's throat.

"Back, or I'll kill him," Wulf threatened.

One of the Wends, a bearded brute with several scars across the right side of his face, sneered at the hunter. "Kill him, Christ-man," he laughed. "Send his spirit to Triglav! Then we take our revenge!"

"All I want is to be shown the way out," Wulf said. He pressed the tip of his knife against his captive's throat, sending a bead of blood rolling down the blade. The other Wends laughed.

"Many Christ-man come into halls of Horjan," the scarred Wend declared. "None of them leave." As he spoke, the raider motioned his fellow pagans forward. The fate of their comrade meant less to them than the escape of an intruder. Wulf had staked everything on this gamble – and lost.

"*Gott mit uns*!" The cry boomed like thunder through the scummy vaults. The Wends, only a moment before ready to converge on Wulf, now swung around to face a new threat that came charging out at them from the darkness. The pagans snarled in fury when they saw the white mantle of von Auerbach and the fact that the Teutonic Knight was alone. Like starving dogs, the raiders rushed to meet the warrior's charge.

Wulf wasted no time seizing upon the reprieve he'd been given. In one vicious motion he slit the throat of his prisoner and ripped the iron sword from his belt. Leaping to his feet, the hunter charged at the other Wends. The scar-faced leader, belatedly remembering the avenger, turned back to deal with Wulf, parrying the German's attack with his own sword. The crash of steel against iron rang out through the tunnel.

It was with a sickening sensation that Wulf came to appreciate that his adversary was a better swordsman than himself. Where such an unwashed pagan had come by such skill was less important to the avenger than how he would overcome the man. Every thrust and slash was blocked by the Wend's intervening steel while Wulf's sword wasn't quick enough to prevent several cuts and slashes to his arms and shoulders. The heavier iron blade from his captive simply wasn't able to keep pace with the reaver's sword.

A mortal shriek rang out as von Auerbach finished one of his foes. Wulf could see the raider crumple, pierced through the breast by the knight. A second scream of agony sounded a moment later, but the hunter was too occupied by his own adversary to see what had happened, or to whom.

The Wendish reaver was prevailing. The blood seeping from the cuts he'd inflicted and the heavy iron sword were conspiring to weaken Wulf's resistance. Skill and strength were in the pagan's favor. All Wulf had left to him was ruthlessness and cunning. Feinting to the left with his heavy blade, distracting his foe with the promise of an opening, the German brought his knee smashing up into the raider's groin.

Coughing in misery, the Wend doubled over, his sword clattering to the floor. Wulf gave his foe the time to neither recover his breath or his weapon. Gripping the heavy iron sword in both hands, he brought the edge cleaving down into the reaver's neck. The blow wasn't quite enough to sever the man's head, but it did reduce him to a twitching mass spurting blood across the walls.

Wulf looked up from his vanquished enemy. Von Auerbach was just putting down the last of the raiders, splitting the man's skull with a crosswise slash of his sword. The knight looked across the carnage to where the avenger stood. He held up his hand, motioning for Wulf to keep silent.

The hunter froze, recalling the voices he'd heard issuing from somewhere ahead. There was no saying how many more Wends were in the tunnels. If the sounds of the fight had carried back to them, an entire horde of angry pagans might even now be charging toward them. Keeping a wary eye on von Auerbach, Wulf listened to the distant voices. Though he couldn't understand their words, they seemed no more agitated than when he'd first heard them.

"It would seem this fray has gone unnoticed," Wulf told the knight. Stooping down, he retrieved the steel sword of the Wendish reaver and tossed the iron blade to the ground.

Von Auerbach shook his head. "Now you would attack me. Then, I imagine that is what brought you all the way from Westphalia. You are fortunate I recognized you when I pursued you into the cellar."

Wulf bristled at the knight's words, stung by the mercy he'd been shown. A moment's reflection only swelled his anger. "You know I'm the Freischoffe the Vehm sent after you! You used me to trail these pagans for you!" He spat on the floor. "That for your mercy!"

"We need each other," von Auerbach warned Wulf. He pointed down the tunnel in the direction of the muted voices. "The only way out of here is through them."

"My quarrel is with you, not them," Wulf snarled.

"It will make no difference," von Auerbach said. "Horjan has twisted the minds of his followers, turned them back to the old ways. He's filled them with visions of a pagan empire built on blood and magic. All civilized men are their enemy." The knight closed his hand around the cross he wore about his neck. "Listen! They are invoking Triglav and the Old Gods, calling to them to accept their offering!"

Wulf glared at the knight. "I hear only gibberish and the ravings of a murderer."

"I am familiar with the Sorbish tongue," von Auerbach persisted. "I tell you they are performing one of their obscene rites. Rites that demand human sacrifice! You call me murderer, but what will you be if you do nothing to stop this abomination Horjan intends?"

The knight's words pierced Wulf like daggers, stinging the Freischoffe's sense of justice. It was one thing to use untoward tactics to overcome a savage, but to abandon innocents to the caprices of pagan captors was something his own sense of honor wouldn't allow. Reluctantly, he nodded to von Auerbach. "A truce then, until these fiends have been stopped. Make no mistake, it is a reprieve not a pardon. The justice of Vehm will not be denied. I am your executioner, not your friend."

Von Auerbach returned Wulf's nod. "For the moment, it is enough that you are my ally."

*****

The Wendish temple was situated in a vast natural cavern cut from the rock beneath Starybogow eons past by primordial forces. The enormity was illuminated by masses of moss that clung to stalagmites and stalactites, creating an eerie confusion of greenish light and deep shadows. At some time in the past, the builders of the ancient vaults had broken into the cavern, but if any use had been made of their discovery, no trace now remained. Instead there were only the geologic formations left by nature and the malevolent constructions raised by Horjan's followers.

So certain were the Wends of the security of their hidden temple that they'd posted no guards to patrol the entrances to the cavern. Wulf and von Auerbach were able to slip inside unopposed, the sounds of their advance muffled by the Sorbish chants of the assembled pagans. The two Germans secreted themselves behind a cluster of stalagmites that afforded them a view of the volkhv and his raiders.

Wulf felt his gaze drawn inexorably to Horjan. The shaman was a small man with a thin build, but he exuded a presence, a sense of sinister power far beyond his physicality. The volkhv wore a heavy wolfskin cloak, his face locked within a mask crafted from a wolf's skull. His arms, bare and pale, were notched with ritualistic scars and inked with arcane tattoos. As he stamped his bare feet against the stony floor, he raised his voice in a feral ululation, howling to his devotees.

The pagan Wends were numerous, perhaps as many as a hundred. While the bulk of them were young, robust men of the sort to carry out the fierce raids and massacres their volkhv demanded, there were some women and children among them. The Wends were gathered together in a wide space that had been cleared of stalagmites and columns, the floor smoothed and etched with crude pictoglyphs and strange runes. Torches set into primitive stands fashioned from bone and horn lent the gathering illumination greater than that afforded by the glowing fungi.

The Wends faced toward a tall wooden idol, a figure that made Wulf shudder to gaze upon. Simple in design and carved in an even simpler manner, the statue had about it an air of unnatural hostility, a smoldering wrath that seemed ready to burst from its wooden shell. The idol was crafted in the semblance of a man, but above its shoulders there rose not a single head but three, each the bestial and horned visage of a goat.

"Triglav," von Auerbach whispered, giving name to the Wendish god. "Horjan has evoked the old ways to draw followers to him. The more horrific the rites, the more completely he rips them away from civilization and into barbarism." The knight pointed to the space between the goat-headed idol and the Wends. Arrayed in a ring were several stout posts. Lashed to each of these with cords of sinew and hide were captives the raiders had seized. Men and women, Pole and German, the prisoners moaned through the ropes that gagged them, squirmed in the cords that bound them.

"What will they do to them?" Wulf asked, though he already knew the answer. These were sacrifices, offerings to their pagan gods. While he watched, Horjan dipped a bone ladle into a big stone pot resting at the idol's base. Even from their hiding place the two Germans could smell the stench of the pasty ooze the volkhv lifted from the pot. Holding the ladle well away from his body, Horjan approached the first of his captives. Shrieking a litany in the Sorbish tongue, he cast the contents of the ladle into the face of the bound Pole.

"He says he has marked them for the dog of Triglav," von Auerbach said. There was both anxiety and disgust in the knight's voice as he spoke.

"I see no dog," Wulf objected, looking about the cavern. Then he saw Horjan turn toward a black patch of floor. The volkhv splashed another spoonful of the smelly paste onto the ground. Wulf was shocked when the stuff disappeared, then chided himself when he realized that the shaman had simply dumped the filth into a hole.

Relief faded fast, however. Sounds began to issue from that hole. Grisly scraping noises, like a dead horse being dragged across stone. Mixed into it was a sullen growl, deep and hungry. Wulf had hunted in forests across Westphalia and Silesia, Bavaria and Styria. The growl he heard now was unlike that of any beast he'd encountered before. All he knew for certain was that the thing must be huge to produce such a tremendous vocalization.

Horjan backed away from the hole, hastily waving a set of armored Wends to move closer to him, axes ready in their hands. The pagan throng fell silent, quieted by a mixture of awed adulation and primitive dread. Even the moans of the captives faded away as raw terror muted their pain.

"Bukavac," von Auerbach hissed, once more giving name to the supernatural horrors of Horjan's temple.

Roused by the paste the volkhv had flung into the pit, the bukavac crawled up from its hole. As Wulf had expected, the creature was huge, bigger than a wisent bull. Its broad body tapered away into a long tail topped by a knobby cudgel of bone. Six powerful legs projected from the monster's sides, each foot ending in sickle-like claws. Its head projected forward on a stumpy neck, the face elongated into a weasel-like snout, the lips curled back by the confusion of fangs projecting from its jaws. The eyes were enormous ovals that bulged from the brute's skull, utterly white and lifeless. Vicious horns projected rearward from the monster's head, stabbing back to defend its neck and shoulders. The bukavac's body was dingy gray in color, covered in a slimy skin that recalled to Wulf the cold flesh of frogs and salamanders.

The monster swung its horned head around, its blind eyes unmoving but the nostrils atop its snout flaring and snorting in agitation. Perhaps it was some enchantment that clung to the stone pot, but the bukavac made no move toward the idol. Instead it scurried toward the nearest of the posts and the German woman lashed to it. The brute sniffed at her, indifferent to her renewed moans of horror. All it cared about was the stink of Horjan's unguent clinging to her. Rearing back on two sets of legs, the monster lashed out with one of its foreclaws. There was a ghastly crunching sound as it snapped the sacrifice's neck.

Fury boiled up within him as Wulf saw the bukavac claim its victim, a fury that swelled when the Wends cheered the monster's savagery. "We can't let this happen," the avenger swore. He looked aside to where von Auerbach had been only a moment before. The Teutonic Knight was gone.

Wulf didn't have long to ponder von Auerbach's disappearance. From the floor of the cavern, the knight's war cry rang out. "*Gott mit uns!*" Sword in hand, the warrior rushed straight toward the hideous bukavac.

The monster swung around at von Auerbach's cry, wisps of glowing red mist seeping from its victim's body and into the grisly claws on its forelegs. The bukavac raised its horned head, snuffling at the air, a grunt of agitation rumbling in its throat. Swinging its head from side to side, the creature's milky eyes failed to find the Teutonic Knight as he fearlessly lunged at the monster. Von Auerbach's steel ripped across the brute's flank, splitting the fleshy hide and drawing a stream of blackish treacle from its veins.

Wailing in agony, the bukavac reared back, lashing out blindly with its claws. Von Auerbach easily dodged the sightless strikes, stabbing his blade again into the monster's flesh.

The Wends shouted in alarm and shock, horrified by von Auerbach's defilement of the ceremony and his profane assault upon 'the dog of Triglav'. Some of them took up axes and swords, enraged by the Christian knight's intrusion but wary of closing upon him while he was near the blind bukavac. Others started running toward the cavern's exits, convinced that von Auerbach was but the vanguard of an entire company of Teutonic Knights.

Horjan was more deliberate in his response. The volkhv dashed back to the pot lying at the idol's base. Again he dipped the ladle into the smelly ooze and then rushed toward von Auerbach, flinging a great dollop of the muck onto the knight's armor. With even more haste, Horjan withdrew, laughing in triumph and calling out to his followers in scolding tones.

Von Auerbach had the better of the bukavac when the beast was blind, but with Horjan's muck splashed across his body, the monster no longer needed to see the knight to find him. One of the great claws slashed down upon his shoulder, ripping through the cloak and shredding the mail beneath. Another claw licked around, raking across his thigh and pulling away the steel plate fastened there. A third claw intercepted his sword as he strove to stab the bukavac once again, the monster's hideous strength swatting aside the blow as though von Auerbach were an insect.

Though he was himself sworn to see von Auerbach dead, Wulf found it impossible to leave the knight's destruction to a crawling monster and its pagan masters. The Freischoffe knew there was nothing to be gained by simply rushing down and joining von Auerbach's fight against the bukavac. Wulf preferred to strike at the one who had called up the beast. With the attention of every Wend in the cavern now focused upon the struggle between man and monster, Wulf knew he had a rare opportunity to fall upon the volkhv before anyone was even aware of his presence.

The vicious shouts of the onlooking Wends and the fearsome growls of the bukavac muffled whatever noise Wulf made as he came around the column and hastened toward the idol. His knife was stabbing up through the chin of a pagan warrior before the man could do more than gape in wonder at the avenger's sudden appearance. The second of Horjan's bodyguards put up a little more fight. Swinging around, the armored raider was bringing his axe up for a cleaving stroke when Wulf thrust the point of his sword deep into the man's side. The Wend collapsed to his knees, coughing a great gout of blood into his beard. He struggled to rise, but his legs gave way beneath him and his axe slipped from numbed fingers.

As Wulf turned away from the dying bodyguards, he saw the grisly volkhv gesturing at him with arcane passes of his clawed fingers. He could see Horjan's eyes glaring at him from the depths of his wolf-skull mask, eyes filled with such hatred and malignance as he'd never believed possible. Though the volkhv appeared defenseless, Wulf felt a strange lethargy coming upon him. The sword in his hand felt impossibly heavy, every muscle in his body was crying out to him to drop the blade.

The steel sword clattered to the floor. For an instant there was a gleam of sadistic triumph blazing in Horjan's eyes, and he let pride in his magic replace vigilance. It was all the time Wulf needed.

The avenger had discarded the sword with less reluctance than Horjan suspected. The blade had no part in Wulf's plans. It was a different weapon he sought to use against the volkhv, a weapon of the sorcerer's own crafting. Even as the sword clattered to the ground, Wulf was sprinting to the base of the idol. Crouching at the feet of Triglav, he wrapped his arms around the stone pot and lifted it. Bellowing with almost superhuman effort, he swung the heavy pot toward Horjan.

Horjan's scream of horror echoed through the cavern as the unguent within the pot splashed across him, inundating the sorcerer from head to toe in the reeking slime. The overpowering stench brought the bukavac's head snapping around. The monster sniffed at the air, its nostrils flaring. With a hungry bellow, the brute turned away from the faltering von Auerbach and scrambled across the floor toward the volkhv.

Wulf retreated before the monster's advance. Horjan hesitated, weaving his hands before his body in arcane passes. The sorcerer was too agitated by the bukavac's charge to focus upon his magic. Realizing that he couldn't concentrate on his spell, the volkhv tried to flee behind the shelter of Triglav's idol. Uttering a fearsome snarl, the bukavac sprang at him, bearing Horjan to the ground. The sickening crunch of broken ribs and crushed limbs echoed through the cavern. Then the monster's claws were raking across the shrieking shaman, ripping the life from him in gory strands of crimson mist.

Sight of the volkhv's brutal demise sent the rest of the pagans fleeing from their secret temple. Crying out in fear, the Wends ran to the tunnels, scattering into the black underworld beneath Starybogow's ruined streets. In a matter of heartbeats, the only pagan raiders left in the cavern were those Wulf had slain and the sorcerer withering in the bukavac's claws.

Wulf circled around the feeding monster, hurrying toward the wounded knight. Somehow, despite the wounds inflicted on him, von Auerbach remained on his feet. The knight was limping toward the surviving captives, his boots slipping in the blood spilling down his legs with each step he took. When the Freischoffe reached him, the knight turned a pallid face to him, a face that already seemed more than half dead.

"Help me free them," von Auerbach begged Wulf.

For an instant, Wulf felt pity for the Teutonic Knight, then hate flared up in his heart once more. "I'll not help you in your penance," he snarled. "Burn for your crimes."

The knight stared at him, a terrible sadness in his gaze. "You would leave the innocent to perish? Is my sin so unholy that others must suffer for it?" Von Auerbach tried to take one final step, then slumped down to his knees as strength deserted him. He looked up at Wulf. "Shall I confess my sin to you? I was in love with a girl beneath my station. When she found herself with my child, rather than shame me she took her own life. I was the one who discovered her body. I was the one who took the crime upon myself, claimed she died by my hand and not her own, that she might lie in hallowed ground and her soul find its way into God's keeping."

The avenger shook his head, trying to fight back the chill provoked by von Auerbach's words, by the conviction in his voice. As Freischoffe, Wulf had hunted down dozens of men condemned by the Vehmic Court. Never had he questioned the justice meted out by the judges. Never had he wondered if the men he was told to execute might be innocent of their crimes.

The bestial roar of the bukavac gave Wulf no time to settle his mind. Horjan's shattered body dripped from the monster's fangs, torn flesh and broken bones protruding from the bloodied wolfskin cloak. A shake of the creature's horned head scattered the volkhv's remains across the floor. Raising its hideous face, the bukavac snuffled at the air, drawing down the stink of the oozy unguent still clinging to von Auerbach. A hungry growl rumbled through the beast as it turned towards the knight and the sacrifices left for it by the Wends.

"Save them," von Auerbach enjoined Wulf. With an effort born of desperation the knight staggered to his feet. Blood gushed from his mangled body. Resolutely he raised his sword and put himself between the bukavac and the captives. "Save them," he told Wulf. "It's already too late for me."

Wulf nodded and hastened to the posts. Playing his knife across the straps and cords, he freed the captives. While he worked he could hear the sounds of conflict, the angry howls of the bukavac as von Auerbach's sword slashed its skin, the pained cries of the knight as the beast's claws ripped into his body. Only when the last of the intended sacrifices was cut loose and sent hurrying toward the nearest tunnel did Wulf turn back to witness the knight's fate.

Von Auerbach's sword was slick with the monster's foul blood. The bukavac's skin was gashed and gouged in a dozen places, one of its milky eyes split by the knight's blade. The violence inflicted upon it had caused the brute to rear back on its hindmost legs, the others slashing about blindly as it tried to fend off the German's attacks. Dodging to and fro, von Auerbach managed to avoid the gruesome claws and continue to thrust at the monster's body.

Focused upon the bukavac's claws, the knight failed to notice a new peril. Wulf cried out a warning to von Auerbach as he saw the monster's tail writhing from side to side. The warning was given too late. The tail darted forward with the speed of a striking scorpion. The club-like knob slammed into von Auerbach's breast, crumpling the mail and shattering the ribs beneath. The blow hurled him backward a dozen feet. Snarling, the bukavac sprang after its adversary, pouncing on him with the ferocity of a lion.

The avenger had no way of knowing if the Teutonic Knight had found penance under the ruins of Starybogow, but it was certain that von Auerbach had found a death more ghastly than any commanded by the Vehmic Court. The knight's head was caught in the bukavac's vicious jaws, the monster's powerful muscles causing its teeth to pierce the steel helm and the skull within. A twist, a contortion of its mouth, and the man's head cracked open like an egg.

Wulf circled around the feasting monster, moving past the residue of Horjan's mutilated corpse. The avenger slipped behind the tall wooden idol of Triglav. The pagan god stood upon a broad base, but the feet of the statue were slender and tapered to a narrow point as they sank to the pedestal. Behind the idol was the firm support of a natural column. Positioning himself in the slim gap between idol and column, Wulf set his back against Triglav's legs and put his feet upon the column.

It was a Herculean task Wulf set himself. Straining every muscle in his body, he pushed against the column, using himself as a lever against the idol. When he would relent, the hunter thought of von Auerbach and the honor he'd shown making his last stand. Slowly, almost imperceptibly, the idol began to creak and groan.

The bukavac looked up from von Auerbach's body, startled by the noise as Triglav's legs cracked. The blind beast didn't see the goat-headed idol as it snapped from its base and came crashing down upon it. Like some immense insect flattened beneath the heel of a god, the bukavac was smashed under the tremendous mass as Triglav fell upon it.

Gasping for breath, every tendon and sinew in his body feeling as though it were on fire, Wulf looked on his handiwork with grim satisfaction. The bukavac was dead, the volkhv who'd summoned it was no more, the pagan cult was broken and scattered. A fitting epithet for Klaus von Auerbach, the man the Vehmic Court had named murderer. The man Wulf Greimmer would always know as a hero.

Sworn to Secrecy

Brandon Rospond

Hanseatic Merchant

This was a strange time to live in. The word on the wind was that the quakes that had shaken the land, demolishing towns, had brought back beings from wisemens' tales and children's nightmares. And the source of it all was centered in a town that was now more ruin than inhabitable – Starybogow. Nothing was sacred anymore; ferrymen feared the stirrings in the water, the woods breathed with strange apparitions, and every cold chill on the back made one think twice about what was behind them.

While this information was more true than tale, the lone rider, clad in all black, traveling horseback across a grass-laden trail, could not believe that word of the mythical returns had spread like wildfire. He shook his head, and within the cowl that hid his face, he felt a smile curl the corner of his lips. They had known about the wodniks that infested the waters and threatened to drown sailors, the leshiye that stalked the forest and snatched away travelers, and the many cultists that believed in their numerous Old Gods; but then again, they were also very well aware of the Eldar Gods and the hooks they had in the knights of the church.

These facts were no less common to him than knowing the sun would rise the next day or that birds took flight with their beating wings. This was because he belonged to the most elite traders – in secrets, information, and items alike – one of the greatest secret societies ever known to man, the Hanseatic League.

Even though he was no rookie to the organization, having been a member of the League for several years now, the thought of their convoluted network of information still widened the smile on his face. In this ever-turbulent time, where the common man fought for control in the name of whatever God or gods he worshipped, the League were the ones that managed to pull the strings behind the scenes to keep the fight balanced in their own best interests. They had eyes and ears everywhere, watching as each side made their every move.

And that returned him to the mission at hand. Geoffrey Winters, better known as 'Bishop', had been watching the forest carefully despite his leisurely trot, but now he tapped his mare on the neck.

"Well, Fiona, I think the leshiye don't want to come out to play today." He winked as she turned her head to snort, even though he knew the gesture would be lost on her. "I think it's for the best, my dear. We wouldn't want to sully your freshly pressed shoes, now would we?"

He clicked his tongue and spurred the dark horse forward, allowing the cloak's hood to drop down on his back. His thick shoulder-length black hair fluttered with each breath of air that passed over him, and he relished how good it felt to be back out on the road. Even though the League's primary cover was that they were merchants, the majority of his brethren were trained as assassins and every member was taught the proper art of swordplay. Surely, he knew how to defend himself and quickly dispose of attackers, but despite the rush of battle adrenaline, the high Bishop enjoyed the most was that of the treasure hunt. He made his fair share from what he brought back for clients, but the exploration of the far reaches of the world was what he craved and had a sort of payout that he could not put monetary value to.

Fiona carried him out from the depths of the forest and Bishop exhaled with relief. The less hassle from strange spirits on his journey, the better. Reacquainting himself with his new surroundings, he spurred the horse onward across the plains. He did not need the map his brethren had made up for him; he had already committed the location to memory as he steered Fiona in the direction of his destination. He stole a quick glance to his right and he could just make out the ruins of Starybogow, looming over the area as if watching his every movement. He shook the trail of icy fingers out of his spine and hurried Fiona forward.

He reached the edge of the town and slowed the horse down; his eyebrow raised involuntarily at the sight before him. Against his better judgment, he pulled out the map to make sure he had reached the right spot, and true to his own memory, he had arrived at the burnt-out husk known as Kukle.

"This… This is it?" Bishop threw his arms out at his sides as he scanned the scattered ruins that loosely traced the city's outline. There were remains of four or five hovels that survived fires, as well as the remains of a barely intact stable, but other than that, everything was gone. He sighed and turned back to Fiona. "Well. The League works in strange ways, and they are always right. Can't dispute them now. Not at least until I've given this place the, ah… proper look around."

He shook his head and led Fiona over to the ramshackle stable. He tested its might a few times, just to make sure that it would not fall with her within, and he was glad when it remained standing. Bishop tied her up to one of the posts, making sure to rub her neck with the fingers exposed from his lightly-leathered black gloves. Before he left, he moved a few pieces of rubble in front of the entrance, as if to ward off any other adventurers; he doubted anyone would be passing this way, but he treated Fiona like any other good woman he met in his life, and always made sure she was properly protected.

As he walked back through the town, he turned his gaze toward the direction of Starybogow and felt a chill creep across his spine once more. He took an elegant thin blade of steel out from his waist, holding it in his right hand. The weapon, along with his fitted stealth gear, had been made by the League's own personal blacksmith.

"Better safe than sorry," Bishop muttered as he faced the ruins around him once more. "So little time, so many towns not ventured… and so many more unsatisfied women I have yet to take care of. Should I live to love another day, I should be wary of my surroundings. Under the watchful gaze of that damned Starybogow is not the way I want the bards to sing of my death."

Using his free hand, Bishop pulled the hood over his head once more as he stalked through the desolated town. He stopped at the door of each building left intact and paused for several moments to listen before disturbing the quiet within. Each time, he was glad to be met with the same result – there was not a soul, neither human nor spiritual, to be found in any of the ruins. Just the simple sound of silence, broken by his own footsteps.

His brows furrowed as he started to think. The League had been amassing an armory of strange relics that were said to combat both the Eldar and Old Gods, but the items that the 'merchants' were always sent to retrieve were often random and rarely showed any symbolic purpose. These 'weapons' were often times not blades of any sort, but trinkets that seemed no different than those often requested by clients; hardly fitting the strange desires of the Leagues' rulers. In one of the more recent – failed – attempts, members had been dispatched to follow some Teutonic Knight who was seeking a cross that belonged to some Saint Boniface; luckily enough for humanity's sake, the knight had decided not to return to the Grandmaster, but still, the League kept eyes on him. But even that strange cross had been kept in the domain of all the darkness, Starybogow. Why had they wanted it in the first place? And what had they expected him to find in this burnt out husk of a village?

He sighed as he exited the last house, putting his free hand on his hip as he looked around. There had been one last house, tucked away in the back, that he had not noticed. He began walking toward it, but as he drew close, something did not feel quite right. The uneasiness grew in his stomach with every step closer, and when he reached the door, he placed his head against the splintered wood to listen closely. Bishop opened the door cautiously, not sure what to expect, his sword at the ready, but he stopped before taking a single step.

He had to steady himself against the doorframe to prevent himself from falling face-first into a hole that seemed to stretch endlessly into the black abyss below. There might have been a foot, if that, of ground before him, but where the floor should have been was instead a pit of darkness. Bishop's eyes bulged as he could hardly believe what he was seeing. He inched his way around the perimeter of the room, finally noticing there had been a staircase built to lead travelers down. He looked back once more to the outside, noticing the sun still high in the sky, and then shrugged.

The League most elite were never wrong about where to look for treasure.

*****

Bishop lost track of how many flights he descended; they kept coiling around the wall of dully shimmering black rock with a landing every thirty steps, until eventually, the outside light had become nonexistent. In odd patches of the wall, there were phosphorescent rocks that projected just enough light for him to see where he was walking, but they only illuminated so much. Luckily enough, he carried several torches with him, just for this sort of event. He was no stranger to catacombs, he thought, brushing his fingertips over the three scarred lines that ran from ear to chin, but he had not expected to find a cave opening in the middle of a ruined town. It had to have been a solid twenty minutes, if not more, before he stepped off the last stair and onto hard stone that led him further into the unknown.

He took note of every twist and turn that he followed, casting his torch across every recess of shadow, and after putting his sword away he traced the wall for divots or depressions with his free hand. If there was one thing he was sure of, it was that he was thorough in his scourings. His hand raised to his cheek again, remembering the spear trap from the one time that he had not been.

After three turns to the left, four to the right, and several long corridors, he heard his first foreign noise. It was distant at first, as if around several corners ahead, but it was coming toward him. He extinguished the flame, pressing his back against the wall. The footfalls were heavy and quick; not hurried, but as if on small legs.

The footsteps would be on him in a moment. Bishop peeked his head around the wall, confident the other being had no idea he was there. Jumping out with his sword aimed at the short person's throat, he grabbed the lantern out of his hand as the other man fell back against the wall, his hands held high in the air. Bishop's expression soured at the thick beard and matted hair, not to mention the putrid smell.

"A *karzełek*. I should have expected as much."

The short man scowled up at the human. He angrily swatted the blade away and tried to jump for his lantern, but Bishop held it just out of reach.

"Ja, and what of it, human?!" The karzełek spat by the man's black sneaking boots when he noticed the attire, and then jumped again at the lantern. "You are with the damn League, eh? Nothing for your kind down here, so just give me my damn light back!"

"Ah, ah, ah!" Bishop waggled his index finger of the hand holding the light source. "Not just yet. I want some answers."

The *karzełek* huffed, putting both his stocky arms over his chest. "What?"

"Where are we? I entered these tunnels at Kukle, and somehow, I have a feeling that we are no longer near there."

"Ha," the dwarf spat, his yellow teeth gleaming in the light. "You humans are all alike. Dummkopf! Kukle is just one of the many entrance points. Welcome to the tunnels of Starybogow!"

Bishop felt his heart drop as he looked around. He had not felt that he traveled that far, but now that he retraced his footsteps mentally, they did lead him in the direction of that damned city. He closed his eyes and gritted his teeth. When they opened, he was staring at the dwarf once more, but a smile painted his face.

"Fine. Wonderful. Storybogow. It doesn't surprise me, to be honest. But since you do know your way around these tunnels, you're going to help me find what I'm looking for."

The *karzełek* snorted. "And just why would I do that?"

"Well," the man shrugged, his face a shadow within the hood

except his glimmering smile. "I'm going further into the tunnels, and from the way you were heading, you're not. I have the lantern, and ah, there doesn't appear to be any others around." Bishop shrugged mockingly with his sword arm. "Oh, no. Quite a conundrum."

The small man snarled, pulling at the ring that seemed to go through both the nostrils of his large, pointed nose that almost resembled a beak. "What is it you want?"

"I'm here to recover an object called the Firstsworn. Have you ever heard of it?"

The dwarf hesitated, opening his mouth, but did not speak. He instead snuffed and turned away, his arms still crossed. "Never heard of it."

"Are you sure?" Bishop stepped in front of him, but the karzełek kept turning away. "Something tells me that you're lying to me. And I mean, if you really haven't, I could always just go wander off to look for it on my own… With the lantern…"

"Fine, fine!" The dwarf sighed, shaking his head. "Why in Perun's name are you after that thing?"

Bishop shrugged. "Because my masters wish for it. That's all I need to know, and that's more than you need to."

"You don't want it. I'm telling you honest."

Bishop rolled his eyes. "And why is that?"

"Because… I…" the short man shook his head. "I can get you close, but that's it. You are on your own after that."

"Close is good enough." Bishop bowed and courteously pointed forward with his sword. "After you, Lord Alebreath."

*****

The duo walked on in relative silence, with the karzełek leading the way under the lighting that Bishop produced from the lantern. The shorter man's heavy footfalls echoed across the walls around them, blanketing whatever noise Bishop might have made. He had hoped the karzełek knew his way around the tunnel enough to know that no one else would be following them. Then again, maybe he just did not care enough; after all, Bishop had taken him by surprise. Eventually, the League member had enough of the silence and cleared his throat.

"Bishop."

"Bis-wha?" The short man looked disgustingly up at him. "The hell is that?"

"My name. It's Bishop. Apologies for the rude introduction."

The *karzełek* giggled heartily and then snorted. "Bishop. What kinda name is that?"

The dark-clad man smiled as well, nodding. "I'm not sure if your people have ever played the game of chess. It's a strategic game, representing real time war in its most basic element – you have to capture the king at all costs. Each piece has its own strengths and weaknesses, and the strongest among them is the bishop. It can sit across the board, away from all of the other pieces, and because it can only move diagonally, it is lethal. All it needs is for the king to think it is secure, hiding behind the cover of a knight or a rook; but as soon as those pieces move, the bishop can slip in and strike the king – as well as any other piece that the player may wish.

"The bishop in chess and myself are both very similar. My job is to slip into enemy lines, find the coveted object that I've been hired to find, and then escape before anyone's the wiser." Bishop nodded to the shorter man. "Much like how I snuck upon you and your heavy footsteps."

The *karzełek* faltered, as if noticing how loudly he was walking, and then made a conscious effort to quiet his steps. After a moment he snorted, the noise being muffled by his large nose ring. "Gorje. It don't got any fancy meaning. Just my name."

"Well, thank you, Gorje, for leading me."

After a few more moments, the disheveled man stopped, peeking around a corner. He put his hands up to Bishop, gesturing toward the lantern. "We're here. There's lights up ahead. Give me mine back and let me be off."

"Woah, wait, hold up…"

Bishop tried to crane his head around the dwarf, but it was the distraction the shorter man needed. He grabbed the drooping arm, yanking the lantern out of it, and ran with heavy steps once more down the corridor. Bishop cursed under his breath. He thought about yelling at him or chasing him down, but in the end, the strange, smelly creature did what he was asked – at least he hoped he had. As for the light, he still had a few more torches at his belt.

He took several careful steps down the hall, once again looking for traps. He was not sure what Gorje had been so fitful about; the room ahead was lit by several torches, like he had said, and there was nothing at all in the chamber except for a small stone table. The high-rising stone walls were empty except for the torch rings. Something nagged in the back of his mind that it might have been too empty…

That worry was soon gone. He could not keep the smile off his face as he stepped toward his prize, his heart swelling with pride. But that elation was quickly snuffed out and he felt his body sag with annoyance. He picked up the item on the table and looked it over several times, hoping he was missing something. A dagger. Much like the one he kept in his boot, but this one shone with a strange gleam. Silver, perhaps? He shook his head as he kept looking it over. Why in the world would the League send him to get a *silver dagger*?

He brought his sword up to attention once more as a sound echoed above his head. It was high pitched, but not like a child, and instead more like some demonic entity. Down they soared from some unknown height, four or five at first. Bishop had to duck, but he got a good look as the little bodies on large wings soared by. Their large orbs of red eyes shone even in the torchlight, their fangs sharpened to viscous points, and the horns on their heads curved only slightly before sticking out straight. Bishop cursed his luck. Skrzaks.

As they made another pass at him, their tiny hands reaching out as their jaws snapped, he ducked once more. He raised his sword toward the last one, impaling it through the open mouth. Its forked tail swung back and forth for a few more moments, but he swung the flailing body in the direction of the others, causing it to fly off and smack one of the other skrzaks into the wall.

The other three flew at him and all at once tried to attack. He placed the dagger into the hidden holster on his right boot and then grabbed his sword with both hands. He brought the weapon up to parry the claws of the first two and then brought it around to sever the head of the third. The insane laughter of the imps grated on his nerves and assaulted his senses, but with each one that he slew, the less noise there was.

He rolled to the left, moving out of the way of the two skrzaks' assault, and grabbed the torch off the wall. He waited for them to come flying toward him once more and threw the blazing brand at them with all his might. The first one was set aflame as it took the brunt of the torch, and as it swerved uncontrollably, it collided into the second, the duo ablaze as their hysterics became shrieks of pain.

Finally, there was silence again, and Bishop exhaled deeply, making sure the dagger was still safely concealed.

"Well that was almost bad. Nasty little buggers."

He walked over to the other side of the wall to take another torche, but something froze his hand on the sconce. It was distant at first, but then the sound escaladed louder than before. The hysteric laughter of the skrzaks was returning and in a fever frenzy. He looked up and saw dozens of red eyes glaring down at him as they swooped down with maddening speed. Snagging the torch off of the wall, Bishop ran back through the halls that his mind had memorized.

At each crossroad, his mind was sharp as a whip, remembering the turn where he once came from. But that did not stop the maddening chant of laughter as it followed him around each corner. His mind worked in overdrive, focusing on which turns held traps. Even if Gorje had been lax in his patrol, Bishop had still been paying close attention to their surroundings. He snapped a tripwire with a kick of his boot and kept pumping his legs forward. He grinned when he heard the splash of acid wipe out several of the demented creatures. But when more laughter took their place, he cursed loudly, pushing his body forward more.

He bolted around another corner, right, then left; held straight for a few dozen feet, and then another hard right, left, left, straight, left. There was another trap. He looked up above the corridor he was rushing through and could just see the large rock that sat oddly above than the rest of his stone surroundings. Smacking his hand into the indent in the wall, he hurdled forward past the boulder that dropped down behind him, propelled forward by the slope it had been sitting on. The sickening crunch of bones and squish of liquid was the reason why he kept so close a vigil on his path, but he groaned in annoyance as the cackles followed still.

No matter how good his memory was and how many traps he triggered in his wake, the skrzaks still haunted his steps. His lungs burned and his legs ached, but he forced himself onward. Left, right, left, straight, right, left-…

And then he could hear something over the hysteria. The sounds was heavy and quick, but these footsteps were hurried. The next corner he turned around, he almost ran into the stocky karzełek from before, holding an axe high in the air. Bishop had to narrowly maneuver out of the way, pinning himself to the wall, as ten other armored men charged forward alongside him.

"I warned ya!" The karzełek bellowed behind him as he charged forward. "If you got what you came for, get outta here right quick! We got beasties to put back to sleep!"

Bishop shook his head, turning back to the path he had been following. "I owe you one hell of a stout ale, Gorje!"

"I'm holding you to it!"

The karzełek's voice was barely above a distant echo as he rushed down the way Bishop had come.

*****

Bishop felt his pace slowing as he tried to catch his breath. It had been some time since he heard the insane cackling of the skrzaks; he just hoped Gorje and his men had survived the encounter. He had had plenty of encounters with strange creatures that had emerged since the earthquakes, several times even with karzełeks that the League had to barter with; and sure he had heard stories about the skrzaks. But nothing in the League's vast network of intel could have prepared him for seeing those creatures up close.

What a rush!

He smiled widely as he laughed to himself. This was why he had joined the League; he loved adventures like this, and the strange creatures only made it that more amusing. It was just a shame that the majority of people had deemed creatures like the karzełeks 'evil' just because they did not understand them. Sure, the odious Gorje had to be forced into helping Bishop, but in the end, he knew just what Bishop was getting into and came back to help. He owed a great deal of thanks to that.

The subject of these creatures always intrigued him and he had often talked about them with others; the women he bedded, the brethren of his order, and even tavern patriots when he visited. Evahn, his main contact for non-League clients, source of outside information, and the gentlemen that sold all of his goods for him, often told him that talking about the Slavic deities would make him a marked man, but it was times like this that those conversations that he held in generally jolliness, he had to consider seriously. There was more to many of these 'heathen' creatures than the church-goers gave credit to.

Another left, right, and... The stairs. Bishop breathed a sigh of relief and then inhaled deeply, preparing himself for the jog back up, taking two of the shoddy wooden planks at a time. His nostrils drank in the odor from above ground, replacing the smell of earth with fresh air, as he held his head high. As his head poked above the broken flooring, Bishop had to pause, pressing his frame against the hastily built railing as he listened.

The sounds were distant, but they were indeed there; the distinct mumbling of those talking amongst themselves and the shuffling of armor. Bishop cursed his luck as he honed in on the voices, listening. They were not speaking in German; the dialect sounded harsher, if that was possible, but he could not make out any words. Trading with people all over the continent taught him many languages – English, French, Italian, German, and even some of the Far East mumbo-jumbo. At this point, it did not matter; he could hear the clanking of metal and with those muttering in numbers like the men outside had to have been, they could only belong to one group.

Bishop snuck his way up the top of the stairs, around the perimeter of the husk, and toward the door. He still had his sword at the ready as he very cautiously cracked the door open. The orange tint of the landscape reflected the sun's descent, but he could not wait until night fell. If they found Fiona, his trip back to the League would be a slow and arduous one; not to mention, he could not let anything happen to his best girl.

Through the slit in the door, he could see several hulking armored shapes patrolling, scouring the ruins lazily while a group sat in the middle around a fire. The cross they bore told him his gut was right; Teutonic Knights. They seemed to be in no hurry and Bishop was not sure if they had picked up his trail somewhere along the way and were searching for him, or if they had been fed the same information he had about the Firstsworn being here, or perhaps they had no idea about him or the relic and they just happened to set up camp here. He did not want to take any chances.

Pressing the door open just enough for him to slink out, Bishop ran around and behind the far side of the house. If he was right, he could follow behind the husks to get him to Fiona and the knights would be none the wiser from where they sat. That was, until he escaped. That part he had not fully worked out yet.

As he peered around the path behind the house, he saw a guard going through the rotting beams of a decayed house, poking items with his foot. Bishop fell upon him in an instant; the cowl of his cloak over his head once more, Bishop dove in with his sword at the knights' known weak point – the neck. As his blade pierced the one bit of exposed flesh, he heard a gurgle and some red fluid expelled out the eye slit of the knight's helmet, but then he fell limp. Bishop caught the body, gently placing it down as he pulled his blade free. Some knights were smart enough to have their lining high enough or even wore gorgets, but many still had not learned that even the smallest of exposed flesh could become the biggest of targets.

As he stood up to continue on toward the stables, another knight rounded the corner of another building. Both men froze as they saw the other, but Bishop's instincts made him the first to strike. Before the man could even utter a shout for help, Bishop swung his legs low, sweeping the knight's legs out from under him. There was an auditory gasp of air as he hit the ground, combined with the rustling of his armor. Bishop dove upon him, blade held to strike when the man let out an ill-fated scream. It was already too late for him though; Bishop thrust the blade down deep into the eye slit, hearing a sickening squish that silenced him.

He pulled the sword free in a spout of blood and broke into a run toward where he left Fiona. He had not expected the man to get the chance to scream. Then again, he had not expected to have to kill anyone today; but Bishop knew better when he saw the cross. He knew, much like many others in his order, just what sort of evils had infiltrated the Teutonic Knights – abominations far worse than the skrzaks or the sacrificing shamans of the Prus.

He rounded the corner toward his goal and another guard stood in his way, just as confused as the last. Unwilling to try something as suave as the last attack, Bishop kept running toward the man and slammed his knee in his groin. The man coughed hard and the black-clad adventurer threw his adversary to the ground. The man clutched his jewels in pain and Bishop pulled the helmet free so that he could slam the end of his pommel into the knight's nose with a crunch.

He knew the man would be knocked out for some time, but something about the way his eyes were shaped, the strange almond form of them, mixed with the thick beard that appeared to be writhing, told Bishop he was correct. Not all of these knights were human anymore, and thus not all of them could easily be disposed of.

Hearing the call across the ruins from his first two kills snapped him back to action. He shoved the barricade aside hastily and then rushed in and grabbed Fiona's reins; the horse did not fidget or become frightened at her master's hurry. She bowed her head, as if giving him a sign she was ready to aid him. Tacking the saddle onto her once more, he brought himself upon her back and spurred her into action.

"Ride, Fiona! Away! We must hurry!"

The horse did as it was instructed without a hint of hesitation, bursting out of the stables and back down the path they had come. Bishop heard a whizzing noise pass by his head, and just to the side of him he witnessed a thick bolt cut the air. He bent down into the ride, gritting his teeth as he realized just how lucky he had been that Fiona had not been a few moments slower.

"Kill that man! Do *not* let him escape!" Someone behind Bishop was shouting, his voice a twisted dark mangle of a man's. It sent a chill down his spine. "Tear his limbs asunder for what he has done!"

Another few crossbow bolts whizzed by his head, another falling just short, and three arrows whooshed forward past him before he heard the sound of horses tearing the dirt road up behind him.

"C'mon, girl. I know you can do it. We have to get this beauty home or else I'm dead anyway," Bishop urged on, his head close to her neck. He knew she was giving it her all, and he began to wonder if his prized steed had what it took to outrun the Teutonic Knights. Had they been mortal men, he would not have had any doubts. But these strange demons… The League still was not sure just how capable they were and what dark magics they practiced. Who knew what they did to their horses? And actually, Bishop did not want to know what they did with their horses…

As the pines he had traversed through came up around him once more, Bishop smiled. If his luck was good, he could lose them in the forest; the leshiye and wood spirits could have their fun with the evil bastards. He turned his head to see just how far back the Teutonic Knights were, but he never saw.

The world around him spun and for a moment everything grew black; darker than the already shadowed realm of the trees blocking the fading orange out. He shook his head hard once he stopped rolling, trying to focus enough to gain his bearings. He saw a tree close by where he lay and hurled his body closer to it. He pulled himself to a crouch at the base of the tree, took several deep breaths, and then his hand rushed to the sword at his side, thankful it was still there, and withdrew the blade. Putting two and two together, he looked up at the tree and noticed the branch that was about a rider's height.

"I didn't mean this bastard, damned leshiye…" Bishop cursed under his rushing breath.

Somehow, he had managed to get out of sight of the Teutonic Knights, as he heard them pulling to a stop several feet from where he hid. He scanned the trees quickly around him and it was bittersweet to see no trace of Fiona.

"Split up and find him!" The demonic voice barked at his troops, who Bishop heard answer with a unison clanking of armor in what sounded like a salute. "His horse threw him around this area. He can't be far. We can't let him escape. Bring the wretch to me as soon as you find him!"

Bishop felt himself leap to his feet, ready and waiting to make a move. He was at the least glad that his armor did not produce the alerting jingles of metal that his foes did, but he would have really enjoyed the company of the boisterous karzełek force of Gorje's right about now. He stilled his breathing, concentrating on the many ringing rivets of armor all around him. Together, the soldiers marching around the forest sounded like one giant beast that prowled its way toward him as it threatened to burst down the tree he hid behind, but pinpointing each sound to a distance and direction allowed Bishop to consider all of his options.

One… Two…

Bishop spun his sword around and swung around the tree at neck height. His blade struck between the armor at the flesh beneath. The man gurgled as the blood rushed through the wound, swinging his arms to try and reach Bishop, but the strength was no longer in his veins. The man had worked the sword in tight and Bishop struggled for a moment before pulling the sword free.

Another man came shouting in behind the first and Bishop just narrowly dodged the incoming attack, using the butt of his sword to knock the man in the face with all of his might. His feet began moving before he could put a plan into motion. He used all of the strength his legs could muster, pumping him through the cover of the trees as the knights around him shouted out. He only hoped he could be a shadow amongst the branches of the trees and that the leshy spirits around him saw his plight.

Bishop duck and wove in between the foliage, trying his best to confuse his enemies as he circled around. As long as he could keep them scattered, he had a chance. He came up behind another one of the knights and ran his sword through his back. Whatever armoring the man wore was useless in its protection as the blade cleaved clean through. Bishop pulled his sword free once more, readying for the next attack as he felt the enemy rushing him, and narrowly dodged. Before he could try to make an offensive push, the man swung again and again, relentless in his attacks. Time after time Bishop wove out of the way, but after the fourth swing, in which he finally had to bring his blade up to parry, his heart sunk as he looked the enemy in the eyes.

"Oh, hell…"

The strange almond eyes of the commander stared ruthlessly down at Bishop as he pressed hard with his blade. He looked like a savage wolf, foaming at the mouth as he bore his pointed teeth, Bishop his prey. The more agile man pulled himself out of the deadlock, swinging low at the man's feet, but the knight was swifter than he appeared, bringing the blade over to block the attack with one hand. He swung up, knocking Bishop's blade back with the force of the attack, and the nimbler man had to roll his body out of the way to avoid a follow-up horizontal strike.

He barely had a moment to get back to his feet before the commander was swinging again. The black-clad man brought his sword up to parry attack after attack, but each time, the Teutonic Knight grew more savage and aggressive; the delay between each swing decreased and the sound as the blades met resonated louder each time Bishop's sword was forced back. He found himself retreating under the weight of the bigger man's stalking and hoped there were no enemies behind him that he had to be aware of.

Something caught Bishop's eye just beyond the knight, twinkling with the slightest of lights, and he took his eyes off of his foe for all of two seconds. Those moments were all his enemy needed as he charged in with his shoulder. Bishop felt the grip on the sword weaken and the blade flew free off to the side; he watched it with twinkles in his own eyes as the weight of the tackle stole all breath from his body. He hit the ground with an exclaimed grunt and watched with horror as the knight stalked over his body.

The man bent down, grabbing him by the front of his cloak; his eyes almost a demonic red.

"Where is it?! Where is the artifact?!"

Bishop grimaced as some of the spittle struck his face. He thought about spitting back at the leering monster, but something in his gut told him it would not be the wisest of ideas. The man leaned down further when he did not answer, almost getting right in his face, as if he could wrap his teeth around Bishop's head to tear it off.

Then, the man snapped back up, turning around. He was looking around him, sudden fear taking over his expression as his eyes bulged and something on his chin twitched. Bishop reached down to his boot and grabbed the dagger. When the man bent back down over him, he pulled the League member up slightly, as if to threaten him.

"Boy, where is the artifact?!"

"Right in front of your eyes!"

Bishop reached up while the man's hands held his cloak, over his arms, and stabbed him in the eye with the dagger. The knight screamed as he dropped Bishop and turned away. He fell to his knees, the agony burning out of his lungs more intense than anything Bishop had ever heard before. There was a bright light that seemed to emanate behind the man's plugged eye. Strange ooze began to seep out of his other eye, down and out his open mouth. As if he were a block of ice set out on the hottest day of summer, the man's flesh began to decay into that strange ooze, his bones disappearing as if nonexistent.

When finally the man became quiet, the last hiss of his scream becoming nothing but a bubble of the ooze, Bishop stood, wobbly at first, and walked over to the remains. The dagger sat on the edge of the puddle, untouched except for the bloodstain on the tip. He picked it up, hesitantly, and wiped the remnants off on the bottom of his cloak.

A silver dagger. He should have known. The League could easily hold the balance against the supernatural if they held a stockpile of their greatest weakness. Shaking his head, he stored the dagger once more.

He retrieved his sword in a hurry and leaned against a tree once more. He was surprised the knights had not come in search of the cries of their commander, but in trying to gain his bearings, he realized that there were more screams of death. He darted from one bark backing to the other, toward the source of the cries that seemed to be in every direction. If he could follow just one of them, maybe he would find out what was happening.

Eventually, he came upon one of the knights, walking in a circle as his blade shook in his hand. His helmet had been discarded and his eyes nervously looked in every direction. Bishop remained as a shadow in the trees as he watched, trying to discern the attacker. His eyes bulged as he watched a branch descend on the man, wrapping its spindly fingers around his face and lifted him in the air. The man tried to scream as he thrashed with his legs to be set free. The thin branches wove their way inside the man's mouth, and then he stopped thrashing, a strange gurgling sound emitting around the branch. The tips of the wood burst forth from the sockets of the man's eyes, exploding the orbs in a gory pop. The body went limp and the tree pulled the arm out from the body, letting it drop to the ground in a heap.

Bishop followed the limb back to the source and saw, for the first time, a leshy. The humanoid-like face seemed old and wizened, with a thick beard carved underneath a long, pointed nose. It stared back at him with inhuman eyes as Bishop froze after stepping away from the tree he was now unsure if it was alive or not. The leshy's mouth curved upward as it smiled at the man, nodding once before standing stock still again, the face disappearing.

"I believe this one is your ally."

Bishop jumped as he heard the deep voice speak softly behind him. When he turned, he saw another leshy, this one's face drawn heavy and down, no beard etched in its plump cheeks. It indicated toward a bush that opened up, and within, Fiona came trotting out to him. Bishop pet the horse on the muzzle and turned incredulously toward the forest spirit.

"Yes… I don't know what to say, but thank you."

"Human one fights against the dark ones. We watched human one when he traveled through our home. We were unaware if human one would cause destruction or simply pass through. This one's ally, 'Fiona' as she claims human one calls her, has spoken on human one's behalf. Fiona says human one is a good friend to her."

Bishop raised his eyebrows toward the horse, but then smiled. "Of course. Fiona's my best gal. I just had no idea she could speak."

"All things can speak. Four legged ones speak, trees of the forest speak, fish of the water speak, birds of the sky speak. All things do not speak the same tongue as humans speak."

"Right, of course, of course." Bishop nodded; it was simple

enough, but this was more than he expected to be dealing with. To see a leshy in person and for it to not want to kill him was amazing! "Thank you, kind leshy spirit. I must return to my people now that I am free of those vile beings."

Bishop bowed to the creature, but it did not move. He watched hesitantly as he got back on Fiona, unsure if he would really be allowed to leave. Before he took off, it raised a branch to call to him.

"Human one, the weapon that you have is imbued with great magic. The silver of the blade is something that the dark ones fear. Not just the Eldar Gods, but the evil spirits that still worship the gods of old, they all fear the blade that you have. Perun himself imbued the strength to ward off the darkness. Keep such treasure safe."

Bishop nodded to the tree spirit, and once he was sure it had finished speaking, he spurred Fiona into action once more, back to the League.

*****

After leaving the forest, his racing heart and mind had many things to think about. The karzełeks, the leshiye, the Teutonic Knight demons or whatever they were… The League had their sources of information, and they knew much about the ever-changing world, but maybe they did not know enough. This was in fact the reason why they had started amassing a storehouse of strange objects. They must have known what kind of effect the silver would have on the demonic knights.

He had been taught that if you were not a disciple of either set of gods, all things supernatural would stop at nothing to end a mortal's life. He did not know how to feel about these strange beings; the creatures of the Slavic Old Gods were real, right before his very eyes, yet he had grown up believing in a higher power, possibly the one God the Catholic faith preached about.

Yet, here, in these bizarre times, creatures he had only read about in information from the League's best spies had helped him and saved his life. Then there was the karzełek, who he also owed a life debt. Yet, then again, there were the skrzaks…

He looked toward the setting sun and smiled. He was glad to have the League's source of information, but there were many treasure troves yet to be discovered; he would learn about all of the strange wonders these earthquakes had brought with them in his journeys, himself, and make up his mind after he had further researched things firsthand instead of listening to the words of others.

The Swamp Hut

William Donohue

Wodnik
by Ivan Bilibin, 1934

The Grandmaster leaned back in his chair, his eyes narrowed behind his steepled fingers as he concentrated on the text. His eyes ached and he realized that the light was fading. With a sneer he noticed the tapers were dying down. "I must beat that boy for forgetting to replace those candles." He shook his head, leaning down toward the book, but the script was too difficult to make out in this dim. Throwing up his hands in frustration, he made an audible growl of disgust before leaning back once more. It was getting difficult for him to make out the words under normal situations, but in this light it was even harder.

"Can you get me some more light?" He then turned toward the doorway when he heard no immediate response; clearing his throat and lacing his words with an equal mixture of disgust and annoyance, "Albrecht, get me some light!"

The boy-attendant came scurrying in with some new tapers. "Yes my lord. Sorry my lord. I was just looking to the visitors."

"Visitors?" The Grandmaster sounded incredulous, half raising his body in the chair, and swatted the short stick he kept by his side to hit the lad.

"The men from the Papal See, Lord." He flinched, raising his arm slightly to absorb the blow.

The Grandmaster slammed the rod to the table, leaning forward to the boy with a vicious look on his face. "Why wasn't I told?"

"I was coming to tell you my lord. They just arrived and wished that I announce them to you while they prepared for Vespers."

"Vespers, oh yes…" the Grandmaster trailed off in thought, then rose quickly, closing the book he had. "Get my robes, Albrecht, and call the brethren to prayer. Do it now, you fool." Once the boy left he picked up the book and put it in his hiding place behind the bookcase. "No need to explain this to the Pope's men."And closed the compartment in the wall, then stopped to shake his head. "I must remember to beat that boy." He reached for the false beard on the table. He hooked it on carefully to hide the tentacles that had emerged from his chin as a blessing of the Eldar Gods. He smoothed out his robes, took a breath, and then moved toward the door. The guards opened the doors to allow him to greet the Papal representatives. He made sure his beard was hidden and hoped the Papal representatives did not notice.

The men rose slowly, but with confidence. "Grandmaster, we had hoped to see you in Vespers. There were not many there. A Holy Order such as yours should take a more active role in faith."

"Yes, brother-inquisitor. Thank you. I was in my private chapel in prayer when you came. Had I known, I would have joined you. My boy was told not to disturb me, but he takes things too literally. I will beat him appropriately later."

To the Grandmaster, it was if the Gods had given him more gifts, and he carefully stroked his beard, careful not to dislodge it, but massaging his tentacles underneath.

"Please do, Grandmaster; do not let him get too comfortable. We have need of your help. Might we speak in your room?" He pointed back toward his quarters and without waiting for a reply continued on through.

The Grandmaster nodded after the fact and motioned with his hand as they went in. He fixed his beard again and joined them. In truth, he was surprised that the Inquisition had time in between rooting out the heretic and hidden Moors and Jews in Spain to ask him a favor in person. But then again, they were supposed to root out heresy everywhere – ironically they didn't know much about his activities.

"We bring news that King Jan Olbrach has died and the Polish nobles are meeting to elect his brother, the Grand Duke as King. We fear that these Poles are bad enough, but the Lithuanians are just heretics beneath the surface. We have championed your cause in Rome that you should be supported in your noble endevor, but the Polish King had friends in the curia. This Alexander, however, has retreated into the pagan past, from what we hear. We just need the proof to push a new crusade against them. We need your help, Grandmaster, in finding evidence – real or otherwise."

The Grandmaster outwardly portrayed a stern, somewhat shocked, expression, nodding sympathetically. "Any aid I may provide, will be my pleasure." It took all he had not to smile broadly, but he could feel his tentacles were wriggling with dark joy.

*****

Michael Glinski found the Grand Duke in his study surrounded by papers. The Ducal Palace was a formidable looking place, but security was lax. There were guards outside the doors, but any well-meaning assassin could have made in it there. Alexander was not like his brother Jan Olbrach – he was more cerebral, not a brawler. He didn't look up but just pointed to the chair across from him, "Sit down Michael. Help yourself to the wine."

"You unnerve me the way you do that. What if it wasn't me?"

"I know the sound of your steps; that clove scent you wear; and the sound you make as you enter a room. If I didn't recognize any of those I would have pulled the dagger out of the pocket in the desk just in case. "

"You worry me, my lord. I'm sorry to disturb you, but I just received two troubling correspondences. Unfortunately, both bad. First, your brother, the king, is dead. The Senate is meeting to prepare for an election to make you his successor." He paused, waiting for a response, but there was just the familiar silence, until the Duke cleared his throat and paused before answering in a very measured cadence.

"I will mourn my brother in my way. I am not sure I want the crown, but it is what is best for the family. I suspect the second is the quakes near Starybogow?" There was no hint of expression on his face when he said it. "If my brother is dead, there is nothing I can do and the ship of state must go on. If there was an earthquake in Starybogow, we have bigger issues we must deal with."

Glinski raised an eyebrow, not so much surprised, but accepting. "I suppose you have your sources?"

Again without looking up from the paper he was reading, he reached to a pile and handed Glinski a document along with a small wooden box with brass fittings and an iron lock, then looked up at him. "Give this to your agents. They need to get to the town and assess what help we need to give the monastery. I had some reports from our agents, but they have abruptly stopped. My Jasek is totally blank now. He gets no messages; senses nothing. We need to re-open the communication."

Glinski looked around, but did not see the King's fool anywhere. He nodded, took the paper along with the box, and left the room, moving down the corridor to his chambers. The haiduk guards presented their halbards as he passed them and entered his quarters. Two men and a woman waited there for him and stood up when he entered.

He slid the contents in his hands across the table he used for correspondence and flopped down in his leatherbacked chair. He motioned to the people standing there. "Please sit down," he pointed to a small table near his desk. "Have some bread and cheese if you'd like." He poured himself a glass of wine and offered some to each, which they all accepted.

"You all know we are locked in a struggle with the Teutonic Knights. You also know that our Duke is trying to protect the Old Gods and our ancient ways. What you may not know is why the news of these quakes in Starybogow is tied to this.

"When the knights first came to the north at the invitation of Conrad of Masovia, they were to help beat back the 'pagan' Prus. At one point they might have been good Christians, but soon after setting up a base at Truso, before founding Elblag on the Baltic, many were infected by the Eldar Gods. Over the past two hundred or so years, several of the previous Grandmasters and senior leadership were 'gifted' special things by the dwellers of the deep. It is not as well known in Europe and many of those who hear this think that we are just spreading rumors, but at Neva and Grunwald, the growing power of the Eldar Gods was beaten back by commanders wielding swords of Perun. The Jagiellonians have kept this secret fight going, knowing what the world would face if they were not successful. We face one of those points in history that could pivot on what may happen next. There are those in the Teutonic Order who do not know the full truth, but many do and have willingly joined for the power they think the Eldar Gods can give them." Glinski got up and walked around, rubbing his hands together, pointing and bringing his hands back together in frenetic energy.

"The minions of the Eldar, in league with some of the minions of the darker Old Gods, have opened the void. Some have escaped, along with some of the Old Gods. The minions will no doubt try to bring more through. We have people in Starybogow to try and stop this, but we have lost contact with them. You need to get there, re-open the communication, and advise me for the Duke as to what is going on. The river has changed course, so you will have to go on foot for part of the journey, but also you will go under cover of tinkerers. A caravan is leaving in the morning, you will join them. Here is some money to get you going," he threw a small leather purse on the table that hit with a clink. "You will go to the monastery and meet with them to appraise the situation."

He pointed to the paper and the box. One of the men looked to the other with a raised eyebrow, the girl gave them a disapproving look. The paper was sealed, not by the ducal seal, but with the insignia of Perun.

Glinski continued, ignoring their motions. "They will have homing pigeons. You take two pigeons with you as well should you need to send a message in route. Here are your silver rings. Make sure you use them."

He held the rings up, studying them carefully before he handed them over. Silver was one of the things that could hurt the Eldar Gods as well as damage some of the darker Old Gods. The rings were good to punch them with and had a point that could do some damage. Even though they all carried silver daggers that were clinched to their wrists, the ring was still a great boon for emergencies. Then he handed them their necklaces with the amber pendants. Amber held the power of the Old Gods and the Eldar ones feared it; that is why it was so prevalent along the shore, acting as a barrier to keep the watchers of the deep at bay.

The three had no questions. They were used to missions for Glinski. They knew that they could die one hundred different ways along a lonely road and no one would be the wiser. Instinct, guile, and a little martial prowess had allowed them to survive this long. There would be no hero's welcome at the end of this, and no one but Glinski would know, but this was for revenge, plain and simple; it would always be about revenge. They simply nodded and left. The first man, Jan, turned to the woman Jadwiga, then to the second man David and asked, "Okay, who do you want to be your husband this time?" They laughed and kept going.

After the hall had quieted down, unbeknownst to Glinksi, a figure moved from the shadows dressed in black. No one would notice the missing guard until morning. He checked to make sure he would not be seen and went out a window into the yard below. From the crack in his door, Glinski noted the man leaving and knew the plan was in place.

*****

The caravan was set to leave Vilnius at dawn the next morning through the Trocki Gate. It was a hodge-podge group that would grow and contract depending how far they were going. It was dangerous to travel alone and caravens like this gave the members a sense of security.

Most of the participants were going to Grodno and who knew where else from there. One of the powerful nobles, Pawel Sapieha, provided an escort for that leg of the journey as they were going to escort some Sapieha relative back to the Lithuanian capital. Since the noble did not pay his private troops very well, and they had no incentive to save the people in the caravan, the members all chipped in a little more money as insurance that the guards would still protect them should they be attacked.

The fourth wagon from the end belonged to Jan Roback and his pseudo-wife Jadwiga, accompanied by her brother, David. Owing to the hour and the distance to travel, the participants were happy, yet quiet as they moved out through the Trocki Gate, past the new walls that were just being started.

The last wagon was a late addition, just a cloth merchant and his assistant. He said they had traveled from the Tartar Khanate with rare cloth and were supposed to be in an earlier caravan going to Warsaw, but delays kept him from leaving and he did not dare venture out on his own to try and catch-up. He spoke with a strange accent, describing himself as Wallachian. He was quiet for a merchant and discouraged his assistant from talking to the others as well. His assistant was a boy who seemed mute and the merchant would speak to him in a guttural tone that the agents could not recognize.

The first night passed without incident. They camped in a protective circle in a hollow off the road, away from anyone that might wander by. They kept the fires low to avoid detection and the Sapeiha guards took turns keeping watch with the travelers. There were plenty of stars and all was calm except for the horses, but they always seemed nervous.

They all talked amongst themselves, swapping stories of their travels or asking about foreign lands; all except the Wallachian. Jadwiga had an ear for languages, which had always done them well in the past, but she could not make out what he was saying when he spoke to the boy. The next morning when they set out, she voiced her fears to the others.

"I can't put my finger on it, but there is something wrong with that cloth merchant." Jadwiga turned to look back down the line at the man bringing up the rear. "I could feel it when we stopped. The horses noticed too. Animals can always tell."

David lay in the wagon behind the seat, cleaning the dirt under his nails with his dirk, then propped himself up on one elbow. "You know, Jan, I did notice the hobbled horses seemed to move away from the area he was parked. And yet, his own horses seem too lethargic to care."

"You know, if you try using water once in a while you would avoid playing with that knife like that." Jan turned to push his compatriot then stopped suddenly with a shiver, as if a cold blast of air was hitting him.

Jadwiga touched his arm. "Its okay, we'll be stopping soon." She then turned toward David with a look of concern.

Jan was sensitive to disturbances in this reality, which is the skill he brought to their party. Jadwiga knew that sometimes his experiences had a lasting effect. "He'll be fine. Just too much exposure to demons." They all went quiet and just kept looking ahead at the rumps of horses.

*****

The next morning, the caravan was slow starting as two of the members had not hitched their horses. The group had pitched their camp in an open section of forest. The area they were traveling was marshy and full of scrub pines, and the leader assured them it was the best place they could stop between rest areas. It seemed like they were not covering the distance they would have expected.

"I think that merchant is pulling us back," Jan laughed." We couldn't be moving any slower." Normally these type journeys had predisposed rest areas, since camping in the open was not recommended, but this trip felt like it was going slowly nowhere.

There was a cry as one of the men who went to use privacy came running out of the woods. The wagon master, a big brute named Osok, ran over to the spot. Jan joined him, feeling as if his head would explode with each step. The man who had originally gone to relieve himself, had done so in his britches. He was standing there pointing when Osok and Jan came up. It was the two members of the spice merchants guild gutted from sternum to groin. Almost by rote, each of the remaining members came over to gape, then turn away.

"Wolves!" the wagon master said it so firmly, everyone in earshot nodded in assent. He acted too calm and matter-of-fact for Jan. "This is why you shouldn't wander too far away from camp, especially at night. There are most likely wolfen in this area. I have heard it before."

Jadwiga, however, turned to Jan."Didn't anyone hear anything? I think we would have heard something." Then she turned to the wagon master, "If there were wolfen in this area why would we stop here or why wouldn't you tell us?"

Osok stopped and the smile disappeared from his face. "You are a woman, you don't understand. Women never understand." Then he turned away and yelled to his assistants,"Bury those bodies before they attract more unwanted attention."

"Yes," David said firmly in agreement, stepping in from of Osok and then loud enough for the others to hear, "if it was wolves we would have heard this. Did anyone hear anything? What about the guards?" It was then he noticed that the guards were nowhere to be seen.

Jadwiga chimed in again,"We would have heard wolves, Osok. Where are the guards?"

"I don't know. It was the guards then!" He stomped around in a circle and once again the rest of the group nodded. "Yes, the guards."

"Where are the guards?"Jan raised his voice to a yell, not believing that anyone would agree with this.

"I don't know. They must have killed these two and run off – and we paid them extra!" Osok threw his hands up as if in disgust at guards reneging on a business deal and the whole idea of wolfen seemed to disappear.

Suddenly one of the other merchants piped up as Osok walked away. "Who gets their goods?"

Osok, turned on his heel, moving everyone out of the way and got toe to toe with the merchant. The wagon master was a full head taller and looked down on him deadly serious as he jabbed his finger into the chest of the merchant, as if punctuating each syllable. "Unclaimed goods are the property of the wagon master. I will dispose of them as I see fit."

At this point Jadwiga piped in."Aside from the fact that we are now defenseless, shouldn't we hurry to bury these poor folks?"

Osok got two adzes, while Jan and the cloth merchant offered to bury the men.

"Why would the guards murder these two when they could

have gotten us all? No robbery, just murder. It makes no sense." Jan looked at the Wallachian expecting an answer, but only received raised eyebrows and stoic continuation of burying the spice merchants. Every other strike in the ground they seemed to find rocks. Jan stopped after a little while of this and looked around. The clearing was man-made. This was once one of the sacred groves of the Old Gods. There was probably a settlement nearby here. These stones, the foundation of a wall.

Carefully, Jan took off his ring and laid it on one of the stones in a way that the Wallachian could not see - the silver ring turned red, indicating the dark ones' trace was present. This was done on purpose to foul the land.

*****

Jan and the Wallachian buried the merchants as best they could and placed some stones over the grave to keep the wolves off. Osok stood, watching them, in turns telling them what they were doing wrong, but not really helping. When the group finally got moving again, Jan looked up to try to locate the sun in order to gauge the time of day, but no matter where he looked, he could not find it. It seemed instead like dawn – or even dusk. There was a haze that hung low in the sky. It did not seem like fog, yet it did not let the sun through.

Osok moved the wagons around. There were originally six, although only five now had their drivers still with them. In addition to Jan, Jadwiga, and David in their ruse as tinkerers, there was the cloth merchant, a tinsmith, the trader who had asked about the deceased spice merchant's goods, the wagon of the spice merchants, and a doctor with his apprentice.

They had traveled for a little over an hour and still saw no sign of humans in the desolate track they traveled down. Jan noticed the landscape began to take on a marshy appearance, to the point that the road narrowed and forced the travelers to stay toward the center at the risk of getting bogged down. Finally this reached a river with some ferrymen there, and Jan turned to his compatriots and gave them an uneasy look. While many ferries were set up to accommodate travelers, it seemed as if these ferrymen knew about their approach, as if they were waiting for this caravan. The mist and fog continued to plague their journey with the air remaining grey.

"Where are we Osok?"

"I don't know for sure, this doesn't look familiar, but I've traveled this road hundreds of times." He crossed himself three times and spit (did the man wince?). He went up to what looked like the leader to negotiate passage.

The men and women that crewed the two ferries all looked slack eyed with high foreheads; almost as if they were all related. Osok spoke and gestured to the men, at times animated as he tried to get his point across. After a few minutes he came back, huffing and puffing before breaking into a big smile.

"I'll use some of the money from the merchants to pay for this. We must have missed a turn off a while back, but crossing with these ferrymen should put us back on course."

Jan tried to make eye contact with the Wallachian again, not feeling comfortable with what Osok offered as an explanation, but the dark man would not look him in the eye.

There was grumbling from the doctor; there was *always* grumbling from him, yet if you asked him a question directly he would smile and act as if you were best friends. Now, however, he was loud in his complaints. "How did you go off course? This is not a boat at sea. You are supposedly an experienced guide. Bah. You are costing me time and money…"

The odd ferrymen moved into position to bring the travelers across the river. The ferries had a gate that flopped down which allowed man and beasts to enter from the ground level along with the wagons. The horses didn't like getting on, making all sorts noises and shying away from entering.

"Looks like these guys have been breeding too much amongst their own kind," David muttered under his breath.

The ferrymen were slow moving and slower of thought. All the time, they stood there with dull looks on their faces – they did not seem very bright. It looked like they had lived along the river and marshes so long they started to take on the appearance of fish. Before Osok left, David noticed that he looked back at the leader of the ferrymen with a pleading look in his eyes and the ferryman seemed to give him a slight perceptible nod. He stared too long and the ferryman caught him looking. David held the look for a second and noticed the ferryman smile before turning away.

David approached his compatriots and started to secure the wagons before loading them on the ferry. His compatriots came over as he fussed with some straps. "I think something is very wrong."

Jan and Jadwiga exchanged looks, but said nothing as they kept helping David.

"This was no accidently meeting. This was premeditated."

"Is this just paranoia or did you actually see something?" Jadwiga gave a quick sideways glance to see if anyone was watching, but Jan tapped her pinkie, indicating that they were being watched.

As a group, they adjusted their daggers and their rings. Jan felt nothing, so there was no Eldar Gods in play. The question was how many of the Slavic dark gods had breached the void and what condition where they in?

*****

The ferries were finally loaded and the ferrymen, which included some women, started to move across the river. Using poles and pull ropes, the flat bottomed boats made slow but steady going, until the ferries suddenly stopped in the middle of the river. At first, the ferrymen tried to keep moving but then David realized they were stuck. Suddenly, the ferrymen dove overboard into the river and the passengers became frantic, trying to move the boat forward or back. Jan, David, and Jadwiga tried to help them, but the other boat was held firmly in place. Jan and Jadwiga looked at each other along with the Wallachian, then over to the other ferry with the doctor, merchants, and Osok. He could see them pointing, waving, and yelling, while Osok kept shouting to the ferrymen swimming away. Then the ferries both 'bounced', as if something ran into them. The passengers kept yelling. Then, the boats started rocking and small hands reached from the water.

Jan felt as if a pit dropped in his stomach. Something or someone had agitated the mermen, the water spirits; the *wodniks*. As they made themselves known, surfacing from the depths as they latched to the side of the boat, Jan noticed that there were also females leading them; the *wodniks* would often be alone, but combined with a *rusalk*a, they were a force to be reckoned with. Someone called out, "I wish we had a bigger boat."

Then, the chaos really ensued.

The men were scrambling while the horses tried to leap out

of the boat, but were still connected to their wagons. Osok fell in the water and as he tried to climb back in, scaly green, moist hands pulled him back under. Jan could see there was a look of disbelief on his face as he was pulled under.

Jan's focus returned to his own boat and he grabbed an oar. The Wallachian, as if he knew what to do, started sprinkling pepper on the water creatures and they recoiled enough that the boat seemed to be floating again. The passengers in the other boat were not as lucky. One was knocked into the water by a frantic horse, another was too close to the side and was pulled in by one of the wodniks, who leaped out of the water and grabbed one of the merchants with webbed hands, and pulled him back into the water. Jan and Jadwiga slashed at them with their silver daggers to help keep them away as they tried to move the boat closer to shore.

On the opposite bank, a ferryman, who was in fact a large, powerful woman, tried to pull them across with a guide rope. As soon as the passengers realized they were free, they all joined in to pull the boat across. The Wallachian took off something from around his neck and dunked it in the water – it was amber! The wodniks and rusalka backed off, but it proved to be another oddity about this 'Wallachian'. Jadwiga could not move quick enough to get off; jumping into the water up to her knees before it hit shore. Immediately, she felt hands pulling at her. She screamed, kicking the water with her back to the shore and almost fell if it were not for David reaching over to pull her along to land.

She fell to the ground, but almost did a crabwalk to get away from the riverbank. She was breathing heavy, almost hyperventilating when Jan came up to her and started to shake when he held her close. It was at that point she started sobbing and babbling, looking towards the water with fear and shooing the air with her hands as if she could will it to go away. A few minutes ago, the water was a bubbling mess, now, except for the wreckage floating away, everything was calm. At that point, they noticed the men of the Teutonic Knights waiting for them just beyond the clearing. With no place to escape, they tried to get themselves as together as they could.

*****

The brothers and the sergeants–at-arms were accompanied by some of the local folk who looked odd, and seemed as if they were inbreed over generations. Nonetheless, no matter how they looked, the spears they poked were just as sharp as the brethren knights who stood by them. The survivors of the water attack were handled roughly by the knights and they were all piled into the Wallachian's wagon. His apprentice was very nervous, but the three spies tried to remain resolved to keep their heads about them.

Jadwiga feigned scared and confused, as they should have been if they were normal people, but having survived a dozen or so missions for the Grand Duke they realized that brashness often made bullies back down.

"You have no right to stop us, we are good Christians of the king. We are simple travelers." Out of the side of her mouth she asked,"Do you think this will work?"

"It won't. Hush." Jan gave her a daggered look as he narrowed his eyes. After a moment, he sighed."This is not going according to plan."

Jan tried to let David know what they were discussing in low tones. They could not trust the Wallachian or his apprentice any more than the knights. In truth, none of them were safe. If the knights knew the trio were on a mission from the duke, they would torture them for information; the Wallachian was a merchant and a foreigner; no one would miss him. This was a no win situation.

"We all are in trouble," piped up the Wallachian. "I have to get my merchandise to Starybogow. Should something happen to me, I need one of you to take something to the gatekeeper." He leaned in closer to the trio. "There's a pouch under my seat. It is of the utmost importance, the boy will know about it. He can help you."

"Given our present situation, why should we, you dark hearted heathen?" Jan had no love for the man who had been silent until now.

"Because we both serve the same master; I also serve the duke, but I bring an artifact that can't fall into the hands of these foul servants of the dark one."

Jan narrowed his eyes, unsure of what to say, but taken aback by the man's words nonetheless. They moved out and Jan looked the man in the eyes, "We will speak more on this in a bit – I hope." The group was pulled out of the wagon and marched through the village.

They remained quiet as the knights jostled them forward into the village.

*****

The knights and their captives wound their way through the brush for a short time and came to a clearing by a marsh. The village smelled of damp and rot which matched the buildings and the people. As they entered, Jan thought he saw figures in the woods. They appeared to be two or three young women. They could not possibly be from the village – they appeared lithe and ethereal, like mists, and moved at the edges of the trees. Jan was transfixed and hadn't thought to ask his other companions when the Wallachian spoke, breaking the spell.

"There are allies here. I'm not sure they can help us, but should the opportunity arise, we must all be prepared."

They were taken from the wagon and had their hands tied and separated. David and Jan were locked in a shack; Jan noticed the Wallachian and his apprentice were taken elsewhere. Jadwiga was moved with some women in another place. As they were being led off, the sergeant called 'Hoff' called out to them.

"We will be coming for you when we are ready. We are going to find which one of you is in the in the pay of the duke and where the artifact is. That person may be of use to us. The rest we will probably kill if you are lucky. Be prepared." Then he let out a cackle that sent shivers down their spine. Jan and David were paraded past a large flat stone mounted near the water. It seemed to have dark stains on it, which did not make them feel any more comfortable.

As Jan and David sat in their hovel, they could see some armed villagers standing outside the porous walls, eyes fixed on them. "They look more like fish then men." David just nodded and looked towards their compatriots in the other huts. "I swear they are making clicking noises when they talk to each other. It is very subtle, but I can hear it." He noticed the village headman was talking to the sergeant. It seemed if the brothers had gone elsewhere, and the villagers did not like what the sergeant was telling them.

*****

Jadwiga was thrown roughly into a stable where one of the fishmen stood watch over her. Behind him, in the background, she could see movement. It was the wood spirits again moving about, looking as if scouting the area. If the men-at-arms and fishmen cold see them, they gave no sign. The soldiers were looking through the wagon.

Jadwiga could see the soldiers rifling the wagon looking for something. Perhaps they knew about the package the trio were carrying. How could they know? Too much didn't make sense, as if the enemy knew about their plans.

*****

The Wallachian stood looking at the Teutonic warriors going through his wagon. His apprentice, Wart, sat on the ground rocking back and forth working himself into frenzy. As this went on, the activity of the wood spirits intensified and the wind picked up. The master looked at him with his palms down and the boy slowed down. He noticed the village headmaster and the sergeant arguing. The sergeant kept poking his finger into the chest of the headman and it seemed to be annoying the leader of the fishmen when suddenly the man was stabbed in the back of his head. A surprised expression appeared on the sergeant's face before he fell to the ground. The Wallachian grabbed his apprentice and moved towards the back wall.

*****

The villagers wanted their sacrifices. That was the agreement. "The Ancient Ones demand a sacrifice."

Hoff shoved the headman hard."You will get your sacrifices when we say – if at all. We'll wait for the commander, and when he says so, and who you get, then you can play with the nice folks."

"No unbeliever. We were promised suitable sacrifices by the next moon – tonight. If you will not give them to us we will take them."

"Only if you want this village burnt down, you savage." He spit at the ground and turned to leave, when the headman pointed to his own ear. A woman walked up to the sergeant to offer him a drink. When he went to push her away she pivoted on her back heel and round-housed a short knife into the back of Hoff's skull. The rest of the villagers had quietly surrounded the men at arms and most were killed.

*****

As David and Jan watched, it appeared as if their misfortune would be relieved. One man was left and he fought until he could fight no more. Wounded and bloody, he was overcome by the villagers. The women were the cruelest to him; they could tell this by his screams. He was brought behind a shed, towards the flat stone. They were followed by the remainder of the village who seemed bent on joining in the blood. One villager was left at each of the huts to guard the prisoners.

*****

From her captivity, Jadwiga could hear the chanting. She thought the villagers might let them go free, but then she realized they were substituting one set of monsters for another. The guard was transfixed on the events going on by the stone. He was sniffing the air as if he was taking in the scent of the blood. Jadwiga noticed movement off to the side. It was the wood spirits who had moved toward the stable. The spirits were part ethereal, part feral. They flitted about with wings, but had bark-like exterior. They sang, sing-song-like in light verse that seemed to keep the guard like stone in place. The spirits moved slowly, but kept singing, transfixing the fishman while others of their kind let Jadwiga go. The spirits released her from her prison and her bonds. While the man was still transfixed, she dispatched him with a small knife she kept in her boot.

The wood spirits moved, fading away back into the woods where they came from. Grabbing the guard by the heels she brought the body back to stable. Taking the dead guard's spear, she moved around to the hut where David and Jan were kept. Getting their attention, they occupied the guard with their shouts when she stabbed him with the spear. Freeing them quickly, they took the dead guard's weapon then snuck up on the guard at the Wallachian's and killed him quietly, picking up his weapon and ready to face the balance of the enemy. The two men worked quickly to get the wagon ready while Jadwiga got the Wallachian and his apprentice.

*****

Jan tried to organize the survivors as quickly he could. Each of them went about their business as quickly as they could, but the Wallachian went to the wagon and pulled the small woolen bag from under the front seat and shoved in into his sash.

"We need to get the boy out of here; now!" There was a sense of anxiety in the man's voice that was not there before. "He is the prize, we need to get him out of here."

Suddenly Jan understood that this was a double blind. The boy had been ignored and in the background. They were led to believe there was a valuable object they were to guard – but the boy was the object. They had been set up as bait, and if not for the delay, the boy would not be here.

The men tried to muffle the sound of the horses and wagon as they pointed them in the direction out of town. The townsfolk were satiated for the moment, focused on the sacrifices, and started to work toward their next victims, walking around in a stupor that seemed like a sense of euphoria. When they finally noticed their captives in the midst of escaping, they were suddenly roused into action and with a roar and charged toward the wagon with their prizes.

Jan, David, and Jadwiga managed to get the horses hitched and moving with the boy protected by the Wallachain. David took the reins and tried to get the wagon moving quickly. Jan saw the townsmen coming toward them on the run and threw a spear toward the lead townsman, which hit him square in the chest. This halted them for a second, while they decided who was brave enough to tempt death again. David didn't wait and started the horses into a gallop, making distance between them and the fish people. The townspeople ran, but could not keep up with the horses and went back to mount up.

Jan was not sure where they were going, but he knew he needed to get away – anywhere – as quickly as possible and tried to direct David down the road. They came to a fork in the path and his natural inclination was to go left.

"Go right!" shouted the boy out of nowhere, and David instinctively yielded to the order, taking the right fork which ran parallel to the water. He could see a ford ahead after a short distance, where the river bisected the road. As they closed on the crossing, figures emerged from the water. They were not the fishmen, but looked like their comrades; those that died in the crossing of the big river.

Their faces were pale, almost white, with blank eyes. David tried to whip the horses into a frenzy, to rush at the bodies at full speed to run them over, but the horses shied at the approach and were hesitant to keep going. The water was only waist deep, but they were stuck in the middle with the dead closing in on them. Jan and Jadwiga poked at them with spears, but it only stuck them without stopping them. They were not close enough to use their daggers and if they waited that long it might be too late.

*****

The fishmen and women got some horses and made their way after the prisoners. They were so far behind they could not see where the fugitives had gone. Rather than taking the right fork, they took the left, sure that was the direction they were heading to avoid the water. They had gone about one hundred yards when they saw a troop of horsemen moving toward them. They were brother knights and they were prepared for battle.

*****

Brother-knight Randolph was talking to Brother-knight Mortimer making leisurely time toward the village. "The Commander will be pleased with this, Brother. Once we get those stooges of the Grand Duke to tell us where the artifact is, the mongrels in that village can do what they want with them."

"It is too bad they have not elevated themselves sufficiently to enjoy the blessing of the Eldar race. Those who do not serve the will of the Eldar Gods sufficiently will always perish."

The force of twelve mounted sergeants and twenty infantry continued in this manner for another twenty minutes when they came upon a man to the side of the road sitting with his back against a tree. He was dressed like one of the infantry and was wounded in several visible places, including the head and hands. One of the foot soldiers came up quickly to examine him, followed by a brother-surgeon. The rest of the infantry came up and set up a perimeter. The surgeon examined him. After a moment he hurriedly called for water and then gently forced some down his throat. The man choked and coughed, but once he settled down, his words were no more than a whisper. The surgeon nodded and ran up to the brother-knight making sure not to make eye contact. "Brother…"

"Yes, soldier. Are you going to leave me in suspense?"

"No, my lord. The soldier is named Franz. He was part of the garrison left at the fish town. The headman wanted to sacrifice the captives at the new moon despite the orders to wait. The villagers rose up against the garrison and killed them."

"How did Granz survive?"

"Franz, my lord. He said he was able to fight some off before they got the better of him. He was only able to crawl off once his attacker was killed by one of ours, sir. He hoped he would find us to warn us."

"Very well then. Sergeant! Get the men in battle formation and get ready to move on the double. Brother Stephen, once we get to that village, kill all of them. They are no use if they can't follow orders. Burn it all. If they want a sacrifice to the Eldar Gods I will give them one."

"Brother-surgeon, will that soldier survive?"

"Yes, my lord."

"Kill him." His words were ice cold as he thrust his arm out toward the wounded soldier.

"My lord…" The surgeon sputtered, staring at the commander in shock.

"He is a coward. He should have fought and died with his companions. We kill cowards." The man sneered as he stared down at the surgeon, his almond shaped eyes never showing the slightest hint of emotion. "Kill him."

"But my lord, he tried to warn us. We may still be in time."

"Do not question me, Brother."

"Yes, my lord." The surgeon turned and went to the wounded soldier asking for his bag. He knelt down beside him and pulled out a jug. He lifted his head to the side to look at a wound in his neck. As the man relaxed, he stabbed the soldier with a small blade and held him there until life drained away. The jug was held next to the stable wound and collected the life blood. When he was done, he dropped the body as if it were a plank of wood and handed the jug to his assistant to put a stopper in. Randolph turned to Mortimer and the knight snapped to attention.

"When we are done here, kill that surgeon too. No one questions my orders. Especially not in front of the men. Bad form."

"Yes, Brother Randolph. Consider it done."

Randolph sneered once more as he turned toward the town. He spurred his horse forward, bending into the stride as he led the charge.

*****

Jan and Jadwiga kept poking the dead specters with poles, but it just stopped one while another moved forward. The Wallachian kept saying incantations and creating small shields that temporarily stopped them. The boy kept rocking back and forth mumbling to himself. The horses were stopped and were shimmying back. The undead were closing in, the horses were panicking, and there was so much noise and motion that Jan felt sick from his head to his stomach. The boy flung his hands out and there was a bright light. Jan raised an arm to shield his eyes, but as the boy cried out, he swore he saw a blast of energy that sent the specters flying back. It stunned friends and foe alike, but the Wallachian and Jan recovered quickly and grabbed the reins blindly and got the horses moving and across the water to the other bank before the undead could recover. In the deeper areas of the water, the mermen watched with disappointment and they went back beneath the surface. Slowly, the dead specters sank back where they came from and the waters were calm again.

*****

The town was still some distance away when they encountered a group of the strange fish people. By the looks on their faces, they were just as surprised to see the brothers as the brothers to find them here. Randolph felt the hatred tighten in his gut as he saw the weapons they were brandishing. Fools,

"Let us pass."

The knights just stood there, stone faced, not understanding the man.

"We need to go after the strangers."

Still, the knight stared at the strange people and did not say anything. Then a sneer formed as he raised one hand, causing arrows to fly from the treeline, knocking village men off of their horses. The fish-people stared in confusion, but the knights charged in, slashing them down.

Most of the people were still by the stone slab, with blood running off it. There were bodies floating away in the water that could not be determined.

Neither man, women, or the small emaciated children were spared the knights' wrath. Those within sword length were cut down quickly. Those that evaded the knights were hunted by the foot soldiers. Torches suddenly appeared and soon the buildings were ablaze. Before long, the whole place was a burning inferno; smoke and embers flew everywhere combined with flames and screams. It was a frenzied hell. There was no thought of plunder, no actions against civilians, just death. Soon the sandy ground and lagoon were awash in blood.

Brother Mortimer was covered in blood and gore as he rode up to Brother Randolph. "The men were upset because there was nothing of value in the village. The people were could not be sold as slave and the women were ugly. When they are done this place will have never existed."

Brother Randolph turned to him and raised his visor, squinting as the sun was setting. "What was that man saying? Not that it mattered; it was probably a lie."

Brother Mortimer screwed up his face and thought. "I don't know. I have never gotten the hang of that language. Our translator seems to have been killed. It just doesn't matter. They are not worth worrying about." Then the brother just trailed off and looked out on the bodies floating in the lagoon. "We didn't find anything in their possessions. Maybe it was never there or these animals buried it."

"The commander was quite adamant on the artifact and the spies. We need to come back with something." Then the knight turned his horse and rode along the water's edge.

*****

Along the river, back in the reeds a small boy lay still. He was the only one who was still alive from his village. He was hurt, having been slashed by one of the men-at-arms, but he laid still as he was taught and knew that the Eldar Gods would watch over and protect him until he was strong enough to take his own revenge, and hopefully ascend.

*****

The wagon started to slow down after about a mile or so. The horses and passengers were tired and dripping with sweat alike, but for different reasons. David dropped the reins and the horse just meandered on the path as the passengers slumped down in the wagon. As far as the Wallachian could tell, they were heading in the right direction, going west.

"It seems we were both a part of the Grand Duke's plan."

"So it seems. Did he alert you about us?"

"No, my friends. He did not." There was a silence between them as they moved along. "My name is Georg. I was born in Constantinople and escaped during the slaughter when it fell. I claim to be Wallachian to keep people from questioning me too much. I was preparing a group of trained fools when the city fell. I wanted to forestall this day, to open the gate, but I was too late. Now fifty years later we are here, but we are not safe."

There was the possibility of bandits, slavers, Teutonic Knights, and wild animals that could stop them, but they needed to keep going to Starybogow. The sun started setting and soon they would be in the dark; probably best to make camp in a hollow and hope for the best, but then they saw the fairy lights and for a second they knew they were safe.

Strength in Faith

Brandon Rospond

Cardinal Carafa,
16th Century engraving

The sun peaked in just enough from the arched window frames to cast its beam of light on his cloth shoes as he strode calmly yet purposely down the stone halls of the monastery. The sister to his left side seemed anxious, constantly having to slow herself when she got ahead of him. He took his time, going as quickly as the gnarled wood cane allowed him. Somewhere, at the end of the deep sleeve of the crimson robe, his hand held the end, but looking down it seemed comical; the cane seemed an extension of the limb hidden within.

They passed many open doorways with men bent over quill and paper, as well as men in earthen brown robes who did not speak but instead bowed their heads as they passed the cardinal. The young woman by his side scrutinized every face they passed. He smiled.

"Elizabeth, you will not find Mathias among these men."

She stiffened, bowing her head slightly.

"My apologies, Your Eminence. I am just-…"

"Eager to meet the man I have talked so very much about?" She looked toward him and he smiled with a wink. "I suppose that I am to blame for your excitement. Mathias is a devout follower of our Lord Almighty and has done much in support of the church. I suppose I have rambled my fair share about the man."

The holy pair continued on, walking slowly through the hallowed halls with the cardinal's cane dictating their speed, until the corridor led to two wooden doors swung completely open, as if welcoming them. When they reached the first pew, he stopped, bending down and crossing himself in the name of the Father, Son, and Holy Ghost. After his young acolyte did the same, he motioned for her to sit.

"Wait here, Elizabeth. While I speak with Mathias, take this time to pray and speak with God."

She did as he asked of her, immediately taking a knee in prayer. The room was much darker than the rest of the monastery, the light reflecting in from the stained glass windows the only illumination as he made his way to the front. Off to the side, away from and past the pulpit, was an extension of the room where numerous red votives were lit, burning softly in the presence of a man who the cardinal knew to be in his early thirties, deep in prayer.

"Your Eminence, your coming here is not something that usually bodes well."

The older man, Cardinal Oliviero Carafa, smiled as he heard the gruff voice. "Ah, Mathias. Ever the clever one. You would not think that an old man such as myself would come here just to check on you? Besides, my friend, how did you even know it was I that approached?"

The man named Mathias D'este turned his bald head toward the cardinal, his blue eyes piercingly bright, and the faintest of smiles peeked through. "My fellow brothers know that this is my deepest time of meditation. Who else should I have expected to come to a monastery in the middle of nowhere to find this specific monk?"

"Fair enough," the cardinal nodded. He forced his brows to conjure a more serious expression as he took a seat beside Mathias. "Then you know why I am here."

Mathias looked away, turning his gaze back toward the votives. "I do my service to the Lord here, in this monastery, praying for the sinners of the world."

"You know that is not the true purpose to this place." The cardinal leaned in, even though Mathias refused to meet his gaze. "As much as you and your brothers are truly monks in this establishment, you know the greater cause that many of you fight for. You must remember that your role is yet a greater one. You fight a battle that not many others can."

Mathias straightened, finally looking back toward the cardinal. "I understand, Your Eminence, but is there not another who can undertake this duty?"

Cardinal Carafa placed his hand on Mathias's, gripping it tightly. "I wish there was, my son, but all of our other agents are on missions of their own importance. This particular one is of the utmost sensitivity, and I would trust none other but you with it."

Mathias sighed and nodded. The cardinal squeezed his hand tighter before letting go.

"I understand your reluctance, my son, to take up the sword again. Going back and forth between both lives must be a burden beyond understanding, but remember my son, we each do our own duties in the name of our Father Almighty." Mathias nodded and the cardinal smiled slightly. "It is work that you and your brothers in the order do that will eventually help to redeem the names of your ancestors."

"I understand, Your Eminence. All my work, both on the field of battle and in prayer, has been in the name of the Knights Templar. If only we are remembered by our fellow brothers of the cloth, it is better than the disgraced and scarred memories that people now associate with our order."

The cardinal nodded. The original order of the Knights Templar had been disbanded by the former Pope Clement V many years ago, all of the members killed and burned at the stake for heresy. The cardinal was from a line of believers in the Church, sworn to secrecy, who doubted that the motives of the Pope and his predecessors were benevolent; they did not believe that so many people who served in the name of God would secretly commit sacrilege and profane blasphemy. And of course, there were the rumors of the Teutonic Knights being more involved than anyone in their false accusations. There were many in the order, like Mathias's father and grandfather, who were good people – Cardinal Carafa knew that personally.

Mathias's ancestor had been part of the order when it was disbanded, and the cardinal had been leader of the new order long enough to see his father and grandfather take up the sword and cloth in the name of the new order, and thus hid them within the cloisters of the monks. The monasteries he organized and watched over consisted of only the most devout of faith and the D'estes were among the most altruistic. Mathias's father had trained his son thoroughly in the art of swordplay and ever since he was young, he had been honed and bred for the day he would take up the mantle. Since he was very young, he served the cloth in every way he could, until the day he was sworn in to the Knights Templar.

Mathias nodded behind the cardinal, toward the back of the church. "Who is that with you?"

"Ah," the red-robed man jolted up, standing quickly. "I almost forgot. Come."

The younger girl finished her prayer and crossed herself as she saw the cardinal coming back. She leapt to her feet, bowing deeply as he approached with Mathias.

"Mathias, meet Elizabeth Baumbres. She is one of the newest members of our order. She will be your companion on this mission."

The Knight Templar cocked an eyebrow at the cardinal. "Forgive me, Your Eminence, but… I am not used to bringing aid on my missions. What task exactly is it that you have for me?"

"Ah, that is a good question." The cardinal bent his knees and almost fell into the pew. He sat with a huff, placing his cane next to him. He smiled as he turned back to the two younger warriors. "But first, let this old man sit and rest a moment."

*****

He wondered how something could feel so uncomfortable, yet so natural, at the same time. He did not need to look down through the slit in his winged helmet to know every rivet and ring. The cold metal felt foreign after donning it for the first time in some months, but after setting forth on his horse and traveling back roads that he knew the Teutonic Knights did not traverse on, he started feeling the pride of fighting for the order that his father and father before him swore to. The emblem had been altered to signify their rebirth, but it still stood for the same thing; the Knights Templar were the sword and shield of God and they would cut down the wicked and sinful.

He stole a sidelong glance toward the girl, Elizabeth. She was not as heavily clad as he, but she wore leather armor underneath her cloak; her vibrant red hair poking out from the hood. He saw the cross-bow slung on her back and the glint of steel on her hip, a pair probably hidden on the other side. She must have noticed the turn of his head, for she looked at him and smiled.

"Cardinal Carafa has spoken very highly about you."

"His Eminence flatters me unnecessarily." Mathias focused his eyes on the path ahead.

"You are an inspiration to all of us in the order. Your deeds over the years have reached many ears."

Mathias did not speak at first, letting the words sink in. "Everything I have done, I have done in the name of God. My work is no different than anything any other man could do."

"But no other man has!" There was a shine of respect in her eyes as she tried her best to balance staring at him and the road. "None other has devoted the time and effort you have to battling the evils both inside and out of the church; with sword in hand and prayer in church."

Mathias said no more even though he knew she expected him to. She was a nice enough young woman, eager to fulfill her duty, but if she were to follow in the same steps Mathias had, it would be a long road paved in blood. Every kill was for a righteous cause, and with every death, he cleansed the world of another blasphemous fiend. But then again, every kill claimed the life of a creature God Himself created and put on the earth. He was told each pagan he encountered was a test in his faith, but not all Slavs fell under that archetype.

These were truly strange times. While the Teutonic Knights worked to abolish and completely eradicate all those who still worshiped the gods of old, the Knights Templar were commonly tasked to aid those pagans that were willing to work alongside them; those whose shared with them the common goal of seeing humanity thrive against the forces of the Eldar Gods. His ancestors would be incredulous to believe such a communion possible, but times had changed. Perhaps years back the church could turn a blind eye to the magics of the Slavs and their beliefs in multiple deities, but in this day and age, there was too much proof to deny that these mystics existed. He had *seen* them with his own eyes plenty of times.

But that did not weaken his faith; no, it only helped to strengthen it and believe more than ever that God worked in mysterious ways that the mortal mind could not possibly comprehend.

The further they rode into the forest, the more the canopy obscured the sunlight, and the darker the woods became. When he realized this, Mathias looked up at the branches overhead and could barely see the sun streaking through the thick swathes of green. Their horses slowed, hesitant, as they tried to avoid the overgrown roots and rotted stumps. Mathias led them on, holding the reins tight as he forced his steed to stay resolute. The cardinal had told them the settlement was tucked deep in the Bialowieza Forest, and so he was determined to continue on until they found it.

When it seemed that the branches would reach out to pluck them off of their horses and smother them in blankets of green, the path opened back up, revealing an open stretch of land. Elizabeth hurried her horse beside him once more and turned to give Mathias a quizzical look.

"This must be it, no?" She nodded before them with her chin at the settlement of huts sprawled across the open field, the sun illuminating the working tribesmen. "Should we be cautious? Will they attack us?"

Mathias noticed the Slavic peasants stopping their fieldwork to stare at the holy warriors, their tools gripped tightly in both hands. He shook his head.

"They will not attack. If they were going to have wards up to stop us, they would have by now. Slavic magic is greater than any tool human hands could craft. They have been foretold of our coming."

He raised a hand up to the tribal people, slowing his horse as he approached. Elizabeth did the same until they both came to a stop. Mathias turned his head and one hand toward the girl as he got off his horse, holding his index finger out to her. She understood and remained mounted as Mathias lowered his arms and approached the crowd that assembled at the edge of the huts. They were very poorly clad, mostly in roughly cut hides; their hair was long, their faces dirty. Mathias took his winged helmet off, placing it in the crux of his arm. The prickles of hair felt odd on his nearly-shaven head now being exposed to the cool air. He gave them all a warm smile.

"Greetings," the words rolled off of his tongue in Polish with no hesitation or strain. He had been in enough parlays with these people that not knowing their language would have been an embarrassment to himself. "My name is Mathias D'este and I am a Knight Templar. Our people have been in talks and you have been expecting me, if I am not mistaken. Which among you is the elder?"

An older man, hunched over a thick walking stick, stepped forward with the assistance of a woman, almost three times younger, holding onto one of his arms. His eyes were sullen and heavy, and despite cheeks that sagged down with age, an almost toothless smile lifted everything momentarily.

"I am the one you seek, knight. My name is Dmitrei. I lead the tribe of this area of the forest and we are loyal servants of Jarilo."

Mathias handed the reins of his horse to Elizabeth and then bowed before the elder, pushing his cape out behind him. "As per the covenant between our factions, we are here to assist you in any way that we can."

Dmitrei nodded and then pointed at one of the younger men, waving him forward to the horses. Mathias watched as the boy rushed forward to Elizabeth and then stared down at the ground. She hesitated, as if unsure of what he wanted from her, but she stepped down from the tack and handed over the reins to both horses. She stood next to Mathias, and when she noticed the elder staring, she bowed down low as well.

"This is my ally, Sister Elizabeth Baumbres."

The elder's smile did not wane, but he hobbled around as best as he could, indicating with his head toward the rear of the encampment.

"Come. We have much to discuss. Our people will see that your horses are properly taken care of."

Mathias gave a look back toward the steeds and then Elizabeth. After her initial excitement to be traveling with him, she seemed hesitant to meet his gaze. It was probably his eyes. He had seen the look on many a face when he turned his stone-cold blue eyes upon them, and even sometimes he found a chill run down his own spine before a mirror.

He walked slowly behind the hobbled old man, looking around at the ramshackle huts as they passed. Each one was unique in their makeup; some had humps at the top while others were on the side; some were tall and lean while others were short and squat; some were made more of hide and others consisted more of leafy natural materials. Mathias had great respect for the people that lived so in touch with the nature of God, even though they did not see it in that fashion; but after living in civilization for his entire life, he could not fathom sleeping in one of those structures.

The young woman detached from the elder as they came close to a hut that did not stand out from the others in any special way. She held open the hide flap that was considered the doorway as the older man led the two warriors inward. The elder limped to the back, nodding with his head toward wooden stumps in the middle of the room, as he himself plopped down on softer looking greenery. The young woman rushed to his side, making sure he was okay, but he waved her off.

Mathias felt the heat of the small enclosure underneath his armor. He exhaled calmly, trying to cool himself down, and he noticed Elizabeth pull her hood back behind her wavy locks of red. He placed his hands on his legs, sitting up as straight as he could as he waited for the elder to speak.

Dmitrei's eyebrows shot up and he leaned forward on his walking stick, his chin almost resting atop it. "Ah, yes. Right. I thank you both for coming here. We approached your order because we have heard other tribes have had successful relations with the Knights Templar. Words spread far of your deeds – especially of Mathias D'este. Many speak highly of you in particular."

He felt Elizabeth's smug grin in his direction, but he nodded politely to the elder. "You honor me wish such praise, truly, but I only do what I know is right."

"As do we all." The elder nodded a few times, but then his smile fell and the droopy skin only made him look sadder. "I sent word of needing assistance because as of late, I feel that we are in grave danger." He indicated to the girl beside him. "Orefia has been blessed with the gift of dreams. She sees things when she closes her eyes that are glimpses of what is to come. Lately, her visions have been dark and clouded, and we fear what that means for our people."

"I… see." Mathias fidgeted nervously. He knew that the Slavs had their unique powers that supposedly came from the deities they worshiped, but sometimes, especially moments like this, he could not help to feel that they were unnatural. "That is not good then. Do you have any idea what it could mean?"

"No." Dmitrei shook his head sadly, the flab of his cheeks swaying with every movement. "But the artifact that we guard is not safe here anymore. This is the real reason why I asked of the Knights Templars' aid. As I have said, many speak your name with high praise, and we needed an outsider that we could trust to recover the artifact and bring it somewhere where it can be protected. If it were to fall into the wrong hands…" Dmitrei sat up straight, his eyes hard. "It could be devastating for mankind."

"Recover?" Elizabeth's voice was a bit deeper than usual, as if trying to force steel in her words. "You mean to say that the artifact that you supposedly guard is not here in the village?"

"No," Dmitrei shook his head. "We are the first bastion, should outsiders attack. We guard the path to the artifact to ward off intruders. The real guardians are the sirins."

"Sirins." As Mathias said the word his brow furrowed. "I have heard of them but have never encountered any."

Dmitrei did not say anything else, but nodded several times. It was Elizabeth who broke the silence.

"Please excuse me for asking, but if you guard the path to these sirins, why is it that you need our help to recover the artifact?"

"Heh." Dmitrei made a sucking motion with his mouth, as if chewing some invisible object. "We cannot fight against the sirins. We are forbidden by Jarilo. And they will not willingly give their treasure. They are loyal guardians, but the time has come to move the item and for new guardians to take up the mantle."

"If that is what you wish, so be it." Mathias nodded and stood. "If you feel you are in danger, we must not waste any more time. If you do not mind, Elder Dmitrei, please tell us where our journey will take us."

*****

It had been difficult getting the horses back into the forest the way Dmitrei directed them in, but after the defensive perimeter of overgrowth had subsided, it was a bit easier to navigate the abundance of nature.

"Are we sure we're going the right way?" Elizabeth had her hood on once more, and the look she gave within seemed a scowl.

"Dmitrei assured us that this was the correct direction the artifact lay in," Mathias nodded, confident and cool as his horse trotted onward.

"Yes, but how could he, or even you, for that matter, be so sure that we are still going the correct way? This forest is so dense and there's growth in every direction we turn. You would have thought he could have at least sent a guide with us."

"You heard what the elder said; it is forbidden by the deity that they worship to stand against the sirins. I'm sure it's a sin – or what have you – for them to directly bring outsiders to the guardians as well. Besides, we need none others than ourselves. The Lord will guide us, as He always does."

When Mathias finished speaking he bowed his head and crossed himself, and Elizabeth repeated the pattern. They continued through the forest for a few minutes more before Elizabeth broke the silence.

"So who do you fight for, Mathias? Who are you protecting? Do you have a family?"

The question caught him off-guard and he almost jerked the reins of his horse. Sitting up straight, he turned a sideways glance to her. She must have noticed his surprise, because before he could speak, she rode up beside him, shaking her head furiously.

"I-I'm sorry… I didn't-… didn't mean t-to…"

He held up a hand to silence her babbling. "Please, Elizabeth. It is fine. It is just not a question I am asked often." He ducked to avoid a low-hanging set of branches, taking the time to form his response. "My bloodline has consisted of Knights Templar for generations. One of my ancestors was a founding member of the order and another was tried and murdered when they were disbanded. At first, it was just my forefathers when men were the only members allowed. But once the order reformed in secrecy, the females in my family took up the mantle along their husbands. Each member of my family that was a part of the order fell in the line of battle, defending the rights of men and women in the name of God."

"That is the noblest of causes – to give one's life in the name of the Lord, in the cause of his people. It is why we fight on every day, so that their names and their deeds will forever be remembered and honored."

Mathias mustered a grim smile, nodding to his young acolyte. "And what of you, Sister Elizabeth?"

"My story is not as benevolent as yours. The cardinal recruited me, as he does most, knowing of my zeal for God and the people alike, and how much I abhorred what the Teutonic Knights had done to the church. I came into the order to try and make a difference and because of that, the cardinal put my parents and younger brother and sister into protective care. I could ask for nothing more than what he has done for us."

Mathias nodded, his smile warming slightly. "Cardinal Carafa is a great man. If not for him and his predecessors, this order would not exist to combat the evils of the Teutonic Knights. He is truly a man of the Lord."

He was half tempted to tell her the rest of his story, to finally trust someone other than the cardinal with the tale that haunted his dreams for years on end, the reason why he was always so reluctant to pick up his sword; but instead, he remained silent.

Around another patch of thick brush, and finally, the path opened up to another clearing. It was more spacious than the one the encampment had been in, with open space in every direction. In the center of the area was a sword standing vertically, glimmering with an otherwordly aura. Both he and Elizabeth dismounted, tying their horses to trees hidden from view before entering the field.

"We have been waiting for your arrival, knights."

Mathias reached for his sword instinctively and looked around for the source of the voice. Standing guard around the sparkling weapon were four columns that rose about seven or eight feet tall, and there was a bird perched at the top of each; or at least, Mathias thought they were birds. He felt his jaw slacken when he noticed that the faces and the busts were that of women! They had long flowing hair that integrated with their back of feathers, bright blue eyes that he drank deep in their twinkles, silky smooth flesh that showed no wrinkle or blemish of age, and dainty pointed features to accentuate their beauty. They smiled warmly at the knight as he stood in awe before them.

"Welcome, Mathias and Elizabeth. We have been waiting for you both."

That gave the lead knight pause. His brows wrinkled and he grasped the handle of the blade in his sheath tighter, staring at the front right sirin. "You have been expecting us?"

"Yes," the back left one spoke this time, inclining her head down toward him. "We saw you traveling through our forest; we felt every step you took across our ground."

"*Your* ground? *Your* forest?" Elizabeth stepped forward, her crossbow swung around to her front. "What gives you ownership of this area?"

There was a light laugh of unison between the four sirins before the front left one spoke. "Silly girl. Acting in affairs you know nothing of. Sir Knight, why do you travel with such a novice who speaks out of turn so openly? Are you not the leader of this expedition?"

Mathias placed a hand out to his side to calm the raging sister beside him. He did not need to look at her to see the clenched teeth or the vein popping out of her head; he could feel her rage.

"Regain your poise, Sister. Be not embarrassed and remember the word of God."

"The word of God?" The back right sirin spoke the words that caused the four to laugh even louder than before. "Ah, you poor fool. You claim belief in God, but how much of that claim is truth? You can see us before you with your very eyes. Those in your holy church would deem us abominations, creatures that your God did not create. But if that were true, how can we exist?"

"I have my beliefs, and they are my shield against darkness. I still believe despite your existence and claim to your own deities. God makes all, and your existence is just a tri-..."

"Do *not* associate us with your 'God' in that fruity place of light and 'holiness.'" The first sirin hissed the last word out, the anger in her face barely blemishing her beauty. "Your God has nothing to do with our creation."

"God is in all things, man or other." Mathias stood resolute, stepping one foot forward.

"Was he in the men who killed your family members?" He paused as the back right one spoke again, the weight of his boot in midair as he dreaded the next words. "Did he help save the men and women in your lineage who fought so bravely under his name? Was he there when they slaughtered yo-…"

"*Enough*!" Mathias boomed, cutting the air with his sword as he pulled it from the scabbard. "You will not take the Lord's name in vain, and you shall not speak ill of the dead!"

"Oh, touch a nerve there, have we?" The back left one tilted her head in mock sympathy, pushing out her bottom lip in a quiver. "You poor baby. The dead is a sore subject for you, hmm? I suppose you fear what happened to them when they left this realm – you wonder if your God really exists. Did they go to be at peace with him? Or maybe they're being tortured every waking moment by that devil you humans hate. What's his name? Sat-..."

The sirin squawked loudly as a crossbolt hit it in the right side of the chest; if its chest anatomy was anything like the human that it mimicked, the arrow must have struck the heart. The creature flailed its wings a few times, trying to gain momentum, but it spiraled to the ground where it smashed hard and then lay motionless.

Mathias swung his head around to Elizabeth. Her anger seemed to only intensify tenfold. "You heretics shall not speak the name of the Devil in our presence! If you wish to speak of him, we will send you to join him in his inferno soon enough!"

She turned to meet his gaze and he nodded his thanks to her. He whirled back around just in time to see the sirins descending, their open claws aiming for them, another bolt this time soaring past them. Mathias's hand jerked up quickly enough to bring his sword to deflect the first attacker's raining blows and then maneuver out of the way of the second. Elizabeth held the third one's attention with her dual daggers.

"Mortal," the first one hissed at Mathias. "You shall neither leave here with the sword or your life!"

"To Hell with you, damnable cretins!" Mathias spat the words as he raised his sword high and feinted toward the first. Stepping back from the incoming talons, he moved toward the second and swept in with his blade. The sirin was caught by surprise, but still managed to dodge most of the strike. He saw the blade find flesh, tearing a spat of blood out of the bird-woman's chest. She shrieked in pain but started flapping her wings in fits at him. Mathias held his sword up, unsure what else to do, but the windstorm created by the creature was so forceful that it actually pushed him back several feet until he fell on his back.

His feet had barely left the ground before the first sirin was on him, trying to tear at him with its monstrous talons. He fended off the attacks as best as he could with his sword, but luckily his armor and helmet were thick enough that the nails left only scratches when they got past his blade. He used his free arm to try and mount a defense by punching the creature, but he could only land a few between her flurry. Those punches were able to weave just enough through her offense to daze her, the assault slowing. He pulled his boot in under her and kicked with all of his might, forcing her off of him.

He leapt up from the ground, gripping the sword with both hands once more to deliver the finishing blow, when the soft sound of singing filled his ears. Something in the melody was so alluring and calming that he could not turn away from the wounded sirin whose operatic voice almost brought him to tears. With one hand, he tore the helmet from his head, barely noticing as it clanked to the ground. He felt the grip on his sword weaken as he stepped toward the woman-bird, the tip of the blade almost kissing the ground, and he was awash with a sensation of regret. How could he have ever wounded such a magnificent creature? Would it be able to keep singing with her wound?

It was speaking to him in the song. The sirin was trying to tell him something, and almost of its own volition, he felt his sword arm rise, the blade turned now on him. Yes, this was the way that he could make up for his error; he could maim himself in a mirror image to make her feel at ease.

Before the blade could pierce his armor, the singing stopped and the tip of a dagger erupted from the open mouth. There was a deep gargling, met with the wings and talons trying to claw for the throat, trying to stop the fountain of blood that was pouring from the gaping hole. Elizabeth pulled her dagger free and kicked the sirin to the ground.

Mathias came back to his senses, sneering at the thought that an abomination such as the sirin could work its magic to make him want to commit such a deadly sin as to kill himself; never such strong magic had been enacted on him before and he would have to say a silent prayer to God later to forgive him to succumbing to man's desires. With one swift motion, he spun around and swung his sword with both arms. The blade tore through the air, severing the last sirin's head from its body, and it remained there for a few moments, unmoving, before the head rolled off and a geyser of red liquid let loose its contents.

The body slumped to the ground to join its other companions, and Mathias wiped his blade clean before sheathing it, turning once more back to his acolyte as he picked his helmet back up onto his head.

"Thank you, Elizabeth. If not for your assistance, I fear what might have become of me."

"It seems even the most devout of God's Christians are susceptible to the heathens' magics." She sheathed both of her daggers, the crossbow slung against her back once more. "I am just glad I could be there to save you. I don't know how I would be able to report back to the cardinal if these creatures had succeeded in killing you."

Mathias nodded, a gruff sound coming from his throat. "I am just a man who serves his Lord Almighty. There will always be more after me that can do my job just as well. As I have said, the cardinal holds me in too high esteem."

"Hmph. He may hold you in high esteem, but I think you are too modest about your abilities and underestimate the weight of your deeds." She crossed her arms over her chest and shook her head, indicating with her chin toward the sword in the middle of the four columns. "Will you do the honors of retrieving the prize?"

"If anyone must, I suppose I should."

Mathias took slow steps toward the sword impaled in the stone. It seemed too mythical to be true. How could a sword be impaled in a solid slab of stone and still remain upright, let alone, that he would be able to pull it out himself? Another Slavic magic trick.

He stood before the blade that appeared to be glowing in an aura of silvery blue, as if some ethereal light was being cast down on it from the sky. He closed his eyes and crossed himself in the name of the Father, Son, and Holy Ghost, saying a silent prayer in hopes that touching the relic would not damn him. He took a deep breath out before grasping the blade with both hands tight.

As he held onto the handle, he waited for something to happen; some other curse that Dmitrei had forgotten to tell him about, some alarm that would sound that he was not of the Slavic people, or even that he would feel extraordinarily strong. But nothing happened. He gave the sword a soft jerk and even though it took a few more forceful pulls, the blade finally began to move, echoing the scraping sound of stone on steel.

When the weapon finally pulled free, he held up in the air to gaze at it in awe. Even out of the resting place, it still gave off an unearthly, unnatural, mystic glow that Mathias had never seen before. There were some strange runes written on the body of the blade, close to the hilt, that Mathias thought he could understand.

"So that is the relic that is so important that it could endanger mankind?" Elizabeth walked up beside him, keeping a few paces back despite the sarcasm in her voice. "Believe me, it's shiny and pretty and all, but why is this blade so important?"

"Because it has been blessed by Perun." Mathias's words were but a mutter as he held the blade close to his face, examining the runes: 'The Valorheart Pure. '. "These words here… They're a bit archaic for my understanding of the Slavic tongue, written in ancient Glagolitic, but if I am understanding it right, it has been made and blessed by their highest deity."

He looked up at Elizabeth and she stared back at him in disbelief. She sputtered out a few sounds, but no words came out.

"I know, I'm just as astounded as you."

"Wh-What does this mean? Is this good? Is this bad?" She looked around nervously. "Are you… Are you damned now for touching such an artifact? Would God approve?"

Mathias shook his head. "I am not damned. God has put these creatures on this earth for some reason. As you know, there are those deities that work for the continued survival of humanity. Perun, from what I understand, is the most supportive of that cause. He is the primary reason why our order exists to work with the Slavic people." He looked down at the sword again; the shock really had not hit him yet. To the Slavic believers, it was the equivalent of holding something blessed by God. "This sword wound up in our hands for a reason of

God's design. No wonder it was being guarded by such vicious creatures."

He had more on the subject to say, but Elizabeth rushed to the edge of the column, looking up to the opening in the sky. He moved to her side, still holding the sword because he had no scabbard for it.

"Elizabeth, what-...?"

He sniffed a few times before taking a deep inhale, and his heart plummeted, adrenaline firing through his veins. She turned to him with a single nod.

"Something's burning."

*****

Mathias rode through the forest as quickly as his horse would allow, which was not very fast because the dense overgrowth caused it to slow constantly. There were times that he worried that he would lose the sister through the thick greenery, but every time he glanced behind him, she was there.

He did not feel like he was getting anywhere, or at least, not back toward the village. Because the path was so overgrown, he was not sure if the pathways his brain thought he remembered were correct; each turnoff in the ocean of green looked identical to the last. They were traveling quicker than they had been when they first entered the forest, yet for some reason it seemed to be taking much longer. There were no signs or indications of where they were, or if they were just going in a blind circle. He trusted his inner compass and God's hand to guide them in the right direction.

"Do you feel that?"

Elizabeth's words barely registered and it took him a moment to realize what she was talking about. He had not noticed how much he had been sweating; it had not been this hot earlier. Steering his horse in the direction of the heat, he rode on. He pushed through the drooping branches as they came into his path, cutting some even with the magical sword that still had no sheath, until he burst through to the scene of the inferno, his horse rearing up and threatening to throw him.

The heat was sweltering. Everywhere he turned there were flames threatening to devour not only Dmitrei's encampment but also the forest itself. Trees cried with huge globs of flame that burned branches to cinders, eating away at the people's homes until nothing remained. He saw, with great disgust and horror, that there were areas where a makeshift gallows had been rigged and several hanging bodies were charred.

He knew whose work this was.

He jumped off his horse, turned around to Elizabeth, and thrust the reins to his horse into her hands.

"Get the horses settled somewhere and save every one of them that you can!"

"What about you?!" She stared incredulously, shaking her head. "What are you going to do alone?"

He brought up the sword blessed by Perun, holding the strange silvery blue against the raging orange red all around them. "It is time to see just what this sword is capable of. If I am damned for wielding it, we shall soon find out."

Elizabeth tried calling out to him, maybe to warn him, maybe to stop him, maybe to wish the Lord at his side, but Mathias did not hear her words. All he could think about was all of the innocent people who the Inquisition tortured and murdered this day – all, they would say, in the name of God.

He came at the first duo of men who were picking over dead bodies and did not hesitate. He plunged his sword through the first one, tearing his glowing blade through the other side. By the time the other realized what was going on, Mathias's blade had already pulled free and he cut the man diagonally across the chest. He tore through the second's lightly armored outfit, sneering at the sign of the cross printed on it. It was because of the Inquisition, more so than the Teutonic Knights, that the church was in such a sad state. They disgraced those loyal to the word of God by, instead of promoting equality and love, tortured and punished all those of different beliefs. Even though the two branches were not aligned, the Teutonic Knights and the Inquisition shared the same goal – to kill all nonbelievers.

"Heretic!" The word boomed across the burning landscape, the crier half-hidden in the wafting smoke. As he stepped forward, Mathias saw the mark of the Inquisition standing violently on the church cloth that concealed his armor underneath. His short hair was a matted mess, mimicking the lunacy in his eyes and the snarl on his face. A cross was held high in one hand, out toward Mathias, while in the other a bloodstained sword was held low. "You would dare slay those that do the work of God? There is no greater sin than yours, blasphemer!"

"Woe to you, inquisitor, for it is you that is wrong. It is your sins that will condemn you eternally. All men are equal in the eyes of God; we are *all* His children." Mathias was keen to notice the pair of guards that flanked the preacher, and he kept his own defense wary. "I have not come to judge you, for that is the work of our Lord Almighty, but I will not let you spread His word falsely."

The inquisitor looked over Mathias' attire and sneered vehemently. "*Templar.*" He nearly spat the word, holding the cross up higher, his fist shaking in rage. "You are the worst of all sinners; a branch that should have stayed dead when it was first purged. You have the gall to stand before me and speak about God's word?"

"If I am to be damned for protecting those who wish to work toward humanity's salvation, then so be it. I will meet my divine judgment when I arrive at the heavenly gates. That decision is for God to make," he raised his left hand, extending a single finger toward the man. "Not you."

The inquisitor laughed heartily, extending his own finger toward the sword in Mathias's right hand. "You lecture me about God's judgment, yet you stand before us with a weapon not from this earthly plane – a sacrilegious blade created by the Slavic heathens and their false gods!" The finger slowly descended and the anger seemed to be mixed with the fear of God. "That helmet you hide behind can save you for only so long. When I pry it from your head and lay eyes on your face, you alone will not only suffer God's holy wrath, but your family, neighbors, and village will be purged for harboring and raising a *heretic*!"

Mathias smiled under the helmet, and thus knowing his enemy could not see such motion, he allowed a chuckle to escape his lips, causing the other man's eyes to madden. "Oh, preacher. If I could recount to you just how many of your branch have said something similar to me. While many have fallen to the most sadistic of your order, both my brethren and other innocents alike, I have avenged them many times over, sending numerous agents of your Inquisition, who claim they carry out the will of God, to meet our Lord Almighty for His true judgment."

Spittle foamed at the preacher's mouth as he let out a howl, his cross raising higher than it seemed possible. His guards rushed out from behind him, raising their swords as they came upon the Knight Templar. Mathias sidestepped the first swipe and then brought his sword up to block the second one. Once the clashing of weaponry sounded out around him, he grabbed his sword with both hands to push his attacker back. Just as he reeled his weapon back, he forced it up just in time to defend against the first one. The duo swung at each other, blocking each swipe as they took turns on the offense, the second member of the Inquisition hanging back, stalking Mathias.

His eyes danced around the battlefield, trying to take in all of his targets, centralizing on the man who was pushing the offense. The preacher was some feet removed, chanting incantations from a book that Mathias thought looked like the Bible. His sword was placed back in its sheath and the cross was still held resolutely high. His eyes, when they looked up, were maniacal as they seemed from the first moment.

Even though his eyes could not be seen through the slit in his helmet, he lingered on the preacher a moment too long and the other guard must have felt it. He tried to pull his body out of the way, but he did not have enough time. He felt the blade sink into his left arm and he winced at the pain and his own inattentiveness. The Slavic blade seemed to spark in its color, which scared the warrior he was in a deadlock with enough to make him pull back, and even surprised Mathias. Sensing his opportunity, Mathias elbowed the man in his exposed nose, causing him to fall over in pain.

The second man was coming around again for another attack and instinctively, Mathias raised the glowing sword to parry the attack; but when he swung to block, his sword did not stop at the blade but instead kept going. He had not fully grasped what had happened until the blood splattered around the Inquisition grunt's face, his scream a maniacal howl. His eyes widened as he witnessed his opponent's blade was no longer whole, but shattered into pieces that were stabbing him in the face, his blood pouring out at every wound as he fell.

He knelt down to the man convulsing on the ground, his screams now a gargle of liquid. Placing the blade at the nape of his neck, Mathias silenced him with a quick pull. When he stood, he looked at the Slavic weapon, astonished at the brilliance of the magical weapon. How could a weapon, *any* weapon, be strong enough to shatter another so effortlessly that he did not feel the swords touch? More importantly, why did it just happen now and not when they clashed before? Did it have something to do with when he was stabbed?

His eyes snapped away from the blade, back to the other man he had knocked down. He was back up and charging toward him, the sword held up high in the air, blood stained down the front of his face.

"God damn you!"

Mathias steeled himself, readying the glowing Slavic sword once more. It pulsated with silvery blue energy as he thrust it forward, through the man's chest, impaling him. The other sword still hung in the air above the Inquisition grunt's head for a few moments longer, even though he was no longer moving. The snarl on his face gave way to pleading, trying to gasp his last breaths of air.

"God has nothing to do with your crimes, except that you take his name in vain."

With that, Mathias pushed the sword further in until his opponent's sword fell from his grip, and then he went limp. Mathias waited until the light faded from his eyes, his head bowed, and blood seeped from it until he pushed the body off of the blade. As it came free, he was astonished once more at the blade's magic. Not a single drop of blood touched the edge of the blade, but instead seemed to run off of it like water.

He did not even feel the dagger that bounced off of the back of his armor. It tore lightly into the cape on his back, but the mail caught the small weapon from doing any damage. He whirled around with his off-hand, slapping the preacher in the face. The dagger flew free and Mathias's opponent spiraled to the ground from the impact. The Knight Templar towered over the man crawling back on the ground, one hand still raising the cross defiantly at him.

Mathias took his helmet off and threw it to the ground as he stalked the preacher. He did not realize just how furious he must have looked until he saw the man's face lose its anger, taking on a complete look of fear. He relieved some of the strain off his brow, feeling the snarl fade away as he straightened.

"You wished to see my face… Now, you have seen it." Mathias held his hands out at his side, as if welcoming the preacher to behold his appearance in its entirety. The holy man's face began to scrunch again when he saw the knight's face, and his mouth moved, as if to speak; but Mathias thrust the sword down before any words could be said. Instead, a gargle came out of the zealous man's mouth, followed by a trickle of blood, and an expression of betrayal. "When you meet the Heavenly Father, and you stand trial for the atrocities you have wrought – killing so many innocent people – make sure you tell him that Mathias D'este was the one that freed you of your mortal bonds."

The cross ascended even higher than ever as the preacher's body fought and climbed up the blade, but then he succumbed to the instrument of his destruction and fell to the ground; the cross laying limp beside him.

*****

At first, Mathias thought the blaze would consume the entirety of the forest. The flames were so hot and burned so fiercely, he was not sure where to start with extinguishing it. Before he could concoct a plan, he saw something through the inferno – the telltale sign of fairy lights twinkling at him all around. As if they sensed that the forces that opposed them had been wiped out, the glow appeared all at once, and the fire fizzled out quicker than Mathias could have even begun to aid.

He set to his own work immediately. In the ruins of one of the huts, by the area he had seen them farming, he found a crude shovel that he used to begin digging. He had been at it for at least twenty minutes, the sweat dripping off his head and down the back of his armor, when he sensed Elizabeth standing by him.

"Did you find Dmitrei?"

His eyes remained focused upon the grave he was digging, but he heard the falter in Elizabeth's steps.

"He… Yes. His body was mutilated and tortured."

"Was he still alive?"

There was pause again in the sister's voice. "He might have been when we came back with the sword, but… He suffered, Mathias."

Mathias winced, his dig hesitating for a moment. He shook his head and stabbed into the dirt once more. "I am sorry you had to bear witness to that. We can rest easy and know that he is with God now."

"Or whatever gods that he worshipped."

It was a good point. He had never really stopped to consider where the Slavic people went after they passed the mortal realm. Were there multiple realms of the afterlife? Was Heaven one version that those of Christian faith ascended to, and did the Slavs have a completely different version of where their people went?

Satisfied with the depth of the plot, he placed the preacher, bundled in his holy garments, into the hole. He fixed the cross so that it rested on the center of the man's chest, just above the mortal wound that Mathias inflicted on him. He stood back from the grave, bowing his head in prayer and Elizabeth did the same.

"Despite his extreme views, he was a man of God, first and foremost. Though he may have interpreted the message of our Lord incorrectly, he lived and served primarily. May God judge his sins accordingly, as he does all men."

Elizabeth nodded her head and then took the shovel from Mathias's hands. He gave her a strange look, but she ignored him and began to bury the preacher.

"We must all do our part, brother-knight." She pulled her red hair tight over one shoulder, preparing for the labor. "And this is mine."

*****

The duo, caked in blood, sweat, and dirt, sat close by to where Elizabeth tied the horses up. He thanked God that the faeries, or whatever woodland creatures, had watched over their mounts and kept them unscathed, but all around them was cinder and ash. Even though the blaze had stopped before the forest's complete destruction, where the village had been, at the start of the fire, had been reduced to a sullen gray graveyard.

He thought that, as he looked toward the markers where the Inquisition members lay buried.

And then he turned back to his sword; the strange Slavic sword that had been imbued with magics that he thought he would never be able to comprehend. The magical aura was gone, the blade seemingly resting from the previous conflict, and it looked like any other mortal blade beside the gem adornments on the hilt and handle.

"So, now what do we do with it?"

He looked toward Elizabeth and shrugged. "We find the next guardian."

"But what if," she shifted to look at him more directly, "what if there is no guardian?"

His brow furrowed and he shook his head. "I don't follow, Elizabeth."

She shifted again, this time uneasily as she tried to hold Mathias's gaze. "Well… We work with the Slavic people in many ways. We aid them and that aid is reciprocated. We share information that benefits humanity. What if God set us on this path to retrieve the sword to seal the union between the Slavics and the Christians?"

Mathias felt his eyebrows rise. There were some in this lifetime that would call such words sacrilegious and exile her as a blasphemer without a second thought. He was not one of those close-minded individuals. He stared down at the sword in his hands and sat contemplating her words for several moments.

"Are... you to say that... we are the guardians of this blade?"

"No," she placed a hand on his that held the sword. "*You* are the guardian. I, only if something should happen."

"I..." Mathias turned the blade over several times before meeting her gaze.

"The blade shone in your hands so brilliantly. I know you might not yet understand the magic that the blade is made off, but you made a connection with it and it seems to answer to your needs. You are the most fit to wield the weapon, Mathias."

Whatever hesitation she had vanished and she now stared confidently at the Knight Templar. He nodded once her words sank in.

"I spoke to you before about my family. They were not the only ones to have died." He closed his eyes and exhaled deeply. "The Inquisition killed my wife and two young sons, no older than six and eight." He raised a hand to forestall the stammering from Elizabeth. "It... it is a pain that still haunts me. The only fact that eases my mind is that they are in God's loving embrace and I do not have to worry about keeping them safe. They and my parents. This is the reason why I say my exploits are nothing more than any other man could do. When you and the cardinal approached me, I was hesitant to take up the blade once more. He and I have been through this song and dance many a time, but every time, he encourages me to fight on, in the name of God.

"And, honestly, I cannot blame him. His belief in me, that I can make a difference with God as my champion that I herald, is why I still have my spirit. And now, yet," he looked down at the blade once more, his mind wrapped around the strange mysteries. "Taking this blade in my grip, my will and resolve has been renewed like never before. Perhaps... Perhaps I am meant to take this blade unto my possession as its guardian. Perhaps this is all in God's great will."

He looked up at her and could not help but let the corner of his lip curl in a smile. She gave him an answering one, much more elated than he.

"You are, Mathias. I believe it, truly."

"Right," he nodded. "Then, young sister, where do you suppose we go from here?"

"Well, what options do we have?"

"Not many." He rose, his bandaged arm still singing from the battle and his joints from the burial after. "I suppose we should return to the cardinal and report in. There is much we must discuss."

"Then so we shall," she leapt to her feet, a wide smile still on her face. As she mounted her horse, she turned to him and nodded solemnly. "Your secret is safe with me, Mathias. I know you seek no vengeance, but I still stand by what I said when we first met – even more so now than ever. You are truly an inspiration to all in our order."

He got atop his horse and shook his head. "And I, Elizabeth, stand by what I said. I am but a man in the service of our Lord."

Appendix I: Factions

Grandmaster Frederick von Sachsen
by Jeff Preston, 2016

-The Church. Among the power struggle between the warring god factions, the religion of Christianity is the prevailing faith. The House of God is ever-present in the ongoing events surrounding Starybogow; both factions and their supporters have been branded heretics by the Pope, but there are still those who sympathize with the Slavic people of the old faith, being aligned with the similar purpose of preserving humanity. There are dark murmurs across the land that Pope Alexander the VIth and his highest ranking officials work in the name of God just to cover their own corruption.

- Eldar Gods. Nicknamed 'the Dwellers of the Deep' and sometimes 'the Dark Ones', these creatures inhabit the Baltic Ocean and thrust their tentacles up from the sea for one purpose – to destroy humanity and replace them with creatures of their own image. They had once been sealed in a Void by Perun in order to protect humanity, but their battle against the Old Gods has been waged for hundreds of years prior. The only people who have truly seen these creatures have fallen sway to their maniacal whims and have lost all sense of their humanity. Those they have wrapped their tentacles around have clear signs – almonding of the eyes, elongated appendages and craniums, and in some intense cases they begin to grow tentacles of their own as a sign of the power bestowed upon them.

-Inquisition. While the Teutonic Knights are the sword and shield of the Church, the Inquisition has slightly more… controversial methods. Even though this zealous group of people is not under the sway of the Eldar Gods, they share the same passion with the Teutonic Knights for ridding the land of heretics. They put people on trial and torture those to death that they find not believing in Christianity. Traveling the land, spouting the word of the one true Lord and Savior, some would rather find themselves to meet a swift end at the hand of a Teutonic Knight's blade than be tortured by the Inquisition.

-Hanseatic League. Once thought to be the world's most elite and elaborate trading organization, their greater purpose and most sacred commodity is secrets. Every member of the guild is trained in the art of swordplay and advanced acrobatics so that they can not only trade valuables across the land, but so that they might spy on the different groups around the realm and adventure to the most desolate ruins to find treasure. They swear allegiance to no overarching group, and even though they fight for the preservation of humanity, their main priority is always protecting their interests and needs above the common man.

-Knights Templar. Originally created to be the sword and shield of the Church, the Knights Templar was disbanded in the 1300's and replaced with the Teutonic Knights; all of the members of the order and their families were condemned to death, as if trying to erase all trace that they existed, as well as whatever secrets the order knew. Even though the Teutonic Knights were ruthless in their persecution of the members, there were those within the Church that did not believe what was happening was of the will of God, and thus sheltered members of the Knights Templar and hid them from the reach of the Pope. After that, the order was restored in secret, its members chosen selectively and they now have an easy relationship with the Slavic people to fight against a common threat – the Eldar Gods. Even though they believe in God and Christianity, they know they must work with the deities that are on the side of life to combat those that would see humanity ruined. Though they do not exist in great numbers, each member is in peak performance and fights like a seasoned warrior. The current leader is Cardinal Oliviero Carafa.

-Old Gods. These deities of legend are worshiped by the Slavic people and, for the most part, wish to see humanity thrive. These beings come in many shapes, sizes, forms, and varying allegiances. Even though there are deities of great power and reputation, such as Perun and Triglav, many minor creatures fall under this category as well, such as the leshiye, the vampyrs, the topielec, etc. The Slavic people worship the Old Gods with statues and totems, and occasionally there are those cults who perform in the dark rites of sacrifices. The gods do not solely represent power, but some represent the elements and everyday aspects of life such as good harvest and household environment. After having escaped the Void, they live in a variety of areas; some underground in labyrinthine caves and tunnels and many in sacred forest groves.

-Romani. Mystic free people that roam the land, swearing no allegiance to any group. They do not really care what happens in the war between the Eldar and the Old Gods, but for whatever reason they try to keep the war ongoing; what stake they have in it is a mystery. The allegiance of many cannot be assured because it changes as each side pulls more victories in the ongoing war.

-Servitors. These nightmarish creatures make up the main force of the Eldar Gods that walk the land. As if born from the very depths of the ocean floor, these creatures have the body shape of ordinary men, but they have gained attributes of sea-dwelling creatures such as the carapace of crabs, their garbs decorated with dried-up starfish and cracked shells, their hair resembling seaweed, and the tell-tale look of tentacles granted by the Eldar Gods. Having lost so much of their humanity, they cannot speak the tongue of regular people, but instead their words come out gargled, as if every word was drowned out by water. They travel primarily by water, but when they walk the land, they do in the dark of night, trying to abduct children and convert adults with a trance-like madness.

-The Slavic People. The majority of people that reside in Central and Eastern Europe in the 1500's; along with the Prus, Lithuanians, Margyars, and Tartars. The Slavs are divided in Czechs, Poles, Ukrainians, Belrus, and Russians, but they all share a common heritage. They struggle to exist in a land where Christianity threatens to overwhelm and destroy those that do not believe. They worship the many different Old Gods, comparable to that of the Greek gods, while Starybogow is similar to that of the Pantheon. In Poland-Lithuania they are led by Alexander Jagellonian; in the countryside they live primarily in swamps and woodlands where they protect the remnants of their statues and idols.

-Teutonic Knights. The strong-arm of the Church, the Teutonic Knights were founded in the Holy Land along with the Holy Orders. After the bloody massacre of the Knights Templar, they became the preeminent military order of the Church. They cleave across the land with their bloodstained weapons, murdering all that do not serve in the name of God. Once seen as knights of Christianity and having model faith, the Slavic people know the truth; most within the order are minions of the Eldar Gods, which explains their unadulterated, relentless violence. Whether the Church is aware of this connection or they believe it to be superstition created by the heathens, they still support the knights and send them to carry out their will where they need it.

Appendix II: Bestiary

Kikikora
by Ivan Bilibin, 1934

-blud. An ethereal spirit who does not walk on ground but instead seems to levitate or fly. It can completely pass through a human body, and in doing so it causes the target to become extremely disorientated; this can result in complete loss of senses, vomiting, and unconsciousness. It is unknown why the blud spirits are able to do this, but they seem to have some control over their ability, as they tend to work with Slavic people.

-bukavac. While most of the spirits of the Old Gods are small or human-like in appearance, this beast towers above the rest. While not many have been known to exist, these blind beasts hunt by scent and are usually kept in check with a paste made by Slavic priests. Only the most skilled tribesmen can train them, and even at that, several have been known to lose their lives from beast-related accidents. Bukavacs prowl around with six legs, ending in sickle-like claws; a horror only matched by the curled horns around their milky-white blinded eyes, or their thick knob-like tail. They are notoriously resilient and it would take a number of the most skilled Teutonic Knights to slay a mature bukavac.

-domovoi / kikimora. Male and female house spirits, respectively. These spirits act as servants or friends to the houses that they inhabit. Much like with any spirit, they have their own personalities and thus each and every one is unique and different. However, as different as they might act, they are always characterized by their short and hairy appearances.

-drekavac. During a time when Christianity is the prevailing religion, one must wonder what happens to those that do not get baptized. Those bodies become the minions of one of the darker Old Gods and get converted into the spirits known as drekavacs. Usually, a drekevac stays hidden in darkness until it can group up with others of its kind, and then one takes over as the leader of the group, directing the others almost like puppets. Depending on how long the body has decayed before being taken over as a drekavac can have varying results on the appearance. Fresher drekavac have most of their flesh intact and can take on a hideous yet translucent look; yet those that have been decaying for a while can end up being naught more but bones. When they find a target to strike upon, they usually shout to be baptized. There are various ways to dispose of a drekavac, but one of the surest is by holy light, namely from a cross.

-karzełek. The creation of the labyrinth of extensive underground tunnels can be attributed to the race known as the karzełeks. These beings are probably the most similar to that of the human race, as they appear to be simply shorter and often times hairier. Why they remain underground seems to be a mystery to the rest of the spiritual world, but regardless they are more skilled builders and tinkerers than any human – and there are rumors they are such master brewers that one sip of their ale would send a human into a coma.

-leshy. One of the most benevolent minions of the Old Gods, these forest-dwelling creatures' main goals are to preserve humanity and the woods of the world. It is hard to tell the difference between a leshy and an ordinary tree when one is standing still. When they are in their natural form, their bodies look completely made out of wood and their limbs like branches. However, as guardians of the mortal realm, they have been given the power to transform their appearance into that of humans when they desire in order to blend in to the world around them – mostly though when they do this, it is in the guise of monks. Being the primary minions of Old Gods such as the like of Perun, they are friend to all those of the Slavic faith; however, that is not always the case to others. They watch vigilantly as those of the new world pass through their forests, ever ready to strike them down should they attempt to sow seeds of destruction.

-polevik. Polevik are often times called simply 'strawmen', because they take the guise of scarecrows in fields. They are usually not aggressive, but unintentionally scare mortals when they are caught moving about. Their main purpose is generally to be another way for the Old Gods to know what goes on outside of the world of Starybogow, as polevik send messages back to the city through crows.

-rusalka / topielec. When a person dies within any body of water, their body is claimed by one of the darker Old Gods. The minion that then rises again from the dead is what is known as a topielec or a rusalka, depending on their gender – male and female respectively.

While these creatures might seem similar to the Servitors, they are starkly different. The creatures wear the clothing they once did when living, their eyes are bulging black orbs devoid of life, and while they cannot speak, they shamble on without the conscious thought or will they once had. The main difference between the two genders is that rusalkas usually retain some coherency when they become spirits and tend to lead groups of topielecs. Topielecs will generally attack anything that they come across, but under the guide of a rusalka they can be a bit more controlled. Because of this, sometimes their dark master can transform rusalkas to resemble mermaids.

-sirin. Stalwart guardians of treasure, dangerously luring men to their deaths at sea, or even as simple as mischievous fiends, these female spirits harbor a number of different agendas. Their bottom half is completely avian; they are completely feathered with wings to match. From the upper half of the breasts up, the form is completely human; the feathers give way to voluptuous, flowing hair. Sirins are one of many different kinds of spirits that can change their appearance. They are constantly transforming their human halfs to epitomize what is considered beauty. Their femininity is not to be undermined – they have the ability to enrapture men in a song that seizes their senses. Many sailors have been known to crash into land or others have been known to slit their throats beyond all control, upon hearing such songs.

-skrzak. Since the earthquakes that have released the gods from the Void, many underground labyrinthine mazes have come to exist. One of the many inhabitants of these tunnels are the skrzaks. Living primarily in dark, high ceiling enclosures, these creatures attack trespassers without mercy. If their target was able to avoid the razor sharp fangs and claws, the maniacal laugh that these imps emit would instead drive a man mad. Their pursuit is relentless and their cackling consistent. These small creatures tend to have human-like appearances, even though their flesh is purplish-black, and they rarely walk but instead fly on the large wings on their backs.

-vampyr. Legend would say that the vampyrs are creatures that only come out at night – but that is but a myth. Vampyrs stalk at night primarily because it is easier for them to hunt their prey. There are many different kinds of vampyrs, but the majority of them are thin, spindly creatures with gaunt features, pale skin, and long hair. While there are those that let their appearances whither to horrible monstrosities, there are also vampyrs that are more refined and treasure and maintain their good looks. Some myths that have trickled down through time have proven accurate, such as the bloodsucking monstrosities able to change form, but even that is slightly incorrect. Myth would have people believe that the vampyrs can only change to a bat, but they can transform into any dark creature they have a mystic pact with, such as even a hound.

-vucari. Once mortal people, vucari have been afflicted with a curse, whether cast upon them or inherited through their bloodline, that forces them to transform into a beast. There have been myths that this is upon the first full moonlight, but there are actually any number of reasons why a vucari's transformation is triggered. The creature that the individual becomes is more wolf than human; the only remaining feature being the ability to stand on two legs if they wish. The degree of humanity loss depends on how advanced the vucari's transformation is. Some transform for only short amounts of time with no control or recognition of human functions; some can change at will and retain full sense of who they once were but perhaps lose the ability to talk; others have fully given in to their bestial side and remain in vucari form permanently but still speak and function as humans would.

-wodnik. A male water spirit said to appear as a naked old man with a frog-like face, with his body covered in algae and muck, usually covered in black fish scales. He has webbed paws instead of hands, a fish's tail, and eyes that burn like red-hot coals. He usually rides along his river on a half-sunk log, making loud splashes. Consequently, he is often dubbed "grandfather" or "forefather" by the local people. Local drownings are said to be the work of the wodnik. When angered, they breaks dams, washes down water mills, and drowns people and animals. (Consequently, fishermen, millers, and also bee-keepers make sacrifices to appease him.). He would drag down people to his underwater dwelling to serve him as slaves.

Appendix III: Dramatis Personae

Alexander Jagellion, King of Poland and Grand Duke of Lithuania,
Contemporarry engraving, 1521

-Alexander I Jagellonian. King of Poland and Grand Duke of Lithuania, he resides in the latter territory. He does not directly support the Old Gods because he cannot of his position, but he does indirectly through the Slavic people. His army is stronger than the Teutonic Knights and thus after beating them in war, they leave him alone for the most part even though they are enemies.

-Baba Yaga. A witch who has some minor control over the darker spirits but also respects the rule of Perun. When she involves herself in the works of humans, it is usually to sow chaos. Sometimes, she even lets them think they have slain her so that she may slip away for some time. She travels in a house that gets up to move on bird-like legs each night.

-Grandmaster Frederick von Sachsen. The Grandmaster of the Teutonic Knights. He works directly with the Servitors and is one of the most influenced humans by the Eldar Gods. Slowly, his whole beard has been replaced by tentacles, and to conceal it he wears a fake one. Even though he works with the Christians, his main goal is to use the Teutonic Knights to bring the Eldar Gods back to their true power.

-Mytiaz. One of Perun's close advisors. He changes colors based on his mood; optimistic yellow-white to sullen red-purple, and a myriad of colors in between.

-Perun. In the Old God hierarchy, certain gods have more power and thus hold command over other gods. The highest and most powerful one is Perun – the god of lightning. He has always seen humanity as being necessary to exist alongside them, and thus fights against the Eldar Gods to preserve them. Even though the war of the gods has gone on for many years, it came to a point where Perun saw the only way to end it was to seal the Eldar Gods away; but in doing so, he ended up sealing the Old Gods away as well. Now, free again from the prison he placed himself in, he looks to reclaim his place in a world that has changed.

-Polunocnica. Also known as Lady Midnight. She is one of the darker spirits of the Old Gods who roams the night, mischievously terrorizing children.

-Pscipolnitsa. Also known as Lady Midday. She is one of the darker spirits of the Old Gods who roams fields during the day and mischievously causes heat stroke to farmers.

-Tłun. One of Perun's closes advisors. His prowess in battle is only matched by his flair for style; he usually wears elegant clothes and keeps his bushy blond beard and mustache well styled. Now that he is free of the Void, an aura of power has returned around his body and his axe glows with strength.

-Triglav. For every casualty of war, for every man slain on the field of battle, for every victory won by the forces of the Slavic people, Triglav grows stronger. Known commonly as the God of War, Triglav has not one head, but three; the left is a ram, the middle a lion, and the right a dragon. Having fought hard against the forces of the Eldar Gods, he objected profusely when Perun decided to seal them in the Void. However, freedom is not what he expected, as when he awoke it was in a mortal form with only one head, his memories gone.

Appendix IV: Concepts

Rusalka
by Ivan Bilibin, 1934

-Amber. Common along the Baltic Coast, this gem has been found to fight the effects of the Eldar Gods and even stunt some of the powers of the darker Old Gods. Because of this, Alexander Jagellonian has made sure to hoard the material so that his agents are always protected.

-Enthralled by the Eldars. Even though the Eldar Gods want to replace humanity, they are not foolish as to the potential that they hold. They send their Servitors out to try and enthrall new warriors to their ranks, and those that do not join perish by the blade. Amongst their enthralled are the Teutonic Knights, and in particular, Grandmaster Frederick. Signs of enthrallment include almonding of the eyes, elongated hands and head, and tentacles.

-Fools. Fools, jesters, funny men – whatever they are to be called, they are the key to channeling the powers of the Old Gods and innately powerful beings. Regular mortals cannot hear the whispers of power from the gods, but the fools, whose minds are clear from all other things, are keen to listen to what the gods ask of them. Because of this, they can channel magic that normal human beings cannot.

-Silver. While amber might stop some dark powers of the gods, silver can completely destroy a force of spiritual nature. It does not have much effect on the benevolent spirits, and there are those that completely are immune to the silver's destructive powers, but it is the more common and effective way to combat the spirits.

-The Void. A realm between the living and the dead where no time passes. There is nothing to see and nothing to do in the Void. It is simply the absence of existence where life is imprisoned so that it might not take place in the world of the living. The Void cannot be exited from within, but requires a great amount of magical power from without to free the trapped souls.

THE GREAT
MARTIAN WAR
INVASION
SCOTT H. WASHBURN

LEGACY OF
SHADOW
CRAIG GALLANT

On
Dave Dougherty

BEYOND
ANTARES
DIMENSIONAL
GATES
BRANDON ROSPOND

Danse macabre,
by Michael Wolgemut, 1493

Zmok Books